THE SHADOWS
OF
CRAZY MOUNTAIN

by H. L. Richardson

WORD PUBLISHING
Dallas•London•Vancouver•Melbourne

Published in association with the literary agency of Alive Communications, P.O. Box 49068, Colorado Springs, Colorado, 80949.

Richardson, H. L., 1927–
The shadows of crazy mountain / by H. L. Richardson.
p.   cm.
ISBN 0-8499-3856-2
I. Title.
PS3568.I3175S48   1996   95-53808
813'.54–dc20   CIP

6 7 8 9 QKP 9 8 7 6 5 4 3 2 1

Printed in the United States of America

*To the Grosfield family and
the pioneers of Big Timber.*

Introduction

Traveling west over the rolling-grass plains of eastern Montana, a mountain chain of unbelievable splendor greets the eye. Magnificent, massive white-shrouded glacier peaks piercing the clouds into the pale blue sky—this awe-inspiring sight was the first real introduction to the mountainous west for the early settlers. Beautiful, but strangely frightening as well.

Hugging the cottonwooded Yellowstone River, while following the tracks of the Lewis and Clark Trail, settlers passed through the shadows of these mountains with a warning by their trailmasters, "Don't wander too close! There's lots of locoweed, death camas, and larkspur in them foothills and what's worse, ya might see the ghost of thet wild-eyed, crazy woman wandering in and out of the shadows. You can bet that'll stand the hair up on the back of your necks."

"Story is she's stalking around with an ax in her hand, lookin' for those red savages who scalped her husband and her two boys. The Indians say her spirit is still up there, bent on killin' whoever she finds. I ain't too sure those redskins ain't right. Them mountains is well-named. . . . Thar's a real good reason why they call 'em the Crazies."

Chapter I

Twilight—December 15, 1883

THEY COULD BARELY SEE the tall cottonwoods bordering the Yellowstone River through breaks in the swirling snow. The two riders plodded slowly down the cold, gray, snow-covered slopes toward the waterway. Both were hunched over their saddles, heads down, protecting their faces from the freezing wind. The horses quickened the pace as they drew nearer to the river. A stall out of the wind and a manger full of hay were on the other side in the town of Big Timber.

David Dodd hoped someone would be tending the tollhouse at the ferry. In weather like this, travelers were few. It was possible that the ferry owner, old man Keiger, had gone home and would not return 'til morning. If such was the case, the riders would have to seek refuge out of the wind, scrounge up a fire, and suffer through the night . . . a most unpleasant thought.

The ferry was a sort of catamaran—two rowboats tied together with a platform on top. The ferry was fit with pulleys and cables to navigate it back and forth, but it was current that actually moved the ferry from one bank of the river to the other. During these times when there was so much ice in the water, crossing could be perilous—particularly in the approaching dark.

"Partner, it's been said it never snows downwards here in Montana, just sideways. It's really blizzarding in Canada, not here," joked Deputy Calvin Davis. "This dang wind whips it down here, then into Wyomin' where it piles up in mile-high drifts . . . and THEN takes two summers to melt!" David could barely hear the deputy's voice, thinned by the driving gale and smothered by the woolen scarf wrapped about his face.

He tried to reply to his sidekick's attempt at conversation but his face just hurt too much. The wise were indoors huddled around glowing hearths; only fools and lawmen wandered out in such frigid weather . . . and for nothing.

A telegram from the county sheriff had instructed the deputy to go to Melville and pick up some legal documents from the blacksmith, Olaf Holmquist, for delivery to Sheriff Jason Sanford in Bozeman. When they arrived at the small Norwegian settlement, it turned out nobody knew anything about the papers, not even Holmquist. They spent the night in the small hotel managed by the widow Coburn, only to be awakened by the warnings of an impending storm—angry wind shifting, then howling from the north.

The scratching of hail on the plate-glass windows and the temperature dropping precipitously told the deputy and Dodd that they'd better start back to Big Timber . . . quick! Fortified by a hurried breakfast of griddle cakes and eggs, they bundled up and headed south. The weather was cold but tolerable on their way north, but now, misery increased with each mile traveled. The blizzard caught them in its freezing grip, erecting deep drifts along the trail, coating horses and riders with blankets of white. David Dodd didn't have to accompany Calvin Davis since he was only a part-time deputy. Davis had cornered him during breakfast at the Bramble Hotel, asking him to tag along as a favor.

"Two can handle a sheriff's papers better than one, pard," joked Deputy Davis. "Besides, it'll be a pleasant relief from breakin' up fights between them danged Texans and our local cowhands, 'specially those hard-cases workin' for the Elk Track Ranch. Me, I'm a peace-lovin' man. I like excitin' work like fetchin' legal papers for the county and tendin' funerals on Sheriff Sanford's behalf. Consolin' good-lookin' widows is my specialty." Cal Davis hooked his thumbs in his suspenders, leaned back in his chair, and beamed. "Yes, sir, I specialize in treatin' womenfolk real nice. That's why I lernt writin' poetry. Womenfolk love good poems."

David had heard Calvin's verse and winced at the thought. Calvin's rhyme was painful on the ears. He grinned widely at the idea of Calvin portraying himself as a ladies' man, a difficult task in frontier Montana where the odds were against it. Men outnumbered women by a large margin and, even if the numbers had been reversed and females were more plentiful than men, the diminutive deputy's scraggly bearded, bucktooth appearance would surely present something of a problem for him in aspiring to such a lofty reputation. However, whatever Cal lacked in looks he more than compensated for in personality and good cheer. The world was one large oyster for Calvin C. Davis.

"Come on with me, ol' pard," cajoled the deputy. "Ain't you tired of arrestin' drunken railroad stiffs and sheepherders? Besides," he added and winked, "with Christmas comin' on, those towheaded Norskie ladies up in Melville might serve up some fine vittles they make fer the holidays. Maybe, by gosh, I might even try that luke fisk stuff."

"You mean lutefiske, that dried fish they cook up?"

"Yeah, crammed between two thick slabs of that dark Norskie bread with a platter full of boiled potaters swimmin' in butter." Davis licked his lips and rolled his eyes in anticipation of such Norwegian culinary delights. "Davey boy, joinin' me is a chore no sensible man can refuse."

David laughed at the deputy's invitation. "Why not?" he said. "Maybe they'll have some lefsa, as well."

"Lefsa? Well, whatever it is, I'll eat thet too!" Calvin joyfully replied

David thought about Melville, the small, isolated settlement of Norwegians on the east side of the Crazies. He admired the rugged people who lived there. Most were sheepmen, surviving a hard life, running their stock on the open range. They were a devout group of industrious immigrants who took their Lutheran faith seriously. David had an opportunity to work with some of them when he arrived in Montana. His first job was logging in the Crazy Mountains, making railroad ties for the Northern Pacific. He felled timber alongside many men whose families lived in Melville. The Norsemen, like their Viking ancestors, were expert with an ax.

Logging was an excellent-paying job. A skilled logger received up to ten cents a tie. On a good day, a hard worker like David Dodd could hew and cut a hundred ties or more. When that job ran out, David worked the spring roundup for the Elk Track Ranch, for thirty dollars a month and board. Eating dust, branding calves, was poor work and seasonal at best. Besides, he didn't get along too well with the hard-cases who worked for the spread. Come winter, when jobs were scarce, he refused to ride "the grub line" as some other punchers would do. Looking for handouts from ranch to ranch wasn't in his nature. He had been successful in picking up work at the feed store, earning enough for his two-bits-a-night room at the hotel.

When the part-time job as lawman opened up he jumped at the opportunity. The pay was adequate and the duties were interesting. Helping Deputy Calvin Davis cover the eastern area of Park County was arduous but satisfying work. The county was vast, covering thousands of square miles of open range, prime grazing land and timber.

Texas cattlemen, discovering the blue gama, needle-and-thread, buffalo, and western wheat grasses of eastern Montana, found it profitable to drive their Longhorn cattle north to take advantage of the abundant sweet growth in the Yellowstone Valley.

Montana ranchers weren't too happy about the Texas invasion. Fights had broken out, some of them deadly. Shootings between the warring factions had occurred in Miles City and more were expected as Texas cattle streamed into the state. Trouble was escalating; concerns about overgrazing and disease became a reality to the northern ranchers, particularly when some Shorthorns were lost to the dreaded Texas fever, carried by the Longhorn cows. Now, the Texans were pushing westward, toward the open range next to the Crazies. The local ranchers, especially the mule-heads who owned the Elk Track Ranch were intent on having none of it.

The problem of enforcing the law was becoming too much in massive Park County. There were rumors that a new county would be formed out of the eastern section, to be called Sweet Grass County.

"If that ever happens, I'll run for sheriff and win for sure," crowed the likable Calvin Davis. He took a loud slurp of his coffee and continued, "Who better for Sweet Grass than a *sweet* guy like me?"

David was amused at the thought of the deputy becoming the sheriff. Cal Davis barely made five-foot-four wearing high-heeled boots and a tall black Stetson. He rode a seventeen-hands-high black Tennessee Walker. First impressions caused some to think Deputy Davis was long on talk and short on grit—that is, until they saw him in action. He feared no one. He'd thrust his right hip out, slap the Colt .45 on his side with a flourish, and confidently say, "This here Mr. Colt makes me as tall as anyone west of the Mississippi." Whoever saw him use "Mr. Colt" readily agreed. His size, however, caused some who were unaware of his reputation with a gun not to take him seriously.

David suspected one of the reasons he was hired by the sheriff was the fact that he stood over six feet, was broad shouldered and obviously well-muscled. Several of the rowdy Texans had ignored Calvin's request to quiet down and he finally had to enforce the demand at the point of his gun. The sheriff knew it was only a matter of time before someone was shot unless he intervened. Hiring David to help on weekends seemed to be a good solution.

David and Calvin were quite a sight. They became known as "the small and the tall of Big Timber law."

The two struck up a fine relationship, mutually admiring the other's talents. Calvin put it succinctly, "Yep, we make a good pair . . . my know-how ability to talk and yours to listen. Yes sir, Mr. Dodd, when I'm elected sheriff of this here new county, I'll hire you as my full-time deputy. Then you can throw all of them drunk sheepherders in the clink while I run for re-election and attend weddings and wakes."

David laughed out loud. "Some honor! First thing we'll have to do is build a jail in Big Timber. We don't have one that I know of."

Until recently, there had been no need for a barred facility. When someone became disorderly, they were locked-up overnight in a back room of the feed store until they sobered up. If they continued to be a problem, they were taken before the justice of the peace and fined. When anyone had to be incarcerated in a real jail, they were taken sixty miles away by train to Bozeman, the county seat.

By and large, Big Timber's residents were law-abiding. Occasionally on a Saturday night, some cowboy or sheepherder would drink too much and have to be corralled. But until recently, there had been little trouble that would require more than one deputy. With the influx of the Texans and the flood of immigrant settlers homesteading the best land, circumstances were changing.

One of the Northern Pacific Railroad workers by the name of Bad Swede Hansen caused some trouble. He was a drunken lout who delighted in intimidating the local citizenry. The sotted bully was arrested, taken before the justice of the peace, and sentenced to be locked up for three days—a dilemma, since there was no jail in Big Timber. Calvin Davis couldn't spare the time to take him all the way to the county seat in Bozeman. The feed store definitely wasn't the answer, which led to Calvin's having to find an alternative.

The clever deputy immediately conferred with a friend who was in the process of digging a new well on his property. He was down thirty feet and had yet to hit water. Being a good citizen, he offered the newly dug hole as a temporary residence for the convicted bully. Deputy Davis readily accepted his kind offer. By rope, the protesting Swede was lowered into the deep pit, along with daily supplies of food and water. Everyone ignored his whining pleas to be raised immediately from its damp confines. Days later, a tame, docile, and repentant Swede was raised to the surface.

CAL DAVIS WAS A GOOD LAWMAN and David enjoyed listening to him ramble on and on . . . but not now, not on this miserable trip back from Melville. To hear his words in this gale would have required David to poke his chin above the collar of his jacket and expose his ears to the stinging snow. He shrugged his shoulders in answer to Calvin's muffled conversation. Soon they would cross Big Timber Creek and be within a mile of the river.

The slate-blue darkness of the sky was meeting the cold, gray landscape, squeezing out the remaining light. Night was settling in when they crossed the creek's rushing water. As they approached the far bank, the shadowy shapes of two figures moved through the cottonwoods directly in front of them. Black on black, the silhouettes meshed with the trees. Without thinking, David drew his Colt .44. Suddenly, a blinding red-orange flash, then another, followed by the violent impact of being hit forced David backward. He fired into the orange flame as he was hit again, this time knocking him out of the saddle, plunging him into the icy waters.

Then total darkness . . . nothing.

CHAPTER 2

DECEMBER 20

SAMUEL DAVID DODD, GET OUT of my clean kitchen with those filthy boots! Do you hear? I have enough trouble mopping up after your children without having to put up with all the mud *you* track in!" Sam Dodd beat a hasty retreat, stepping backward through the kitchen door onto the porch, mumbling apologies.

"Sorry, Mary, I wasn't thinking . . . forgot to scrape 'em off."

Mary followed him outside, vigorously sweeping the snow and muddy ice out behind him. "Samuel, you are always forgetting. I doubt if you *ever* think of anything but cows!" Mary Dodd was more than agitated. Tracks of mud, snow, and frozen bits of cow manure adorned her newly-scrubbed floor. The soft pine was difficult to keep clean, but at least it was washable; not the packed-dirt floor of the sod home they had tolerated in the past years.

In a few short days, neighbors and family would brave the winter weather and be arriving for the Christmas celebration. The Dodds were hosting the event and, by Mary's standards, the house had to be spotless. The floor looked almost as new as when the dwelling was built just a few years ago. Only the exterior was showing wear, due to the severe high mountain

winters. The house was a rugged, unpainted log-and-stone structure surrounded by a wide porch. It bore more resemblance to a
small fort than a typical ranch home. To the Dodds, it was a
palace, a four-room mansion! It was spacious compared to their
past sod residences, with a private bedroom for Sam and Mary,
a smaller one for the boys, and yet another for the girls. They'd
built a very large room with the kitchen area at one side and a
big open fireplace surrounded by comfortable chairs at the other.
A Christmas tree colorfully decorated with strings of popcorn,
red bows, and homemade ornaments nestled in a corner. An
enclosed portion of the porch connected to the kitchen, a de-
pository for dirt-laden boots and jackets. Close by was a table
which held a pitcher of water, soap, and wash basin.

Mary's tolerance for indoor dirt was nonexistent. Right up
close to the porch, next to the pathway, was the luxury of all
luxuries . . . a hand pump! No more bucketing water from a
distant creek, no more dipping from a rain barrel; all one had
to do was pump away! Another pleasurable comfort was their
two-hole privy, one seat for adults and a smaller one for the
children, affording a grand view of the mountains if one was
immodest enough to leave the door open.

The ranch house was strategically located on a small rise,
the terrain sloping gently downward in all directions. The site
offered a spectacular view of the valley and the mountains rising majestically around them. The view was an added benefit
but hardly the reason for the home's location.

The Dodd ranch was far from civilization, existing in the
midst of the primitive high frontier of northern Colorado. The
spread was tucked in a secluded valley and often snowbound
during the harsh winter months. It was a beautiful but hostile
land. Until recently, it had been populated by warring factions
of Indians. Now it was sparsely occupied by a rugged breed of
homestead families, the nearest being several hours' sleigh ride
away. Sarah, their oldest daughter, and her husband lived just
five miles down the valley.

Sam and the boys had cleared the slopes of all trees and shrubs for a thousand yards around the ranch house, making it virtually impossible to approach without being seen or detected by the dogs. The barn and outbuildings were log-sided with shingled roofs. Lodgepole pine corralled the sizable remuda of horses.

The Dodds were one of the few families in the remote Colorado Territory who could boast of such a fine home, although they weren't ones to brag about anything.

"Cleanliness is next to godliness," was one of Mary Dodd's favorite quotes. In fact, the adage was appropriately framed above the wash basin, in scrolled needlework.

Sam often said that if cleanliness was the criteria for entry to heaven, there wasn't a soul in the territory closer to God than his wife. "Why, the kids and I are bound to make it through the pearly gates just by being related to her!"

Sam, now without boots and feigning sheepishness, asked, "Is it all right if I come in?"

"Brush off your pants. You still have hay all over them."

He took a couple of swipes at his overalls, then entered the kitchen. "What's for dinner?"

"Bean soup, sandwiches, and apple pie. You still have some hay on your pants . . . but sit down and eat before the soup gets cold."

Sam smiled. Mary was still a little hot under the collar about the mess he'd tracked in and, as usual, too sensitive about how her home looked with the advent of guests looming so near. He took it upon himself to be understanding of her idiosyncrasies, particularly on the eve of hosting such a momentous occasion.

A warm glow overcame him and a bit of a grin touched his lips, just at the thought of her. To him, she was the most beautiful woman in the world. "Yep," he said to himself, "pretty inside and out."

Mary Dodd was, in fact, a beautiful woman; her reddish-tinted hair abundantly framed her round face. Soft brown-hazel eyes, clear and sparkling, gave ample evidence of a bright, strong-willed mind. Twenty-three years of marriage, six children, and middle age had added extra pounds to her well-shaped body. *Just more to hug*, thought her adoring mate. Sam would do anything within reason to please her. Frontier life was difficult for the hardiest of women and, up until a short while ago, Mary had experienced her share.

After years of saving and scrimping they had accumulated enough to buy good stock, decent land, and sufficient equipment to make a go of it. The last few years had been extremely profitable, a welcome change. Barring the loss of his right arm and the former rough times endured by his family, Dodd was content to forgive and forget anyone or any past hardship.

He rubbed the perennially bothersome right shoulder. *If the Lord could forgive His tormentors while sufferin' on the cross, I reckon what pains I have to bear ain't worth thinkin' about.* Sam's Christianity allowed him to let the ugliness of the past fade from memory like wisps of smoke on a windy day. The war, the killings, the desperate men with whom he contended both as a soldier and a lawman, the amputation of his right arm from a gunshot wound were nothing more than faint images, more difficult to recall with each passing day.

A wide grin split his craggy, weather-beaten face as he contemplated the coming week. "Mary, in just a few days this ranch will be bustlin' with all kinds of good friends, with kids runnin' this way and that, to help us celebrate our Lord's birthday. Sarah and her husband will be here with little Jake. Can't wait to see our first grandbaby again. Must admit, I'm lookin' forward to all that good eatin'. Hope you can relax and enjoy yourself and stop frettin' about a little mess here and there."

"It would be better if David were here," Mary sighed wistfully.

"Hon, you're right about that."

"I'm not too happy about his runnin' off to Montana, chasin' after that Dills girl," she added.

"Well, they've been sweethearts since childhood. They planned on getting married on Deborah's seventeenth birthday and her folks up and moved before that happened. David couldn't help it if her pa decided to sell out and move up north. You know as well as I do that Homer Dills wasn't the best at raisin' cattle, and he was sure headed for trouble if he stayed in the business of punchin' cows. He and Matilda are city dudes and runnin' a general store in Big Timber, Montana suits them a lot better . . . don't you think?"

Mary said nothing. Her silence bothered her husband.

"Something troubling you, sweetheart?"

"Yes," she finally replied. "Deborah was only weeks away from her seventeenth birthday before they moved. There was no reason they couldn't have been married before they left. I don't think the Dillses approved of their daughter marrying our son."

Sam was mildly shocked. "Why do you say that?"

"David's been gone almost a year. Deborah turned eighteen several months ago and still no wedding. Something is keeping it from happening. David's there and I'm here and can't see what's going on and it frustrates me no end. I can't tell much from his letters. Everything seems to be all right but . . . I have a funny feeling inside that there's a problem."

"Women's intuition?"

"No, a mother's. Something's not right. I just feel it in my bones."

"Don't worry, honey. David will soon be coming home with Deborah in tow. They love each other and I'll bet by this time next year, they'll not only be wedded but maybe expecting as well." Grinning, Sam added, "We need more grandbabies about us."

Mary laughed. "You're probably right. I do, however, have a right to worry about David's new job as a lawman."

Mary shuddered. Vivid memories still haunted her about Sam's role as a peace officer in the unruly mining town of

Silverville, Colorado. The gunshots resounding through the night.
. . . Was it her husband on the receiving end or was it just another drunken cowboy or miner shooting at the moon? She never knew until Sam walked through the door whether one of the bullets just fired had had his name on it. She remembered one night when their home had been peppered by bullets. Sam had gunned down the two culprits, but they had to live with the threats from the family of the dead men. Sam incarcerated countless drunks and rambunctious cowboys, pistol-whipping some in the process, knocking others senseless with his fists. Sam Dodd had a reputation as a tough hombre, no one to mess with, fast with fists and gun. The thought of her son exposed to comparable danger sent chills through Mary's body.

Sam knew what was going through her mind and tried to console her. "Don't worry, sweetheart. Big Timber is a sleepy little railroad town where the greatest threat David will face is getting run down by sheep or blown over by the fierce Montana winds. Besides, he says the job is part-time and he'll be coming home as soon as he and Deborah are married. Better be soon. I can really use him around here; he's a good hand."

"Oh, Sam, I hope you're right. Guess I'm a born worrier."

Sam also knew something was amiss, but he didn't want to upset Mary needlessly with his own intuitive concern. He'd tried to ignore that sense of danger, the cold tingling of the skin, the knot within his stomach when he thought about his son.

CHAPTER 3

ONSCIOUSNESS RETURNED SLOWLY and David fought against it, aware that pain was its only reward. Something or someone was dragging him by the leg through the shallow stream, bumping his head over rocks. Icy water gushed around his face. Hazily, his eyes began to focus on the gray sky and the tree branches overhead. Where was he? Who had hold of his foot?

"Let go!" he cried out in excruciating pain as his face scraped over the rocks, tearing his cheeks. He was jerked about violently, then suddenly he was free . . . whatever had hold of him had yanked the boot from his foot. He heard a horse whinny and shod hooves clattering over the rocks. As he struggled to roll over on his side, he saw his animal trotting off through the trees, headed for the Yellowstone River. His boot was dangling from the right stirrup.

"Whoa!" he yelled, but his feeble shout just provoked the frightened horse to trot away at a faster pace.

David shook his head and rubbed his eyes, trying to clear the fog from his aching head.

What happened? David agonized, *I've got to think clearly.* The throbbing in his right shoulder and recalling being violently knocked from the saddle told him he had been shot.

"Calvin," he suddenly shouted, "where are you?" David struggled to his knees and frantically looked about. The dark, huddled body lay facedown on the rocky bank close by, draped over a partially submerged log. Painfully, he crawled over to the silent deputy and rolled him over on his back. The right side of Calvin's face was a bloody mass of dirt and gore. A gurgling sound came from his lips. David felt for his pulse . . . faint, but there. Cal was still alive!

David grabbed the deputy's coat at the shoulders and pulled his legs from the icy stream. He laid back on the rocky bank to examine his own wounds. His upper body ached immensely and his face was covered with sticky blood. His forehead and cheek were swollen and lacerated. Reaching inside his shirt, he gingerly felt his chest and stomach, still bleeding from several small puncture wounds high up on his right shoulder. The amount of warm dampness told him he had lost a considerable amount of blood.

He knew that he and Calvin had been blasted from their saddles at close range, in all likelihood with buckshot.

Were we robbed? David felt for the coin purse inside his vest. It was still there; so was his watch, but no gun. With his heart pounding, he looked quickly in all directions. *Are the gunmen still hanging around, hiding in the cottonwoods and willows?* Frantically, he fumbled about searching for the Colt strapped to Calvin's leg. Drawing the gun from the holster, he cocked the hammer while hugging the ground, searching the dense brush bordering the stream, looking for any movement. He waited and listened a bit before being fairly satisfied that the assassins were probably long gone, then lowered the hammer and holstered the pistol.

David's shoulder was stiffening and he began to shiver violently, the shock and cold taking their toll all over his bruised body. *What'll I do? I can't lie here or we'll both freeze to death. The ferry . . . I've got to get us both down to the ferry and get help!* He stared at his bare right foot, then groped around in his coat until he found the pocketknife.

Shivering, the handle slipped from his grasp and disappeared into the snow. David dug down deep with fingers almost as chilled as his toes before he found it. Holding the knife in his shaking left hand, he cut the right sleeve from his coat and pulled it over his exposed foot.

He rolled Calvin over on his back and yanked open his jacket. "Hope you don't mind, partner, you won't be needing this bandanna for awhile." David removed the silk bandanna from Calvin's pants and wound it around and secured the fabric on his foot.

"That should help some," he muttered as he struggled to his feet, thankful that he had some protection from the cold on both feet. His underclothes were partially drenched with sweat so that the outer woolen garments were becoming stiff in the frigid air. *Better get moving. I'll turn to ice standing here.* David knew his chances of making it to the river were questionable, but he had to try or it was sure death for both of them. Leaving Calvin was not an option; any chance of keeping him alive depended on reaching the ferry. Fortunately, he was a slight man, weighing no more than one hundred thirty-five pounds— about as much as two sacks of grain. David reached down and with more difficulty than he imagined, placed the dead weight of the deputy over his left shoulder and headed for the river.

Although the wind had abated somewhat, the snowing had increased. With the approaching darkness and the lack of light, everything blended into a shadowless dark blue-gray mass of swirling flakes.

Dear Lord, we sure need Your help. David began to pray, silently at first, then aloud . . . it comforted him. He knew God was with him as he struggled down the slope, falling occasionally, each time rising with greater difficulty, hoisting Calvin to his good shoulder.

God's will be done! The thought gave him strength. David forced himself to think clearly, struggling to remember Bible verses his mother insisted he memorize as a child. Chapter 35 of Isaiah dimly crossed his pain-wracked mind. Out loud, speaking into the wind, he mumbled the verses, remembering most, forgetting some. "Strengthen the weak hands, and make firm the feeble knees . . . be strong and do not fear. Behold, your God will come with a vengeance . . . will come and save you." David stumbled on. Now he had reached the flat, only a short way to the ferry, maybe no more than a mile.

The dark settled in around him like a black shroud; the snow was quickly obliterating the tracks of the horses he had been following. He continued with blind instinct and faith. *Where's the river? I should be there by now.*

Again, he fell down. The strength had left his right arm which now hung useless by his side; trying to rise seemed so futile. "I think we'll rest here a bit. Okay with you, Calvin? It's a relief not to move." His thoughts wandered to his younger brother, Matthew, and the ordeal he suffered—the loss of his right hand from frostbite. The face of his mother floated into his fading consciousness. He focused on her strength and the "make firm the feeble knees." David pushed himself up and struggled in vain to again lift the deputy to his shoulder.

After several tries, he spoke to the inert form on the ground. "Cal, everybody said when I was growin' up that I was goin' to be as strong as my pa. You better hope they were right." David bent down and grabbed the collar of Calvin's coat and began dragging him through the snow. He concentrated on what a powerful man his father was in character, courage, and strength. *What would he do if faced with these same circumstances? Would he give up? Oh no, not Sam Dodd, not my pa.* David's hopes rose.

Hope! David desperately searched his fading memory for the Scripture—*where is it? Romans, Hebrews? No matter. Doesn't it say, "Now hope does not disappoint, because the love of God . . ."*

David fell again, headfirst into a shallow gully. This time he didn't get up.

CHAPTER 4

T**HE POUNDING ON THE DOOR** was barely discernible above the howling wind. Not until she heard voices did she roll out from under the quilts and place her warm feet on the cold floor. She sat there for a moment, shoulders sagging, her tired sixty-six-year-old body aching, listening to the snores of her exhausted husband. It seemed just moments ago they had laid their heads to rest on the pillows . . . now this infernal intrusion.

Martha Collins lit the kerosene lamp by the bed, pulled the old wrapper over her nightdress, and shuffled downstairs. Emerging from her bedroom under the stairwell appeared Amy, the sleepy-eyed hired girl.

"Better open up, Amy, and see who it is. They won't stop pounding until you do."

"Yes, ma'am." Amy Rostad held her burning candle out of the way of any draft, then opened the door a crack and peeked outside. Snow quickly swirled into the room, extinguishing the candle and sending shivers through both women.

"Who is it?" the frightened girl asked.

"It's me, Amy, Mrs. Collins . . . it's me, Abe Keiger. And here's Frank Sorby. We come to see the doctor."

Martha Collins poked her head over Amy's shoulder and said irritatingly, "Abe, can't it wait 'til morning? The doctor's dead-tired; in fact, he just got into bed a short bit ago. Can you come back in the morning?"

"'Fraid not, ma'am. We got two shot up men in the back of George's wagon; one's Calvin Davis and the other is that new deputy."

"Sure they're alive?"

"Don't rightly know; they barely was hours ago when we found 'em. Ain't too sure about now, bein' as cold as it is."

"Good Lord, man, bring them inside quickly. I'll fetch the doctor. Amy, put more wood in the stove; it's freezing in here."

"Yes, ma'am." Amy quickly tended to the fire while Mrs. Collins climbed the stairs to awaken her husband. Moments later the physician, yawning and stretching his aching arms to awaken all of his sleepy muscles, descended the steps.

"Well, what do we have here?" The doctor knelt down beside the two bodies stretched out on the floor, their clothing frozen stiff and particles of ice clinging to their hair. He felt for the pulse on the throat of one. The clammy cold skin gave him advance knowledge of what he would find . . . no heartbeat. "This one's been dead awhile; he's cold as ice." He examined the facial wound, then shied back in surprise. "Why, this is Cal Davis!"

Then turning to the other, Doctor Collins asked, "Now, who's this poor fellow?" He reached over and pulled back David Dodd's coat and saw the caked blood on his head and neck. His skin was also cold to the touch.

"That's the new deputy, or I should say, that *was* him. He seemed like a real fine young feller."

"So was Calvin Davis," piped in Frank Sorby. "He'll be sorely missed."

Doc Collins stood up and sighed, "Not much good I can do for these poor departed souls. Could you boys help me carry them out to the back room? That's where I do the autopsies. It's good and cold out there. Come morning, I'll take a look at the wounds."

"Sure will, Doc. Glad to oblige." As Abe and Frank were about to bend down to pick up Cal, Martha Collins came in with cups and a pot of fresh brewed coffee. "You boys look chilled to the bone. Appears to me you could use a hot drink."

"Why, that's mighty kind of you, ma'am." Both men eagerly reached for the offered mugs and quickly poured themselves the steaming black brew.

"Can you tell us what happened?" asked the doctor, nodding his head toward the bodies on the floor.

"Don't rightly know how they got shot, but I can tell you how we found 'em," answered Abe. "I was just about to close down the ferry when I saw Frank with his wagon comin' up."

"Yeah, I was in town gettin' supplies and figgered I better get on home when the storm was brewin'. My bad luck to have the axle break on the wagon and get stuck in town at the blacksmith's gettin' it fixed. I knew my missus would be worried if I didn't get back, 'cause the snow drifts up pretty bad on the road home," added Sorby.

"Yeah," said Abe excitedly. "Just as we got to the other side of the Yellowstone, up comes this spooked riderless Tennessee walker. Took us awhile to ketch him."

"Yep," stated Frank. "We recognized it right away as Deputy Davis' mount. We feared trouble was afoot."

"No sooner did we get that horse under control," Abe interrupted excitedly, "than another horse came trottin' up. We knew somethin' was mighty wrong then." Both men nodded strongly in agreement, Frank Sorby spilling an ample amount of coffee on the rug.

Apologetically, he mumbled, "Sorry about that, Mrs. Collins."

"Pay no mind, Frank. Amy will take care of it." Mrs. Collins turned toward her hired girl who had been silently standing in the alcove, taking in every word. She said, "Amy, please get some rags and water."

Amy disappeared into the kitchen while the men continued their tale.

"We was sure somebody was hurt bad. The light was fading fast and the snow was kickin' up so we both piled in the wagon and took off backtrackin' the horses' trails before it got too dark to see. We were just about to give up when we found a boot stickin' out of the snow."

"Yep. Notice that one feller over there ain't got but one boot on." Frank nodded toward David. "We figgered the foot belongin' to it shouldn't be too far away."

"In the next gully, there they was," said Abe. "We loaded 'em in the wagon and brought 'em here, sure they was still alive then."

"Jus' barely," added Frank.

"Yeah, barely is right," repeated Abe. "Both had been shot up pretty bad."

"Have any idea who shot them?" asked the doctor.

"Nope. Nary a soul in sight. No other tracks around but ours. Couldn't tell, though, being as dark as it was gittin," added Frank Sorby.

Amy returned to the room with cloths and a pail of water and proceeded to scrub the coffee stains from the rug while the men went on to speculate about the shooting. When she finished doing her best, she couldn't help but stare at the face of the young man stretched out on the floor. He was handsome, though covered with grit and dried blood. She felt a deep pang of sadness in her chest, pondering the circumstances that could allow such a young life to be so brutally snuffed out. She thought about his mother and the grief she would soon suffer when informed of her son's death.

Amy had lost her parents a few years before to smallpox. The bitterness of watching them die came flooding back as she gazed at the two bodies. Her own loss had left her with not only ugly memories, but physical scars as well. The right side of her face bore pox marks, a permanent brand of the sickness. To Amy, each small scar was a never-ending avenue to the past, dredging-up frightening images every time she looked in a mirror. The left side of her face was unaffected—creamy, healthy, smooth skin—a sharp contrast to the other.

Amy helped the doctor care for the sick of Big Timber, so death was certainly no stranger to her. After her parents died, Doc Collins and his wife took her in and gave her a job as housekeeper. As time wore on, she discovered she had what the doctor called "healing hands." Amy was a good nurse and she enjoyed the work. Tending the sick gave her great satisfaction. She sat back on her heels for a moment and sighed.

I wish, she thought, *I could have helped them. I guess I can at least improve their appearance.* On her knees, she crawled over beside the bodies and with the wet cloth, wiped the caked blood and grime from Calvin Davis' face. *When his kin come to get him, he shouldn't look so bad,* she thought. Then, tenderly, as if he were still alive, she cleaned up David Dodd, exposing the red welts and cuts about his face and head. Amy dabbed at the remaining dirt around his eyes . . . which fluttered open.

She didn't even try to hold back the choked gasp that escaped from her throat. "Blessed Savior, he's still alive!"

CHAPTER 5

MARY, COME ON OUT HERE. It's a mighty pretty day to celebrate Christmas Eve!" Sam leaped up the porch steps, two at a time. "Come on out, woman, and share the beauty." He turned at the top step and looked at the panorama of the valley, letting out a pleasurable yell of exhilaration.

"Whahoo . . . what a day!" A broad smile filled his rugged face. The early rays of morning light were breaking over the mountain ridges to the east, turning to cream those in the west. There was fresh snow during the night and now the sky was a clear azure blue, a canopy of fresh cool air.

It was ideal for Christmas. The storm had passed and the weather was expected to hold for the next couple of days, a great time for friends to come neighboring. The sun was ricocheting off the newly fallen snow with exploding brilliance, while the pine boughs were heavy with white crests. The entire landscape was covered with foot-deep unblemished powder, except for tracks leading to and from the timber, made by the nocturnal Wapiti. Several cow elk could still be seen, slowly grazing their way up the slopes, following the bulk of the herd which had already disappeared into the ponderosa and aspen.

"Here, Sam, have your coffee."

"Why, thank you, sweetheart." Sam gratefully accepted the hot brew, carefully took a sip from the steaming cup, and said, "No one should have any trouble getting here; in fact, the snow should make it a lot easier, perfect for a sled or wagon."

Mary shivered, "It's too chilly for me, standing out here without a coat. Call the boys, then come inside and have your breakfast."

She marveled at her husband and how the weather never seemed to bother him. The temperature hovered around zero degrees and he was out before sunup, feeding the stock with no more than a flannel shirt and ducking overalls on his tall, lanky frame. "Come in now before you catch your death, and wipe your feet." Sam grinned and knocked off all the snow and mud clinging to his boots. The aroma of bacon and toasted bread acted like a magnet, drawing him into the warm kitchen where Mary had set out, on the long table, her usual array of mouth-watering breakfast fare. Her griddle cakes and blackberry preserves particularly pleased the children, while Sam really appreciated a bowl full of white beans flavored with ham.

With the stomping of boots and a slam of the door, two teenage boys came bursting into the room. They tossed their coats at the hooks on the wall and slid into place on the wooden bench at the table.

"You boys hungry?" asked their father with a wink.

"Pa, right now, with a little bit of ketchup, I could eat out the south side of a bear headin' north," bragged Matthew.

"And I could eat the other end," chimed in Daniel.

"Nobody's going to eat anything until you boys wash up."

"Aw, Ma, we were wearin' gloves," complained Matthew.

"The food will get cold by the time we get back," whined the famished younger brother.

"Git!" ordered their mother.

"Aw, Ma . . . " they groaned in unison.

"Mind your mother, boys," Sam quietly admonished.

Their father's voice set them in motion. Begrudgingly, Matthew and Daniel slowly raised one leg at a time from the bench, then with a mad dash they rushed to the washtable, each trying to be first. Amid good-natured shoving and pushing, they both quickly managed to splash some water and rub soap on their hands and faces, then dry their grinning faces on the opposite ends of the same towel. Then it was back to the table at a dead run.

Sam watched in quiet amusement. Ten-year-old Betsy was not impressed by the uncivilized antics of her older brothers. The youngest Dodd, eight-year-old John, was gleefully taking it all in, in total admiration of the older boys and wishing he had been part of the playfulness.

"All right everyone, time to say the blessing. Matthew, would you lead us this morning?"

As soon as they all joined hands, Matthew rapidly said, "Lord, thank You for the Christmas tree. Thank You for the food. Thank You for Jesus, Amen. Pass the toast, please."

"Don't you think that was a little too fast, Matthew?" asked his mother.

"I figgered God knows how hungry I am. With chores and all, breakfast is a might late this morning," answered Matthew, stuffing a piece of toast in his mouth.

Sam couldn't help but smile. Ranch work did take longer than usual in the snow and no one was allowed to eat until the stock was fed. They had plenty to be thankful for; this was just about the best of all Christmas Eves and their six children were healthy and doin' fine. *Only four left at home*, pondered Sam. *Sarah's a married lady now and a mother, but fortunately, she's not too far away—just up the head of the valley. Lookin' forward to this afternoon when she and her husband arrive with their little Jake.* The only member of the family not present was David, and thoughts of him furrowed Sam's brow and troubled his mind. His sense of foreboding and uneasiness recurred.

Mary was right; David *had* been gone too long. He and his son had talked about the section of the ranch where he and Deborah would build their first home, where the barn and corrals would be. David had even cleared the brush and small trees away from the site. They had often discussed plans for expanding their breed of Morgan horses and the possibility of mining some small gold deposits on Bacon Creek. Sam knew David was intending to come home. Montana had never been in his long-range plans; nor was being a lawman.

Sam wasn't as worried as Mary was about his son wearing a badge. David was cool-headed, strong as a draft horse, and extremely good with guns. His son had badgered him into teaching him how to use weapons properly. It was a good thing he did. When three grubby prospectors camped on their property and began panning for gold, David politely asked them to leave. Noting the request came from such a young man, one of them threatened to shoot him if he didn't take off and leave them alone. The intruder made the mistake of drawing a gun and taking a wild shot in David's direction. It was his last. Before he could thumb back another round in his single-action .45-caliber Colt, David dove from the saddle while drawing his Winchester carbine from the scabbard. Hitting the ground rolling, David jacked a round in the chamber and as soon as his excited horse moved out of the line of fire, slammed a bullet into the center of his assailant's chest. The force of the .44-.40 shell knocked him backward into the arms of his companions . . . stone dead.

Looking down the barrel of David's carbine as the muzzle swung from one prospector to the other took the fight right out of them. When he firmly asked, "Are you ready to leave *now?*" the two trespassing miners hastily mounted their mules and rode into the woods leaving behind all of their mining equipment, a slab of bacon hanging from a tree limb, and their dead crony. Providentially, the intruding prospectors had brought them good fortune. One of the pans left by the stream showed some color—small flakes of gold.

The Dodds had no idea that this precious metal could be found on their property. They had called the small stream Deer Creek due to the abundance of white-tail nearby. The younger boys wanted to rename it Dead Man's Creek, or Gold Creek.

Sam thought it best not to press their luck, that either name might cause too much curiosity, so they decided on Bacon Creek. They brought the body back and buried it next to the graves of some renegade Indians Sam had to kill years earlier. As in that case, Sam offered this unknown interloper a Christian burial, upon Mary's insistence. The family begrudgingly complied. "It is no small matter, praying over the remains of any departed soul," she solemnly stated.

Sam was surprised at how well David handled the dangerous confrontation and the subsequent killing of a fellow human being. He knew, from personal experience, that it affected each person in a different way. Most panic at the very thought of killing or being killed; very few delight in it. For a Christian, it can be gut-wrenching even when defending life, family, and country. David never broached the subject and Sam never asked. *There's some things a man doesn't talk about—killin' and lovin' being two. If you got to talk about it, take it up with the Maker.*

After breakfast, Mary had plenty of chores for all of them, since guests would be arriving the following day. Snow needed to be swept from the porch and walkway, two geese had to be plucked, and there were lots of special foods to be prepared. She had already assembled the mincemeat pies which would send their fragrant aroma throughout the house as they baked to a rich gold-brown.

"Sam, do you think old Eb will be tagging along with the Wilsons?"

"If he's still alive. He's past seventy, I would guess. Why do you ask? I didn't think old Eb was one of your favorites, especially his particular command of swear words."

"Oh, he's a hard old cowhand, no doubt about that, and I do hate his cussing so much; but last year when the Wilsons hosted the Christmas party, do you remember what he said?"

"Vaguely."

"I wrote it down," Mary replied. "Let me see if I can find it."

She disappeared into the bedroom and emerged with her special box containing souvenirs, tintypes of the family, letters from Sam when he was in the war, pressed flowers, and drawings by the children.

"Here it is." She carefully removed the slip of paper. "Remember what he did? He had this small bottle of rum which he shared with us. You can't have forgotten. Jenny Wilson made us all hot toddies."

Sam grinned, and answered, "Yes, I remember the hot toddies."

"You would." Mary waved her hand at her joking husband. "No, I mean when Clem Wilson held up his cup and said, 'Merry Christmas!' Old Eb stomped his foot and let out a string of swear words and said, 'That ain't the way to do it! Bow yer heads now, and I'll say what's fittin.' Remember that?"

"Well, sort of," answered Sam. "What exactly did he say?"

"I'll read it to you." Mary unfolded the paper and read:

> Dear Father of Jesus, here we be; just a bunch of critters out in the hills but we got meat and drink and fixin's for Christmas and we are going to remember tomorrer about the manger and the Babe. Amen. Now, folks, drink her down.

Sam reflected for a moment on Old Eb's words. "I don't think the finest preacher could have said it any better."

"Nor do I, Sam. I hope he comes, but . . . let's keep him away from the children; they pick up things so easily."

Sam laughed heartily and hugged Mary tightly. "We'll do the best we can, Mary, we'll do the best we can."

"Hey, everybody, someone's coming up the road!" yelled Daniel as he burst into the house.

"Well, it looks like we have an early arrival," smiled Mary. "Come on, Sam, let's go welcome our first guest."

They both donned their coats and hurried outside into the cold, looking to see who it was. A lone rider was approaching, leading another horse.

"That can't be one of our neighbors. They'll be comin' by wagon or sled," commented the tall rancher. He stepped back inside and slid his Colt from its holster hanging next to the doorway. He placed it in his belt, beneath his coat, then quickly returned to Mary's side. He did it so silently, she hardly noticed. The rider reined up a short distance from the gate and called out, "Howdy. Is this the Dodd ranch?"

"You're at the right place," answered Sam. "What might your business be?"

"I'm Deputy Ellis from over Laramie way. I have a telegram for you." He hesitated and cleared his throat before he continued, "The sheriff said I should bring it by." The tone of his voice was solemn as he dismounted and walked to the porch.

A small cry escaped Mary's lips. "It's about our son, David, isn't it?"

"Yes, ma'am. I'm sorry to say it is."

CHAPTER 6

HOMER DILLS LOOKED SADLY at the countertop, stacked with the newly arrived merchandise from the east—toys, bolts of cotton fabric, linens, needles, embroidery threads—all supplies he wished he had ordered weeks earlier for the holiday season. Now, just before Christmas, most of his customers had already done their shopping. All of the items had been in great demand . . . several weeks ago. The toys would certainly be collecting dust for awhile. Homer supposed he should have ordered the material earlier but he just didn't get around to it.

Frustrated, Dills stuck his hand in the peppermint jar and found nothing left but tiny particles of broken candy. He loved sweets and consumed more than he should of his own merchandise. "Dang . . . wish I'd known we'd be out of peppermint sticks. We've sold a bunch for stuffing Christmas stockings." Homer licked his finger, stuck it back in the jar, and ran it around the bottom to pick up particles of sugar. He was enjoying the tiny morsels when there was a voice behind him.

"Good morning, Mr. Dills."

Homer whipped around and hastily withdrew his finger from his mouth. He nervously wiped it on his apron before extending

33

his hand in a cheerful greeting. "Why, good morning, Colonel. It's good to see you," adding without a pause, "and how is your son these days? My girl, Deborah, has been asking about J.D."

The colonel ignored Homer's hand extended before him, keeping both of his own on top of the golden-topped cane. He smiled politely and drawled, "J.D. is fine, suh. My best to your lovely daughter and I'm sure those are the wishes of my son, as well. Now, suh, I need some supplies for the ranch." Reaching inside his vest pocket, he brought forth a piece of paper and handed it to the storekeeper. "Here is the list; fill what you can. I'll have one of my hands pick it up later. Thank you kindly." Colonel Malachi Raven bowed somewhat, leaned on his cane, and limped slightly from the store, cutting short any further conversation.

"There's a fine Southern gentleman," said Homer, emitting a deep, envious sigh. Although no one else was in the store, he continued to talk out loud. "He's a real credit to our community. What a son-in-law his boy, J.D., will make for my sweet Deborah." Then in a lower voice, he said, "A much better catch than that Dodd fellow."

The colonel was his best customer and very wealthy, owning the largest spread in the county. The Elk Track Ranch was one of the oldest cattle operations in Montana, covering many square miles on the eastern and southern slopes of the Crazy Mountains. Dills shuddered a little when he thought of the Raven ranch house, tucked into the bowels of a deep canyon. The dwelling was a fortress of adobe, log, and stone, built to withstand Crow and Sioux Indian raids. Such attacks were not uncommon for the early settlers.

HOMER WAS RELIEVED TO HEAR the colonel say he was having someone pick up the order. Once he had to deliver supplies to the Elk Track and, even in broad daylight, it was a chilling experience. He had to cross the river and guide the horses along miles of rutted roads across the windswept flats up to the foot of the mountains. Then, he traveled through a precipitous canyon whose granite walls reached up dramatically, blocking out all but a thin slice of the blue sky. It was slow-going through the pass, where the trail picked its way over boggy Swamp Creek, bordered by thick stands of aspen and cottonwoods forming a shadowed canopy over the trail.

Once across the creek and out of the trees, the road led up a thousand yards to the face of a massive granite wall. At its base was the Elk Track Ranch, fortified on the remaining three sides by a high, thick adobe barrier, with bastions strategically placed to defend from any approach. Inside the bastions hung lances, sabers, and guns, ready to repel anyone trying to scale the walls. A huge wooden gate protected the entrance and on the overhead beam were fixed dozens of sun-bleached elk antlers, stark white against the granite backdrop. The residence itself was hardly a welcome sight, more like a collection of interlocking one-story adobe buildings scattered against the face of the steep rock. Cut into the face were several storage caves. Two housed ranch equipment and a third was an icehouse, storing the frozen blocks that had been cut during the winter for use throughout the hot summer months.

The Elk Track was constructed for defense against attack, not for beauty. It was easy to see why the Indians left it alone. Inside the living quarters, home for the colonel and his son, Homer expected quite a different scene. He thought a man of the colonel's standing would have objects reflecting his wealth such as fine furniture, paintings, silver, velvet draperies, and perhaps imported woven carpets. There were none. Scattered about were pieces of rough-hewn furniture, buffalo rugs on both floors and walls, and guns everywhere . . . on tables, hanging up, and standing in the corners.

There were Winchesters, Sharps, breach-loading Springfields, outmoded 1860 Army Colts in decrepit leather holsters, Kentucky flintlocks from years past, and scores of other weapons. The old ones were covered with dust, but the newer models were all in excellent repair. Memorabilia from the Civil War, sabers, regimental flags, and a large stars-and-bars flag of the Confederacy adorned one expansive wall. Two huge dogs lay curled up on a buffalo rug, growling ominously at Homer.

There were only two pieces of decent furniture—a billiard table in the middle of the main room with multiple kerosene lamps overhead, and a large cherrywood bar filling one entire corner. The bar was amply stocked with bottles of bitters— McBryan, Old Crow, and Squirrel. The essence of liquor, sweat, old leather and wet dog filled the air—definitely a man's environment. There was no sign of a woman's influence anywhere.

The colonel, when entertaining, sent his men into the mountains to collect wild mint for the Southern drink he preferred. He graciously offered a mint julep to the grocer. Dills had quickly carried the supplies inside in hopes of an equally quick departure. The place depressed him and daylight was fading fast. Having to trail the empty rig back alone in the dark was a frightening thought, but Homer felt it unwise to refuse the whiskey and mint concoction.

Although the drink was strong, Dills gulped it down and bid the rancher a hasty farewell, the story of the Crazy Mountain ghost welling up in his mind. The tale had fascinated him when he first heard it. But in reality, having to ride over the lower reaches of the Crazies at night, Homer wasn't so sure he wanted to confront the spirit who gave the mountain range its name. The mere thought of viewing the wild-eyed woman, driven insane by the brutal murder of her husband and children, gave him the chills. Several of the local citizens swore they had seen her roaming about, seeking revenge. Homer wasn't eager to share their experience.

As the sun disappeared, darkness fell like a dropped anvil. Riding into the trees seemed like being immersed into the fold of a witch's black robe. The wind whistled and moaned through the dry branches, gaining in volume at the narrows. Homer, feeling the effects of the liquor, was sure the ghost of the crazy woman was in the canyon waiting for him, ax in hand, watching his every move. It was too dark for him to see, so he had to trust the horses to pick their way through the black, hoping they would stay on the trail. He was wet with fear by the time he cleared the pass and reached the flats. Then, he whipped the team into a dead run.

Homer winced just thinking of ever having to make another delivery to the Elk Track. "That place sure gives me the creeps," he muttered.

WHEN JASPER SHANK, the Elk Track cook, was in for supplies one day Homer had prodded him with an offer of a plug of tobacco and whiskey. Jasper told him most of what he knew about the Ravens.

"Yep, them was one of the first settlers hereabouts, drivin' a big herd of cattle to the base of the Crazies. The Crows, Sioux, and Blackfeet hunting parties still roamed about lookin' for shaggies. Them buffs were still in abundance when them Ravens crossed over the Yellowstone."

"Did they come alone?" inquired Homer.

"Naw," replied Jasper, looking down for the spittoon. "The colonel and his baby boy, along with his cousin Dorsey, were the only ones in the family. But he also had with him the orneriest bunch of gunslingers, Mexicans, Indian fighters, and rough-ridin' cowboys a man could hire." The cook let a stream of brown juice fly at the nearby cuspidor, hitting it dead center. "One thing, though; they had to be Confederates and Democrats *besides* bein' handy with a gun. There's nuthin' the whole family hates worse than a bluebelly, Yankee Republican."

"I agree on that," piped in the storekeeper. "I'm from the South, myself."

"Didya fight in the war?" asked the cook. But before Dills could answer, Jasper continued to ramble on. "I did. Served the whole war under the command of Longstreet. Look here. See this?" Jasper pulled up his shirt and pointed to an ugly scar across his shoulder. "Got this in Gettysburg and this . . ." he unbuckled his pants but was immediately stopped by Homer.

"Better not. Some womenfolk might drop by any minute."

Shank buckled his drawers and boasted, "That there scar got me the job cookin' for the colonel. Number of fellers wanted the job but none could show a Minie ball wound." Jasper grinned from ear to ear, displaying a crooked assortment of stained brown teeth.

"Tell me some more," said the inquisitive merchant, while trying to disregard the tobacco juice running down Jasper's chin. "What about his cousin?" That question wiped the smile from Jasper's face.

"Dorsey? He's a mean one. Likes to kill things."

"What kind of things?" probed Homer.

"Any kind." Jasper then hesitated and added, "That's all I'll say about that one." He spat at the container once more. This time he missed!

"Well then, tell me more about the colonel," Dills persisted, while intentionally ignoring the tobacco stain on the floor and offering another whiskey to the receptive cook.

"It's a sorrowful story. Learned it from some of the hands who knew him way back when." He took another swallow and handed the bottle back to the storekeeper. Then, with a sad look on his face, he unfolded the tragic story.

Dills listened intently, taking in every word about the Raven war experiences—the wounded leg, being captured by the Yankees, and the colonel's heroic escape.

"Malachi Raven was a fine officer in the Confederate army and his cousin, Dorsey, served under his command." The cook rambled on, "His sweet wife was a lady, a real good-looker, I hear. Came from one of them wealthy Louisiana families an' so did the colonel."

"Lots of money?" asked Homer, offering Jasper another drink.

The bewhiskered old man grabbed the bottle and took a healthy swig. "Thet bunch had more money than the Louisiana swamp has gaters."

"Gaters?"

"Yeah . . . ally gaters. Big ugly lizards with sharp teeth. Swamp's full of 'em." Jasper Shank stretched his arms wide. "Got mouths on 'em big as this!" He then brought his hands together in a loud clap. "Cut a growed man in half with one bite. Fearful things, them gaters."

Homer brought him back to the subject. "What happened then?"

"Where was I?" asked Jasper. "Oh yes, they lost all their money."

"They lost all their money?" exclaimed Dills.

"Well, not all. They'd stashed a whole lotta gold away when the war started. Raven's pa was a smart ol' bird who did lots of tradin' with the North. He jest didn't believe the South could win and guessed what was goin' ta happen. Raven dug it up and headed west with his boy and Dorsey after the war. Went to New Mexico for a spell and didn't like it. Too many Yankees settlin' there. Sold his spread and headed up here to Montana with his cattle."

"What happened to his wife?" asked Homer.

"I heared she died birthin' their babe . . . poor thing. The colonel came home from the battle to find her dead and buried, the plantation house burnt to a cinder, an' a boy he knew nuthin' about. Broke his heart, thet's what it did." Jasper took out a soiled red bandanna from his back pocket and blew his nose loudly. "I durn near tear up jest thinkin' about it."

"Not too hard figuring out why he hates Yankees," added the grocer.

"Yep, that's a fact fer shore. Like a brand on the forehead, it's hard to forget."

"I hear the colonel had a distinguished military career."

"That he did," reflected Jasper. "He was on General Pemberton's staff at the siege at Vicksburg an' with a handful of good Rebs 'round him, he fought his way out afore it fell to General Grant. Then he joined up with General Hood in defendin' Atlanta. 'Twas where he got wounded in the leg and captured."

"Did he spend the rest of the war in prison?"

"Not that Reb. On the way north, he got free an' worked his way back to Louisiana." Jasper looked hungrily at the whiskey bottle. "Can I have another swig?"

"Be my guest." Homer handed the almost empty bottle to Jasper and asked, "By the way, why does he call his son J.D.? What do the initials stand for?"

"Why, Jefferson Davis, that's what!" Jasper staggered to attention with a frown on his face. "I thought every Southern boy knew that," raising one eyebrow suspiciously and leaning forward, the drunken cook slurred, "Whose command did you fight under?"

Homer Dills nervously fidgeted about before he answered. "I had a bad back, suffered a terrible accident bein' thrown by a horse." Homer quickly changed the subject because the South he came from was southern Ohio and he escaped military service by paying for someone to serve in his stead . . . in the Union Army. Homer couldn't afford to have the conversation dwell on his past so he said, "Tell me more about the colonel's wife."

"Well, let's see. Oh yes, the colonel came home and found his dear wife dead an' buried and the big house burnt to ashes."

"You told me that part."

"I did? Well, anyway, tha's all I know. If you want to ask some more, see Dorsey."

Though Jasper was drunk, he was clear-headed enough to know maybe he had talked too much. The colonel was pretty secretive about his business and wouldn't be too pleased that his cook was jabbering on so much. *Tellin' the storekeep to ask Dorsey should shut him up.*

Dorsey was a mean one. Wouldn't tell a blind man if the sun was shining, much less talk about his own kin. His business was shutting people up and just taking a long look at them usually sufficed. Small, charcoal-colored steely eyes peered relentlessly from under heavy black brows; the unkempt, gray beard covered his gaunt, perennially sour countenance. Dorsey was tall and slump-shouldered with long, sinewy arms dangling at his sides. His right hand was always in close proximity to the gun strapped to his thigh.

Dorsey Caine was the ramrod of the Elk Track, in charge of the everyday operations. He also was the troubleshooter and enforcer of the colonel's policy decisions. No one knew of anyone who had bested Dorsey . . . with either gun or fist.

Jasper tilted the bottle and drained the last drop. "Well, pard, reckon I'll be moseyin' back to the spread. Much obliged for the drinks." With a wave of his hand, Jasper staggered for the door, empty bottle still in hand. Before he could exit, a beautiful young lady rushed frantically through the door, tears streaking down her flushed face. She rushed up to Homer and threw her arms about his neck sobbing, "Oh Pa, have you heard? David's been shot and they say he's going to die!"

CHAPTER 7

THE NORTHERN PACIFIC LOCOMOTIVE was grinding to a halt as Sam Dodd threw his bag to the Big Timber station platform. He stepped off into the swirling snow which swept over the icy boards, making the footing perilous. Greeted by an unfriendly blast of frigid Montana gale, the wind ripped his hat from his head and sent it spinning down the snow-covered planks. Fortunately, it was retrieved by an agile cowboy waiting to board the train.

"Gotta' pull it down over yer ears, sir," smiled the cowman as he handed Sam his Stetson.

"Much obliged," answered Sam, who continued without a pause, "Can you tell me where Doc Collins lives?"

"'Fraid not; jest passin' through." With that parting comment, the young waddy boarded the train.

Further down the platform, the stocky, bundled up stationmaster was busily loading a stack of frozen hides into the baggage car. Sam approached and asked the same question of the visibly cold and irritated station attendant.

"I'm too busy right now!" he barked. "Wait inside and I'll be with you shortly."

"But this is very important," insisted Sam.

"So is loading these hides," the attendant responded sarcastically. "Wait inside."

Sam could do nothing but comply. There was nobody else in sight, the train was due to leave momentarily, and he was the only passenger left on the platform. Begrudgingly, he entered the stifling-hot depot. The potbellied stove in the center of the room was glowing red, emitting waves of heat and the faint smell of tobacco spit from its hot exterior. Sam opened the collar of his coat and nervously paced back and forth. He reached in his pocket for the telegram and read it again:

> Dear Mr. Dodd. Stop.
> Son David shot. Stop. Might live few days. Stop.
> D. K. Collins, M.D.
> Big Timber, Montana

Seven words in the text, that was all. Nothing about the extent of the wound, no prognosis, no hope, literally nothing. All the information contained in the wire led him to think David could already be dead. It was a cold, impersonal communication, more frigid than the weather outside.

He had to find David, consult with the doctor, and telegraph Mary the information. The family and neighbors were worried sick. Mary had been praying constantly and hadn't slept soundly since the fearful message arrived. Sam had, in short shrift, saddled the mules and taken off on the long ride to Laramie.

They had all prayed and, trusting in the Lord, placed the fate of David in His hands. Sam knew the family and their friends were praying even now; he could feel it in his bones. The thought of God's presence comforted him somewhat, but being so close, being here in Big Timber, he needed to be with his son.

Through the window, he anxiously watched the unconcerned railroad hand slowly approach the waiting room. Sam hurried to the door, impatiently asking, "Where does Doc Collins live?"

"What's the matter, you sick?" he smirked, while kicking the snow from his feet. He turned his back on Sam, whose patience was wearing razor-thin. Sam immediately grabbed him by the shoulder and spun him around, demanding to know where to find the doctor. Seeing the empty sleeve on Sam's coat, the burly station master huffily sneered, "Find him yourself!"

Sam leaped forward and with his outstretched hand, pushed violently against the man's startled face, slamming his head hard against the wall, sending him crashing to the deck. In one quick motion, Sam seized his coat collar, jerked the sprawled figure from the floor, and propelled him through the door, knocking it open, shattering the glass window. The dazed attendant rolled over in the snow, totally intimidated by the strength and anger of the man towering over him.

"Now," Sam said through clenched teeth, "take me to the doctor's house."

Still stunned, the station attendant staggered to his feet. As he led Sam toward the main street, he contemplated how easily he had been manhandled by the one-armed stranger. He'd always thought of himself as stronger than most, handling heavy baggage that daily tested and strengthened his body but . . . to be tossed around by a middle-aged cripple . . . well, that bothered him. After slogging through the snow for a few blocks, he stopped and pointed to a large two-story gray Victorian.

"The Doc lives there."

Sam faced him and said, "I'm sorry, I shouldn't have been so rough with you, but I've no time to spare." Without waiting for a reply from the befuddled stationmaster, Sam hurried to the door and began knocking, far louder than need be, his heart pounding.

SAM STARED AT THE MOTIONLESS FORM of his son. He had been standing silently beside the bed for quite awhile, watching over David and quietly praying. He had yet to talk with the doctor. Mrs. Collins had answered the door and led him into the room where David was resting. When he asked about his son's condition, she skirted the question by saying as she left the room, "My husband will be home soon. He's the doctor. I'd rather have him consult with you."

The situation appeared ominous as Sam continued to assess David's pale, still body with his sunken cheeks, yellow pallor, the wheezing and shallow breathing. The red welt on his forehead and the deep gash across the cheek made him wince. And the bullet wounds . . . Sam had seen enough of them in his life—too many, in fact. An indescribable, constricting pain balled up in his chest. *What greater agony is there than seeing your offspring in pain?*

Helplessness engulfed him and he felt a burning behind his eye lids. Sam fought back, gritting his teeth until it hurt. *Tears may come later, but as for now, thank You, Lord, for keeping him alive.*

A girl carrying a tray of dishes came into the room, circled behind Sam, and sat on the edge of the bed. "Are you his father?" she asked.

"Yes I . . . " Sam stopped to clear his throat. "Yes," he said more forcibly, "I'm Sam Dodd, his father."

"Glad to meet you, sir. I'm Amy. I work for the doctor."

Her decided accent prodded Sam to ask, "Are you Swedish?"

"Oh, no! Norwegian," she stated emphatically.

Sam couldn't help but grin. In Colorado, the immigrant Swedes and Norskies who worked for him in the Silverado Mines made very clear that ethnic differences burned bright under the northern lights—bright enough to be transported to distant America. The blue-eyed, blonde Amy removed a damp cloth from the tray and began to dab at his son's face. David stirred slightly under her gentle touch.

"Wake up, David, yer lunch is here and you have company."

"How's my boy doing?"

"Much better than when he was delivered to us. When he first came here, we thought he was dead."

"What happened? I know nothing, other than what the telegram said. Please tell me."

"I truly don't know. He and Deputy Davis were brought here just before Christmas, shot up so very bad. We thought them both to be dead but only the deputy was. Your son wasn't as bad shot up and the doctor took out a lot of buckshot from his shoulder. The gunshot wounds were not the worst of the trouble so much as the cold in the chest and fever."

As David continued to stir, his eyes blinked open.

"Ah, good." Amy placed her hand under his head and raised it from the pillow. "Now, open yer mouth." She placed a cup of broth to his lips and encouraged him to drink. With difficulty, he took a few sips.

"David, can you hear me?" asked his father.

The young man's brow furrowed. Then as recognition set in, he answered weakly, "That you, Pa?"

"Sure is, Son." Sam couldn't hold back the tear about to roll down his cheek at the joy of hearing David's voice. As he reached down and clasped his son's left hand in his, Sam squeezed, hoping some of his own strength might flow into his boy's body.

"Whatcha doin' here in Big Timber, Pa?" he whispered with a small smile.

"Oh, just passin' through," Sam responded, with a grin. "Thought I'd stop off and see how you were doin'."

"Little under the weather right now. Reckon I'll be all right by tomorrow . . . maybe the next . . . " His voice trailed off and his eyes closed as he settled back into a restful sleep.

At that moment, Sam knew his son was going to be well again. *Humor goes along with living, not with dying*, Sam thought. As he felt the weight of worry and fear lift from his shoulders, he was eager to telegraph Mary as soon as possible with the good news. Sam marveled how strong young bodies can take severe punishment and recover, unlike older ones which collapse under the strain. It was obvious from the attention David was receiving from that tall young blonde that he was in caring hands.

"That's the most he's talked 'til now," beamed the pleased young nurse. "We better leave him and let him rest."

"Good idea," responded Sam, as they left the room and closed the door.

"I'm sorry I've missed Deborah Dills," said Sam, "but I guess she comes pretty often. She and David are plannin' to be married."

"Ya . . . I know," softly replied Amy. "She came by once or twice."

"Once or twice?" asked a surprised father.

"Ya. It seems David's condition frightens her terribly and it upsets her to look at him. But she does stop by every day or so to ask how he is doing."

"Is that all? She doesn't come in . . . ?" Sam's curiosity was cut short by the sound of someone banging the snow from their boots on the front porch. Amy ran to the window. "The doctor's back and he's with the sheriff."

"Good!" exclaimed Dodd. "Maybe I can get some answers as to who shot my son."

The two men entered the front hall and removed their coats. "Amy . . . get us some coffee," barked the doctor.

"Ya, sir," was her quick response as she hurried to the kitchen.

"Who might you be?" snapped Doc Collins as he spied the tall figure standing in his living room.

Without moving, Sam replied, "I'm Sam Dodd, David's father."

"Oh, you got my telegram . . . good."

"Yes . . . what there was of it."

"Anything over ten words costs too much. I doubted it would ever get to you, so why spend the extra money? I imagine you've seen your boy."

"Yes, we've even spoken a few words. He's still pretty sick, isn't he?"

Without answering, he turned to the man standing beside him. "Mr. Dodd, like you to meet Sheriff Jason Sanford."

Sam stepped forward and extended his hand. "Sam Dodd." He quickly studied the powerfully built lawman. A well-worn brown Stetson still on his head was pulled down to the tips of his ears over his graying hair. The eyes were cold blue, the jaw square, and weathered wrinkles lined his blocky face. His head and neck looked to be a part of his broad shoulders. He offered his big hand and shook Sam's vigorously. The grip was like being seized by a vice.

"Are you Jason Sanford?"

"I reckon," was his reply.

"I've heard of you," Sam cordially stated. *But who hadn't,* he wanted to add. Jason Sanford was one of the most famous lawmen in the West. As a young man, he was an Indian fighter with Colonel Crook and took part in the surrender of Chief Joseph's Nez Perce tribe, south of the Canadian border. Sanford served as a deputy in Miles City where he earned the reputation of blinding speed with a Colt, having gunned down in a street shootout three of Texas' most wanted desperadoes. Rumors were, he was one of the vigilantes who hung out the cattle rustlers in the Madison Valley.

Raising one eyebrow, the sheriff said, "Sam Dodd. I know that name. You be the same Dodd who was a lawman in Silverville, Colorado a few years back?"

"I was with Sheriff Will Poole, one of his deputies for a short spell in the seventies."

The sheriff chuckled, "If I'd knowed David was your whelp, I'd have given him a full-time job." Turning to the physician, he asked, "Doc, didya know you've been lookin' after the boy of one of the West's toughest officers of the law?"

Embarrassed, Sam quickly changed the subject. "Sheriff, Doc, what can you tell me about the shooting?"

"Not much, I'm afraid," replied Jason Sanford. "I rode out to where the shooting musta taken place and couldn't find anythin' worthwhile. There were three of 'em doin' the killin'. Found their boot tracks amongst the trees where they'd lit a fire. Tracks led from the fire to the edge of the cottonwoods where, I'm sure, they could watch anyone approachin' from the north. Whoever them bushwhackers were, they musta been waitin' for someone for quite some while—most likely my deputy and your David. Out in the open, the drifting snow covered up any hoof prints leading away. No tellin' which way they went. Nobody saw anything, no riders crossed the river from town. The ferry operator said no riders crossed all day and I doubt that anyone could safely ford the river, as iced up as it is. Whoever they are, they're from the north side of the Yellowstone."

"Was it robbery or maybe renegade Indians off the reservation?" asked Sam.

"No, both David and Calvin still had money on 'em, not to mention their guns and horses weren't taken. If it was Indians, they'd of taken the horses, for sure."

"Both were hit by double-ought shot, the deputy getting the worst of it," added Doc Collins. Your boy must have been further away because the shot didn't penetrate as deeply, probably due to distance and the heavier jacket he had on." The doctor went over to a corner cabinet and removed a small bag from the top drawer. "Look at this." He poured the blood-stained shot on the table. "I took enough of this out of your son to kill them both."

"From the evidence so far, seems like it was a planned killin'," added the sheriff. "And as I said before, those three bushwhackers waited for them awhile, tellin' from the ashes left by the fire."

"Was your deputy not too friendly? Did he have enemies?" inquired Sam.

"Not likely. Cal Davis was an extremely popular feller. Everybody liked the little guy. Even this sour old doctor thought highly of him."

Doc Collins nodded his head in agreement and added,

"Couldn't have been David either; he hasn't been around long enough to make such deadly enemies."

"A lot could be cleared up in a hurry when David is well enough to talk to us. He might identify his assailants," stated the sheriff.

"It's a miracle he's still alive," said the doctor. "I wasn't giving him much of a chance to make it. Even now, it's touch and go. The gunshot wounds don't worry me but the chest congestion could worsen."

Just then Amy came in carrying a tray of cups and saucers, along with a plate piled high with buttered toast and jam. "The coffee is ready. I'll bring it right in." Once more, she disappeared into the kitchen.

"There's the reason your son is still alive," said Collins, nodding toward the kitchen. "She stayed up for two nights straight nursing that boy of yours, keeping the fire tended, forcing soup down his gullet, changing bandages." The doctor's harsh voice softened when he spoke about Amy.

Quietly, almost under his breath, he added affectionately, "The good Lord gave her healing hands." Then returning to his normal tone, and addressing Sam, he blustered, "If he pulls through, it won't be because of me—but be assured, I'll send you a bill anyway."

Both Sam and the sheriff laughed and then poured themselves cups of steaming hot coffee. They had barely touched the cups to their lips before they heard a pounding on the front door.

Amy hurried to see who it was and as soon as the door opened, a cowboy rushed in, excitedly brushing by Amy.

"Excuse me, ma'am," blushed the young man as he deferentially touched the rim of his hat, "is the sheriff here?"

"You don't want to see the doctor?" asked Amy.

"No, ma'am, too late for that. I need Sheriff Sanford. I gotta see him now."

"I'm right here," said the sheriff, as he stepped into the foyer. "What can I do for you?"

Rapidly, the young cowboy blurted out, "Found two dead men, Sheriff, frozen stiff and both shot to pieces."

CHAPTER 8

THE COWBOY SHIFTED NERVOUSLY from one foot to the other while twisting his hat in his hands. "Sheriff, my name's Omer Smith. I ride fer the J Bar B over near Livingston durin' the spring and fall roundups. Jest now, I've been movin' rocks, repairin' corrals, and chasin' strays fer ranchers hereabouts—that is, 'til this mornin'." He paused to take a deep breath and continued. "I come across a couple of five-year-old cows hidden in a draw, tryin' to keep out of the wind. I rode in to chase 'em out and herd 'em back to the ranch. They was cagey ol' critters and jest as we got close to the river, they dove up this draw and tried to circle back. I spurred in after 'em and right there in the shadows of the north face of the slope were these two bodies, froze stiffer'n a board, arms and legs stickin' out of the snow. Looks as how some varmints was chewin' on 'em, but they was froze too stiff for the critters to get much of a chaw."

"Who are they? Did you know them?" inquired Stanton.

"They was Texicans; I can tell by the spurs they're wearin'. Them were old geezers, musta been in their fifties, gray beards and all. Must be from the Box X spread that's been pushin' Longhorns into the range hereabouts and causin' all the trouble."

"Could you tell how they died?" asked the sheriff.

"Shore could. Both was kilt by buckshot—no mistakin' the work of a sawed-off shotgun."

"Wonder how long they've been dead?" asked the sheriff.

"I shore have no way of knowin'," responded the young cowhand.

"It shouldn't be too hard to ascertain," stated Doc Collins. Turning to the nervous cowboy, he asked, "You say they weren't too chewed up?"

"Yassir, that's a fact."

Doc Collins continued. "The weather was pretty mild up until the blizzard hit. If they had been shot much before the freeze set in, the bodies would have suffered more from the birds and varmints. It's a safe guess they were killed no more than a day or two before David and Cal were gunned down."

"Makes sense," added the sheriff. "Well, better get a wagon and go out to get 'em."

"I have to telegraph my family and tell them David's still alive. Then, if you don't mind, I'd like to tag along," said Dodd.

"Glad to have you. Could use the help," replied Sanford. "I'd guess there may be some connection between the two shootings."

"Seems like all parties were shot with the same kind of weapon," observed Dodd. "Whatever the reason, it must be danged important for someone to want to kill three men in cold blood, and one of them a lawman. What worries me, it could happen again."

"Why do you say that, Sam? You actually think there might be more?" asked the doctor.

He couldn't answer immediately. It'd be too hard to explain the feelings boiling up inside, the aura of evil touching his senses, the uneasiness, the crawling tingle up the spine when the angel of death was near. How could he describe the premonitions, like his ability to sense perilous circumstances that had been with him during the war? He dreaded the sensation, even though it had warned him of imminent danger. It was with him now.

"I think . . . it's just too coincidental that three men were murdered, and one wounded, by the same type of gun in such a short period of time. Some killer or killers are out there, maybe plannin' to strike again."

"Aren't you being a little melodramatic?" queried the doctor.

Sam smiled, then agreed. "Maybe I am, but what else can I say, since I feel it in my bones."

They all laughed a bit, but Sam's was more subdued.

"THEY SHOULD BE RIGHT OVER YONDER." Omer Smith pointed toward the side of the wash, "Right there, next to the willows."

The snow had drifted, covering the bottom of the wash and the two bodies. All they could see was an arm sticking out of the snow, the frozen hand partially opened in a silent wave, a gruesome greeting from the dead. The two rigid, blood-splattered bodies were frozen to the ground and had to be pried loose. Their immovable arms and legs were grotesquely angled away from their torsos. Loading them into the back of the wagon like scraggly tree limbs was clumsy. After covering them with a tarp, Sam and the sheriff spent an hour scouring about for any evidence . . . but it was useless. The pristine snow hid the gruesome details of the killing. They agreed that finding any clues would have to wait 'til spring.

"Let's get these bodies to town and have Doc take a look at them—once they've thawed out, that is," said the sheriff.

"I saw you going through their pockets," observed Sam. "Find anything?"

"Nothin'. These boys were cleaned out. No papers, no guns, not even pocket change. Maybe this was just a robbery," answered the sheriff.

"Maybe," replied Sam, "but look how they died. There's no mistaking they were gunned down with a sawed-off greaser."

"I got another idea," said Sanford. "Let's get the Doc to clean 'em up, then we'll take these poor souls down to the icehouse and keep 'em there for awhile."

"Why ya want to do that?" asked the curious cowboy.

"Well, I'll tell ya'. We'll put out the word and maybe somebody will identify 'em. I intend to ride over and talk with the Texicans. Maybe they'll know who they are. Besides, the ground's too hard to dig decent graves. These boys will keep real nice in the icehouse."

"Ain't that bein' disrespectful of the dead?" asked Omer Smith.

"Naw," the sheriff replied jovially. "Last year in Butte we had a shootout with some itinerant Irish miners and we had 'em stacked up like cord wood in the icehouse 'til spring."

"Didn't that upset their kin?"

"Not a bit. Gave 'em an excuse to have a four-month-long wake. They seemed real sorry when the ground thawed out and they had to bury the lads."

"Well, don't that beat all," said the awed young cowboy, not noticing Sanford's wink to Sam.

"YEP, I KNOWED THEM," stated Mark Riser, the tall Texas foreman of the Box X. Pulling the canvas tarpaulin back, he exposed the heads of the dead men and sorrowfully added, "The one with the big nose is Rob Hurtt and the long, skinny one is—or I should say *was*—ol' John Lewis. They was pards and both worked fer me a long time." The sad-eyed drover gently, respectfully placed the tarp back over the bodies. "Appears they was shot up pretty bad."

"A shotgun at close range can be awful messy," responded the sheriff.

"Had a hard time recognizin' ol' John. Not much left of his face." The cowboy turned away from the still forms on the cold floor. "Sheriff, let's get out of here; I could use a shot of whiskey."

"Not a bad idea. I've some questions to ask you, and the saloon next door is a lot warmer than here."

The Fast Buck Gaming and Drinking Emporium was just a few steps away, down the boardwalk. The town of Big Timber and the surrounding area was growing fast and new buildings were cropping up almost overnight. It was becoming the wool capitol of Montana, with sheep steadily replacing cattle as the main industry. Most of the buildings were unpainted wooden structures, hastily built. The Fast Buck saloon was no exception. The bar was a long table made up with saw horses and two-by-eight timber.

An assortment of tables were scattered about with a few chairs and wooden crates to sit on. Gas lamps hung from ceiling hooks, a player piano pumped out melodies in one corner, and a pot-bellied stove radiated heat from the other. The only touches of refinement were a very respectable oil painting behind the bar and a large number of polished brass cuspidors on the floor. Fresh sawdust covered the rough-hewn boards to soak up any errant spray.

The saloon was empty save for a bored bartender, washing glasses in a galvanized tub, and an old man vigorously polishing a spittoon by the alley door.

The sheriff ordered a beer and the ranch foreman asked for a shot of rye whiskey. They retired to a table by the stove where Mark Riser leaned back in his chair, downed the whiskey with one gulp, then shook his head slowly, expressing remorsefully, "They both was good hands. Hated to see 'em leave. Most times, there's nuthin' but youngsters workin' for me; these two knew what they was doin' all the time."

"Did they have any enemies that you know of?" asked Sanford.

"None I can think of. Both were likable cowpokes, seemed

to get along fine with everyone; but most times, they kept to themselves bein' older than the rest of us."

"Can you tell me much about them, where they came from, who they hung around with, anything you think of that might be of help?"

"They was both Civil War veterans and would sometimes talk about it. Around the campfire, they'd tell all kinds of stories about fightin' Yankees and how the South shoulda' won. Most of our hands are young fellers who lost a pa, a granddaddy, or some other kinfolk in the war. They liked to hear about the battles, especially ones where Stonewall Jackson and Nathan Bedford Forrest beat the bluebellies' hides into pig dust." A wide grin crossed the wrangler's face. "One night in Miles City, after we had sold the beefs, both of 'em went on a tear and got whiskied up. They started givin' that Rebel yell. Y'all know the one I'm talkin' about? That wild scream the butternut boys let rip when they charged the Yankees?"

Sanford nodded his head. "I heard about it."

"Good thing they never did it when they was ridin' herd. It woulda' scared the cows clean back to Texas. It's no wonder the bluebellies wet their britches when they heard it. Right on the main street of Miles City, Rob and ol' John let out this high-pitched bloodcurdlin' holler and guess what?"

Riser didn't wait for a response but continued excitedly. "Down the other end of the street, some other Reb did the same. Next thing, all sorts of old cowboys started stickin' their heads out of doors and windows and givin' the same yell and shootin' their guns in the air. Sounded like the whole Confederate army was hidin' out in Miles City." The cowboy slapped his leg and said, "Dang! I shore can't figger out how we lost."

"Did they have any kin?" inquired Sanford, getting back to the subject, figuring this was no time to recall the Civil War.

The foreman thought for a minute. "Not that I knowed of. They was both from Alabama and headed west right after the war. They cowboyed around the New Mexico Territory, looked for gold in Colorado, were bullwhackers on the Santa Fe Trail, and I think they pushed stock to Abilene, Kansas in the early days. That's about all I can tell you."

"You said earlier that they had left you. What did you mean?"

"They quit. Rolled up their gear and took off sudden-like," Riser said bitterly. "Left me shorthanded. Just a few weeks ago, they came to me and said they was movin' on, headin' west to California. Both seemed pretty happy about it. I sure wasn't."

"Did they have much money on them when they went off?"

"Only about a half-month's wages. Both spent every dime they made on rotgut and soiled doves. I said to m'self, they'd be back in a week lookin' for work. I was shore wrong on that 'count." The Box X foreman reached into his vest and pulled out a plug of tobacco, offered a chew to Sanford, then took a big wad between his fingers and stuffed it in his mouth. "Shore is a sorry state when a man can be robbed and kilt for a lousy fifteen dollars."

The Texan fumbled in his pocket and brought out two small gold coins, then tossed them to the sheriff. "That should take care of buryin' the boys."

"You don't need to do that."

"Yep, I do. Both of 'em worked for the Box X. Myself and the rest of the hands would want them to have a decent burial. We'll be movin' the herd north in a couple days and by spring, we'll be long gone. Could y'all take care to see they get a pastor to say some partin' words over 'em?

"I think that can be arranged," offered the sheriff.

"We'd be much obliged," said the drover as he looked around for a nearby spittoon. Since none was handy, he spat on the hot stove, as was the custom. "Well, I better get back to headquarters. Lots of cows to look after."

"Before you go, we have one more matter to clear up." As the sheriff's voice turned serious and official, the foreman stiffened in his chair. "Your Texas hands have been gettin' into scrapes with some of the local cowboys. It seems to be gettin' worse. Fistfights and broken noses is one thing but drawin' down on each other brings *me* into the picture. You understand what I'm sayin'?"

"Are you threatening us, Sheriff?" Riser's tone changed as well, a belligerence having crept into his voice."

"No threat, just a fact," Sanford replied emphatically. "What I just told you, I've also said to the Elk Track hands. I'll hang any one of you who kills the other."

"Even in self-defense?" inquired the wrangler.

"I'll hang 'em or shoot 'em down, just for the fun of it," the sheriff promised, leaving no doubt that he meant exactly what he said. Jason Sanford's reputation as a hard-case reached into Texas and to all corners of the West. His word was not to be taken lightly.

The foreman's hostility subsided somewhat, but he wasn't going to let the sheriff go unanswered. "We got just as much right to the open range as anyone else. Raisin' beef is as much our business as it is theirs."

"Yes, you do; tendin' cows is your business. But shootin' people is mine, and I want all of your boys to know that." Sanford looked the Texan steadily in the eye until he glanced away. The sheriff thought it better to change the subject once more. "If you can think of anything else about the killin' of Lewis and Hurtt, I'd appreciate hearing from you."

"Yeah, I can think of somethin' else. Could Rob and ol' John been kilt by those gunslingers over at the Elk Track? They got reason to hate the Box X brand." The idea pleased the foreman. "Yeah, they got a good reason."

"There's no cause to blame anybody yet. It could have been robbery, it could have been anything. Don't let that idea fester . . . hear me?"

"I hear you."

The sheriff, however, wasn't convinced. The cowboy nodded

solemnly, shot another stream of tobacco spit at the sizzling stove, tromped to the door and out into the cold without saying another word.

In the back corner of the saloon, the grizzled, stooped Norwegian janitor was listening intently to every word, taking it all in while slowly polishing the cuspidors. Old Lute Olsen was rarely noticed as he swept floors, emptied spittoons, washed glasses, or tended to the stove. He moved silently among the patrons clearing tables and scattering new sawdust on the floor. The elderly immigrant had lost his wife to scarlet fever shortly after arriving in America. He could have stayed on and lived with his children in Wisconsin, but having an independent spirit, chose to move west and be on his own, burdening no one.

Old Lute's spoken English was poor, but he had no trouble understanding the language. Most of the saloon patrons assumed he was hard of hearing and spoke no English. He thought it wise to feign deafness—much safer that way. Over the years, Lute had heard many an ugly or frightening comment made by unsuspecting customers, careless about who might be within earshot. Lute ignored most of it; what they said and did was none of his business. *Isn't that what they say is the code of the West . . . live and let live? But what if they talk of murder?*

CHAPTER 9

THE BRIGHT SUN SHONE through the window of David's room, bouncing off the snow with an iridescent brilliance. The wind had stopped and a touch of warmth was in the morning air. The young Dodd sat up in bed and eagerly attacked the tray of breakfast. As he mopped up the last bit of egg yolk with a hunk of bread and stuffed it into his mouth, he said, "Amy, can I have some more toast and maybe some coffee?"

"Ya," said the lithe, towheaded young nurse, smiling. Amy had been sitting nearby, happy to witness his ravenous appetite. She was overjoyed that David was still hungry and as she hastened out the door, she said, "I'll get some right away." This morning, the labored breathing was gone and a healthy tone colored his cheeks. He was alert, had no problem sitting up in bed and, more importantly, he was man-hungry.

"Well! What do we have here?" blustered the doctor as he entered the room, having just been informed by Amy of the change in David's condition.

"Good morning, Doc. I *do* feel a bit better."

Doc Collins sat down on the edge of the bed and leaned forward. "Let me have a look at the bandages." Carefully, he untied the white cotton cloths, lifted them gently, and examined the ugly puncture wounds. The swelling had subsided and the flesh looked and smelled healthy.

"Fortunately, I didn't have to dig too deep to get the slugs out and it doesn't look like any lead poisoning has set in." The physician sat back with a pleased expression. "You, Mr. Dodd, are a very fortunate young man."

David was suddenly downcast. "I wish Calvin was as lucky."

"David, there was no way Calvin could have lived," he answered. "Several of the slugs entered his brain. Whoever shot him must have been close up. The ones that hit you weren't anywhere as deeply imbedded."

"Yeah, guess so. I was riding behind Calvin and I stopped my horse when I saw some figures moving through the trees. I don't think Calvin saw them."

Just then, another voice interjected from the doorway: "How many men did you see, David?" His father, accompanied by the sheriff, came in and crowded around the bed.

"Howdy, Pa!" A beaming smile lit up his face. He vaguely remembered his father being in the room over the past few days, but sleep had overcome him every time. This morning was different; he felt alert and full of questions. *Who found me? Who shot me and Calvin, and most of all, why?*

"David," asked Sheriff Sanford, "did you get a look at 'em?"

David's brow wrinkled in thought; his head wasn't as clear as he had imagined. "Two, maybe three. It was dark; there could have been more."

"Any idea who they were?" inquired the doctor.

"Nah, I saw them in the cottonwoods and then, all at once, they were blastin' away. I got off a shot but the next thing I remember, I woke up with my head in the creek, my foot stuck in the stirrup, and my horse draggin' me over the rocks." David slouched down in bed and wrinkled his brow. "Whew, guess I'm not so up to snuff after all."

"Feel like answering some more questions, son?"

Taking a deep breath, he rose to his elbows painfully and replied, "Sure, ask away."

"David, I looked at the artillery you were packing and it hadn't been fired. Are you sure you got off a round?" asked the sheriff.

David frowned again. "I think so—it all happened pretty fast." He sank back in the bed and closed his eyes, then raised his head up with a jerk, his eyes wide open. "Do you have my gun here?"

"Yes," answered Doc Collins, "it's hanging up over there in the closet."

Sam quickly went to the closet and opened it. The holster was there on a hook behind the door. As he brought it over to the bed, he said, "This here's an ivory-handled Colt .45. Don't you pack a Colt .44?"

"That's Calvin's gun, Pa. Musta lost mine when I got blown out of the saddle."

"Do you think you could've hit one of them?" asked Sanford.

"I have no idea. It's all kinda fuzzy to me right now." David was quiet for a spell, then with firm determination added, "I hope I did; for Calvin's sake, I hope so."

They could see David was tiring fast but he raised up on his elbows and asked, "Pa, have you seen Deborah? I sure would like to see her; she's probably worried sick." He slumped back down on the pillow, obviously drained by the conversation.

"I'll go fetch her," answered Sam. He replaced the gun in the holster and put it back in the closet. The doctor motioned for everyone to leave the room.

Amy had coffee waiting for them in the kitchen and David's turn for the better was the topic of discussion. Doctor Collins excused himself to see a patient in his office. As they were about to leave, Sanford asked Sam if he could speak with him for a moment in private. Nodding toward the hallway, they both excused themselves and slipped into the quiet of the front room.

"What's so secret we can't talk about it in front of others?" asked Sam.

"Well, I didn't want to put you on the spot, in case you said no," replied Sanford.

"Say no to what?" inquired Sam.

"Hear me out. It's important that you do . . . for both of us," the sheriff stated emphatically.

Sanford began to pace, his body tense and voice serious. "I've just had one of my best deputies murdered and another wounded so bad he can't work. This county is enormous, bigger'n most states back east. It stretches over several mountain ranges and covers a lot of territory. What I'm sayin' is that I can't spend all my time in Big Timber. I've got a trial comin' up next week in Bozeman, and a killin' down in Ennis, not to mention some ranchers screamin' about cattle rustlin' in the Madison Valley." He stopped his pacing and faced Sam. "Do you know what I'm trying to say?"

"Not quite," puzzled Sam.

"I'm sayin' I've got to leave. I can't spend all of my time here, as much as I might want to. The trouble is, I don't have a man to spare to send in my place, and this area shore needs the law."

"Isn't there anyone here that you could deputize?" asked Sam.

"Dodd, you know as well as I do that few have the stomach for bein' a lawman." The sheriff walked to the window and looked out, taking a minute before he spoke again. "There is, however, one man who could do the job temporarily."

"Who might that be? Do I know him?"

The sheriff turned and looked him straight in the eye. "It's you, Dodd—it's you."

Sam smiled broadly, "Jason Sanford, you're joshin' me. Whoever heard of a one-armed deputy?"

"Who better'n you? Don't try to fool me. I heard about your law work in Colorado. You tracked down and shot to death one of the most deadly killers in the West. There's more than one notch on your gun, Sam Dodd!"

"That was long ago . . . times I'd like to forget," he said solemnly.

"Long time ago? How about a couple a days ago! When I arrived in town, I no sooner got off the train when the stationmaster was all over me like ticks on a Texas steer, wantin' me to arrest some tall ugly guy for deadly assault—showed me bruises on his cheek and a lump on his head as proof positive. When I asked him to describe his assailant, he told me pretty sheepishly that he had an arm missin'. Didn't take me long to figger out who he meant."

"I was sorry to do that to him, but I truly had to find out if my boy was alive or dead, and that one was sort of sullen and very uncooperative."

"He's a big man and you seemed to have no trouble handling *him*," stated Sanford. "I notice you carry a gun under your coat. I imagine you know how to use it."

Sam just shrugged his shoulders in reply, then said, "I'm complimented, Jason, but I'd appreciate it if you would consider someone else. I've got a ranch and a family to look after."

"Do me a favor, Sam—think about it. I wouldn't expect you to do more than look after the Big Timber area. If the rowdies know the law is still around, it would be helpful. Besides, I'm only askin' you do it until David is back on his feet."

"I'll think about it, but that will be about all I'll do. My days of wearin' a badge are over."

Sanford put his hand in his vest and pulled out a badge. He moved over next to Sam and slid it in his pocket. "I have to leave soon. I won't be back for a couple of weeks. If you decide to take the job, just pin it on."

Sam smiled wide again, retrieving the badge and handing it back to the sheriff. "Oh, no you don't. I got cows to look after and I'm catchin' the train back to Colorado tomorrow. Now that David's on the mend, there's no need for me to stick around."

The sheriff stuck out his hand and retrieved the badge. "Well, I understand. Can't blame me for tryin', now can ya?"

"No, I guess not, but I sure appreciate the compliment," Sam said, then laughed. Gripping the sheriff's hand mightily, Sam bid him farewell. Turning toward the kitchen, Sam said, "I better find out how to find the Dills place." Jason Sanford stepped out the front door into the stubborn cold while Sam entered the warm kitchen where the welcome aroma of fresh-baked bread filled the room. Amy was sitting at the table reading. She looked up, marked her place, and cheerfully said, "Care for another cup of coffee and a slice of fresh buttered bread, Mr. Dodd?"

"No, thank you, Amy."

Seeing the Bible she had pushed aside, he nodded toward it. "Pretty good stuff, isn't it?"

A big smile lit up her face. "Ya, the very best. It is a long letter from my best Friend." Amy's Norse accent was almost musical.

Sam glanced warmly at the girl and quickly reflected on what she had said. He had never thought of Scripture as a personal letter from God, but that was certainly a good way to look at it. He'd have to remember to tell Mary. She'd like that.

"Amy, I'll be leaving tomorrow. I'm going home. But I won't be headin' out until the afternoon, so I've time to catch Sunday services. I haven't been inside a church for months. Is there one you can recommend?"

Amy looked a little perplexed. "We don't have yet a church building, so we get together in the homes. The pastor talks to us in our own Norwegian." Her eyes lit up, brightly. "We will be so happy to have you."

"Good, I'd appreciate it. Now, how do I get to the Dillses?"

Her attitude changed perceptively, from enthusiastic to cool. "Oh, they live closer to town on this street—a brown house on the corner, just a few blocks away."

Sam, not wishing to probe her change in attitude, walked to the door. "I'll see you here tomorrow; we can walk to church together."

She smiled warmly again. "Ya, see you here at nine o'clock."

Sam swung up on the saddle of the stable horse he had rented and headed towards the Dillses' residence, down the icy windswept street. Sam had been in Big Timber for three days now and had yet to see any of Deborah's family. He knew she'd stopped by the clinic yesterday while he and the sheriff were on the road. Deborah had inquired about David's condition but, once again, hadn't gone in to see him, claiming she didn't want to disturb his rest. Neither of her parents had visited him either. Sam found that strange behavior for his son's future bride and her parents. Sam was sure David loved her deeply; however, he suspected the feeling might not be reciprocated.

He was well aware that her mother and father weren't thrilled about their little girl marrying a cowman. Both of them disliked ranching intensely and, being city bred, they preferred urban life. When Homer inherited a small fortune some time ago, he was convinced the road to real riches was through raising livestock on the open range. Enthralled by the romance of it all, he was eager to give it a try. Dills bought a small ranch in the Laramie River drainage, sight unseen. Nobody mentioned that such a life was a commitment to labor from dawn to dusk, or that a ranch wife would likely endure some hardships . . . such as the joys of a sod-roof house infested with insects and an occasional snake.

The Dillses had only one child and they pampered her excessively. Deborah was bright, beautiful, and exciting with soft brown eyes that sparkled, particularly when treating anyone to her infectious laughter. She was instantly likable, especially when her brilliant smile was on display. A mass of seemingly unmanageable black hair surrounded her delicate face, composing a paradoxically wild yet sophisticated look. David was besotted by her, as was every young buck who laid eyes on her.

While growing up in the back country of Colorado, David had Deborah pretty much to himself. But now, in a bustling town like Big Timber with men outnumbering the women five to one, he was bound to have plenty of competition for her affection.

Sam didn't care much for Homer Dills, never having had much time for men whose prime occupation was thinking up excuses for not working. It was clear that Homer wasn't cut out for ranching; nor was he much for hiring good hands. When one of them absconded with part of his herd and sold it off, it was months before Homer found out since he rarely rode his property to check on how his stock was faring. Dills often disappeared for weeks at a time, even during the fall roundup. He'd leave the ranch's care to his hired hands and take the family to Denver. The women enjoyed shopping while he joined other cattlemen at the Denver Club, playing billiards and drinking. Homer never failed to drop by the Dodd ranch to let Sam know what important people he had met at the club. Sam listened politely as Homer basked in the status of others.

When they first became acquainted, Sam found Dills to be deeply imbued with the importance of his own opinions on all subjects. He thoroughly enjoyed arguing over the most trivial and insignificant details. Sam soon tired of it and remembering the biblical admonitions about arguing with a contentious person, let Homer ramble on uncontested. Besides, the conversations ended more quickly that way.

Sam didn't miss the companionship of the Dillses. Now, here he was riding up to their residence in Big Timber. He hoped Homer wasn't at home. He reigned in the horse and swung effortlessly from the saddle.

"About time you were here," sang out Deborah. Sam looked over the neck of the horse to see her rush through the door, only to stop suddenly when she saw who it was. She was dressed warmly, bundled up in a long coat and scarf.

"Oh my, Mr. Dodd! What are *you* doing here? I mean, how nice to see you."

"Were you expecting someone else?" Sam said with a smile.

"Oh, just one of my friends said they might come by." She blushed, then said, "I'm truly glad to see you and I'll bet David is delighted to have you here."

Sam couldn't help but notice that this was not the young girl he had known in Colorado. In her place was a beautiful, vivacious woman; gone was any vestige of childhood. She appeared flustered. Sam wondered, *Hardly over my appearance at her door.*

"Yes, David was happy to see me. I'm sure you're pleased to hear he's quickly regaining his strength. In fact, this morning he ate a big breakfast and said he's looking forward to seeing you. I told him I'd come and get you."

"Ah," she sighed, "that's wonderful news. He's been so sick, only a few of us thought he'd pull through." She looked both ways, up and down the street, then said, "Tell him I'll be by this afternoon. There's something I promised my mother I'd do this morning." She made no move to ask Sam inside the house, nor did she seem to want to continue his visit. After an uncomfortable pause, she terminated the conversation by saying, "It's cold. I'd better go back inside."

"Yes," he said softly, looking directly in her eyes. "It *is* a bit cold." Sam swung into the saddle and slowly headed back through town as Deborah disappeared into the house. A block away, he swung the horse around and waited in the shadows of a building, watching.

Deborah appeared too eager to see him leave and it seemed peculiar that she asked no questions about David or the family . . . nothing. For fifteen minutes he waited, out of sight, in the cold. Then he started to feel guilty, spying on his son's girl. Sam gently nudged his horse into motion when a rider, at full gallop, passed by him leading a saddled Indian pinto pony. They skidded to an abrupt halt in front of the Dillses' home. The young man dismounted with a bound and hurried toward the entrance. Even at a distance, Sam could see he was stylishly dressed. A glint of silver flashed from his black Stetson. The ebony gelding was beautiful—a thoroughbred, definitely *not* common stock. Sam noted the saddle also glittered a bit with more of the precious white metal.

Deborah rushed outside, glanced up and down the street, then greeted him with a hug. In a matter of moments, they mounted the horses and spurred them his way. Deborah was an excellent horsewoman. Leaning forward over the saddle, she whipped the pinto into a dead run. She was laughing as she encouraged the pinto to greater speed. Sam eased his horse into the light just as they were about to pass. Deborah twisted her head away as they raced by, but not before Sam saw her shocked look of recognition.

CHAPTER 10

THE MIDNIGHT SKY WAS CLEAR of clouds and a full, bright moon competed with the stars in lighting the night. Its beams bounced off the gleaming snow, casting deep shadows everywhere. David's room was illuminated by the outside glow, interfering with his desire to find sleep. He lay awake, his mind racing. He rolled over on his right side, but then thought better of it as the pain uncomfortably reminded him of his wounds.

It brought back anxious memories of Calvin Davis shot down in the snow, blood seeping from his wounds. *Why would anybody want to lay in wait for us? There's got to be a reason. Robbery? Hardly. Who would choose that spot to hold someone up?* The trail between Melville and Big Timber was lightly traveled, a poor choice to rob a passerby. But the well-used road from Big Timber to Bozeman had far more potential victims. Robbery seemed such a remote possibility. *Could someone dislike Calvin so much as to plot to kill him?* That, too, was hard to believe. He couldn't think of anyone as personable as Calvin Davis; he didn't have an enemy in the world.

A knot welled up in David's stomach as he contemplated the loss of his friend. Calvin was a good man, full of fun and horseplay. He may have talked more than anyone else, but he was a real gentleman, respectful of women, true to his word and a peace-loving, God-fearing soul. A sizable number of cowboys and sheepherders obeyed the laws about drunkenness and rowdy activity more out of a liking for Calvin than fear of him. David ruled out anyone bushwhacking him due to hate; it was too ridiculous to even contemplate. He also ruled himself out as the victim of revenge because he hadn't been in Big Timber long enough to make any real enemies—leastwise, any who'd like to see him dead.

Come to think of it, a few dandies would probably like to see me leave town, allowing for a clear path to Deborah's door. In the dark, David smiled when he thought of how fortunate he was to have such a beautiful, desirable sweetheart. Soon she'd be his bride. Mr. Dills had intimated they could marry this spring, just a few short months away. David knew the Dillses wanted to give their daughter a big wedding, complete with a reception where the best people in the whole territory would be invited. By May, the roads would be easier to travel and, as Mr. Dills suggested, it was wise to wait until David had a steady job. Deborah and her mother didn't want her moving to the Colorado back country, where the Dodd ranch was located.

David's job with the sheriff's office would be regular employment and, with the extra money he made at odd jobs, it'd be enough for them to live on. He thought about the money he'd saved while working for his father, sure it would be plenty to build a modest home in town where he and Deborah had already picked out a lot.

David winced when he thought about not returning to Colorado. How could he tell his folks of his change in plans? His father was counting on him to help manage the ranch. There was certainly enough work for both of them and the financial rewards were much greater raising stock in Colorado than being a deputy in Montana. However, it was not possible to convince the Dillses of that. Having lived as ranchers, they were convinced it was a miserable and lonely existence. Homer Dills said it loud, clear, and often that his daughter would never be saddled with the hard life of a backwoods frontier woman.

David resigned himself to living in Big Timber after he and Deborah were married and he had already promised that to the Dillses. Now, he had to tell his parents of his decision which would be a disappointment to them both. He knew they'd be hurt, especially his mother.

Being in love with Deborah wasn't easy. It was like riding the rapids—violent ups and downs, but always exciting. In spite of her temper, which could ignite at the slightest provocation, no one could be sweeter or more affectionate. David's face grew hot thinking about some of the things she had whispered to him. She aroused in him emotions that he had difficulty controlling. His heart pounded just imagining being a husband to Deborah Dills.

Though vaguely, he was pretty sure he remembered her being by his side recently. But the only girl he had seen clearly was Amy. She was always near, always handy. He was emotionally moved when he first saw her in the lamplight. She appeared as a fair-haired angel bending over him, blonde tresses bound loosely and rolled into a bun at the back of her neck. Her cool, soft hands gently wiped his fevered skin. When she turned her head, he saw the little scars on the side of her face, made all the more evident when contrasted to the perfect beauty of the other. At first he felt pity; then, as each day passed, the scars became almost unnoticeable. Her quiet, good nature and bright smile obliterated any awareness of the smallpox affliction.

Amy was good company; she read aloud to him daily, saying it would help her speak the language more clearly and understand the country better. The doctor had an excellent library; his selection of good literature varied from medical journals to political philosophy. Amy chose wisely from the wide assortment. One day she would read from Adam Smith's *Wealth of Nations*, the next a tract on freedom by the French author Frederick Bastiat or excerpts from *The Federalist Papers* by Hamilton, Madison, and Jay. She began each time by reading from Scripture. David told her of his family and how he was raised on Bible text by his mother, that Bible-reading was a daily occurrence around the Dodd household.

They had only a few books to learn from, for the Dodd library was still small. In the back country of Colorado there were no schools and all of David's basic education came through his mother, gathered around the kitchen table with his brothers and sisters. He could quote many passages from the Old and New Testaments, especially Proverbs. So could Amy. She liked starting a quotation and calling upon David to finish it; then he would do the same with another verse. Amy had a curious and facile mind, grasping abstract ideas, understanding complex subject matter. She, like his mother, loved delving into Scripture. David told her that his father once said the Bible was an amazing document—shallow enough for a baby to wade in but deep enough to drown an elephant. She laughed joyfully at the simple but profound statement.

Although Amy tried hard to improve her diction, she still had trouble pronouncing some letters in English. David enjoyed teasing her; in fact, he looked forward to seeing her every morning. As soon as the sun tipped above the eastern horizon, Amy cheerfully entered his room with a cup of steaming coffee and a plateful of sweet, hard bread for dunking. He was now strong enough to swing his legs out of bed, get up, and eat seated in a chair. His strength was returning quickly.

In a matter of days, Doc Collins said he could bundle up and go outside for short walks. It wouldn't be long before he'd be back in the saddle, and real soon he might be able to figure out who attacked them and killed his good friend Calvin. "I'll never get back to sleep, thinking about this," he mumbled.

David tried unsuccessfully to force thoughts of Calvin out of his mind, then shifted in bed onto his side. He lay looking through the window at the peaceful scene outside, finally relaxing.

What was that . . . a moving shadow? There was a faint noise near the house, the sound of something breaking through crusted snow. *Was it an animal? No, unmistakably, those were footsteps.* David rapidly swung his legs to the floor and, as swiftly as his weakened condition would allow, headed for the closet and the gun inside. Just as he opened the closet door, there was the crashing of broken glass followed by blinding light as shotgun blasts filled the room. He whirled to see a black form reaching through the broken window.

David tried to pull the gun from the holster but the butt was tied down. He pulled back the hammer of the Colt still in the holster, aimed it in the direction of the figure, and fired. The shadowy image quickly disappeared back through the shattered opening. Still struggling mightily to free the gun, David ran toward the open window and slipped on the broken glass, crashing to the floor. A torrent of freezing air filled the room, mixing with the white smoke from the burnt powder. The bedroom door flew open and he saw Amy standing there in the light of the oil lamp she was carrying.

"Get back!" he screamed. But she rushed into the room, thinking only of David, injured on the floor.

"David, what happ . . . oh, dear God!"

He was sprawled on the broken glass and with each attempt to get up, cut himself again. He was bleeding from a score of small wounds on his hands, knees, and feet. Amy reeled at the profusion of blood on David's body. Had it not been for Doc Collins entering the room, she felt as though she might buckle to the floor, but he grabbed her swaying body and squeezed her tightly. "Not now girl, not now!"

The stern sound of the doctor's voice and another blast of cold air in the room brought Amy back to her senses. He snatched the lamp and lowered it out the window near to the ground. Clearly, there were footprints in the snow leading away. In fact, the doctor saw more than one set of prints. "Whoever it was is gone," he barked. Turning to David who was now struggling to his feet, he examined the cuts and determined all the wounds were superficial, none very serious. "Let's get into my office and I'll pick that glass out of your hide and do some patching up before you bleed all over my rug."

IT WAS BARELY DAYBREAK before Sam heard what had happened. Amy had dressed and braved the freezing temperature to awaken Sam at the Bramble Hotel. The rancher was already up, having breakfast in the dining room, when she spotted him. As soon as he saw the look on her face, he dropped his forkful of food, grabbed his coat and hat, and left for Doc Collins'.

David was sitting up in bed, in Amy's room, as he told his father what had happened. "It was a lucky thing we stowed Calvin's gun in the closet or I'd be a dead dog. Pa, did you see what those shotgun blasts did? Played Holy Ned with the beddin'!"

Sam had already seen the mess in David's room. The destructive force of buckshot, fired at close range, tore the bedding to shreds, leaving gaping holes in the mattress. Feathers were scattered all over. It gave Sam the shivers to see where his son had been lying. If he hadn't gotten up to get the gun and if he hadn't been awake at such a late hour, he would certainly be dead by now. It was chilling to contemplate. Someone tried to murder his son, again.

"Yes, David, I saw it. Thank God that His providential hand kept you awake last night." Sam reached for his coat and pulled his hat tightly about his head. Anger swelled up inside him as he thought of such a cowardly act. *Are fiends out there who would shoot a helpless man while he slept? No way is this going to go unanswered.* He headed for the door, saying, "I'll be back in a short while, Son. Keep that gun close by your bed." He turned and addressed the doctor. "Don't let anyone go stomping around outside the bedroom window. I want to look at those tracks, soon as it's light enough."

Sam went back to the shot-up room and rummaged through David's clothes where, after a moment, he found what he was after and stuffed it in his pocket. Now that the sun was rising, the walk back into town was a bit lighter. Sam went directly to the train station and the adjoining telegraph office, appearing to be the first customer of the day. At the counter, he quickly scribbled out a message.

"May I help you, sir?"

"Yes. Send this to Sheriff Sanford in Bozeman."

The telegraph operator looked at the note and inquired, "Is that all? You can have ten words for the same price."

"No, thank you. That will do it." Sam paid the fee as the clerk tapped out the message on the key.

> Sheriff Jason Sanford
> Bozeman, Montana
> Wearing badge. Stop.
> Sam Dodd

"DAVID, LET'S REVIEW the last few months and see if we can come up with any idea why someone wants you dead."

"Pa, I've done that a hundred times over and I just keep comin' up with nothing," answered his exasperated son. "It got all the more confusing when you told me about those two Texas cowpokes who were shotgunned down. Nothing figures, nothing ties together."

"Yes, something *does* tie together," replied Sam. "It all could've been happenstance, until last night. The killing of Calvin and the cowhands could have been coincidental but not now. Three times? Not a chance. All three shootings were planned attempts of murder; we just haven't figured out the reason why."

"Or *who!*" added David.

"That's right, or who. We need someplace to start, some thread that can lead us to the center of this ball of mystery." Sam paced about the room, thinking. "Let's go over what we do know."

"We don't know anything, do we?" queried a disgusted David.

"Yep, we do," answered the senior Dodd. "We know that there's more than one assassin out there. We know it wasn't robbery. We know the reason is important enough to kill three men and," Sam turned to look straight at his son, "we know they'll try again."

"You're real serious," frowned David.

"Yes, I am. Chances are good they'll not try to kill you here. To repeat what they did last night is pretty remote, 'cause we're on guard now. But when you leave here, when you're up and walking around, they're bound for certain to try again."

"That's a sobering thought," growled the younger Dodd.

"You bet it is. So while there's time, let's find *them* before they find *us.*"

"Pa, I just remembered something that didn't make any sense until now."

"What's that, Son?"

"Calvin and I rode up to Melville to get some documents for the sheriff and when we got there, nobody knew anything about 'em. We were shot on the way back."

Sam was animated as he asked, "Did the sheriff personally ask Calvin to get the papers?"

"No, he received a telegram from Sanford, saying that Olaf Holmquist was holding them and for Calvin to fetch 'em. Now that I think about it, I wasn't supposed to go along. That was Cal's idea."

"That sets up an interestin' bunch of *ifs,*" said Sam. "*If* the sheriff sent the telegram or *if* he didn't, then maybe someone set you up. And, *if* Calvin was the only one the telegram addressed, then maybe he was the one they wanted to kill and you were just what some call an innocent bystander."

"Well, if that's all I was—'an innocent bystander'," David put in, "then what was last night all about?"

"Good point to ponder," answered his father. "But first, instead of assuming anything, I'm going to find out if Sanford did send that wire—and there sure is a quick way to find out. I'm going back to the telegraph office after I check those footprints. And don't forget, keep Calvin's gun by your side . . . be careful."

"I will, Pa. You do the same now that you're wearin' that badge."

Sam nodded and stepped out the door into the bright daylight. He circled the house to the broken window. The sun was reflecting with intensity off the pristine white. There were two distinctly different sets of tracks. Their depth in the snow indicated that one was much heavier than the other. Sam followed them and he found evidence of where three horses had been standing, plus footprints of a third person. Obviously, one stayed with the animals in case a quick getaway was necessary. But why did he dismount? Why not hold the reins while seated in the saddle?

Sam retraced his steps back to the house and took a closer look at the broken window. They probably knocked in the glass with a gun barrel and immediately blasted away. Most of the glass and split window frame were strewn around inside, but no shell casings or anything unusual were discernible. He was about to leave when, on closer inspection, he noticed some tiny dark spots on the window sill. To be sure, he hurriedly went back inside for some hot water, then dabbed it on the spots. Blood! The water thawed the frozen particles into tell-tale red. David must have winged one of the killers, leaving a small spray of blood dotting the white ledge.

At a good clip, Sam returned to the spot where the horses were held. Maybe the rider dismounted to help the wounded one into the saddle. He bent down on his knees to closely inspect the trampled snow. There it was, a small bit of red blending into the white. Again, he retraced his steps to the clinic and David's room, looking for any sign of a slug in the wall. Nothing. Sam could only conclude that somewhere, in the shadows of the Crazy Mountains, a killer was carrying around a lead memento from Calvin Davis' gun, compliments of David Dodd.

CHAPTER II

Y EAH, I'VE SEEN 'EM BEFORE," Tom Nugent, the bar
tender of the Lone Steer Saloon, sullenly answered. He'd
begrudgingly followed the request of Sheriff Sanford,
who'd asked every merchant and saloon keeper to stop by the
icehouse to see if they could identify the two murdered cowhands. Most complied out of curiosity more than civic duty.
Tom Nugent recognized them but he didn't like answering questions about his customers. It just wasn't proper to pry into the
affairs of others, dead or alive. It wasn't safe, nor was it too
bright to stick one's nose into someone else's business. Live
and let live. He looked at the star pinned to Sam's vest and the
empty coat sleeve, deciding he had no cause to volunteer much
information. Whoever this soft-spoken new deputy was, he
didn't look too formidable.

Sam didn't cotton to asking the questions anymore than the
barkeep enjoyed answering them. "Mr. Nugent, I'm tryin' to
find out who murdered these men. So far, I haven't got much
to go on. Anything you could tell me might help."

"Bartender! We need some drinks!" shouted one of the patrons down at the end of the bar. It was the excuse Nugent
needed to leave the conversation with the new deputy. "I'm

busy right now; it's Saturday night. Have a drink on the house. I'll get back to you."

Not letting Sam refuse, the bartender drew a beer from the tap and placed it before him. "Here, I'll be back when I can." Quickly, he moved down the bar to tend to the other customers.

Sam wasn't much of a drinker, although a cold beer on a hot day could sometimes be pretty enjoyable. A cold beer on a *cold* day was hardly refreshing, so he slowly sipped the beverage, waiting for the bartender's return. The saloon was getting crowded. Hands from the Elk Track Ranch were having a grand time throwing dice and downing whiskey at one end of the long bar, while several Box X Texans were gathered at the other. Sheepherders, railroad switchmen, a lively mix of local cowboys, and a few ladies of the night added to the crowd.

All the tables were occupied, including a couple of hot and heavy card games going on in the back. The plinking of a piano, accompanied by a fiddler, were but a small part of the din of loud laughter and cigar smoke. Sam thought about coming back later, but time was important; maybe the action would slow down long enough to talk to the bartender. With each passing hour the crowd grew larger and more raucous, reminding Sam that there was a full moon shining outside. To him it was most peculiar, but it seemed a fair number of men became more edgy and combative when the moon was full. He remembered the bright moonlit nights in Silverville and Leadville, Colorado, when there always appeared to be more latent violence boiling to the surface. On such nights, those in law enforcement joked about, yet dreaded, being on duty when the moon reached its full size, filling the sky. *Could be it's different here in Montana,* Sam thought, hopefully.

It wasn't.

One of the young Texans tried to cut in on an Elk Track hand who was dancing with a little red-haired dancer. Neither one appeared to be older than nineteen or twenty. Hot words were exchanged and suddenly the Texan swung a roundhouse-blow that knocked the Elk Track hand sprawling to the floor. Both were swagger-drunk and red-faced mad. Amid a flurry of foul words the Elk Track cowboy staggered to his feet, spitting blood. With the back of his hand, he wiped the gore from his mouth. Unsteadily, he backed up, right hand poised over the butt of his gun. "I'm goin' to kill you, you Texas swine; fill yer hand!"

The piano and the fiddle were suddenly silent. The barroom became deathly still as both young rowdies backed apart, each of them ready to draw but too afraid to be first. Neither one had ever drawn on another, nor had been forced to defend himself with a gun. In a matter of seconds, one could draw and the other would be dead. The patrons noiselessly shuffled away, crowding together to give the two plenty of room.

"Go ahead, Clyde, put a hole in his Yankee hide," shouted one of the Texans.

"Nobody's going to shoot anyone! Keep your guns holstered or I'll have to arrest the two of you." Both combatants seemed to be relieved and moved their hands away from their guns, as they turned with the rest toward the authoritative voice. Everyone, still silent, parted as Sam Dodd strode to the center of the room. Eyebrows raised at the tall, middle-aged stranger; there were whispers and several gasps as the badge and empty sleeve became evident. Murmurs increased when they saw no gun strapped to his leg, no rifle tucked under his arm. From all outward appearances he was unarmed.

"Okay, you boys better join your friends and quiet down or I'll have to lock you up in the feed store." He turned to the young doxie and said, "I suggest you find someone else to dance with."

"What do we have here, the short arm of the law?" Out of the crowd swaggered an older customer. A sneer spread across his unshaved face as others laughed at the sarcastic tone in his voice. Sam knew the type—big, abrasive, and a braggart to boot—ever ready to take advantage, whether picking on a smaller man or shooting a good one in the back. The loudmouth wore his revolver lower than most and Sam could see he'd loosened the strap over the butt of his gun, for quick action. There was no doubt in Sam's mind that the yahoo would use it if he thought he had a sure-fire advantage.

"Do ya know who I am, Mr. Lawman?" he sneered.

Sam just looked him over, sizing him up, not answering immediately. Mistaking Sam's silence for timidity, he continued, "I'm Red Murphy and I'm a wanted man. Yeah, there're wanted posters out on me down at the depot, even at the store. What do you think 'bout that?" Murphy started to slowly circle Sam, keeping his gun hand to the far side, hiding it with his body. "Uh-huh, just passin' through town, havin' a few drinks with the girlies and playin' some faro." Again, some of the crowd laughed, goading him to continue his diatribe.

"I've shot up a few men but never kilt a lawman before. Always wanted to. You a real sheriff? I wouldn't want to gun down just some ol' war cripple. Wouldn't be right."

"Don't let that bother you; I didn't loose my arm in the war," Sam softy replied.

The inebriated bully moved threateningly toward Sam and slobbered, "Gotya scared, huh? Do ya know what they call me by?" He raised both arms wide, then folded them over his chest and struck a haughty pose. "King . . . how 'bout that!" He glanced over at the crowd and smiled; they were taking it all in, hanging onto his every word, intimidated by his bravado.

The smile left his face as he turned once more to face Sam. "I was enjoyin' watchin' the boys wantin' to shoot each other, but you breakin' it up—that made me angry!" A deep scowl crossed his ugly face as he thrust his chin menacingly toward Sam.

"Bow down to the king, lawman, and do it quick!"

"Certainly," obeyed Sam, quickly bending from the waist, then deftly gripping the bully's trouser leg and straightening up. He jerked "King" off his feet, crashing him hard to the barroom floor. Flat on his back, Murphy scrambled for his gun, only to find the muzzle of Sam's .45-caliber double-action Smith & Wesson just inches from the bridge of his nose.

"Don't that muzzle hole look big enough to crawl into?" Poking the gun ever closer to the spot between his eyes, Sam firmly repeated, "Well, don't it?"

Murphy nodded, wide-eyed.

"Roll over, on your face," Sam commanded, "with your hands over your head." Without looking at anyone in particular, Sam asked for some rope. One of the Elk Track boys disappeared outside and returned with a lariat. "Will this do?" Sam saw he was one of the same young men who, only moments ago, was the center of attention.

"Tie 'im up tight and leave his feet free." The cowhand did a good swift job, binding Murphy's wrists, then Sam yanked him to his feet and marched him to the back of the saloon. He tossed the end of the rope over a beam, hoisted Murphy's arms high above his head, and raised him up until his toes just touched the floor. Sam looped the rope to the nearest wall support and tied it off, leaving the ruffian helpless.

Murphy, regaining a bit of his bravado, started to cuss but his foul language was cut short when Sam stuffed his red silk bandanna in his mouth.

The pack of Saturday night revelers stood by, pretty much in shock over the speed with which Sam had subdued Red Murphy. This blustering, intimidating desperado was now trussed up like a calf at branding and hung up like a slab of beef.

"Going to take 'im to the feed store?" asked the proprietor.

"No, not this one. I think I'll pack 'im off to the county jail in Bozeman, come tomorrow."

Sam walked back down to his place at the bar where Tom Nugent was refilling Dodd's mug and broadly smiling, thoroughly impressed with the one-armed lawman. Looking again at the subdued Murphy hanging from the rafters, Tom ignored the customers clamoring for more whiskey. With the wide smile still on his Irish face, he deferentially asked, "Now, what was that you wanted to know?"

It was six o'clock in the morning before Sam and Tom Nugent could finish their talk over breakfast at the Bramble Hotel. By then, Sam had already hiked Red Murphy to the depot to make the Bozeman-bound train. Sam shackled him to the floor of the baggage car and telegraphed the sheriff's office to expect the incoming prisoner on the next train from the East.

The bartender had given Sam enough bits and scraps to assemble a large jigsaw puzzle; unfortunately, no two pieces fit together. Both Lewis and Hurtt had frequented the Lone Steer Saloon almost every weekend, ever since the Box X spread settled in the open range around the Crazies. There was nothing unusual about their behavior; they acted like any other cowboys. That is, until a little over a month ago. One Saturday night they were buying drinks for everybody, picked out two doxies apiece, and got roaring drunk.

As the night wore on, they bragged about a store of riches they'd found, but when pressed as to what they were talking about, they both grinned and clammed up. Whatever it was, they sure weren't letting on, but it was clear they had plenty of gold coin on them. The two jabbered on about going to eastern Oregon and buying a small spread, maybe even getting married and having kids. Strange talk for a couple of middle-aged, dirt-poor cowpokes.

"Didn't they give you any inkling about where the money was comin' from?" inquired Sam.

"No," replied Nugent, scratching his bald head, "nothing comes to mind. They talked a whole lot about the war and about killin' Yankees, the siege at Vicksburg, the fall of Atlanta. Got real excited about it and the drunker they got, the wilder they was. Once, both of 'em pulled out their guns and started blazin' away at the ceiling. Shot it up pretty good but they was good-natured boys, and paid handsomely for the damages. Reminiscin' about old times, I guess."

"They came in again and did the same thing. Bought drinks for everybody and bid us good-bye. That was the last I saw 'em alive." The barkeep frowned and added, "They was good guys, not a mean bone in either one; but one thing's for sure, they shouldn't have bragged about their poke. Sure as shootin', someone heard 'em and dry-gulched 'em. Betcha didn't find a dime on 'em."

"You're right; both were stripped clean," replied Sam.

Nugent yawned. "'Bout time I get some shut-eye." They both shook hands and parted.

Sam went upstairs to his room and sat heavily on the edge of the bed; he was bone-tired and his eyelids felt as though there were anvils attached to them. He hungered to lie back and stretch out but sleep wouldn't fit into his immediate plans. He put his hand on the bedpost and pulled himself to his feet. He had prom-ised Amy he'd attend Sunday services and take communion. He shuffled to the washstand and poured some water from the pitcher into the porcelain bowl. He grabbed the shaving mug, lathered his chin and cheeks, and stropped his razor.

As he shaved, he gazed in the oblong mirror that hung over the washstand. He found himself squinting at his image, see-ing the tired, haggard reflection. "Stayin' up all night is for young folks," he mumbled. Returning to the task at hand, he reached for the scissors. "Better trim this mustache—it's gettin' a mite shaggy." He noticed the gray hairs were multiplying, slowly but surely catching up to the darker brown. Why did this bring Mary to mind? *Oh, yes.* He remembered seeing a few silver strands in her wealth of auburn hair last month, and had casually mentioned it . . . to his regret.

"Do I *really* have to know that?" was her caustic reply.

I better get her a little something before I head back, chuck-led Sam, as he brushed back his hair. Donning a fresh shirt and a string tie, he reviewed himself in the mirror. *That's better—not much, but at least I shouldn't embarrass the girl.* He put on his coat and headed for the door. It was a new day.

TIRED AS HE WAS, SAM REALLY ENJOYED CHURCH. The service was held in the Halvorsen home and conducted by the circuit-riding Lutheran minister, Pastor Paulsen. The congregation was mostly made up of Norwegian settlers and their children. It was noisy and crowded, but comforting to see entire families worship together. Sam had never attended a Lutheran church and was happy to see there was not an appreciable difference between their litany and that of his own. It had been a long time since he had taken the body and blood of Christ for the remission of sins.

The receiving of the wafer and wine swept much of the tiredness from his body; he felt the blanket of peace engulf him, renewing his strength. He even enjoyed the music. Although the hymns were in an unfamiliar language, some of the melodies were familiar, so Sam hummed along. Singing wasn't his strong suit. No one would miss his sonorous offerings.

After the service, when the congregation lingered over coffee and cookies, Amy had the chance to introduce Sam to the Halvorsens, Mr. and Mrs. Nordstrom, the Weatons, and the elderly Lute Olsen. For some reason when she mentioned that Sam was the new deputy, the old man was visibly startled at the news.

Sam needed to talk with David to go over his conversation with the bartender, Tom Nugent. The message he had received from Sanford bore the startling news that there had been no telegram sent to Cal Davis requesting that he ride to Melville. The communiqué was a phony.

As they approached the house, Doc Collins was leading his mare to the front of the residence, to the hitching rail.

"Goin' somewhere, Doc?" inquired Sam.

"Yep, I have to ride out to the Elk Track. Dorsey Caine, the colonel's cousin, is hurt and the colonel wants me to come out and see him."

"What's ailing him?" inquired Amy.

"The rider didn't say. He just reined up and said Raven needs me out there to patch up Dorsey. I didn't have a chance to ask for details; he rode off too fast. Most likely, Dorsey got thrown from a horse and broke a bone or two. I've been out there before puttin' splints on broken arms and legs." The doctor adjusted the heavily laden saddlebags and tightened the cinch again. "I sure hate the ride out there."

"Why's that?" asked Sam.

"I don't know, can't put my finger on it, but the place puts a sour taste in my mouth. Just thinking about it augers up the bile."

"How about I ride out with you?" offered Sam.

"Nah," the doctor responded lightly. "The colonel doesn't like uninvited guests. Besides, you being a newcomer, you might see the ghost that haunts the Crazies and she might frighten you to death. Then I would have two people to look after." He climbed into the saddle and said, "I'll probably stay the night but I'll be back tomorrow." With a sly wink, he smiled at Amy. "Take good care of David."

Her face flushed as she nodded her head affirmatively. Sam noticed her embarrassment and wondered, *What's going on here?*

Over the kitchen table, Amy told him the story about the woman who haunted the mountains but not a word was said on the cause of her embarrassment.

CHAPTER 12

THE CRIMSON-RED EASTERN HORIZON stood in stark contrast to the ridge of black pines outlined against the sky. Sam spurred his mount into a fast walk and settled in for the long ride. The pre-dawn air was cutting cold and the frosty breath of his horse could plainly be seen as he labored up the draw. Sam thought of the old seaman's adage, foretelling of bad weather: *Red sky in the morning, sailors take warning.*

He hoped not. The last few days had been relatively pleasant. The sun was shining, wind moderate, and the cold was tolerable. It was a half-day's ride to the Box X—maybe more. No telling how far he might have to go to find the foreman. With any luck, Mark Riser would be at the ranch headquarters. Sam wished he'd been with the sheriff when the foreman identified the bodies; might have saved him this long, chilly trek. There were a few more questions needing answers. Though Sanford had filled him in on the conversations with Riser at the icehouse and saloon, that was before Sam learned about the two cowboys' newfound wealth. Maybe one of the Texans' cronies could provide some answers.

It turned out to be a fairly nice ride up and out of the valley, through scrub oak and pine-filled canyons; then higher to the flat bench filled with sagebrush and dry buffalo grass. Sam rode to the southwest toward the snow-covered Granite Peak, reaching twelve thousand feet skyward. Beyond were the headwaters of the Yellowstone with its erupting geysers, steaming ponds, and alpine clearings.

The Box X cows were grazing on the plateaus above and east of the Boulder River. At midday Sam topped the ridge, reined in the puffing gelding, and gazed down upon the ranch's headquarters in the distance. A lazy wisp of smoke wafted from the chimney in the dead calm, a brief respite from the persistent wind. A ranch hand was outside gathering wood while another was culling a mount from the horses in the corral. All the structures appeared to be temporary, built of logs, mud, and sod, surrounded by lodgepine corrals, wagons, and stacks of firewood.

The wood-gatherer looked up and spotted Sam as he descended down through the wash. He peered intently at the approaching stranger, sizing him up while stepping closer to his Winchester leaning against a stump. As was the custom, Sam halted his horse and called out to identify himself. "Box X? I'm Deputy Dodd from Big Timber." The man waved a greeting and only then did Sam ride in.

"Howdy," Sam called, as he swung down from the saddle. "Is your foreman around?"

The cowboy nodded toward the bunkhouse. "He's inside."

Sam pushed aside the buffalo hide that served as the door and entered the dimly lit interior. It was a typical boar's nest. The ceiling was low and Sam, who was taller than most, had to take off his Stetson or stoop down to keep it from being knocked off. He chose the latter and sat down on a wooden box next to the door. He could see the silhouettes of three men watching him, saying nothing.

The smell of unwashed garments, bacon grease, tobacco, and wet saddle blankets saturated the air. On the walls he could make out pictures cut from the *Police Gazette*, clippings from hometown papers, and a poster advertising a stage show. There were tintypes of families and girlfriends, a calendar, and a tattered Lone Star flag. On the far side, a pot of coffee was boiling away on the hot stove. Sam finally broke the silence. "One of you gents Mark Riser?"

"Who do ya be?" came a voice from one of the three.

"I'm Sam Dodd, one of Sheriff Sanford's deputies. I'm here 'bout Hurtt and Lewis."

"Find out who kilt 'em yet?" interjected one of the hands.

"Nope, not yet," responded Sam. "That's the reason I'm here. I have some more questions."

Out of the haze stepped the belligerent foreman. "I'm Riser. What more can I do for ya? I was of a mind I answered all the questions for thet nosy sheriff."

Sam ignored the antagonistic tone and went right to the point. "I don't like asking anymore than you like answering, but I thought you were interested in finding out who killed your friends."

Sam's abrupt response caught the foreman by surprise and he stammered, "Of . . . of course, I am." Realizing he had no cause to be rude, he offered Sam a cup of coffee and, without waiting for a reply, he picked one of the stained tin cups from the table, emptied the grounds on the floor, and poured Sam some steaming brew.

Sam took a sip and smiled, "Been on the stove since mornin'?"

"Nope," replied the wrangler, grinning and breaking the tension. "Last night. Now, what else can we tell ya?"

"I heard the boys came into some money. How did they get it?"

"Don't know. They sure didn't get it from us. Only thing I can figure, they mighta won it gambling," answered Riser.

"Nah, ain't that," said one of the other hands. "Never saw them two go near the card tables or play much faro. They was bunkies, a couple of buck nuns. They'd buy a bottle of bug juice, set in a corner jest watchin' the girls, and get drunk."

"Yeah," piped in another, "onest in awhile, they'd whoop it up, but mostly they'd just watch the rest of us."

"Yep, 'til right before they left. One of 'em musta had a rich aunt die or somethin', 'cause all at once they was buyin' drinks fer all of us."

"Did they receive anything in the U.S. mail you know of?" asked Sam, scratching for a reason why they were suddenly so affluent. The Texans looked at each other and shook their heads. None had any idea where they could have found such a large amount of gold.

"What were Hurtt and Lewis doing just before they came into their newfound poke?" inquired Sam.

"What do ya mean by that?" asked the foreman.

"Just that. What were they working' at—ridin' the range, gatherin' wood, tendin' cows?"

"What difference would that make?" asked Riser.

"Maybe they found some money along the trail traveled by settlers heading west. Lots of those folks were killed by Injuns," offered Sam. "The Shoshone, Blackfeet, and Crow burnt a lot of wagons along the Yellowstone River. Were they ever working close to the trail?"

"Nope. Most times they were here around the ranch. They was our remuderos. Their job was tendin' the stock. Both Hurtt and Lewis were good at shoein' hosses and breakin' the wagon mules." The foreman shook his head, "We're in sorry shape without them. Needed 'em yesterday to take the rest of the bulls over to the Elk Track Ranch."

"You say they delivered stock to the Elk Track? I thought your two outfits didn't get along."

"We don't usually. However, business is business. The colonel made us a good offer on some of our Shorthorns. We had a few to spare so we sold 'em. John and Rob drove some of them over." Riser wrinkled his brow and thought for a second. "Maybe that's it—maybe they won some money at poker when they was over there. They didn't come back right away—stayed the night, now that I think about it."

"That could be," offered one of the others. "The following Saturday, they had pockets full of coins."

"Too bad that deputy got kilt; you coulda asked *him* about the boys," added the third man.

"Why do you say that?" asked Sam.

"Both Rob and John palavered with him quite a bit the night they was buyin' drinks for all the waddies. The three of 'em kilt a bottle of red-eye before staggerin' out of the Lone Steer together."

"Yeah, that's right," claimed the other hand. "We saw 'em later at the Fast Buck Saloon, workin' on another bottle of Old Squirrel."

Sam's curiosity was now at the razor's edge. "Did they mention anything later 'bout getting drunk with the deputy?"

"Shore did!" laughed Riser. "We all kidded 'em pretty good, right up 'til they took off."

"How did they handle that?" asked Sam.

"Oh, they just grinned and said he was a crony and knew a lot of good jokes. Besides, they said he warn't workin' that night and for a pan-sized deputy, he was good company."

"Was that all they said?" queried Dodd.

"Yep, that's all I can remember," said the foreman as the others nodded in agreement. Sam and the cowboys talked for a while longer but nothing new came to the surface. Sam rose to go. "Gettin' late. If I leave now, I can probably get back before dark," said Sam. "Think I'll be moseyin' along."

"Not a bad idea. Looks to be a blue northern is comin' up."

"Think you're right—red sky this morning," answered Sam.

"Before you leave, you might want to see this. The boys left it behind." The wrangler handed Dodd a tintype, a picture of a group of butternut-clad Southerners around their company flag. Riser pointed to two of them. "That's John right next to the flag and Rob is there on the end." The soldiers all looked very serious, as was the way a fighting man thought he should be when his picture was being taken. In the background were the fortifications at Vicksburg.

"The men who defended Vicksburg fought well," remembered Sam.

"Were you there?" asked Mark Riser.

"Yes . . . I was there."

"Blue or gray?" asked one of the hands.

Sam glanced at the young, inquisitive face. Between hay and grass, the lad was barely older than his second son, Matthew. It was not uncommon to see fifteen- and sixteen-year-old Rebs mixed among the battlefield dead, particularly toward the end of the war.

"Son, that was a long time ago and the colors have faded together. It really doesn't matter anymore."

BLUE NORTHERN, IT WAS. Sam barely beat it back to town before it hit with ferocious intensity. The temperature dropped fifty degrees in a matter of hours, accompanied by gale winds magnifying its killing nature. He left the gelding at the stable instead of riding to the Collinses' place. It was no time for man or beast to be exposed unnecessarily to the elements, especially since the horse was exhausted and in need of a rubdown and a bucket of oats. Sam had pushed him hard to make it to Big Timber before the blizzard. The saddle blanket was sopped with sweat and the large head was drooping. "I can walk to the Doc's; you did a good job, ol' hoss, gettin' me here afore the storm."

Sam needed the walk to warm him up; the last few miles in the saddle were bitter cold and he was chilled through. Mingled with the wild wind and swirling snow, the familiar smell of burning firewood greeted his senses as he hurried up the porch steps. Martha Collins opened the door and waved him quickly inside.

"Get in, Sam, before I freeze to death. Looks like we're in for another cold spell."

"Reckon you're right, Martha," he replied, removing his coat and brushing the snow from his hat. "Is Doc around?"

"No," she said immediately. "I'm worried about him. He has yet to come back from the Elk Track Ranch and that's a miserable rough ride in the best of weather." Martha Collins was obviously exasperated as she continued. "That man! He will probably stay there 'til this storm blows over and I'll be worried sick the whole time."

Sam tried to console her. "You shouldn't worry about that tough ol' badger. Betcha it's happened more than once, bein' a Doc in these parts."

"Yes, it has," she replied curtly, "but it doesn't get any better with time." Then, changing the subject quickly, she asked, "Had any supper? I'm about to set the table. Would you care to join us for a plate of antelope stew? David would be pleased."

"Thank you, Martha. If it won't put you out any, I'd be more than obliged." Sam was hungry. Other than coffee with the Texans, he hadn't had anything since breakfast at the hotel. "You say David's eatin' at the table?"

"Sure is," Martha said, with a smile. "That lad's healing faster than anything. By the way, you just missed seeing that pretty little thing your son is going to marry. She spent quite a bit of time with him this afternoon."

"Deborah Dills was here?"

"Who else would she be? He talks about her all the time," answered Martha as she busily set out the tableware. Leaning into the kitchen, she called, "Amy, bring in that kettle of stew. Sam, you go fetch David; he's back in the front bedroom again."

Sam opened the door to his son's room. It was dark inside.

"Howdy, Pa, come on in. I'll get some light in here." David struck a match and lit the kerosene lamp. "Room looks a little bit different, doesn't it?"

Sam saw that the broken window had been boarded up and the bed had been moved to a side wall, giving David a better view of the doorway. The ivory-handled Colt .45 lay beside

David on the bed, within inches of his hand. Evidence of the buckshot was still on the walls.

"Supper's on," were his father's only words as he held open the door.

David got up and walked with his father toward the Collinses' kitchen.

"Pa, Deborah spent most of the afternoon with me. It sure was good to see her." David was animated as he continued on during supper—detailing their long visit, about his job with the sheriff, her father's business, their wedding plans for the spring, living in Big Timber, and the lot they were going to purchase. David was so wrapped up in his own plans, he was oblivious to the others around the table. Amy sat quietly with her eyes lowered, staring at the plate of food. She hardly touched her stew and halfway through the meal, she excused herself and returned to the kitchen. Martha was thoroughly enjoying David's enthusiasm and absorbing his every word. Sam ate heartily but the conversation wasn't pleasant to his ears. "What's this you said about a lot?"

David suddenly realized what he had said and the implications his father must have read into it. It was time to put all of his cards on the table.

"Pa, Deborah and I are goin' to live here in Big Timber. We're buying some property come spring; we're goin' to build a home." It was awhile before the senior Dodd replied, "Made up your mind for sure, Son?"

"For sure, Pa," he firmly but respectfully answered.

"Your ma and I hope the two of you will be happy here." Sam was heartsick that his son and bride wouldn't be returning to the Dodd ranch in Colorado, but he had no intention of showing it. His son was a grown man and had a right to make up his own mind. The matter, as far as Sam was concerned, was settled. He was very much aware that he wasn't the only one upset by the conversation; Amy was visibly shaken by the discussion of the impending wedding. Sam sure didn't cotton to the idea either, not after seeing Deborah ride off with another man.

Suddenly, the front door burst open and Doc Collins, along with a freezing gust of wind, entered the house. He immediately headed for the pot-bellied stove, yelling, "Martha! Amy! Get me a cup of hot coffee! I'm froze solid from cranium to colon and all parts in between!"

The doctor dropped his snow-laden coat, scarf, gloves, and hat on the floor as he made his dash to the stove, scattering them all the way from the door. Rushing up to the heat, he placed his hands just inches from the glowing stove, then rubbed them together while dancing from one foot to the other. "I'll never go out to that place again, even if they promise me my weight in gold!"

"You talkin' about the Elk Track?" asked Sam, having left the table to join Collins by the stove.

"No place else," Doc Collins said through shivering lips. "It's a miserable ride out there and the unpleasantness is only surpassed by the miserable, lying curs living in that miserable place." The doctor turned to warm his backside while vigorously rubbing the circulation back into his body. Angrily, he rambled on. "Treating Dorsey Caine is tantamount to trying to pet a rattlesnake. They had the audacity to tell me that the hole he had on his rump was caused by falling on a pitchfork. He had a big puncture wound in his gluteus maximus—in one cheek and out the other. I could tell someone had been trying to fix him up but when it festered, they decided to call on me."

Amy came in with a cup of hot coffee and handed it to the shivering doctor. Without a thank you, he continued, "Dorsey, he's a tough one. Laid there on his stomach gritting his teeth while I probed away, not uttering a sound. Musta hurt like the dickens."

"Is he going to be all right?" asked his wife.

"Probably. Won't be sitting a comfortable saddle for a spell. All the time I was working on him, that lying son of the colonel was telling me how he saw Dorsey trip in the barn and impale his butt on the pitchfork. Bull!" The doctor was finally warming up and he stopped shivering. "It was enough to insult my intelligence."

"Why do you say that?" inquired a most curious Dodd.

"I've been doctorin' a long time," replied the physician, "and I know a bullet hole when I see one."

CHAPTER 13

THE WIND POUNDED AGAINST THE Collinses' house with savage intensity, piling the snow ever deeper on the wayward side. It had been coming down continually for two days with no relief in sight. The walk from the Bramble Hotel to the doctor's house had been relatively easy with the gale at his back, but Sam knew his return into the stinging snow and whistling wind would be painful. He hoped the meeting with Jason Sanford and David would be productive, that the sheriff had some worthwhile information.

It was warm sitting by the stove with a cup of hot broth in hand. The doctor called it "love-apple soup." Sam had no idea where canned tomatoes got such a silly name, but that's what they were called. Whatever the moniker, it sure tasted good. David sat quietly on the couch, fully dressed for a change. Jason Sanford sat in a squeaky rocker, which was overburdened and strained with each movement of the large man.

Doc Collins was fidgeting through his pockets looking for his pipe, as Sam asked, "Doc, what can you tell me about the Elk Track outfit? Who is this Colonel Raven?"

The doctor went over to his desk, rolled back the top, and poked around inside before he answered. "Sam, I really can't tell you a whole lot except he was one of the first ranchers in the area. Came here in the early seventies with his cousin and son, plus a whole herd of Longhorn cattle."

Sam said, "I hear he's tough as rawhide and keeps pretty much to himself."

"Oh, yes," added the doctor, "he was in the Confederate Army, and badly wounded, and because of it, hear tell, he still hates Yankees. I'm told he's a Southern aristocrat by birth."

Doc found his pipe and tobacco, then after tamping it down with his forefinger and lighting up with a match touched to the potbellied stove, he went on. "I've been out there only two times before tendin' broken bones, and I've treated a couple of their riders here in town. They're a close-mouthed bunch, every one as ornery as a wolf on the prowl."

"I don't know much about 'em either," offered the sheriff. "But I do recall that the colonel squatted on foothill land and had his hands file claims on much of it. I understand he bought it from them, all legal-like."

"That's true. He's the first to buy out anyone who's in trouble, provin' up their claim. Or, for that matter, any settler hereabouts who can't make it and wants to sell. There've been plenty of those around here," added the doctor.

"Has the Elk Track had any run-ins with the sheepmen on the open range?" asked Sam. "There've been some real wars in other parts of the country."

"Hardly any at all," said Collins.

"That's good. Wonder why not?"

"It's the graze, Pa," explained David. "The cows and sheep don't compete as much for the same feed and, in some cases, they even benefit from each other. The sheep can graze on larkspur with no bad effects, while it kills cows. The woollies like the forbs and weeds which the cattle won't touch. These Montana cows favor the rough grass; they'll graze on death camas with no trouble, but it will sure kill any sheep who ate it. Fact is, in the hills, they do each other a favor."

"That sure is different from other parts of the West," stated Sam.

"That's true," interjected the doctor. "The foothills of the Crazies are absolutely beautiful in the spring, covered with lovely wildflowers and, unfortunately, death for the sheep. The hilltops are lush with feed and covered with death camas. The herder has to keep his flock on the side hills and along the creeks or he'll be in big trouble. I've seen whole flocks trembling in death throes from feedin' on camas. It's not a pretty sight."

"I rode for Raven for a spell and the mutton-punchers didn't seem to bother the colonel much," David mentioned.

"You rode for the Elk Track?" asked the sheriff.

"Yep, I did," answered the young Dodd. "But only for a short spell, during the fall roundup. It didn't work out too well."

"I didn't know that," remarked his father, carrying a surprised look on his face. "When did all that happen?"

"First job I had in the area was riding for them, chasin' mountain boomers out of the Crazies. It was interesting ropin' those critters out of gullies and draws," David said, with a grin. "I enjoyed that part of the work."

"What didn't work out too well?" the doctor asked specifically.

"It was around the ranch. I ran into a little trouble with J.D."

"The colonel's son?" asked the doctor.

"What kind of trouble?" the elder Dodd quickly put in.

"Well, wasn't much. I didn't rightly want to talk about it, but I guess I better. It was cause enough for me to leave in a hurry. Besides, Pa, there isn't much I can tell you about the Ravens, since I spent much of my time in the hills roundin' up strays. I never did palaver much with the colonel or Dorsey Caine, who handled the crew. I can tell you one thing—their regular hands were a shaggy lot of mavericks, hard-cases to a man."

David didn't want to tell his father that he and J.D. had engaged in a grisly fistfight. The memory wasn't pleasant, but it might have some significance so, reluctantly, he told the story, leaving out the bloody details.

ON A SUNDAY NIGHT, the colonel allowed the hands access to the ranch house to play pool, gamble, and hoist a few. During roundup, extra men were hired to augment the full-time crew and David was one of them. It was hard work with little time off. Sunday was just another day, but in the late afternoon, the cowhands were given the opportunity to relax and even get drunk. As long as they could fork a saddle the next day, Dorsey didn't seem to care. This particular day, Dorsey and the colonel had gone to Livingston leaving J.D. in charge.

David didn't immediately take part in the festivities with the rest. He pulled a small Bible from his saddlebag, found a spot in the shade of the bunkhouse, and read a few passages before joining the other waddies playing pool in the main house. Several of them spotted him reading Scripture and good-naturedly started calling him "Preacher." David took it with a smile. Later on, when they noticed he wasn't drinking and the teasing magnified, he continued to take it in good stride.

Joshin' around and playing practical jokes was a cowboy's pastime and David knew that to take offense would just increase the humorous jibes. As the evening wore on, the drunkenness became more prevalent and the talk more vulgar, turning to the attributes of the local females of ill repute. Most of the funnin' was directed at J.D. Raven, who was deemed by one and all as the premier ladies' man among them. J.D. wallowed in the praise, looking peacock-pleased, and expanded upon the already acknowledged exploits. He'd been drinking more heavily than the rest, adding to his boastfulness about the hookers of his acquaintance in Miles City and Livingston.

David didn't think much of the conversation, while the other hands were soaking it all in and joking about the soiled maidens as well. He thought it a good time to leave and started for the door, only to stop short when he heard J.D. mention Deborah Dills. Hearing her name bandied about in such ribald company shocked him to the soles of his boots. David whipped around, the blood rushing to his face as he spat out through gritted teeth, "Don't ever let your dirty mouth utter her name again! Do you hear me?"

All in the room were shocked into silence, then one started to chuckle, another guffawed, and the rest broke out in nervous laughter.

"Well, lookie whut we have here, the preacher callin' J.D. a flannel-mouth!" snickered one of the hands.

Everyone was amused, except J.D. Raven. He stepped in front of the others and glowered threateningly at David. His shoulders were hunched, right hand hovering over his Colt, anger and humiliation his lot, galled by the threatening tone in David's voice.

"No one calls me down and tells me to shut up—no one who lives to brag about it."

"He ain't packin' iron, J.D.," announced one of the new hands. "You can't go gunnin' down an unarmed man," said another. Just about all mumbled in agreement.

J.D.'s hand quavered over his gun; he desperately wanted to shoot David, standing there defiantly. But he was sober enough to figure killin' an unarmed man in front of so many new hands hired for the roundup. They could bring the law down on him. J.D.'s hands went to his belt. He unbuckled his gun and hissed so all could hear, "There's nothin' stoppin' me from kickin' him to death! Outside, Preacher!" J. D. handed his holstered gun to one of his cohorts and gestured at the door.

With heightened excitement, all the hands shoved and stumbled behind David into the dusky light of late summer, whooping it up, eager to watch the fireworks.

David was burning with quiet anger, ready and willing to take on the foul-mouthed Raven. Before he had barely cleared the doorway, a fist smashed into the back of his head, sending him sprawling and his hat flying. Dazed, he rolled over in time to see a boot headed for his face. As he twisted away, J.D.'s foot grazed the side of his cheek with the spurs cutting a deep gash in his jaw.

The momentum of the vicious kick carried J.D. awkwardly past David, giving him time to regain his feet. J.D. immediately went at him, swinging fists, arms, and knees in rapid-fire blows. Lefts, rights, and ferocious kicks were hurled at Dodd, some landing painfully but most absorbed by his arms and shoulders. Ducking and weaving, David tried to shake the fog from his brain, fighting to recover his senses. Suddenly, the blows stopped. J.D. backed off, breathing heavily. He collected his wind, fists jabbing at the air as he circled David, taunting him.

"How did ya like that, Preacher?" J.D. gasped between deep breaths. With sneering bravado, he moved closer. "Come on, Bible boy, put up a fight; let's give the gang a good show."

David had yet to throw a punch and he looked a gory mess. The spur slash on his jaw had exuded blood all over his face and shirt and was still bleeding. The Elk Track hands were screaming for Raven to finish him off and the twisted smirk on J.D.'s face spoke of his confidence in the final outcome.

David was taller than Raven, though not as heavily built. He was every bit as strong and more accustomed to the rigors of outdoor life. Although his head had cleared, the anger was still boiling and the pain only intensified his resolve. David circled as well, facing the smirking Raven. He knew that after J.D. captured his breath, the onslaught would go on with a vengeance. Raven's style of fighting was to swarm all over his opponent and pummel him, then kick him senseless.

David stood braced, arms at his side, knuckles clenched, waiting for the next attack. The young Raven wore his long black hair tied back, Indian fashion. It was now wildly loose, framing his clean-shaven, profusely sweating face. With a roar, he lunged at David, throwing a wild right at his jaw. David ducked forward, slipping under the blow, and with his left hand grabbed J.D.'s mane and pulled him off balance, keeping a firm grip on his locks. With blinding speed, he hit J.D. flush on the mouth with his free hand, sending blood flying. Again and again, his right fist smashed into Raven's face, striking brutally, and each time David yanked him forward by the hair.

The blows were loud and ugly, the crushing of human flesh and bone. *Bam . . . bam . . . bam!* Then it was over.

Raven's seemingly lifeless body crumpled to the ground as soon as David let go of his hair, a limp heap collapsing into a cloud of dust. Glancing around, David retrieved his hat and pulled it down firmly on his head. He wiped the blood from his mouth and cheek, then defiantly looked over at the gawkers. "Anybody else?"

They were astounded over the abrupt finish of the fight and the prostrate body of their boss's son lying facedown in the dirt. They were equally awed by the speed and power they'd witnessed in David's fists. Not a one had the slightest desire to test him out.

One of the cowboys seemed to speak for them all. "It was a fair fight, right boys?" Their grunts and nods signaled agreement. A waddie stepped forward and said, "If I wuz you, I'd get my bedroll and vamoose. I wouldn't wanta be you when J.D. wakes up. He'll try to kill ya fer sure."

"Yeah," added another. "So will Dorsey and the colonel when they get back."

Concurring, David said, "I'll mosey along but not before I'm paid up. The outfit owes me three weeks' wages. A dollar a day—that's twenty-one dollars."

"Ya ain't goin' to get it from any of us," snidely remarked one of the cowboys. "We'd get skinned alive if we gave you the hair offa a dead skunk."

"No problem, I'll get it from *him,*" David said, motioning to Raven's senseless body. He squatted down by the unconscious form and rifled through his pockets. Extracting a twenty-dollar gold piece, he held it up to the shocked cowboys and said, "This will do. I'll call it square." Within the hour, he'd packed his roll and ridden away.

"DAVID, I THOUGHT YOU TOLD US you had no enemies. Now I find out you tangled with the son of the most powerful rancher in these parts and cleaned his plow, to boot," stated his mystified father.

"Aw, Pa, it was just a fistfight—nothin' to get excited about. Besides, after it was over, he looked a lot better than I did," his son said humbly.

"You humiliated J.D. Raven in front of his men. If he's as much of a dandy as you say, I doubt he will forget about it."

David paused, then responded, "Wanting to face me in a gunfight is one thing; waiting around for hours during a blizzard, hoping to dry-gulch me with a greener, is another. J.D. has a reputation as a gunfighter, and a good one, at that. If I somehow damaged his honor, he's sure not going to redeem it by cutting me down with a shotgun in the dark. He'd more likely challenge me in the street, in broad daylight, with other folks watchin'."

"David's got a point," interjected the doctor. "The colonel's whelp is a proud one; what David says is probably true. What's more, from all of the facts gathered so far, there would be no way J.D. could have known David was coming back from Melville with Deputy Davis. He'd also have had to know Calvin would take David along. That's stretching it—too complex for a vain young buck like J.D."

"You're probably right," replied Sam. "However, the Elk Track Ranch is hooked up in these shootin's somehow. Too much coincidence for me. The Texans suddenly wind up with pockets full of gold after they deliver some bulls out there. Both are done in soon after and then . . . the latest attack on David. What about the shot my son fired at the assailants?

Could that be David's bullet hole in his backside? I don't know, but somehow the Elk Track could hold the key to who's doing all the shooting."

"But why?" asked the doctor. "The colonel's the richest man this side of Denver; money isn't his problem. Dorsey is meaner than a rattlesnake but why would he want to kill off David? What possible reason could he have?"

"I just don't know," answered Sam. "But whatever it is, that reason's a serious one. Murdering three men, one of 'em a lawman, has got to be important to someone."

"I don't get it, either," added the sheriff. "And right now, I don't have the time to find out. I have to get back to Bozeman right away."

"What's the rush?" inquired Doc Collins.

"Ask *him*," scowled the sheriff, pointing a finger at Sam.

"Jason, what in the world are you talking about?" asked a surprised Sam Dodd.

"Remember that bad hombre you shipped me by rail last month?"

"You mean Murphy?"

"Yeah, that's him. I was down in Ennis chasin' rustlers when he arrived in Bozeman. My new deputy didn't know how to handle the matter, so the vigilante committee took him out and hanged him."

"They didn't!" answered an incredulous doctor.

"Shore did!" replied Sanford. "Can't say he didn't deserve it. Coulda plastered the jailhouse wall with the circulars out on 'im."

"If he's dead, why do you have to get back?" asked David.

"Get a lot of nervous folks on my hands ever' time someone gets strung up without a trial. We're gettin' real civilized over in Bozeman."

"Sure seems like it," agreed Sam.

"I'll try to get back as soon as I can, but it wouldn't hurt for you to ride out to the Elk Track and ask a few questions," instructed the sheriff.

"Good idea," agreed Sam.

"Don't even think of going out there until this blizzard subsides," offered Doc Collins. "It's trouble enough finding the doggone place in the summer, much less locating it with a blue norther' blowin' in your ears."

"This is Saturday, isn't it?" asked Sam.

"Think so," answered his son.

"If the weather lets up, I'll ride out there Monday. Tomorrow," Sam said, addressing his son, "I can attend services and write a letter to your mother. Wouldn't be a bad idea if you wrote a few words to her too. By the way, want to try to make it to church with Amy and me?"

"No thanks, Pa. Amy already mentioned it. Deborah said she'd be over."

"Deborah would be welcome too," added Sam.

"Thanks, Pa, but the Dillses still haven't found a church to their liking. Leastwise, that's what Deborah says. Her ma has yet to pick out a preacher to perform the wedding."

Sam wanted to offer his opinion but thought better of it. It isn't what Mrs. Dills liked that was important, it was what David and Deborah wanted. He felt sure the Dillses were stalling, looking for excuses to delay the marriage. *Unfortunately, David doesn't even seem to be aware of all the games being played.*

CHAPTER 14

SAM REINED THE DUN TO A HALT after crossing icy Swamp Creek. Upon reaching the top of the ridge to the east, he swung down from the saddle and tied the horse to a twisted spindly pine, giving him a perfect vantage point to view the mountain ahead and the valley below. The animal shook itself, relieved of the weight on its back. Sam lifted a stirrup, hooked it over the apple, and tightened the cinch. "Well, ol' hoss, what do you think of this beautiful place? Think the Lord knows how to paint a pretty picture?"

Beautiful, it was. A cloudless blue sky and the high plateaus appeared to be swept clean. The wind randomly piled the snow in sparkling white drifts. The magnificent snow-covered Crazies loomed before him, cuts of dark green pine slashing down the sides into a myriad of canyons and draws. The Crazies were an old mountain chain—white-topped giants thrust up from the high plains, awesome in sheer size with the jaggedness smoothed by erosion and time. Steep granite cliffs and massive rock formations abounded but were less dramatic than the younger mountains to the west.

The plateaus and valleys supplied good graze for elk and huge swaths of black virgin timber where they could bed down.

There were plentiful caves for hibernating grizzlies, black bear, and wolves to lair their cubs. Swamp Creek drew its strength from the glaciers above, nurturing the cottonwoods, aspen, and willows along its winding path to the Yellowstone. The trees were a backdrop to the ever-alert white-tail deer; though browsing, they kept a close check on the distant horse and rider. Sam waved his hat and watched them disappear into the thicket, snowy tails erect, flagging danger.

Above him, no more than three hundred yards away, stood a magnificent mulie four-point buck, grazing on bitter bush. The mature deer had lost one of his antlers, pushed out by the new growth. He soon would be growing new ones, bigger than the last. He raised his head as Sam signaled with his wide-brimmed Stetson; he stared for a moment, then went back to browsing.

"Mulies sure aren't as smart as white-tails, but the dumbest one of them is brighter than you'll ever be," he said to the dun-colored mare as he mounted once more. Sam wished he had one of his own horses to ride. Big Timber's stable had little to offer—nothing but a motley assortment of range horses. There was not a mule in the lot, which he'd requested. Be it snow, rugged rocks, or sloppy wet weather, he preferred a good sure-footed mule. The last animal he rented was adequate, but none measured up to the Morgans and the mules he had back home. If he were to stay much longer, he'd have to seek out and buy a decent mount or borrow David's. His son's poor roan was now recovered from the buckshot wounds inflicted during the slaying of Calvin Davis.

With buckshot in his neck, why didn't the horse panic and run off, dragging David to his death? Why, at the right moment, did David's foot come out of the boot? And, how did the men at the ferry find David in the dark, just in time to keep him from freezing to death? Providence? You bet! There was no doubt in Sam's mind that God's will ruled the lives of men, as it did in all creation. Once more he drank in the beauty that surrounded him and marveled at the symmetry of it all. At that point, he thought of the business at hand—getting on to the Elk Track Ranch.

The doc's instructions were explicit. The frozen, rutted wagon tracks and the multiple sign left little doubt the canyon entrance was just ahead on the right, over the next ridge and down along the valley floor. Sam was assured when he caught sight of a rider leading a string of horses, headed in the same direction on the far right. Sam spurred the gelding into a trot, hoping to intercept the wrangler before he entered the narrow canyon. As they were about to converge, Sam was sure the horseman looked familiar.

Sam reined up and hailed the rider, identifying him as the young hand who faced off against the Texan in the Lone Steer Saloon.

"Howdy!" was the friendly greeting he offered. "Remember me? I'm Sam Dodd."

The cowboy's frown disappeared and as the name registered, a wide smile lit up his face. "Sure do, Deputy . . . sir, now that I heared yer handle. What's a feller like you doin' out here?"

"Two things. For one, this." Sam bent forward and untied the saddle string and removed the coiled rope. "This belongs to you. Thanks for lettin' me use it." Sam tossed the lariat to the young cowboy, who caught it easily. "I never thought I'd see this hunk of braided rawhide again," he said while inspecting the rope. "Much obliged, sir, for returnin' my reata."

"Heading to the Elk Track," Sam said, adding, "mind if I ride along?"

"Not a bit," the young waddie replied, smiling. "Give me the chance to thank you fer keepin' me alive. I don't win no prizes packin' iron and I was so drunk, I was seein' two Texicans afore me. I wouldn't know which one of 'em to shoot."

Sam laughed out loud at the wiry, good-natured lad riding alongside him. He was a towhead and about David's age, full of life and energy. It would have been a tragedy, had he been shot down in a barroom quarrel over the attentions of a soiled dove. He had seen too many like him, their lives seeping scarlet from their wounds. Sam's four years of Civil War and his service as a lawman could be chronicled in the blood of young men like this one. "What's your name, son?" he asked.

"Arlis Thadius McKay, sir. Most folks jus' call me Arlis."

"How long have you been ridin' for the colonel?" inquired Dodd. Then he added, "Hope you don't mind me askin'."

"Don't mind at all. Y'all have more trouble shuttin' me up than gettin' me started."

Sam couldn't help but chuckle; he liked the affable young buckaroo. He seemed out of place, not the sort of regular working for the Elk Track.

"Well, let's see now—when did I, fer true, start bustin' broncs fer this outfit? Since yer the law, I better be shore. Lessee now. Oh, yes. 'Twas last year sometime, maybe the year afore." He busted out laughing at himself as Sam chortled along with him.

"My memory's not so good, Deputy Sir. Been throwed by 'bout ever' bronc I've forked in the last few months and landed on my head most times."

He rocked back and forth in the saddle, giggling at his own humor until tears rolled down his cheeks. "Doggies! That was a good one." He wiped his face with the back of his glove and said, "Guess it's time to stop the funnin'. In truth, I went to work for them in the fall of last year. Been with 'em about six months. They needed someone to handle breakin' the broncs. They couldn't spare any of their regulars. Most of 'em are too old fer rodeoin' unbroke range hosses, so they hired me. 'Spect I'll be leavin' come spring. Got some work up in Fort Benton." Young McKay looked over at the tall lawman and wondered aloud, "Say, what's a deputy doin' way up here, anyway?"

"Arlis," Sam asked, "do you remember two older Texans delivering some bulls to the Elk Track?"

"Sure do. They brought in several head of good-lookin' stock."

"Did they stay the night before they went back to their out-fit?"

Arlis thought for awhile before he answered, "Yep, they shore did. Slept next to me in the bunkhouse. Both of 'em got sloshed and one snored so loud I had ta throw a boot at 'im."

"Do you remember anything special about their visit?" asked Sam.

"What do ya mean, *special?*"

"Did they play cards . . . gamble . . . win some money?"

"Now that you mention it, they delivered the cows on a Saturday an' that night they went up to the ranch house to play pool with the rest of us. I won fifty cents off of the one with the big nose. I forgot his name."

"Rob Hurtt was his name; the other was John Lewis," stated Sam. "Both were shot to death."

"Yep, I heard tell when I was at the Lone Steer Saloon. Know who done it?"

"Not yet. They came into some money and I'm tryin' to find out where they got it," he answered, shifting his weight in the saddle. He looked up the sides of the steep canyon walls they had entered.

"They shore didn't get it gamblin' with the hands out here. You should ask the colonel about 'em—he seemed to know them from somewhere."

Sam's ears perked up at this tidbit of information. "How's that?"

"The colonel ain't big on mixin' with the hands but he spent a lot of time talkin' to 'em. Early on, when they first showed up, they kept lookin' at the colonel funny-like and whisperin'. Then, after awhile they seemed ta be old pals."

"Could be, since they were in the Confederate Army to-gether," offered Sam.

"Come to think of it, there was a lotta war stories floatin' around. That was rightly it, relivin' the war an' all."

They rode silently along for a time, picking their way through the rocky canyon shelf that served as the road before Sam spoke again. He decided to throw a little bait out, wondering how Arlis would respond. "I hear Dorsey had an accident and got himself shot in the rear end."

"Shot? That ain't what *he* sez happened," answered McKay. "Fell on a nail or a pitchfork in the barn. Dobie Johnson's the one who got shot accidental. Came ridin' in with a bullet in the gut a month or so back. We'll be ridin' by where we buried 'im."

"How did that happen?" Sam asked quickly, trying not to show his heightened curiosity over this unexpected news.

"Accordin' to Dorsey, Dobie took out his revolver to shoot at a coyote and tripped over some sagebrush—somethin' like that. I figgered they shoulda taken him to town, but for some reason they brought him all the way back to the Elk Track. They was pretty upset about it. Dobie was an old hand—been with the colonel from the beginnin'.

"We was all asked to keep quiet about it as a favor to Dobie's memory. They said before he died he asked that his passin' be kept quiet. Seems like he was pretty good with a gun and to be kilt in such a dumb way woulda mortified his ghost. Didn't make much sense to me. There's dumber things to get kilt over . . . like fightin' over a dancehall gal." Arlis broke out laughing again. "And gittin' kilt bustin' broncs is another!"

They rode out into the open; the creek and trees lay before them, the ranch house beyond, well within a short ride. It was fortuitous meeting Arlis McKay; much had been gleaned from their conversation. Sam doubted that Arlis had any idea of the significance of his remarks. Or, that if innocently repeated—especially to any of the Ravens—his very life could be in danger. Dobie Johnson could very well have been one of the assailants, and was probably shot by David at Big Timber Creek. If so, he could be the reason they rode off instead of robbing both David and Calvin, making it appear like a holdup.

The fact that the two Texans seemed to have known Raven was highly interesting. Could he have given them a lot of money? And if he did, why?

The sense of foreboding was back. In spite of the cold, Sam's skin felt like he was crawling with hot ants. There was no question in his mind that he had put this young cowboy in peril. Sam reined to a stop and signaled the young bronc-buster to do likewise.

"What are you stoppin' fer?" asked his congenial companion. "The ranch and hot grub is just beyond them trees. I bet there's a batch of Mexican strawberries cookin' on the stove."

Dodd pointed to a pile of rocks and a makeshift wooden cross, and asked, "Is that where Johnson is buried?"

"Yep, that's the place. They just heaped rocks on 'im and left him be," Arlis solemnly commented. "I put the cross up an' offered a few words later on, after everyone left. They don't take much to religion at the Elk Track spread."

Sam's voice and manner were deadly serious as he spoke. "Arlis, please pay close attention to me. I can't tell you why 'cause I don't know for sure, but I'm going to rest here a spell and ride in later. I don't think it's wise that we're seen together. Do me a favor and keep quiet about us talking to each other."

"What's the matter," he asked, with a grin. "You shamed at bein' seen with a bronc-buster?"

"One of these days I'll tell you all about it, but for now, your silence would be deeply appreciated," answered Sam with a worried expression.

"Well, all right," Arlis replied, "but I shore don't see any harm in two fellers ridin' and jokin' around together."

"There probably isn't, but I'd sure appreciate it, nonetheless." Arlis was taking his request too lightly but there was no way he could confide what he'd learned, or the suspicions he held. Neither could he share the anxiety he was feeling, nor express the fear inside . . . fear that came from years of experience.

Sam dismounted and watched young McKay ride on, expertly sitting firm in the saddle as he led the string of horses off at a gallop. He waited better than an hour before he rode to the trees and across the creek. He hoped no one had seen them together.

CHAPTER 15

TWO RIDERS APPEARED OUT OF THE RANCH at a dead-gallop toward Sam, throwing snow in the air as they pounded over the frozen ground. Sam could see they were anything but friendly. He reined his horse to a standstill and sat immobile, gloved hand on the horn, watching the two bring their mounts to a sliding stop. "What calls fer you bein' on this property?" one asked gruffly. Before Sam could answer, the other added, "If yer lookin' fer work, we ain't hirin' so rattle yer hocks outa here."

They were along in years, with telltale gray scattered through their scraggly beards. Both had the hard look of men who had seen their share of trouble. The taller one's young horse was fidgeting, full of energy, refusing to remain still. He jerked the reins violently, viciously driving the bit deep into the horse's mouth.

Sam gritted his teeth, the muscles in his jaw pulsating. He immediately disliked these two, but now was not the time to vent his displeasure at the bad manners and cruelty to dumb animals.

Most ranches greeted strangers hospitably, offering freely of food and shelter. Sam remembered times when his hosts didn't have two slices of bread to spare, but put forth both graciously to a visitor. In most cases, homesteaders and small ranchers alike were poor and struggling but, as a rule, were kindly to strangers. A cowpoke looking for a job was never rudely chased away. A meal, neighborly conversation, and overnight lodging were common. Westerners were few and far between and the stranger usually had interesting news of the world outside. The reception Sam was receiving was most *uncommon*, and Sam resented the rudeness.

"I'm one of Jason Sanford's deputies," Sam crisply declared. With those brief words, he spurred his horse to a lope and rode between the startled bullies. They had nothing to say, and no alternative but to fall in behind and follow him through the gate to the hitch rail in front of the main house. The two hands hastily dismounted and the tall one barked, "Roy, you wait out here with the deputy while I tell the colonel we got a visitor." He pulled open the large front door and disappeared inside. In a matter of seconds he reappeared and beckoned to Sam with a cursory wave. Once indoors, he pointed to the huge fireplace, and said, "The colonel's over there by the fire."

It took a moment for Sam's eyes to adjust from the white glare of the outdoors to the relatively dark interior. Several large hides hung over high-backed chairs facing the hearth. A mass of white hair was visible above one of them. A soft-spoken voice greeted him. "Come here, suh; sit beside me and enjoy the fire. I'm sure y'all are frozen to the bone."

Sam walked across the room, put his back to the fire, and stood before the seated man . . . who made no attempt to rise. Neither hand was free; one held a heavy crystal glass filled with whiskey and the other rested on the golden knob of his cane. His shock of white hair was slightly disheveled and a marble pallor defined his sunken cheeks. Save for muttonchop sideburns and a small mustache, his face was clean-shaven, accented by a sharp Roman nose. It was a face not easily forgotten.

"Please forgive me, suh, for not risin', but my leg has been actin' up durin' this cold spell." He raised the glass in his right hand, examined it ardently, and slurred, "Fortunately, there's a favored remedy from the Old South. Bourbon, suh, fine Kentucky bourbon. Do you care to join me? Of course, you do." Without waiting for a reply, he called out, "Elmos, come here please!"

Out of the kitchen area hurried a small silver-haired Negro. "Yessuh, Colonel?"

"Elmos, take this gentleman's coat and fix a drink for our guest. Bring me another too," requested Raven.

Sam interrupted, "May I have coffee?"

"Good idea," added the Colonel. "On a cold day like this, a shot of bourbon in the coffee is just the right thing."

It was obvious the colonel could hold a great deal of whiskey, but it was just as apparent that he had been imbibing steadily and was inebriated; his speech and his deep-set black eyes bore the glazed look of a heavy drinker.

Sam thought better of refusing the whiskeyed coffee. He took off his heavy coat but not the shoulder-holstered gun before seating himself. The colonel bent forward and peered at the Smith & Wesson double-action revolver, then the empty right sleeve as it caught his attention. He pointed at it with the tip of his walking stick and with a raised eyebrow, inquired, "Did y'all get that in the war?"

"No, it happened at home in Colorado," answered Sam. The colonel sunk back into the chair and tapped his knee smartly with the edge of his cane. "Got that fightin' under General Hood, defendin' Atlanta from that rapist of the South, that bluebelly defiler of women."

"Just who was that?" asked Sam.

"General Will Sherman! Ah would guess y'all being raised in Colorado, ya wouldn't know much about that fiend." To emphasize his hatred, he leaned forward and spat into the fire before continuing his diatribe. "But ah got in my licks, yes ah did, ridin' with Forrester before ah was transferred to General Pemberton's staff at Vicksburg."

"I hear Forrester was a great cavalryman."

"The very best. He put the fear o' God in Grant and every other Yankee swine. If we had 'im instead of that Yankee-lovin' Pemberton, we never would have lost Vicksburg."

The colonel became deeply engrossed in the past and couldn't stop talking about the battles surrounding the fall of Vicksburg. The whole affair seemed to stick in his craw like a lodged fishbone, and he was noticeably agitated over the memories. Small beads of sweat appeared on his forehead; his heavy eyebrows pushed together over the bridge of his angular nose and formed a frightening scowl. The corners of the colonel's mouth twitched perceptibly, damp with saliva. He called for another drink and continued his biased disparagement against Lincoln, the North in general, and its military leadership in particular. It was clear to Sam that the colonel assumed he was never an active participant in the War Between the States.

Sam had been a master sergeant in the Illinois Thirty-seventh Regiment. Having enlisted shortly after the war started, he served under General McClernand until Grant assumed full command of the Army of the West. Due to his expertise in scouting and hand-to-hand combat, Sam was assigned to the advance units of William Tecumseh Sherman's attack forces and saw action until the conclusion of the war. Sam fought at Vicksburg, Jackson, Atlanta, and participated in Sherman's march across Georgia. Throughout the entire conflict, he never received a single bullet wound, although he suffered from the hardships of disease and dysentery, as had most all soldiers who had served as long. He knew the red-headed, hot-tempered Sherman personally, and admired him a great deal. Sam had been his chief scout for months on end.

It wasn't easy sitting by silently, hearing his former commander defamed in such a vile manner. Restraint, however, was important and as long as the drunken Raven continued his dialogue, Sam would pay attention. Besides, there was a certain vicariousness, listening to the open anger spill out of this enemy of bygone days. In the past, the colonel had tried to kill him as he'd tried to do the same to any grayback who crossed his sights. The bitterness, on the other hand, had left Sam years ago; he had no trouble forgiving an enemy who fought valiantly. Plainly, there was no forgiveness in this man.

In the late spring of 1863, Raven had evidently been just across the lines directing his men—a battalion of Johnnies dressed in butternut garb, screaming their Rebel yell as they charged the blue forces. They had fought against each other many times—at Champion Hill, at the battle for the Capitol at Jackson, Mississippi, and then through the summer heat at Vicksburg. Sam was tempted to add his side to the story but discretion kept him silent.

"We woulda whipped them if we hadn't followed that fool Yankee, Pemberton," added Raven.

"Yankee? I thought he was a Confederate general," baited Sam, knowing full well what the response would be.

"No one, suh, born and raised in Pennsylvania can be called a true Southerner," fumed the Colonel. "And what's more, his own kin were bluebellies; his two brothers fought for Lincoln." Raven again leaned forth and spat into the fire before continuing. "Pemberton let his Yankee blood and his Northern sympathies be known when he once uttered during a staff meeting, 'Ah am a Northern man, ah know my people.'" The colonel jammed his cane loudly on the floor several times, and said, "How is THAT, suh, for a slip of the tongue? We shoulda hung him right then and there."

"What else should he have done?" asked Sam, keeping the conversation going.

"Followed orders, suh? General Joe Johnson sent him instructions to join forces with him northeast of Vicksburg. That would have given us the manpower and strength to push them all the way back to Chicago. But, it was not to be. Split asunder, our fate was doomed. We retreated like whipped puppies to the fortifications at Vicksburg and waited for the inevitable end—which came, coincidentally, on the Fourth of July."

Sam remembered the occupation of Vicksburg as clear as yesterday. They marched into the town on Independence Day and were surprised at how little real destruction their constant bombardment had accomplished. Every glass window was shattered but no major structural damage had been inflicted. The siege, however, had left its mark upon the populace; the Rebel soldiers and the townspeople were starving.

The graybacks' daily rations were reduced by a fourth, to one biscuit and a small piece of bacon. The Johnnies were in no condition to fight a well-fed opponent. Their four division commanders—Forney, Stevenson, Bowen, and Smith—knew their men were not fit to fight their way out and suggested to General Pemberton that surrender was the only humane alternative.

When Sam's regiment marched into Vicksburg and saw the rampant hunger, the quartermaster of his division stopped his wagons and distributed all of the food supplies to the butternut scarecrows. He doled out coffee, sugar, and hardtack to the thankful Rebs. Afterward, when his own men complained, he lightheartedly said, "I swore by all the saints . . . that the wagons had broken down and the Johnny Rebs had stolen all the grub."

The Southerners were concerned there'd be a whole lot of Yankee crowing since the surrender occurred on the Fourth of July, but such was not the case. General Grant gave orders that there was to be no cheering or hoopla. In fact, he later stated, "The men of the two armies fraternized as if they had been fighting for the same cause." Sam recalled being amazed at the joking and good-natured ribbing that took place between the gray and blue. One bluecoat called out to a Reb officer, whose duties kept him riding back and forth in view of the Yankees, "Danged if you ain't the hardest feller to hit I ever saw. I've shot at you more'n a hundred times."

The memories came flooding back to Sam as Raven talked on. *But, wait a minute! What in the world is he saying now? No way does it set with what I've seen with my own eyes!*

"When the bluebellies tromped into Vicksburg, y'all should have heard the braggin' and gloatin' that went on," the colonel stated indignantly. "They intentionally humiliated those gallant men. The pillage that occurred to the local citizens was despicable."

Sam gnashed his teeth together and held himself in check before commenting on Raven's statement. "I never heard about that," Sam answered, still not letting on to his whiskey-soaked host that he had been there as well.

"Well, it happened, all right. You don't think those Northern newspapers are goin' to report the truth, do you?" The colonel slobbered as he emphasized the remark with his drink, spilling the contents over his waistcoat. "Ah was there, suh. Ah was there. And do y'all know the humiliation of bein' sent to a Northern prison? Well, ah do, suh."

Raven staggered to his feet, then steadied himself. He said, "Excuse me, Deputy, ah'll be right back," then limped out of the room. Sam was surprised at how tall he was when he stood, a good head above the average man. Seated in the chair with shoulders slouched, his long, angular frame was disguised.

Sam sat quietly in deep thought, trying to make sense out of what he had just heard. Grant's orders that there be no gloating or jubilance by the federal troops were obeyed. In fact, the only hurrah was from Sam's outfit and that was a hearty cheer given for the brave defenders of Vicksburg.

The Rebels weren't sent north to prison; in fact, to their joy, they were paroled. Sam could only conclude that Raven's hatred was so intense, it blinded his memory and warped his judgment. Either that, or the colonel was an unmitigated liar. There was no doubt he had fought at Vicksburg, for his knowledge of the siege was too detailed to be acquired in any other manner.

Sam watched as the colonel, reeling slightly, returned with a fresh whiskey in hand. He stood before the hearth and peered sullenly into the fire, poking at the logs with his cane and said, "See those flames? That's what Sherman did to Atlanta."

Sam knew that if the conversation continued along the same vein, and if more lies were forthcoming, he'd be compelled to interject the truth. He thought it better to change the subject.

"Colonel, was your kin from Mississippi?"

"No, suh. Our family plantation was in Louisiana. That's where my dear wife is buried; ya see, the war killed her too," he answered sadly. Suddenly, Raven straightened up and inquired, "Enough of my troubles; what brings you to the Elk Track, particularly on such a cold day?"

Sam was more than pleased the conversation had taken a turn. It might not have been long before Raven would, out of politeness, inquire about his own family. Sam was convinced that Raven did not remember or perhaps not hear his last name, let alone know that he was David's father. The Southern gent was more intoxicated than Sam first suspected, maybe had even forgotten his visitor was deputized. Sam immediately asked about the two Texans and their visit to the Elk Track.

At first, he seemed confused, acting as though he didn't remember them. Then he exclaimed, "Oh, yes. Ah believe Dorsey—that's my foreman—ah believe he bought some bulls from the Box X. If the memory serves, they still owe me five more Shorthorn bulls."

"That's what I've been told," replied Sam. "The Texans who drove the cattle here to your spread were killed. I'm trying to find out why."

"Ah heard that some Box X boys were bushwhacked, but I didn't know it was those two. Ah'm sorry to hear it," Raven solemnly droned. "What would their killin' have to do with us?"

"Probably nothing," responded Dodd, "but I have to check out everyone who spoke to them and maybe I can get a lead."

"Ah'm not the one to ask, then; you better talk to Dorsey," the colonel calmly lied. "He handled the transaction. Ah never spoke to either of them."

"Were they given any cash for the stock?" asked Sam.

"No, we paid by bank draft when first we bought the bulls."

"Do you know if they played cards or did any gambling with your hands while they were here?"

"No, ah don't think so. They left shortly after delivering the animals. As ah said before, best y'all talk with Dorsey."

"Is he here?"

"Unfortunately not. He rode over to Livingston to buy some horses. He'll be back in a week," the colonel said, smiling. Malachi Raven was showing signs of sobriety. Seemed the conversation about the Texans was rapidly sobering him up. A suspicious glimmer appeared in his eyes, replacing the watery dullness. The slurring of words had diminished remarkably and his answers were now brief and to the point.

Through the entranceway, a well-dressed young man entered. Sam immediately recognized him as the one who rode off with Deborah Dills. He, too, had trouble adjusting his eyes to the darkened room.

"Jefferson," called his father while turning in his chair, "come over here by the fire. We have a guest you should meet." Bending his head toward Sam, he said, "My son, suh, is a student of the law."

So, Sam thought, *this is the heir to the Elk Track*. He noticed that J.D. Raven was exceptionally handsome, with a rugged, cavalier air about him. He took off his gloves and sheepskin-lined jacket, letting them drop to the floor. Raven's manservant suddenly appeared, picked up the jacket, stuffed the gloves in the pockets, scurried to hang them up on a rack, and then disappeared into the kitchen. J.D., with his black, silver-buckled hat still in place, was smiling as he sauntered over to his father . . . that is, until Sam rose from his seat

With a disapproving scowl, he demanded, "What the devil are *you* doing here at the Elk Track, Dodd?"

"Dodd!" exclaimed the senior Raven, struggling up from his seat in confusion. "You never told me your name was Dodd."

"You never asked," calmly replied Sam. Turning to face the younger Raven and ignoring his befuddled father, he asked him the same questions regarding the Box X Texans. He received substantially the same answers but far more abruptly. Jefferson's tone of voice reeked with contempt, to the point of rudeness. They both warily watched Sam cross the room to retrieve his coat, well aware of his reputation with a gun and that he was armed. After he had collared Red Murphy in the Lone Steer Saloon, the word had spread that he was no one to trifle with.

The three walked outside in silence; J.D., however, couldn't seem to restrain himself. Knowing Sam had seen him in Big Timber riding by with Deborah, he smirked, "I hear your boy's havin' trouble settin' a wedding date with Deborah."

Sam studied the sarcastic young whelp and noticed his nose had been broken, marring his perfectly chiseled looks. He shot back a quick response, knowing better as soon as it was out of his mouth. "A word of advice, J.D. You're already sporting a broken nose for mentioning that young lady's name; it's not wise to try for a broken jaw. David wouldn't take it lightly."

As the blood rushed to the face of the young Raven, his hand moved dangerously close to the gun strapped low to his leg.

"Don't do it, boy," Sam said firmly. "I don't want to shoot you."

"Jefferson!" his father shouted. "He's a guest in our house. Mind your manners." Quickly moving between them, he turned to Sam and added, "Suh, you must excuse my son's bad manners." J.D. whipped around and disappeared into the ranch house.

"No, I owe you an apology," said Dodd. "I should have kept my temper and not goaded him. One fool is enough." Without further comment, Sam untied his mount while keeping an eye on Raven, and on the door his son had just slammed shut. Backing his horse away, he slowly pulled himself up into the saddle, turned and made tracks for the creek and the cottonwoods.

Moments after Sam disappeared from view, a man hobbled out from the bunkhouse doorway and approached the main house. From his stilted gait, it was clear the walk was painful. J.D. emerged from the house to stand by his father as the man spoke.

"One of the boys told me a deputy was nosin' around. Ah thought best to hide out 'til he left."

"Y'all did right, Dorsey. It was Dodd," said the colonel. Then he continued in a daunting tone. *"That* is a dangerous man. Ah'm afraid one day soon we might have to do somethin' about that nosy lawman."

CHAPTER 16

THE LONG, COLD NIGHT along the upper reaches of Little Timber Creek seemed to race by, even though little sleep was forthcoming. Contrary thoughts beat new trails through Sam Dodd's mind, keeping him awake and passing the time swiftly. The sub-zero temperature was no threat, the embankment of the creek working as a heat reflector to the fire. And with the horse blanket and heavy jacket, it was tolerable. Sam kept jerky and hard tack in the saddlebags for such occasions, so hunger was no problem either. He'd hobbled the gelding, keeping him close by.

When the first glimmer of light cut the eastern horizon, Sam saddled the dun, stuffed a piece of jerky in his mouth, and climbed into the saddle for the remainder of the scouting that he felt was necessary. For five days he had been circling the Elk Track Ranch, staying out of sight, observing their operation, counting the number of hands they employed, and checking out the various approaches to the principal buildings. The canyon where the ranch was located afforded great protection from Indians and also gave anyone who cared to sit on the high ridges with a telescope a perfect spot to survey their daily operations. Sam spent several full days and frigid evenings watching the activities. He learned a great deal.

Sam discovered that Saturday night was a time for rowdy drunkenness and Sunday was for sleeping it off—at least, during the winter.

It didn't take him long to spot the limping foreman, Dorsey Caine, and recognize another lie the colonel had told him. Distinctly, Sam could see that Dorsey was hurting too badly to fit a saddle and ride the long way to Livingston.

Sam watched Arlis McKay work with the unbroken broncs. He was good—very good, the best Sam had ever seen. Not one broomie could unseat him as they sunfished around the corral. When one tried to roll over on him, he quickly dismounted, then leapt again into the saddle as the bronc rose. Not once did he grab leather or look as if any of the wild mustangs could give him trouble. It was a pleasure to behold such a good professional at work. The rest of the regular hands seemed to be a motley crew of misfits and castoffs. Sam wondered how the large ranch could succeed with such a lazy crew.

After he had pretty thoroughly satisfied his curiosity, Sam rode back into Big Timber. An intricate web of concerns was weaving through his mind, connecting one fine thread to another. He was awash with facts that seemed to lead nowhere and statements that didn't add up. He was reasonably sure the Elk Track crowd knew much more about the Texans than they were willing to admit . . . *but why? Could they be mixed up in the shootings and, if so, for what purpose?*

The colonel had bald-faced lied to him about knowing Hurtt and Lewis, claiming he hadn't even spoken to them, saying that they left shortly after delivering the bulls. The young bronc-buster had stated the opposite. Sam remembered clearly Arlis McKay telling him the Texans were friendly with Colonel Raven and that they had spent the night drinking and gabbing with him before leaving the following day. Someone was lying—and Sam was confident that it wasn't the young wrangler.

What was the reason for all this deception?

SAM CONTINUED TO PONDER the puzzle as he rode into town. Darkness had settled in and fortunately, the stable still had the light burning inside the small cubicle that served as an office. The portly owner stuck his head out of the door and hastily said, "Take off the saddle and put 'er in one of the empty stalls. Throw 'er some hay if ya have a mind." He closed the door quickly, trying to keep his small office from losing too much heat. Without a doubt, he had no intention of helping Sam bed down the horse in the cold and drafty barn.

Sam lit one of the railroad lanterns hanging on large nails by the office door. In the dim light, he led the tired mare to an empty stall and, grabbing a pitchfork, tossed some alfalfa in the bin along with a can of ground oats. While she ate, he unsaddled her and removed the damp blanket. He swung the saddle over a stall rail and placed the blanket beside it to dry. After Sam had finished the chore, the stable owner appeared, lantern in hand, with a patronizing smile on his puffy, cherry-cheeked face.

"Did he give ya a good ride?" he asked, showing a tobacco-stained, toothy smile.

The weary lawman answered curtly, "The mustang got me there and back."

Sam wasn't at all happy with the cayuse—too small for the arduous journey, even though the stable owner had assured him the gelding was up to the long climb. Sam had to rest him an inordinate number of times. Without another word, Sam walked down the line of stalls, inspecting each of the horses while the proprietor disappeared once more into the comfort of his little room.

A solid buckskin gelding caught his eye, standing at least a hand taller than the rest. He appeared to have good conformation, well-muscled hindquarters, and a quiet disposition. Sam unlatched the gate and went inside the stall, proceeding to run his hand over the gelding's flanks and withers. He lifted all four feet to inspect the hooves and pulled each leg up and back to see if any abnormalities existed in bones or tendons. He checked the teeth for age and health of gums while the animal withstood the inspection calmly.

Sam's activity heightened the curiosity of the fat-faced stableman. He left the comfort of the office once again, sauntering over to where Sam was inspecting the buckskin. "That's a fine gelding you're lookin' at," he exclaimed with a broad smile. "He's fer sale—best horse in the whole stable."

Sam said nothing for a moment, then inquired, "Do you have a halter handy?"

"Got one right here," he replied as he quickly retrieved a worn halter from an adjoining stall. "Are ya interested in buyin' this fine animal? I can make you a fair deal," he said, offering Dodd a toothy grin.

Sam put the halter on and led the gelding out into the long aisle between the stalls, then handed the lead rope to the owner and instructed him to run the animal. Abiding by Sam's request, he trotted the horse to the stable entrance. "Now, what?" he hollered.

"Trot him back."

"Isn't he a beauty?" beamed the proprietor as he ran back, panting heavily from the exertion.

Sam didn't answer but reached up and ran his hand along the horse's spine, pressing, pushing hard. Just before he reached the withers, the buckskin sagged slightly under the pressure. Sam looked at him dead on as he asked, "How long has this horse been sorebacked?"

"Sorebacked? Why, there's not a durn thing wrong with that hoss. Ride 'im myself," the indignant stableman said, puffing.

"Yep," Sam said, grinning as he headed for the barn door, "and the wind doesn't blow in Montana, either."

He mumbled to himself and continued to smile at the un-ethical antics as he made his way to the Bramble Hotel. "Horse traders! That fellow would sell a sunfishing outlaw to his own grandma. Best I look elsewhere."

Sam wanted to see David but it was getting to be too late. Darkness had engulfed the town and he was hungry and dog-tired; visiting with his son would have to wait 'til morning. Entering the hotel's small lobby was a bit of a shock, having been in the cold outdoors for a week. The warm interior was positively stifling but was made more than welcome by the enticing aromas coming from the kitchen.

Without bothering to stop by his room, Sam went directly to the dining hall, drawn by the distinctive smell of fried chicken and hot biscuits. Draping his wool jacket over the back of a chair, he sat down heavily . . . only to rise up immediately.

Better get upstairs and wash up a bit, he thought sheep-ishly, as he scrambled back into his coat and headed for his room. *Mary would skin me alive if she were to get a whiff of me like this.* The image of his wife was both pleasurable and pain-ful at the same time. Sam loved and cherished her immensely; a warm glow encompassed him, just thinking of her. He missed her sorely. This month of separation was getting more difficult by the day; he wanted desperately to go home. He tried hard to put Mary out of his mind. The quicker he could get to the bottom of the present trouble, the quicker he could leave. He had to keep his mind on it.

At the door to his room, he stood for a moment and rum-maged through his pockets for the key, then hesitated. *What was that, footsteps?*

The muffled sound came from the other side of the door; who was in his room? He pressed his ear close to the wall and froze at the almost imperceptible stirring of someone moving about. His hand darted inside his coat and drew the revolver. Moving back a few feet, he threw his right shoulder violently against the wooden door, shattering the lock, slamming it open.

Sam swung the gun in a quick arch and settled the sights on the frightened figure standing in the center of the room.

"Sam Dodd, what in the world? You scared me out of my wits!"

"Mary!" mumbled her shocked husband. "What are *you* doing here?"

"I'm here to see my son and my husband—the best of all reasons, I'd say!" With that, she moved quickly toward him, wrapped her arms about his neck, and kissed him intensely. Sam eagerly returned the favor. They hugged each other hungrily, as Mary whispered lovingly in his ear, "Darling, you need a bath."

IT WAS FIVE O'CLOCK IN THE MORNING, time to get up; in less than an hour the sun would be pushing the dark sky toward the western horizon. Sam lay quietly in the warm confines of the feather bed, comforted by the touch of Mary's leg draped over his. She was breathing heavily as she was prone to do when sleeping on her back. Sam tried to move, but Mary caught his leg with her heel; even in her sleep, she was not willing to let him go. They had talked late into the night about David, the family, the shootings, and why Sam had not been able to return home. He cursed himself for not being more explicit in his letters. He should have known she would read between the lines and not be satisfied with so little information. Writing that he had been deputized and wouldn't be returning to the ranch within the immediate future did nothing but increase her fears.

Sam was surprised to learn that Mary and Matthew, their sixteen-year-old son, had arrived in town nearly a week ago. There'd been a break in the weather so she and Matt jumped at the opportunity to join him and David. They rode the mules north along the river to the town of Laramie, Wyoming, where they caught the train west to Salt Lake City, then on to Butte, Montana and east through Bozeman to Big Timber. She told him that Matthew was bunking with David at the Collinses'.

When Sam asked about their ranch operations, Mary assured him that their daughter, Sarah, and her husband had everything well in hand at home.

Riding out from their back-country spread in the dead of winter was a dangerous journey. However, the trail was not unfamiliar to Matthew, since he had traveled it several times before—once under the most adverse winter conditions. Sam would never forget three years ago, when his boy was just thirteen, how he accompanied his wounded father to the Laramie Hospital where Sam's arm had to be amputated due to a gunshot wound. They made the punishing trip during the worst of blizzards—so bad that Matthew was victimized by frostbite and ended up having to lose his left hand above the wrist.

Sam shuddered at the painful memory and what frightful consequences there could have been, had Mary and Matt been caught in a high-country snowstorm. He never would have permitted such a risk; but Mary, once she made up her mind, was not to be denied. He was relieved with their safe arrival and delighted that they were with him now. But under no circumstances would he let them return until spring. Hopefully, they could all travel home together. Mary was beginning to move about in the bed, half-awake. She turned on her side, nestled her head into Sam's shoulder, and mumbled, "How soon can we get a cup of coffee?"

"Well, bright-eyes, we have about half an hour before the dining room opens but there's usually a pot brewing by now. Want me to see if I can get you a cup?"

"Would you please?" She stretched her arms above her head, yawned, and rolled over on her back. "Sam, this is like a second honeymoon."

He mirthfully exclaimed, "Second? We never had the first." Then chuckling, he swung his legs out of bed, fumbled around for a match, and lit the kerosene lamp on the nearby table, illuminating the cold, dingy room.

"Sweetheart, this is hardly the bridal suite." Removing his pants from the post at the foot of the bed, he pulled them over his long underwear. Sam scratched as he headed for the wash basin, still grinning. "Second honeymoon! If that don't beat all."

Mary was now totally awake and sitting up in bed with the quilt pulled up around her. "Sam, I forgot to tell you about something that happened to me last Sunday."

Sam scrubbed his face and while toweling the cold water from his brow asked, "What was that, sweetheart?"

"Matt, David, and I went to church with Amy last Sunday. A strange little old man approached us with a real worrisome look on his face. He took me aside and whispered something about not knowing our family were Christians and it was important that he talk to you. He seemed terribly frightened."

"Was it Lute Olsen?"

"Yes, that was his name," Mary answered. "His lower lip trembled the whole time we talked. He was scared, Sam, scared bad. He wanted to tell you something about a Hal or Cal somebody. He was speaking so low, I could hardly hear him."

"I'll drop by this afternoon and see him at the saloon where he works. Maybe he has some information about Cal Davis— the deputy who was killed."

"Oh," Mary exclaimed, suddenly remembering. "You can't do that. He wants to see you alone; he was quite emphatic about that. He told me he lives by himself in a house down by the river and that he's home most mornings."

"Well then, guess I'd better go see him this morning." Sam leaned over the bed and kissed her on the top of the head. "I'll go get that coffee for you while you get dressed." He dislodged the chair propped under the knob and struggled to open the jammed door. "That is, if I can figger how to get out of this busted-up mess I made last night."

"Come in, Mr. Dodd, come in quick-like!" At first, the small, withered man had opened the door just a slit, peering out with only one eye. But upon recognizing the lawman, he opened it wide and beckoned him inside with a hurried motion of his right hand. Sam had to duck his head down in order to enter the little shack Lute Olsen called home. The inadequate wooden walls provided little protection. It was cold inside, in spite of the red glow from the stove that doubled for both heating and cooking. Sam noted the meager comforts, the cot covered with a buffalo robe tucked in the corner, a lamp on a hook dangling over the table along with three wooden crates for chairs. Firewood was stacked along one wall beside another crate holding a wash basin and a pitcher of water.

Two things caught Sam's attention—a gold-framed photograph of a plain, stoic-faced woman holding a child with another clinging to her dress, and a large, luxurious leather-bound Bible on the table. It looked old, but appeared to be in excellent shape. Sam nodded toward the picture and inquired, "Your family, Mr. Olsen?"

"Ya," he warmly grinned. "Dot's my Anna und my two boys, Sven and Knute. My sons are both married with kids in Wisconsin und my poor Anna passed away a few years ago." He sighed deeply, "She vas a goot woman."

"Do you see your children often?" asked Sam.

"Sometimes, yust sometimes. They vant me to come back und live with them, but I not be happy," Lute answered.

Sam thought about asking him why not, but he'd already posed enough personal questions so, to change the subject, he brought up the reason he was there. "Mr. Olsen, my wife told me you knew something about Cal Davis."

His eyes grew wide and tears appeared, then his hands began to tremble. "Ya!" His voice and lips quivered in excitement as the words tumbled out in stuttered, broken English. "Ya, I know wh-who kilt da deputy und sh-shot yer boy!"

CHAPTER 17

COURAGE, BRAVERY. WHO HAS IT AND where does it come from? Sam pondered these questions after he left Lute Olsen's shack. *What is it that makes that gentle old man able to face danger even though he's scared half out of his wits? Where does the strength come from . . . the strength that puts starch in a man's backbone?* Sam felt great respect for such a courageous individual—a fine, moral citizen. There was little doubt in Sam's mind that much of the little Norwegian's grit came from his faith. Sam had seen others of far greater physical strength wilt under much less pressure. *Guts is more of the mind than muscle*, Sam thought.

It was important that he keep Lute's identity secret until there was a trial. He would be too easy a target for the thugs at the Elk Track if they even suspected anyone was aware of their evil chicanery. Much had to be done before he could seriously consider going after Dorsey Caine. *First off, I've got to get a decent horse or two. With what I have to do, good ones are necessary.*

Sam quickened his step up the hill. It was quite a jaunt from the rundown shacks at the river's edge to the more substantial residences where the doctor lived. He was anxious to tell David and Doc Collins what he had just learned from Lute Olsen—particularly in case anything unforeseen happened to him. For now, no one else needed to know.

Sam was also going to require the cooperation of some of Big Timber's local leaders to seek their advice on just how to go about making the arrest. Hauling in the cousin of the largest and wealthiest rancher in central Montana could prove to be difficult. Sam remembered Proverbs' admonition to seek more than one's own advice: "In an abundance of counselors there is safety." It might well be foolish to apprehend Dorsey by himself, but it could cost the lives of others if he tried to ride in with a body of deputized men. The ranch was well fortified. *Best I talk this over with some other folks about what would be the right way to handle it. Doc Collins ought to know who to ask.*

Sam's thoughts about Dorsey Caine were rudely interrupted when, a few long blocks from the Collinses' residence, a series of shots rang out, cutting like a jagged razor through the cold air. The hair rose on the back of his neck and a chill shot through him as he bolted into a fast pace toward the house, gun drawn, ready for use. He forced himself to slow down; no sense getting out of breath and not being able to aim accurately. Too many men in the Civil War rushed to their death when caution would have kept them alive and victorious.

Cutting to the right, Sam kept a thick row of bramble bushes between himself and the doctor's as he closed in on the residence. His eyes darted back and forth, taking in everything, missing nothing. No horses were tied to the hitch rail and he couldn't see anyone, not even inside through the windows. The sound of five more exploding shots blended together as in one continuous roar. The gunfire was coming from the back of the house. Sam moved into the shade of the building, peering into each window as he passed. With his back pressed to the wooden siding, he sneaked a look around the corner. Instantly, he recognized the grumbling going on and the familiar sounds of a revolver chamber being opened and shell casings hitting the ground.

Sam immediately relaxed and holstered his gun, then quietly stepped around the corner of the house. A warm grin split his weathered face as he observed his son angrily reloading a pistol, jamming shells into the empty chambers. He watched David reload the Colt and place it in the holster, then bend over and pick up one of the empty tin cans piled next to his left boot. With his right hand he flipped the can high in the air. When it began its descent, David's left hand flashed to the handle of the single-action and with a fluid motion drew, fanning the hammer and firing all five shots before the can hit the ground.

Sam was astonished at the speed of his son's reflexes. He hadn't hit the small falling target, but David was quick, very quick—the fastest left-handed draw he had ever seen. While he reloaded, Sam approached his preoccupied son from behind and casually asked, "Trying out Cal Davis' hogleg?"

David jumped with surprise at the sound of his father's voice, causing him to fumble and drop several .45-caliber slugs to the ground.

"Where did you come from, Pa? You scared the holy Ned outa me, sneakin' up like that," blurted his startled son.

Sam laughed. "I didn't mean to rattle you, Son. You know me; it's just my way of walkin'. After all my years, it's second nature." During the years as an advanced scout for the Union Army, Sam learned to be stealthful and quiet, moving silently through wooded areas during the day and unobserved through open fields at night. It also served him well as a deputy in Colorado and as a rancher when hostile Utes roamed the mountains.

Most men walk with the heel first, noisily touching into the ground. Sam moved as an Indian, the ball of the foot reaching for the dirt and the heel quietly following. Sam knelt down to help retrieve the dropped shells. Picking one up, he handed it to David and said, "When did you learn to slap leather that fast? You weren't ever that quick when you left home."

David grinned. "Cal and I used to practice together. It was a lot of fun, Pa, 'cause he was pretty good. At first, I was all thumbs but it got so I could beat him and it would sure make him mad, bein' beat by a left-handed gunslinger."

"How's your right shoulder, Son, any better?"

"Gettin' so, Pa." David reached across and rubbed his upper arm. "It's still pretty sore and stiffer'n all getout, but much better than before."

"What were you grumbling about before I startled you?" asked Sam.

"Plain and simple," answered David. "I can't seem to hit that durned can."

"Like me to show you how?" asked Sam.

David's face lit up with a doubting grin. He knew his father was a good shot but to toss the can, draw from a shoulder holster, and be able to hit it would be next to impossible. Trying not to be disrespectful, he chuckled, "Why sure, Pa, show me how."

Sam reached down and picked a bottle from among the cans. Grabbing it by the neck, he threw it a distance away and while it was falling, drew his pistol and took aim. As soon as it hit the ground he fired, shattering it into a thousand pieces.

"Ha! You didn't even *try* to hit it in the air," David humorously exclaimed.

"I didn't say I was going to," his father soberly replied. "I said I would hit it . . . and I did. Now *you* try it."

"What do you mean?" asked David.

"Let's see if you can do as I just did . . . hit the target."

David threw another bottle the same distance, and fired all five shots rapidly at the glass object on the ground, bracketing but missing the bottle. Before he could say anything, Sam drew once more and pulverized the target with one shot, sending pieces of glass everywhere.

"Son, no one needs to draw fast to hit an antelope or shoot a snake. The only reason anyone needs to be quick is when somebody's out to kill you. When that happens, you better hit what you're shootin' at. Bein' quick might still make you second best. I've seen men draw fast, then drop their guns when faced with someone out to kill 'em. Under attack, I've watched men forget to fire, then reload their Springfields several times, blowing the barrel when they finally touched off. I've even seen so-called hard-cases wet their britches and run away when death stared 'em in the eye." Sam reached over and affectionately punched his son on the arm. "Know what I'm sayin'?"

"I think so, Pa. You're tryin' to tell me it isn't easy shootin' someone who's comin' at you with a gun blazin'."

"That's part of it. If someone does, you have to kill 'em good; you have to put 'em down hard. It's no time to be thinkin' peaceful thoughts."

Sam turned and looked seriously at David. "Son, I've also seen wounded men—soldiers with lead in their guts—run fifty yards and still have enough life in 'em to stick a bayonet through some Johnny Reb. Men with mortal wounds can live for days. The only way to make sure is to hit 'em in the head or heart. Head shot, they drop like a rock; heart-shot works pretty good most times." Sam looked back at the broken bottles. "Shooting a gun must be instinctive under pressure. You don't have time to think . . . just act. Hittin' what you're aiming at takes practice until it becomes second nature. Getting a gun out quick is helpful, but it isn't the most important."

"I get what you mean, Pa. I'll take it to heart."

Sam wrinkled up his face in a wry grin. "You better, or you might take one in the heart—a lead slug right through that badge you've been wearin'."

Sam nodded his head toward the house and asked, "Is the doc home? We need to go in and talk to him; something very important has come up."

"He was here a few minutes ago, talking to Mother. She's been visitin' with Martha Collins and Amy." David bent down, picked up the empty brass, and put them in his pocket.

"What's so important?"

"We'll talk about it inside, but I can guarantee you'll be real interested."

"WELL, I'LL BE DANGED! Are you sure?" spurted the incredulous doctor. Sam had related the entire story to him and David.

"That's exactly what old man Olsen told me," responded Sam. "Lute actually overheard Dorsey Caine and Dobie Johnson plan the murder and even name the spot on Big Creek where they intended to dry-gulch Cal Davis. They even joked about the telegram J.D. had sent to the deputy."

"Did Olsen say why they wanted to kill Cal?" queried David.

"No, he didn't say," replied Dodd. "I asked the same question and ol' Lute said if they mentioned it, he didn't hear." Sam scratched his head before he added, "But it's a good question. The *why* is still a mystery to me. It seems evident that Cal was the only one they were after. David, your name never came up."

"If that's the case," asked the young Dodd, "why did they try to kill me the second time?"

"Good question again," answered his father. "The only thing I can come up with is that whatever Calvin knew, he musta told you. Or, at least they think so. Calvin was chummy with the two dead Texans and I figure they knew something that was a mighty big threat to the Elk Track."

"Wonder what that could be?" mused the doctor.

"I haven't the slightest idea, but it has brought about the death of three men."

"That we know of," the doctor added sarcastically.

"Yes, that we know of," echoed Sam. "One thing I'm sure of is that Dorsey Caine murdered Cal Davis and I have the responsibility to arrest him and bring him to trial and to do that, I'll need some good advice and plenty of help."

"Well, Deputy, what do you say we do now?" asked the physician.

"Doc, could we get together with some of the town's leaders, just in case I have to put together a posse? I need information and, of course, their support. It's a whole lot easier if the good people in town know what's going on."

"How many do you think we'll need at this meeting?"

Sam thought for a moment before replying. "For now, I'd say not more than three or four. Just make sure they're concerned, law-abiding men who know how to handle a gun."

"I know just the right ones. Anything else?"

"You bet. Where can I get a good horse or two?"

"That's easy. Head up Swamp Creek a few miles 'til you hit the Abraham M. Grosfield ranch. A.M.'s got a pasture full of fine animals and I hear tell he wants to sell some. He's got a great big stud named Blackie who has sired some fine colts. Buy one of those beauties and you'll be more than satisfied. You can borrow one of mine to ride out there and by the time you get back, I'll have everybody here after supper."

"Pa, I'd like to ride along. I need to stretch my bones a bit," requested David.

Sam carefully appraised his son's condition before agreeing. David was obviously much stronger and from all outward appearances, he looked healed. "What do you think, Doc? Should I take him along?"

"Might as well get him out of the house for awhile and give him a break from the womenfolk. All they do is fuss over him all day. Isn't that right, Davey?" the impish old doctor wisecracked.

"Son, why don't you saddle up the horses so we can get on out to the Grosfields' and look over their stock." David hurried on with his coat, grateful for the opportunity to leave.

THE WAY TO THE GROSFIELD RANCH branched off the trail to Melville, and the crossing at Big Timber Creek where David was shot lay just ahead. David remembered the spot all too well and suggested they dismount and look around for his lost

Colt .44. They reenacted the shooting, trying to figure the exact location where David drew, then fired the revolver. Since the spring thaw was still a month or so away, the creek had yet to overflow but, when it did, the firearm would probably be washed away or submerged under rubble and rocks. David had spent a half-month's wages to buy that .44 revolver and he wasn't too happy about losing it. Fifteen dollars was nothing to sneeze at.

"Well, lookie here," joked Sam. "Look what's stickin' out from under this rock."

David came splashing through the water toward his father. "Did ya find it?"

"Yep!" Sam squatted down and lifted the gun out of the water, angling it to pour the icy water out of the barrel. With his thumb, he released the cylinder and exposed the shells. Two had been fired.

"Looks like you got off a couple of rounds, Son. Dobie Johnson probably got in the way."

"Pa, I sure don't remember firing twice."

"Hard to remember when you've got a load of buckshot in your body," his father responded.

"Guess you're right." David raised the Colt in the air and looked at it carefully, spun the cylinder, cocked and dry-fired the .44 pistol. His face broke into a grateful grin. "Water didn't do it much harm. Nothin' a good polishing and a spot of oil can't fix."

"Come on, David, we better get a move on if we hope to be back by supper."

DARK HAD SETTLED IN as they rode up to the Collinses' house with two new horses in tow. The doctor had been right; A.M. Grosfield had some fine mounts for sale and Sam and David had a grand time selecting from the lot. They finally settled on a gelding and a young stallion, two sons of A.M.'s big black stud. They carried much of their sire's color; the gelding was dark brown with black points and the stallion was coal black with star, stripe, and snip. Both were well-broken, gentle, and sound as a gold dollar. In the stallion, Sam found exactly what he was looking for, having every intent of shipping him back to Colorado. A stud of his temperament and breeding was hard to come by.

Talking about the big stallion brought pure enthusiasm to Grosfield's face. One story about Blackie, among several, happened in the middle of the previous winter. A.M. was riding him far afield, miles from the ranch house, inspecting hay pens and fencing. Blackie stepped in a badger hole and fell, throwing A.M. violently to the ground, knocking him unconscious. When he awakened some time later, badly shaken and injured, right beside him was Blackie. The stallion had always been full of spirit and tough to mount, but there he was standing stock-still while A.M. struggled to get his battered body up in the saddle. No question, had the great horse trotted off, A.M. would have frozen to death in the night since he could barely walk.

Sam enjoyed seeing the deep affection Grosfield held for the muscular, coal-black animal. He hoped the same characteristics were passed on to his offspring—especially the young stallion . . . the horse he intended to use for breeding.

Several horses and two buggies were tied up in front of the Collins residence. David took the horses around to the shed while Sam entered the front door. He was getting out of his coat in the hallway as the doctor's voice rang out. "Come on in here, Sam, and meet everybody." The warm room felt good, even though it was thick with cigar smoke. Through the haze, he saw five men standing around the stove, talking. Collins waved, inviting him forward.

"Sam, I'd like you to meet some people. Since you were late, I took the liberty and filled them in about Dorsey Caine; and everyone of 'em is pretty shocked about it all. This here's

W.Y. Fisher, our blacksmith." A full-bearded, middle-aged man with huge arms busting through his shirt stepped up and put out his large hand in greeting.

"Willie was in the Confederate Army and fought under Longstreet," added Doc Collins. He turned to the next man. "Now, this here is Colonel Brown, our postmaster."

Brown was tall, lanky, and gray-haired with a warm, personable smile; he extended his left hand in deference to Sam. "I'm the Yankee of the lot, but I still let Willie shoe my horses."

The group laughed as the irascible physician continued the introductions. "Now, this handsome feller is the politician of the bunch. Meet Mayor Walt Allen. Believe it or not, he's another bluebelly. Walt was cavalry and was at Five Forks with Phil Sheridan. Underneath that girth is a good fightin' man who still knows how to fork a horse; leastwise, that's what he tells me."

The portly mayor greeted Sam and shook hands, revealing the partially obscured figure of the man standing behind him. Turning, the mayor said, "I hope you don't mind but I brought along a friend of both of ours. You know Homer Dills, don't you?"

CHAPTER 18

IT MIGHT BE SMARTER *to form a posse of the willing citizens of Big Timber and it certainly would be much safer than the plan I'm about to try. I probably should go to Bozeman and talk it over with the sheriff, but that's neither practical nor expedient.* Sam knew it was up to him to bring in Dorsey Caine, his responsibility to arrest him and take him to Bozeman for trial. It would be next to impossible to boldly ride up to the Elk Track Ranch, arrest Caine, and take him away without getting destroyed in the attempt. All logic, including the mayor, told him that the colonel wouldn't tolerate anyone riding into his domain and arresting his kin for murder. Walt Allen was emphatic about the Elk Track being Raven's private world, his fiefdom, the colonel's kingdom in the land of Montana. On his spread, the only law Malachi Raven recognized was his own.

Will Fisher doubted Dorsey would volunteer to go peacefully. He was familiar with Caine's reputation as a gunfighter and firmly believed it was well-earned. Dorsey's background was laced with the mashed faces and broken bones of those he disliked. His repute of being the meanest foreman in central Montana was legendary around Big Timber.

Postmaster Brown suggested a posse, and both the mayor and the blacksmith agreed, all personally volunteering and offering to help round up others.

Homer Dills argued vociferously against any action at all, defending the Ravens and seriously questioning that the charges made against them were true. He kept pressing for the name of the witness and became livid when Sam wouldn't divulge it. He was especially upset when J.D.'s name was mentioned. "Hold on, now," he shouted. "How do we know the witness is telling the truth? For all we know, it's likely some hallucinating drunk who has a grudge against Dorsey or J.D. I hardly would want to go riding off in a posse unless I know more about it. I suggest we form a delegation and go out there and talk to the colonel. I'm sure there's a good explanation for all of this."

Brown came to the crux of the matter when he said, "Do that, and Dorsey will disappear for sure, if he's guilty. That's why we have courts and trial by jury. Sam says we have plenty of evidence to arrest Dorsey. The concern at hand is how to get it done without getting anyone killed." Everyone but Dills nodded, and uttered agreement.

The mayor advised Sam to take the morning train over to Bozeman and discuss it with Sheriff Sanford. Everybody, including Homer Dills, agreed with that . . . everyone but Sam. He said nothing, allowing them to assume it was the proper course to follow.

After the men said their good-nights and left, he asked Martha Collins if she could supply him with enough provisions on hand to last him a week in the wild.

SAM KNEW PERFECTLY WELL the following day would see Homer Dills making a beeline to the Elk Track Ranch. In all probability, he would make sure Sam boarded the train before he left. If Homer were observed anywhere around the station, it would be all the confirmation necessary that his sojourn to the Elk Track was inevitable. Homer wasn't in evidence, but his wife was, doing a good job of making a particularly big fuss over sending a telegram to a supplier, ordering merchandise for the store.

Sam boarded the train as it noisily pulled out from the depot. When the locomotive slowed to make the grade west of town, he effortlessly swung down from the caboose and greeted David who was waiting for him with the two new horses and supplies. His son desperately wanted to accompany his father but admittedly wasn't up to the rigors of perhaps as much as a week in the rugged cold. Just the trip to the Grosfields' the previous day had worn him out. Days of hard riding and sleeping nights on frozen ground could aggravate the infection and kill him. The plan had begun to formulate in Sam's mind as soon as he noticed a tight-lipped Homer fidgeting in his chair whenever apprehending Dorsey Caine was mentioned. Plainly, Homer Dills wasn't buying any of it.

Dills had always been impressed by moneyed people and spoke reverently of the wealthy. He was that way in Colorado and he hadn't changed one bit. Colonel Raven and his son filled the bill when it came to whom Homer thought important. The delay in the wedding plans of his daughter to David now made sense. He had someone else in mind for Deborah's bridegroom and there was little doubt that it was Jefferson Davis Raven. Homer's incessant objections at Doc Collinses', then his wife's appearance at the station, confirmed it was a family decision; she was as deeply into the deception as Homer. Sam wondered just how much Deborah had to do with the schemes of her parents. He couldn't help but feel heartsick for his son, for too soon, he would surely find out what was going on.

For the present, Sam had other more important things to consider—matters pertaining to life and death. *Sure as can be, sometime today Homer will reach the Elk Track and spill out what he knows, jabbering like a jayhawk 'til the colonel hushes him up.* Sam tried to figure what the colonel and Dorsey would do. *Will Dorsey stay and bluff it out? Not likely.* Sam suspected Dorsey would conveniently disappear until the witness was located and done away with.

Time was on their side. J.D. wasn't directly involved in the killing of the deputy. He could claim sending the telegram was nothing more than a practical joke, with no knowledge of the planned murder. Dorsey was the only one who could be implicated.

J.D. would undoubtedly stay at the ranch, but Dorsey Caine was bound to run. *But when, and where?* They were sure to count on having a few days to make a decision, since it would take Sam two days to Bozeman and back, then another to get a posse together. They'd figure they had at least those two days for Caine to go to cover and hole up.

Now . . . the question is, where! Dorsey could head up higher into the mountains but that was unlikely. With a wound in the backside, it'd be mighty unpleasant living out of a line shack. Sam guessed Dorsey's age to be about his own, somewhere in his forties. Having been used to a relatively comfortable life, chances are he'd choose someplace with plenty of creature comforts and he could certainly afford it.

More than likely, he would make tracks for the depot in Livingston and catch a train for San Francisco. Or, maybe backtrack to Denver, figuring by the time the posse arrived at the Elk Track, he could be just about anywhere he chose. Sam reckoned if that were the case, he'd trail out southwest from the ranch. *Wonder if Dorsey might go it alone? Possibly he'd have company. The ride to Livingston should take a couple of days in his condition, and no matter where he goes, he's sure to have a sore rump when he gets there.*

What the heck, all of this ponderin' is nothing more than conjecture. He might even choose to stay, ride east to Billings or north to the mountains, and rough it. There's really no way to know for sure except to hide out close to the ranch and keep a watchful eye on it.

With some hard riding, Sam could be perched on the high ridge above the Elk Track, telescope in hand, observing Homer's arrival. He gave the black stallion a light touch of his spurs. "Let's get a move on, Smoke—we're burnin' daylight and we've a piece to go." Smoke liked to run. The horse responded quickly into a comfortable lope and Dodd could feel the power beneath him, sensing the animal's eagerness to break into a full-bore gallop, if so allowed. This magnificent animal was nothing like Big Timber's stable broomtails he'd previously had to rely on. The sure-footed bundle of muscle and grit could go all day and into the night, as could his half-brother, Dusty, pacing comfortably behind him. It felt good to be sitting a quality horse, moving effortlessly over the ground, "punchin' the breeze," as the waddies would say.

RIGHT ON TIME, JUST BEFORE DUSK, Homer Dills crossed the creek on horseback and climbed the hill to the ranch headquarters. He jumped down fast, skedaddled to the front door, and disappeared inside. There was little doubt he would be there for the night.

A veil of dry snow was falling; time to get back to the horses hidden in the little draw on the far side of the ridge. Sam had selected a spot where he could start a small fire, undetected. He watered both mounts, then hobbled them so they could graze for awhile before being tied securely for the night. From one of the packs, he shoveled several handsful of oats into his Stetson and fed the grateful horses, one at a time.

To satisfy his own hunger, he unwrapped the antelope jerky, dried apples, and a couple of Mrs. Collins' biscuits. When the deep tin cup of water by the fire began to simmer, he threw in some coffee grounds and let it steep a bit, then tossed in a handful of snow to settle the grounds. The snowing would probably stop, since glimpses of stars appeared through the clouds. Small storms often hovered around high mountain peaks while the valley sky remained crystal-clear. If enough new snow fell, any tracks leading away from the ranch could easily be followed.

Waiting for Dills' arrival, Sam glassed the surroundings, observing all trails leading to and from the ranch. He'd already selected an area where he could easily get the drop on any riders leaving, heading for Livingston. From his vantage point on the ridge, he could see the pile of stones that covered the body of Dobie Johnson and right next to it appeared to be another mound of the same size rocks. This was troubling. *Had one of the other hands died?* Sam's curiosity tempted him to sneak down and look for any identifying marker, perhaps a name scratched on a rock or a piece of inscribed wood. The graves were too far away and, even through the telescope, were barely discernible. *If one of the Elk Track hands is buried there, some pard, some fellow waddie might have left a memento or sign of recognition.*

Thinking abut the new grave kept Sam awake late into the night. *Could it be Arlis McKay? Could he have innocently mentioned their meeting up on the trail, or had someone seen them riding together?* Arlis had taken Sam's warning so lightly; it was entirely possible he'd let something slip. Sam's imagination ran wild and the colder the night grew, the more jumbled his thoughts. He finally resolved to steal down the slopes in the dark and be at the grave site at dawn. Figuring that chances were slim that Dorsey would leave at first light, he should have enough time to scout out the burials and make it back to his lookout post on the high crest. Going down at night would take about an hour, but climbing back undetected in broad daylight would take much longer.

At last, Sam was able to sleep, but only in short segments. He awaked to the sound of his horses' whinnying and straining repeatedly against their halter ropes. He sprung to his feet, gun drawn, startled by a string of elk bolting by no more than fifty feet away. In the downhill wind, the lead cow was followed by at least seventy-five head and the swift-moving Wapiti didn't see the horses until they were right on top of them. In a matter of moments, it was all over and the herd of elk was out of sight as Sam went over to calm the two horses with a hatful of oats.

The animals having quieted down, Sam knelt by the burning embers to stoke the fire and place another cup of water on the coals to boil. He took out his watch and by the dim light of the fire, squinted to read the time.

Four o'clock—be light enough in about two hours. He wasn't hungry but Sam knew he needed the energy food would provide and before long, his stomach would be nagging at him. He chewed on a hunk of jerky and, as a precaution, stuffed some extra, along with a hard biscuit, into his coat pocket.

Sam leisurely finished his coffee and after checking the horses once more to see they were securely tied, headed down the dark slope, following the convenient elk trail and blending his tracks with theirs.

He reached the grave site earlier than he had expected. It was still too dark to see anything legible, although a half-moon cast dark shadows through the trees. The wind had picked up dramatically, churning the snow, fashioning ghostly shapes as it swirled about. Boughs swayed, dropping snow in dull thuds to the ground while an eerie moaning of frigid air meandered through the pines. Sam was not superstitious but he undeniably understood how the tale of the Crazies' ghost remained alive; particularly so when a huge clump of snow, big as a bushel basket, thumped to the ground right behind him. A cold chill not prompted by the weather ran roughshod over his backbone. He shuddered involuntarily, then muttered, somewhat ashamed of himself, "I'll shore be happy when the morning light breaks over that eastern ridge."

At the first glimmer of daybreak, Sam brushed the light coating of snow from the unidentified pile of rocks. There was absolutely nothing to determine who or what lay beneath the stones. Sam was sorely tempted to uncover the body to see who it was, but desecrating a grave for curiosity's sake was more than he cared to stomach. At the moment, it was more important to get back to his point of observation without being noticed.

He could only retrace his steps over the elk tracks for a short distance if he wanted to avoid being spotted from the ranch. Sam had to swing to the right, climb up through the trees, and get the ridgeline between himself and the valley floor. The ascent was difficult, climbing over snow-covered deadfall and through the thick growth of lodgepole pine. Every so often, Sam veered back to the edge of the trees to see if he could detect any movement below. In the fresh layer of white he could make out steps leading to the woodpile from the house, plus several more from the bunkhouse to the stables. He watched as a cowboy led Homer Dills' saddled horse to the main house and tied him to the hitching rail.

There was more activity than Sam had expected so he hastened his pace. Before him lay an open stretch that necessitated swinging still further off to the right. If he tried to cross the bare slope, he would stand out like a skittery black bug on a white linen tablecloth. By the time he reached the trees above and could again be hidden enough to keep watch on the Elk Track, many minutes had passed. Sam saw that Dills and his horse had already departed, leaving a series of clear tracks toward the trail leading back to Big Timber. Two other mounts and a pack mule were now tied up at the same hitching rail; two horses saddled and the pack-saddle panniers on the mule appeared to be carrying a full load.

He was furious with himself. His assumptions had been dead-wrong. No doubt Dorsey was getting ready to leave and Sam was still a good half-hour away from his own horses. Spending time and energy to inspect the grave had been a rotten idea. "Curiosity has killed more than a cat," he grumbled. Now, he had no other choice but to cool his heels and watch from the pines; it was no time to let them out of his sight, not while saddled horses were tied to the rail.

He didn't have long to wait before two men emerged from the ranch house. Dorsey was limping slightly and the other, Sam was sure he'd never seen before. They quickly mounted and to Sam's surprise, headed toward a small opening in the sheer rock face, which from all outward appearances led nowhere. Within moments, Dorsey and company disappeared from sight.

"Well, I'll be danged," Sam said outloud. "There must be a passage through that crack leading up to the high ridge. I sure missed that when I was here before." Sam impatiently moved through the trees, worrying far less about being seen, for time was critical. He thanked God for giving him the wisdom to saddle the horses and secure his gear before he took off to check out the graves. With no minutes to spare, he had to climb to the top of the ridge, circle to the high plateau behind the ranch, and cut their trail to follow them. Sam's previous plan of intercepting Dorsey on the path to Livingston was no more than dust. Somewhere in the vast expanse north of the ranch, Dorsey Caine was going to hole up.

Sam had saddled Dusty and placed the pack on Smoke, giving the big black a rest, knowing both horses would be strenuously worked the next few days. Remaining unobserved while in pursuit was hard on a horse, a "hurry up and wait" situation.

Reaching the high plateau where Dorsey and the cowboy had to have emerged from below took Sam until midmorning. He discovered their tracks among some scrub oaks, discernible and easy to follow. Sam dismounted and backtracked to a narrow ravine that wound precipitously downward. Unless one already knew of the site, it would have been next to impossible to know that a path—especially one sizable enough to allow a mounted horse to climb up through the rock face—could possibly be there. Before getting back up on the dark gelding, Sam made a mental note, locking in the route's exact location. Fortunately, enough snow remained on the ground, still undisturbed by the inevitable late afternoon wind which would sweep the dry granules away. Although they had a good three-hour lead, Sam could determine from the signs that they were traveling slowly—in fact, slower than driving a herd of feeding cows. Every two miles or so, they obviously stopped to have a smoke and give Dorsey some rest. His wound must have been painful, hindering their progress.

Sam was now sure of the reason Dorsey didn't go as far as Livingston. It would have been too agonizing a ride. *Probably hide out 'til he feels better. Likely, Dorsey's destination isn't too far off.*

Sam rode hard to catch up. Topping a rise, he reined in and viewed the open stretch of meadow ahead, where scrub pines and clumps of sage dotted the landscape. Less than half a mile from where a creek wandered through the flats, Sam caught sight of the two riders traveling through a grove of bare aspens. Midway into the vast meadow was a small shack surrounded by holding corrals.

It wasn't long before he saw smoke rise from the chimney, causing Sam to feel a little envious. He hoped they would both settle in for the night. If Dorsey's companion decided to return to the Elk Track right away, he'd soon discover they had been followed, definitely complicating matters. Sam had no alternative but to stay put. As night approached, the temperature dropped drastically and Sam's waiting place gave little protection from the wind. He was bone-cold and knew he couldn't stay there much longer.

Cold, mud-colored clouds rolled in overhead and turned the landscape to shades of dark blue-gray. The only sign of warmth was the spot of yellow light emanating from the cabin window. The figure of the cowboy appeared and set about unloading the mule, taking everything inside. He emerged again and removed the saddles from both horses, then let all three animals loose in the corrals.

Good, Sam thought. *They're in for the night. Now I can find some cover and start a fire.* The snow started to fall again, this time with more intensity. *More good fortune. The tracks will be covered over and even if the other rider leaves early, all signs will be sufficiently obliterated to arouse any suspicion.*

A thick growth of virgin timber lay off to the right. Sam pushed the horses deep within the trees to a small clearing where he hobbled them and loosened the saddle cinches. Bunches of needlegrass poked up through the snow and with adequate protection from the wind, the animals eagerly began to feed on the ample tufts of dry growth. Soon, Sam was warming himself by the flames flowing out of the dead limbs he had pulled from the surrounding pines.

While chewing on some of Mrs. Collins' biscuits, he cut enough pliant boughs to make a bed and set up his tarpaulin for protection from the falling snow. Wrapping the wool blankets about him, he crawled beneath the canvas. Last night was short on rest and long on effort. Before the coming daylight, he needed every ounce of strength to figure how to go about arresting Dorsey Caine.

Dawn came quietly and undramatically. The slate-gray clouds rested close overhead, touching the snow-covered distant peaks. In the still murky light, Sam moved silently across the meadow to the side of the shack, waiting, cocking his ear close to the slat siding. All he could hear were the sonorous sounds of sleep—deep, rumbling sleep.

Sam stealthily circled the cabin to what served as the door—a large buffalo robe hung across the entry. With the barrel of his gun, he moved it slightly aside, seeing both men asleep in the same bunk, covered by layers of heavy blankets. There was no vestige of heat from the small potbellied stove. On the floor next to the table was a broken whiskey bottle, on top was another, a half-full quart of Old Squirrel. The sour, acrid smell of red-eye hung in the frigid air. Outer garments and boots were scattered about the floor, among withered leaves blown in during a former autumn.

Sam shouldered by the buffalo hide and quietly stepped into the small, one-room shack, confident that the two men were sleeping off a night of heavy drinking. They would be groggy when awakened and slow to register to the threat of his presence. Several rifles and one shotgun, a Greener, were stacked in a corner and a pistol hung over the arm of a chair. One was missing, probably Dorsey's, and in all likelihood, it was close at hand somewhere under the covers.

Sam picked up one of the chairs and silently placed it by the head of the bed. He sat down and bent forward enough to place his .45 right beside Dorsey's ear. Then, he cocked the hammer. There was no mistaking the metallic sound; instantly Dorsey's eyes popped wide open. He had no problem identifying the cold, hard object pressing against his temple.

"Good morning, Mr. Caine," Sam stated firmly. "Now, if you'll be so kind as to hand me the gun you have under those blankets."

CHAPTER 19

"SAM DODD, YA SHORE STIRRED UP a hornet's nest!"
Sheriff Jason Sanford leaned forward in his chair, picked
up several telegrams from his cluttered desk, and
thumbed through them again. "Got some more this mornin'.
Some pretty important dignitaries wantin' me to release Dorsey
Caine until the trial is held. I got wires from Marcus Daly, and
from some powerful Democrats up in Helena. Colonel Raven's
been pretty busy gettin' high-powered friends sendin' me all
these messages. It's hard not to listen to 'em."

Sam paced about the sheriff's small office, plainly upset by
Sanford's comments. "Jason, you can't let him go. He's locked
up proper 'cause he's bein' tried for murder. He'd vamoose
quick as a gopher goes to hole if you let 'im out."

"Ya better be right about him bein' Calvin's killer. Ever since
you brought him in two days ago, I've been gettin' lots of heat
from some pretty important people. Raven's got a lot of muscle
with the railroad crowd, copper-mine owners, cattle buyers,
and a whole herd of Helena politicians. Never had such a fuss
lockin' someone up."

"He's guilty, that's plumb sure, no matter whatever anyone
else claims. You shoulda heard him squawkin' when I rode

him out. Not once did he deny killin' Calvin or claim he was innocent. Instead, he spent his time braggin' how we could never convict a kin of Malachi Raven. Cocky, right down to his rotten core."

"You weren't too gentle on him, Sam. Those rope burns about his neck are pretty raw. Raven came in yesterday to visit Dorsey and went loco when he saw them. He claimed you tried to hang him and couldn't, 'cause of you havin' just one wing. He said Dorsey talked you into bringin' him in alive."

"He's a liar; maybe I *shoulda* hung him for all the trouble he gave me," scowled Sam.

"All right, I'll keep him under lock and key 'til trial but you better make sure your witness shows up. Outside of him, all you have is a lot of flimsy evidence. Nobody knows why Cal Davis was killed and we can't prove it was Dorsey who tried to kill your son either. We have no solid evidence that Caine even knew the Texans, much less dry-gulched them. The only solid thing we have is your witness having overheard their plan to kill Calvin and that's about as thin as the wall he heard it through. The bullet wound in the butt don't mean much, even though Dorsey lied about how he got it."

"Sheriff, I know he did it; I spent two days on the trail with that foul-mouthed heathen. I watched the smirks appear on his ugly face and heard the veiled threats on my family's lives. He has the raw cockiness of a killer who believes he is beyond and above the law because of who he is. The man is pure, ugly evil and a sidewindin' sack of trouble. I've seen the type before; he enjoys killin' folks. Maybe I shoulda hung 'im and got it over with."

"Well, they're gonna claim you tried," shrugged the sheriff. "By the way, Sam, how *did* he get those ugly neck burns?"

"He was a handful and a half. Pure lucky that I remembered to bring along some manacles and rope. I had his cohort, whose name was Morty Pitt, shackle Dorsey's hands up front so he could ride. While I held a gun on both of 'em, I had Pitt saddle their horses. Then, I put a rope around both of their rotten necks and tied 'em to the saddle horn of Pitt's animal. And with me on Dorsey's animal, I marched 'em on foot over the hill to where I had my own two hosses. When I told Dorsey to mount up, he no sooner touched the stirrups than he tried to ride off quick-like."

"How far did he get?"

"To the end of the rope. I jerked him plumb clean from the saddle. Dociled him up for quite awhile."

"How about the other cowboy; did he give ya any grief?" Sanford was grinning ear to ear over the image of Dorsey Caine flying off his horse to the ground.

"Morty? Nah, after seein' me dump Dorsey, he was wide-eyed and tuck-tail timid," smiled Sam. "Morty was yes-sirrin' me at every turn. Dorsey was the nasty and hot-tempered one. Every so often, I had to yank him again from his horse and drag 'im through the snow to cool down his foul mouth."

"Didya drag 'im by the neck?"

"Yep! Shut him up real good. Most times I made sure he could reach out and grab the rope with his hands. The rope did worry his sorry neck a bit."

"What did you end up doing with what's-his-name—Morty Pitt?"

"I tied his horse to a tree and walked him ahead of us for half a day, then turned him loose. I didn't want Pitt goin' back to the Elk Track too soon and have a passel of hard-cases chasin' after us. By the time he made it back to the shack, it woulda been nightfall. I figured after walkin' all day in his high-heeled boots, he wouldn't have been too eager to ride to the ranch after dark. Even if he had, they couldn't have caught up with us."

"They shore didn't waste any time burnin' up the telegraph wires." Sanford tossed the sheaf of telegrams down on his desk with a flourish. "Raven must have contacted every politician in Montana, claimin' his cousin was at the ranch at the time of the murder and that he has a dozen people to prove it. Your witness better be a good one 'cause they'll be more than a couple of Elk Track waddies sayin' he's a liar."

Sam thought about the frail old man he had to depend upon as a witness and how terrified he was. *Could Lute hold up under the cross-examination of a good defense lawyer?* The sheriff said they had hired the best one in Montana. Sam had no way of knowing how Lute would handle the pressure, but one thing he was sure of. Arresting Dorsey Caine put Raven on notice that they could no longer work in secrecy. They'd be the first suspects if any more shotgun killings occurred.

Sam had picked up the rumor that Malachi Raven had political ambitions for his son. Since Montana was soon to become a new state, and with relatively few people scattered here and there, it was a great opportunity for anyone interested in politics—especially if they were rich.

The impending trial could be rough on the Raven reputation. Since members of the family could now be implicated in conspiring to commit murder, it might be very damaging to J.D.'s future—particularly if Dorsey was convicted.

Both Dodds were rapidly chinking away at the Raven clan's thin veneer of civility. Sam learned the colonel was a blatant liar and the last few days, bringing Dorsey to Bozeman revealed his glaring viciousness. David wasn't the only one who had witnessed the drunken, bully-boy makeup of J.D. However, their wealth and influence had turned many a head, forgiving their crude attributes, convincing many that the Ravens were the noble Southern gentry they pretended to be. The trial would do much to reveal the Raven family's true nature, Sam was convinced.

Elderly Lute Olsen was certainly credible; a jury of working people would more than likely believe in the honesty of his testimony. They couldn't help but see he was a Christian man who had nothing to gain by lying. Sam was still keeping Lute's identity secret, having told only Doctor Collins, his son, and now Sheriff Sanford. He hadn't even confided Lute's name to Mary; the fewer who knew, the better.

Sam concluded his business with the sheriff and headed straight for the train depot, where he loaded his horses in a freight car, thankful to be leaving the crowded Bozeman, whose population had swelled to more than two thousand. He longed to be away from populated areas and return to his high-country ranch, spend time with his children and new grandson, just lie back and watch the grass grow. After the Caine trial, he and Mary would immediately be on their way home to Colorado. The thought gave him much pleasure.

MARY WORE A STRAINED LOOK as she opened the door to the hotel room and greeted Sam with an unusually prolonged embrace. She pulled away to sit on the edge of the bed and patted the spot next to her. "Sit down, honey—there's something I have to tell you, especially since you're so deeply involved." Tears were in her eyes as she looked at him.

"Sam, did you know there is real trouble between David and Deborah? She's called off the wedding and David's fit to be tied. I've never seen him so low in spirit. The boy's heart must be breaking. I don't know all her reasons, but she blames *you* for some of the trouble between them."

"Blames *me?*" Sam asked, incredulously. "Blames me for *what?*"

"Deborah is furious; she says you've defamed the good name of the Ravens. It seems she's developed a rather strong friendship with the son and believes they are innocent of any accusations. She and David got into a terrible fight over your arresting J.D.'s kin. She said he insisted Dorsey Caine was at the ranch when the killing took place. David, of course, defended you and told her there was a witness, but when he wouldn't say who, she became very indignant."

"That girl sure takes after her pa. He reacted the same way at the meeting we had at the doctor's." Sam put his arm around

Mary and gave her a small squeeze. "Don't you take it too badly, sweetheart; we've seen this split coming for quite awhile. The trouble is, David hasn't." Sam shared with her what he had observed about Deborah and her family since his arrival in Big Timber. He related the affectionate hugging and horseback riding with J.D., the lame excuses for delaying the wedding, and Deborah's obvious absence at David's side when he bordered on dying. Mary stiffened upon hearing Sam's words and the tears stopped abruptly as she curtly inquired, "You mean she wasn't at his bedside every minute?"

"Nope, she wasn't. In fact, some days she didn't even inquire as to how he was doing. Deborah simply wasn't there, but Amy was," he added.

"Well! What do you know about that! What kind of an excuse did she give for THAT behavior?" Mary was fuming. She often stated it was a woman's responsibility to care for her man in both sickness and in health. The very idea that Deborah wasn't constantly by his side was appalling to her, an affront to her sense of values. "Well, I never!"

Sam couldn't help but grin. "Don't get all huffy, sweetheart; maybe it's for the better."

The sadness returned to her eyes. "Maybe so, but for the time being, that isn't going to help David. He loves her so much that he can't concentrate on anything but the affection they seemed to have had for each other. He's very confused right now." Mary got up from the bed and stepped over to the window, looking down on the street. "Is there anything we can do to help him?"

"I don't think so. Time is the only cure for David's ailment and only God has herd over that. Let's see how the trial works out. If Dorsey is convicted, Deborah might think a bit different about the Ravens." Sam suddenly brightened. "Sweetheart, I've got a good idea. You haven't seen much of this area—just this hotel and visiting David's place. There are some pretty spots along the river. Sunday's only a couple of days away;

after church, let's rent a buggy and we can take a ride along the Yellowstone. This March wind's been blowin' a bit warmer and the weather's not too bad. Sound good to you?"

"Oh, Sam, it sounds lovely, but I don't think we will have the time."

"Why not? What's so important to keep us from going on a ride together?"

"The funeral we should attend." Mary exclaimed, "Oh . . . I guess you didn't hear what happened yesterday."

"What happened?" Sam instantly felt a knot in his gut.

"One of the members of Amy's church just up and died," Mary sadly sighed. "He was having supper with the Swensens when, like a bolt out of the blue, he grabbed his chest and keeled over dead. The burial's Sunday afternoon."

"Was it Lute Olsen?"

"Yes, it was!" Mary surprisingly exclaimed. "How did you know?"

"It wasn't a hard guess."

CHAPTER 20

H E'S DEMANDING A PUBLIC APOLOGY, Sam." Jason
Sanford paced back and forth in his office, waving the
newspaper in Sam's direction. "Raven says his good
name has been dragged through the mud by an irresponsible
sheriff who's lost control of his hirelings." He thrust the paper
at Dodd. "Here! You read it."

Sam took the publication in his hand and spread it out on the
table. "Well, I'll be doggoned, it's right smack on the front page!"

SHERIFF'S DEPUTY FALSELY ARRESTS
MONTANA RANCHER

"Read the text of the story; it gets much worse," groaned Jason.
Sam continued to read:

> "Dorsey Caine, foreman and part-owner of the Elk
> Track Ranch, was arrested, incarcerated, and falsely ac-
> cused of murder. All charges were dropped by the county
> attorney when no substantial evidence or witnesses could
> be presented. Colonel Malachi Raven, majority owner of
> the Elk Track and first-cousin of the accused, was highly

incensed by the false charges and swears his cousin was with him and others when the murder was committed. Colonel Raven is demanding an apology from Sheriff Jason Sanford and calling for the dismissal of Deputy Samuel Dodd. Dorsey Caine said Dodd tried unsuccessfully to hang him and displayed ugly rope burns on his neck."

Sam stopped reading. "They sure didn't miss a trick, did they? What are you goin' to do, Jason?"

"Don't rightly know, Sam." A mean glint appeared in his eyes. "But I'm not *that* easily pressured. The colonel came into my office yesterday with the mayor and a reporter from that paper. Raven tried to run roughshod over me, demandin' I oust both you *and* your son."

"And what didya say?"

"I listened to 'em and told 'em I'd think about it. I'm still thinkin'."

"Jason, is there any doubt in your mind that Dorsey didn't kill Calvin?" asked Sam.

He responded by looking Sam straight in the eye. "None whatsoever. If I had any doubts, Dorsey Caine erased them yesterday when I let him out of jail. His smug 'you-can't-prove-nuthin'' 'crowin' made me want to shoot 'im on the spot. He was so arrogant; he demanded I give him back his Greener shotgun. He didn't say it outright like a man, but that sidewinder beat a path around the barn, suggestin' he was goin' to blow off your other arm and kill ya dead. There's no doubt in my mind he'll back-shoot ya the first chance he gets."

"He'll have to go to Colorado to do it. Mary, Matthew, and I will be heading there as soon as I get back to Big Timber. It's time to take them home. You can tell the newspaper you fired me, if it would help . . . makes no mind to me."

"I won't do that; Sam, you weren't wrong."

"Wrong or right, we can't prove it, nor are we about to convince a jury. Dorsey and J.D. will go unpunished unless we can figure out why Calvin and the Texans were killed and then prove it. We aren't one step closer to the answer than the day we started and there's no sense being bitter about it. Vengeance belongs to the Lord. He knows they're guilty and will hold 'em accountable on Judgment Day, for sure."

"By the way, Sam, I just remembered. As Dorsey was leaving, he said somethin' I couldn't figure out." Jason scratched his head and said, "Dorsey wanted me to repeat it to you, but what he said don't make any sense at all."

"Just what did he say?"

"He said, 'Tell that one-armed SOB that the broncobuster is next to adobe' . . . or somethin' like that. Do ya know what he was gettin' at?"

Sam was lost in thought for a minute or two, then his shoulders sagged as he answered, "I'm afraid I do. It's not *adobe*, it's Dobie—Dobie Johnson—that he was talkin' about. Arlis McKay is dead. Caine is telling us he's buried next to Dobie. Remember, I told you about the extra grave at the Elk Track?"

"Yeah, I remember," responded Sanford. "They must've found out about that conversation you had with Arlis."

"Yep, they sure did." Sam slapped his leg hard in frustration. "I told that kid to keep his mouth shut but he didn't seem to take it very seriously."

"Well, it shore looks like the Ravens did," Jason lamented ironically, "and one more dead witness."

The killing of Arlis deeply saddened Sam. The young broncobuster was such a happy, easy-going young man without a whit of guile or meanness in him. His slaying could be so easily explained, a blow to the back of the head blamed on a bucking bronc. This sorrowful news just added to the frustration and helplessness that he already felt inside.

"What about David; is he goin' back to Colorado with you?" asked the sheriff.

"Not for now, Jason. David's planning on moving back into the old shack he shared with Calvin. He wants to stick around for awhile. He's fit enough to ride and work and he wanted me to ask if you could keep him on as deputy. I'd be obliged if you would consider it, even though the Ravens won't like it."

Jason shrugged his shoulders, "I don't see any reason why not. David's a good man and . . ." He looked at Sam and grinned. "It so happens, the deputy who had that territory has just resigned."

They both smiled and warmly shook hands good-bye.

EASTER SERVICES AT THE DODD RANCH brought neighbors from miles around, each one bringing some special dish for the feast that followed. The happy occasion was celebrated as good friends greeted one another with the glad salutation, "He is risen," and the joyous reply, "He has risen, indeed!"

The weather was quite pleasurable. A southwest wind moved the warm air over the land and the roads were a little muddy, but passable. The festivities were over and everyone was trying to get home before dark. Sam waved farewell to the last guest and went into the house, where Mary and the girls were busy cleaning up the last of the dishes and chatting among themselves.

"Any pie left?" he asked impishly. He got the response he expected. None—merely the clanging of pots and pans. "Well, I think I'll find my pipe and have a smoke on the porch and read some."

Sam went over to the bookcase and reached for the Bible. Beside it was a small notebook of scribbled poetry which David had brought with him from Big Timber. It was one of Calvin Davis' few treasured possessions, his book of cowboy rhyme. Curiously, Sam flipped it open to read the first poem entitled *Ode to a Lonesome Cowboy*:

> Out wer the wether is wet
> is wer i'll get
> me and my hoss Rex
> that I stole frum a Tex.

David was right; Calvin *was* a lousy poet. Sam stuffed the small journal in his pocket and walked out onto the wide porch. He sat quietly on the steps and viewed the peaceful valley below. It was good to be home. Sam, Mary, and Matt had been back in Colorado for close to a month and David returned just three days ago, all doing their best to forget Big Timber. The frustration still burned a hole in Sam's innards every time he thought of Montana. The Ravens were free as the vultures that soared around the Crazy Mountains. To make matters worse, the Dodd name was being sullied by them at every opportunity. Dorsey was bragging that he had chased Sam out of the state and that he would have killed him if he weren't a one-armed cripple.

Matters had worsened between David and Deborah. Not only had she avoided any chance of reconciliation, she announced her impending marriage to Jefferson Davis Raven. Adding insult to injury, the Dillses sent a wedding invitation to the Dodds. Mary was fit to be tied.

David resigned from serving as a county deputy and was home to help his father with the spring roundup. The entire Montana experience had been one of disappointment, travail, and suffering for the Dodds.

It was too bad because they had come to know some wonderful people there—the Collinses, the Grosfields, Amy Rostad, and quite a few others. Sam couldn't help but feel he had let all of those good folks down. He had prayed about it, knowing for sure that God listens to all supplications. A pastor by the name of W. Mees once told him, "Mr. Dodd, the Lord answers our prayer requests in three ways—yes, no, or wait awhile." So far, yes hadn't been the answer and Sam had a difficult time believing that such evil would go unpunished. "I guess I'm stuck with 'wait awhile,'" Sam mumbled.

Maybe I'd like a little vengeance over the pain the Ravens have caused and I tend to forget that revenge is the sole prerogative of the Lord. Sam looked up to the heavens and asked aloud, "Lord, when You get around to fixin' the Ravens's wagon, if I'm still kickin', wouldya let me know about it?"

Having David safe at home was comforting. He was much quieter than usual and every so often, a distracted, faraway look crossed his face. He kept his hurt to himself, never mentioning Deborah's name. The last few years had erased his last vestige of youth. He was now a full-grown man, steeled and tempered by the fires of experience. David had faced death and survived . . . and he had killed. Two men lay dead because of his proficiency with weapons and the nerve to use them. Rowdies and belligerent drunks had witnessed his agility and strength; all came out second-best when they challenged him with their fists.

What's more, he was a God-fearing man, trusting in the Lord. Sam was proud of his son but now saw within him a new restlessness, a freer spirit. The two years working in Montana had brought about an independent streak in him, and both he and Mary knew it was only a matter of time before he left for new horizons. David Dodd wouldn't be satisfied as a rancher—at least, not at this time in his life. He had tasted the excitement of being a lawman, a lot more challenging than punching cows. No longer was he planning on marriage—not until he got the sour-pickle taste of the Dillses out of his mouth. Sam couldn't help but crack a smile at this last thought. *Dills and pickles. It fits!*

Sam pushed the reflections of Montana to the back of his mind, for there were more important things to consider. It was spring roundup time. New hands would need to be hired. The cows would soon be dropping their calves, easy prey for numerous predator wolves, coyotes, and mountain lions in the surrounding terrain. Horses needed to be shod and fences repaired; the necessary upkeep and chores were endless.

Sam was optimistic that David would stick around until the fall, but at this point, he could only hope. Each day, David found time to practice with his guns. *Why every day?* Sam wondered. *He sure doesn't have to be fast or even very good to punch cows.* He was taking his father's advice to heart, making sure the shots were true. Now, he was combining speed with accuracy and was becoming deadly efficient with his .44 Colt. Sam trusted that David would never have to use his guns, but was relieved that he knew how.

Something was up with that young man; some heavy thinking was definitely riding around in David's head that his father didn't know about. In all probability, it had something to do with Deborah. It must have been galling to realize the love of his life was soon to marry J.D. Raven who, in his mind, was a despicable cur. *It must hurt to the quick to lose your sweetheart, even more to a Raven.* J.D. had a reputation for being skilled with a gun. Sam hoped that challenging him wasn't what David had in mind.

When Sam reached inside his pocket for the tobacco, he also brought out the little book of Calvin's poems. Turning his attention to one of the family dogs who had muzzled his nose under Sam's arm, he said, "Rusty, how would you like to hear some Montana poetry?" The dog wagged his tail at being recognized.

"Oh, you would? Well, let's try this one called, *Luv thet Gal.* Sam cleared his throat. "Here goes, Rusty, listen closely."

> Met her in a bar
> saw her over thar
> leanen on the bar
> over thar.

"How do you like that, boy? Doesn't that tug at your heartstrings?" Sam thumbed through pages and pages of Calvin's heroic attempts at writing verse. Metrical pattern had never entered Cal's mind, but his words did come within the width of a barnyard to rhyming.

A loose piece of paper fell out as Sam came to the few remaining blank pages in the back of the book. He picked it up and said to his attentive dog, "Rusty, can you stand another one?"

Rusty barked affirmatively as Sam read, "Dere sheriff."

Sam stopped reading out loud; it wasn't a poem, but an uncompleted letter to Sheriff Sanford.

> Dere sheriff, funny things are happing over here in Big Timber. Met a cuple of waddies frum Texas when full of red-eye told me some bad things about Raven. They was drunkern two skunks suckin on a wine jug so can't tell how truthful they whar. They called him ther Vicksburg gold mine. Both new him ther durin the war. They sed he

That's all there was to the letter. Something must have interrupted Calvin's finishing the message. Sam guessed that he folded it up and put it among his poems, intending to complete and mail it later. *Whew, this bit of information sure tightens the cinch!*

Whatever those Texans were in on was sufficiently incriminating to get them bushwhacked. Somehow, Raven must have gathered that Calvin was their confidant and became a target as well. Though David was just an innocent bystander, when they found him with Calvin, they probably assumed he also knew the story.

David had said the shack that he and Calvin shared was ransacked, literally torn apart. It was likely Raven's thugs were looking for anything incriminating Calvin or David might have written down. Fortunately, the notebook wasn't in the shack at all, but in Calvin's saddlebag which was, at the time, still attached to his saddle at the stables.

Eager to share Davis' letter with his son, Sam hotfooted down to the barn where David was feeding the stock. He called into the dark interior, "Son, come on out here, I've got something for you to read."

David strolled through the door, wiping the sweat from his brow and brushing the loose flakes of alfalfa from his clothes. Spotting Calvin's book of poetry in his father's hand, he ventured to say with a glint in his eye, "Don't tell me, Pa, you found one good enough to repeat!"

"Shore did." Sam handed the letter to David without another word.

David's eyes opened wide. "Well, I'll be danged! Where did you find this?"

"It was just among the pages of Calvin's notebook."

"It certainly ties a few pieces of loose string together, doesn't it, Pa?"

"It also tells me something else, Son."

"What's that?"

"It tells me you'll have a lot of extra work to do around here for the next few months. I'm goin' to get to the bottom of this, which means I have to go to Vicksburg. Can you handle it for me?"

A broad smile broke out across David's face. "If it means we have a chance to expose the Ravens for the dry-gulchin' liars they are, I'll work 'til my caboose drops off."

Now somewhat solemn, Sam stated, "Another door has been opened, and it leads to the deep South. The last time I was there, I had a Springfield rifle in one hand and a torch in the other. We made a pretty big mess of the place, burnin' everything in sight. It ended the war sooner, but it was a sorry thing to do. I hope they have forgiven us."

"That might take awhile, Pa—maybe a hundred years."

"Yep, or maybe even longer."

CHAPTER 21

THE PHYSICAL SCARS OF THE WAR Between the States were gone; the shell holes in the cobblestone streets had been fully repaired or completely replaced by neat rows of red brick. The buildings along China and Walnut streets had been restored to their pre-war state and businesses appeared to be booming, accompanied by all the sights and sounds of commerce. Wagons and carriages noisily clattered over the steep roadways; the harsh hammering of new construction and conversation of merchants and shoppers filled the town center. Laden paddle wheelers docked along the levies emitted volumes of smoke as sweating Negro laborers moved up and down the gangplanks, unloading farm machinery, crates, and bales of cotton onto the railroad platforms nearby.

Vicksburg had changed dramatically since the first time Sam Dodd had walked its streets. It was a pleasant uphill stroll from his downtown hotel to the Warren County Courthouse on Cherry and Grove. The slate-gray overcast was breaking up as he crossed Clay Street, allowing filtered sun to glorify the prolific display of white, pink, and red azaleas. *Quite a marked difference from the burned landscape and ugly bomb craters that marked the face of Vicksburg the last time I was here*, Sam noted.

The city and Confederate embattlements had been subject to forty-seven days of incessant shelling from Union gunboats along the Mississippi River. The iron-clad warships had poured more than sixteen thousand rounds of cannon shells into the South's fortifications. Tens of thousands more rounds rained down from the encircled forces of Ulysses S. Grant's federal army. The bombardment seemed never ending. Untold numbers of exploding Parrott shells, weighing anywhere from ten to two hundred pounds apiece, spewed lethal cluster balls of shrapnel in all directions. Thousands of twelve-pound Napoleons, each filled with lead balls and yellow pitch, spread sulfuric fire to whatever they struck. Terrified Vicksburg residents took shelter underground, burrowing into the hillsides. Women and children packed together in damp, man-made caves. The town soon came to be called "Gopher City" by its inhabitants.

Sam became melancholy when he thought about the vicious fighting that occurred at Jackson, Champion Hill, and the crossing at the Big Black River. The march to Vicksburg was a bloody affair; assaults upon the fortifications were very costly in loss of life and limb. Several of his closest neighbors—boys he knew from primary school in Edgar County, Illinois—were buried just north of town. Mark Bates, his closest childhood buddy, rested there with many other friends. *Before I leave, I best go visit them.*

Sam hastened his step; the Warren County Courthouse was just ahead, unmarred by the battle. The large brick building was a familiar sight during the siege, standing out like a sore thumb on the bluff above town. Union artillerymen were dying to level the multi-storied brick building and pound it into dust, but none dared to fire a single shell in its direction, even though Rebel artillery spotters daily were seen in its high tower. Sam smiled, "Cagey fellers, these graybacks." The second floor of the courthouse was used for interning captured Union officers and the Rebels made sure the Yankee brass knew it.

Sam wondered how he would be received by the local citizenry if they were aware he was one of the Union soldiers who fought there. He didn't want to open any old wounds in his search for information; it could seriously complicate matters if anyone found out. Sam certainly didn't think it advisable to let on that he'd spent the latter days of the war under the command of General Sherman. There was no Union general more universally hated by the South . . . and for good reason.

William Tecumseh Sherman intentionally, purposefully, burnt a wide, ugly swath through the South on his march to the Atlantic, setting afire plantation, farm, and town, pauperizing many a family. His scorched-earth policy was geared to destroy the Southern will to resist and it accomplished its purpose. Sherman's fire seared a brand of loathing hatred into the hide of the Confederacy. Famine also followed his footsteps; the Union Army lived off the land, robbing whatever food could be carted away. General pillage of valuables by Northern soldiers was commonplace. Economic ruin was the lot for those who stood within reach of General Sherman and his hardened Western troops. Plundering bummers and vengeful slaves picked the landscape clean.

Sam recalled being personally appalled by the policy, bringing to mind the Lord's admonition of, "As you sow, so shall you reap." Even then, he knew the war would end someday. But the scars, the Sherman brand, would be passed on from generation to generation. "The sins of the father are passed on to the fourth generation, so said the Lord."

Thankfully, Sam wasn't directly involved in the procurement of supplies. Because of his skill at scouting, he was assigned to Sherman's staff as an advanced observer, reporting directly to general headquarters. Sergeant Sam Dodd had ample opportunity to know the red-headed, fiery-tempered Sherman. Winning, crushing the enemy consumed his every thought and the general's comment, "The very object of war is . . . death and slaughter," spoke volumes about his objectives. "The nature of war," he said, "demands immediacy of action; there is little time for contemplating tomorrow, much less years later."

Sam thought about his close association with the general. *Yep, it would be wise to keep quiet about it, especially here in Mississippi.*

During his stayover in Fort Collins, Colorado to catch the train south, Sam wired Sheriff Sanford in Bozeman, informing him of the contents of Cal Davis' letter and his travel plans. Jason immediately wired back that he thought it was a wild-goose chase . . . at best. But, since Sam was so inclined, he was redeputizing the senior Dodd, suggesting his inquiries might be more easily answered if he was an officer of the law. The sheriff's postscript read:

> Do not tell them you are Yankee.
> Do not expect pay or expenses.

Sam laughed out loud when he read the return message. The sheriff was right; investigating as a Montana officer of the law would be much easier, particularly if he stressed the fact he was trying to solve the murder of two former Confederate soldiers from Mississippi.

Sam felt Jason might also be right about the wild-goose chase; it was like he was looking for one specific Southern Minie ball in a war-torn battlefield. Four divisions, more than twenty thousand Confederate soldiers, were crammed into the Vicksburg defenses. Locating anyone who might know one of them was bound to be very difficult. Telegraph inquiries to the War Department in Washington D.C. had indicated that war records of the federal troops were extensive, but those of the South were still being gathered by the states. Data was scattered, incomplete, and in some instances nonexistent.

Sam's only alternative was this trip to Mississippi to pore over records in the state capitol at Jackson. Copious records were available, but nowhere could he find the name of a Colonel Malachi Raven who had been at Vicksburg. He did, however, glean the names of three Rebel officers who served under General Pemberton whose homes were in and around Vicksburg. Sam jotted down their names, then caught the train west for the city by the rivers. *If they still live in the vicinity, their whereabouts should be known, probably at the court-house.*

The county clerk was helpful; all three were listed as property owners and resided within the town. In fact, a Lieutenant R.G. Koopman lived on Adams Street just a few blocks from the courthouse. With a feeling of guarded anticipation, Sam quickened his steps past rows of well-kept homes with cropped lawns and patches of colorful azalea bushes scattered about. All looked neat and orderly until he reached the Koopman residence—a sorry sight, a neighborhood blemish, like an ugly scab on the nose of a pretty lady.

The two-story Victorian was in sad need of repair and paint, its gray coat peeling, exposing the rotting wood underneath. One of the shutters was hanging by a lone hinge, while another lay against the side of the sagging foundation. A split board on the first porch step creaked under the pressure of Sam's weight; another was missing altogether. The handrails, worn free of finish, were a dirty sheen of grime, sticky to the touch. Rubble was strewn on the porch and boxes of empty bottles were stacked by the entry. On the weather-beaten door, Sam could see a configuration wehre the door-knocker was once located, undoubtedly removed long ago. He knocked . . . then again, louder.

"Come on in! The door's not locked." The man's voice was soft, faint-sounding. Sam reached out for the door handle, but it too was missing, so he pushed against it. The heavy door swung open awkwardly, pulling on the loose hinge-screws. It was dark inside. The windows were shuttered and the interior walls were covered with dingy, peeling wallpaper. It took a moment for Sam's eyes to adjust, but his nose was immediately assaulted by the distinct putrid smell of age, whiskey, and sour bile which saturated the dank air. The floor was bare and there was little furniture.

Across the room sat a slumped silhouette of a man, outlined by the light flowing through a partially ajar shutter behind him. The shadowed figure spoke in a whiskeyed, but gentle voice. "What, suh, may ah do for you? If y'all are heah to buy any more of my belongings, ah'm afriad ah've got nothin' else to sell exceptin' those bottles out on the front porch, if y'all are interested."

"I'm not here to buy anything, sir. Are you R.G. Koopman, formerly Lieutenant Koopman of the Mississippi Artillery?"

For several long moments, Sam waited for an answer. Finally, almost inaudibly, he responded, "Yes . . . yes, suh, ah am. May ah inquire who are you, suh, and what may I do for y'all?"

"Mr. Koopman, my name is Sam Dodd. I'm a sheriff from Montana Territory. I'm here to garner information on some of the officers and men who served here during the siege. I've been told you were here at that time."

"Oh my, ah was here, all right," he whispered. "so were my wife and daughter, God rest their souls."

Sam, his eyes having adjusted to the dark, was mildly shocked at the appearance of the thin, flushed man who sat before him. The ash-gray skin contrasted the black, hollowed eyes buried deep under a protruding brow. A once well-tailored jacket was now threadbare, hanging loosely on his gaunt frame. One leg of his trousers was rolled up and fastened, the limb clearly amputated near the hip. A twisted left arm lay in his lap, two fingers missing from his hand. Crutches leaned against the table within easy grasp.

Koopman's age was difficult to ascertain—maybe fifty or even seventy. The toll of liquor and depravation had been paid in full measure. The glass in his right hand was empty, as was the whiskey bottle on the table. He held up a glass as if proposing a toast. "I'd offer y'all a drink, suh, but it seems ah just ran out." Noticing Sam's sewn-up sleeve, he said, "Ah see you also left some muscle and bones on the battlefield."

"No, I lost my arm just a few years ago." Sam quickly changed the subject, not wanting to dwell on the matter. "Mr.

Koopman, do you happen to know of a Colonel Raven who fought here at Vicksburg or of two enlisted men by the names of Rob Hurtt and John Lewis?"

The old man was not to be dislodged from his train of thought. He continued talking, seeming to ignore Sam's request for information. "See this, suh?" He raised his distorted left arm. "Ah got this memento from the Yankee artillery at Fort Donelson." "And this, suh," he turned his wrist, displaying the three remaining fingers, "ah gave my thumb and forefinger to the Southern cause at Champion Hill, compliments of a Northern Minie ball. "And this," he quietly continued while rotating in the chair and thrusting his right hip clumsily forward, "ah lost in the street right in front of this very house." Then with a touch of pain and sarcasm, he added, " . . . along with my wife and little girl."

"I'm sorry to hear that, sir," said Sam.

"Oh, ah guess they were the lucky ones; they didn't even know what hit them." His voice cracked with emotion as he slurred dramatically, "They were dead . . . but not me! Ah laid out there for an hour with the blood of my little Ella splattered all over my body."

"My deepest sympathies, sir. I hope the Lord will help ease your pain."

"Well, suh," he replied, "ah haven't noticed any help so far. He was nowhere around when the bomb hit my family." The wounded veteran picked up the whiskey bottle and shook it above the glass, anticipating drops that were not there. Shrugging his shoulders, he muttered, "Despair is a bottomless pit, isn't it? Ah've been to its edge and have looked over . . . more than once." Koopman paused and added reflectively, "Victory moderates personal loss; there is something noble about sacrificin' life and family fortune for a cause that succeeds, but dying for one that fails? What glory's in that?

"One can justify and rationalize defeat, but it assaults logic to forgive your mortal enemies, much less forget what they did to you. We Southerners are now asked to do just that . . . forgive and forget. Forgiveness, suh, is simple for the victor, but a bitter pill for the vanquished. We'll nevah forget, no suh . . . nevah!" With that, he brought the glass down hard on the table, the sound echoing off the bare walls.

The heated diatribe appeared to exhaust him, but without taking a breath, the crippled Confederate launched into a long, jumbled dissertation on the war, the Reconstruction, carpetbaggers, and the plight of veterans. "Did you know, suh, the second-highest expenditure of the 1870 Arkansas Legislature was for artificial limbs for our forces? Did y'all know that?"

"No, I did not," answered Sam. "In 1870, I was in the mountain country of Colorado." Sam stared down at the pitiful creature and asked, "When was the last time you ate?"

Silence. Koopman's chin had dropped to his chest in exhaustion; he'd fallen asleep. Sam turned on his heel and left.

WHEN SAM RETURNED with a gunnysack of groceries, the old man's head was still slumped forward. Dodd went into the kitchen and, as he expected, there was no food except for a handful of flour infested with weevils. The kitchen had practically no cooking utensils—just a greasy iron skillet, a cracked porcelain soup kettle, and a coffeepot. Sam guessed the rest of the kitchenware, like the furniture, door knobs, and knocker, had been sold to acquire food and drink.

He kindled the stove and placed a pot of coffee on the fire. After cleaning out the fry pan, he threw in some thick slices of bacon and boiled up some water in the kettle. In less than half an hour, he was holding a plate of bacon, eggs, and grits under Koopman's nose. He awakened groggily and, without a word, began to ravenously shovel the food down. Wiping the plate clean with a chunk of bread, he reached for the coffee mug and gulped a big swallow. He looked up at his benefactor and asked,

"What was the name of that colonel y'all asked about?"

"Raven," Sam eagerly replied. "Colonel Malachi Raven."

The wizened old lieutenant thought for a moment, then broke off another piece of bread and stuffed it in his mouth. He gruffly said, "Nevah heard of 'im."

CHAPTER 22

S
O KOOPMAN HADN'T KNOWN of Hurtt or Lewis either. Sam doubted that he was conscious of anything but the bitterness he harbored inside. He was hopeful that Koopman would've been the exception to the rule, rather than reflecting the attitudes of the average Southerner. Sam hated the carnage that was the soul mate of war, but he agreed with Sherman on one or two points. Sam agreed: War *is* death and slaughter and, truly, there is no such thing as a "civil" war. Although the general's planned pillage of the South hastened the war's end saving untold lives on both sides, expressing this opinion to someone who'd felt the flame of Sherman's torch was wasted breath. Lieutenant Koopman was right about one thing; it *is* easy to forgive if you are on the winning side.

The second name on Sam's list was Captain S. P. Roundtree, of the Twenty-third Mississippi, whose home was located just south of town. The house sat on the side of the hill, overlooking the Father of Waters, the mighty Mississippi River. Unlike the place he had just visited, this structure was newly painted and well-kept; a warm pale-gray paint covered the white-shuttered antebellum-style home. Sam walked up the red brick walkway, neatly bordered with yellow pansies and iris. He was relieved to see smoke curling from the chimney and assumed the occupants were at home.

Sam lifted the highly polished brass knocker, rapped twice, and waited. An attractive young woman answered the door carrying a rosy-cheeked, squirming infant boy in her arms.

"Mrs. Roundtree?" asked Sam.

"No," she smiled, "that would've been my mother. Ah'm Mrs. Lofton."

Sam frowned and hesitatingly asked, "Is your father still ali—is he home?"

The young matron shifted the wriggling child to one arm, holding him tightly to her hip and sweetly drawled, "Ah'm sorry, suh, Momma and Daddy passed away just this last yeah. My husband and ah live heah now. Is there anythin' ah can do for y'all?"

Sam shrugged and smiled again. Though discouraged, he was enjoying hearing her soft Southern voice and watching the bobbing young lad trying to free himself from his mother's grip.

"I think not," he replied, then added with a grin, "quite a handful you've got there."

"Yes, he surely is . . . hold still, Robbie!" Exasperated, she gave him a tiny slap on his bare leg, saying, "Ah declare, ah don't know how anyone can have more than one boy." Shifting the now crying child to the other hip, she asked, "Are you sure ah can't help? Were y'all friends of my folks?"

"No. I never met them. I wanted to ask your father if he knew a Colonel Malachi Raven during the war," answered Sam.

"Why, yes, he did," she beamed. "I remember Daddy mentioning the name several times. Raven's an unusual name, hard to forget."

"Did your father know him well?"

"That, ah can't answer, but ah know my daddy thought highly of him, spoke of him more than once. Daddy said he was a very brave man, a fine soldier."

Sam eagerly pursued the subject. "Can you tell me anything else about Colonel Raven? What state he was from or maybe where his home was located, who his friends might have been? Anything you can remember could be helpful."

She pondered all the questions for awhile, then said, "No, ah'm so sorry, but ah can't remember a thing. Ah was pretty young the last time ah remember Daddy mentionin' his name." Then, knitting her brow, she inquired, "Why, suh, do you want to know?"

Sam didn't want to tell her he was investigating a murder, but he didn't want to lie either. "I'm doing research on the Civil War and some of the men who fought at Vicksburg."

The baby was now screaming so loudly, Sam was having a hard time hearing her. He thought it best to leave so he bid her farewell and turned to leave. Halfway down the steps, he barely heard her call out above the wails of he child.

"Mister!"

Sam turned to hear her say, "If y'all want to find out anything, anything at all about the fightin' around Vicksburg, y'all should go see mah daddy's best friend, Major Charles Knowles. He lives down in Port Gibson, a short spell south of heah."

"Do you have his address?"

"Don't need one. Y'all just ask around; ever'body knows him."

Sam clearly recalled Port Gibson. Twenty years ago to the month, Sam had crossed the Mississippi River as one of the vanguard pickets, scouting for the Thirteenth Corps under the command of General McClernand. When the main body landed at Bruinsburg, they were unopposed; but shortly thereafter, they fought their way northeast to Port Gibson, battling through the most difficult terrain imaginable.

Two narrow roads twisting along ridges were their only access. Both were flanked by steep draws, overgrown with thick almost impenetrable stands of pine, oak, dogwood, and bramble. The gully bottoms were bogs of tangled brush, possum vine, and willow, with visibility severely restricted to less than twenty yards.

Out of the tangle charged screaming gray-clad Rebels, bayonets fixed, muskets firing. *They were upon us before we could reload and vicious hand-to-hand fighting ensued.* He vividly remembered turning quickly and witnessing an elderly, bearded foe about to ram a bayonet in his side, tripping over a vine and sprawling at Sam's feet. Without a moment's hesitation Sam drove his own bayonet through the Reb's back, then held the dying, wrenching man down with his foot while he yanked the bloody weapon free. Before he could reload, a much younger wild-eyed Rebel charged, intent on doing the same. Sam knocked the bayonet aside with the barrel of his Springfield and struck the lad flush in the face with the butt of the gun, then speared him as he fell.

It all happened in a flash. *No time to think, no time for remorse, no time to lie in wait during an advance by the enemy . . . take cover. To dawdle is to die.* After resisting the enemy, the Union forces attacked. Sam's division charged through the tangle of canebrake and deadfall toward the Southerners' lines, where for two lengthy hours they were involved in repulsing the charge of Tracy's Confederate Brigade . . . only to gain but four hundred yards. It was a miserable place to fight an entrenched enemy.

Fortunately, the Confederates—under overall command of General John Bowens—were undermanned. Due to superior numbers the Union Army finally prevailed and marched into Port Gibson. Bowen retreated under the cover of dark to north of Bayou Pierre.

Sam shook his head, trying to dislodge the memories. Were it not for a providentially located vine, he, rather than an old, bearded Reb would be buried nearby.

General Grant had once commented that Port Gibson was too pretty to burn. Sam observed through the Pullman car window the beautiful oaks adorned with Spanish moss, prolific flowering bushes and flower-lined walkways, as the train clanged to a halt in the station.

Mrs. Lofton was right; the first person Sam spoke to knew where to find Major Knowles.

Pointing with his finger, the man on the station platform cheerfully offered, "He lives on the cornah of Vine and Coffee, suh. Just head ovah that-a-ways."

In no time at all Sam was climbing the wide steps of the large, two-storied home where flower-encircled, giant trees shadowed an expansive lawn. A broad veranda surrounded the front and sides of the Georgian structure and pots of blue iris bordered the railing. The swing, cushioned wicker furniture, and several comfortable-looking rockers prompted Sam to think, *What a relaxin' place to spend warm summer evenings.*

An aging Negress answered his knock. "Yessuh," she asked, "what can ah do fo' y'all?"

"I would like to see Major Knowles if he happens to be home."

"Ah'm sorry, suh, but he ain't home right now but ah's expectin' him and the missus will be back soon. Y'all like to wait fo' him inside?"

"No, thank you. Is it all right if I wait for him out here on the porch?" asked Sam.

The white-haired servant cocked her head to one side, closed one eye, and inquisitively said, "Y'all ain't no Southern boy. Is you a Yankee?"

Sam smiled, then answered, "My home is in Colorado."

"Oh, then y'all is a Western Yankee; that's different. Care for some coffee? Ah's got a pot brewin'."

"Yes . . . thank you. I'd like that, if it's no trouble."

"No trouble 'tall." She disappeared into the darkened interior and returned shortly with a silver tray, heavy with a platter of cookies, and a pot of steaming-hot coffee. She placed the laden tray on the wicker table beside Sam's chair. Before he could offer a thank you, with a twinkle in her eye, she quipped, "Ain't met a man yet who'd pass up mah molasses cookies."

Sam laughed and jovially responded, "And I'm not going to be the first." He was hungry and eagerly reached for one, took a huge bite, and nodded approvingly as he chewed. "Mighty delicious, ma'am. Don't reckon I've ever tasted better."

The portly Negro lady grinned from ear to ear, immensely pleased by his response. With a wink, she aimed her finger at him and giggled, "Lordy, ah been tol' how y'all Yankees lie like a rug on the dinin' room flo'. Finish those off and ah'll get some mo'."

Sam poured himself a cup of the strong coffee and settled back to await the arrival of the major. Thoroughly enjoying the time out from travel and the serenity of the setting, he couldn't help but contemplate the stark difference he'd just experienced at the ramshackle home of the pathetic Koopman. During the short train ride from Vicksburg to Port Gibson, nothing but the old veteran occupied his mind, actually pushing aside all thoughts of Montana and Colonel Malachi Raven.

Being part of the army that wrought destruction upon Vicksburg and the thought of killing Koopman's wife and child brought a sense of remorse, a distinct emotional pain to his heart. One could justify the shelling of a town as an impersonal act of war, but killing certain individuals—people with names—was a different matter. He tried not to think about it but he couldn't let it go.

Sam wished that he could help the crippled Confederate officer but knew not how. When he had mentioned the Lord to Koopman, he was bombarded with sarcastic commentaries. The lieutenant had summarily cut off any help from God, the Alpha of all mercy, the only One who could really be of any lasting assistance to bring him any peace.

Sam was just finishing the last cookie when a horse and buggy rounded the corner and pulled into the carriage barn behind the house, bringing his thoughts back to the task at hand. Through the open window behind him, Sam heard the Negro servant saying something about a guest; then out stepped a dapperly dressed middle-aged man, clean-shaven except for neatly trimmed graying sideburns and mustache. He had warm brown eyes and wore a reserved but pleasant smile as he extended his hand. "Good mornin', suh. I'm Charles Knowles, and who might you be? Amanda says you're a friendly Western Yankee."

Sam grinned broadly as he gripped the outstretched hand. "My name's Sam Dodd, sir. It's difficult not to be friendly, being plied with such good coffee and delicious molasses cookies."

"Well said, suh," said the major. "You must be a Yankee with Southern sympathies."

Sam immediately liked the man. His entire demeanor was casual and hospitable, so unlike the resentful Lieutenant Koopman.

"Amanda, bring me a cup of coffee too . . . do y'all hear?"

"Yessuh," came the distant voice from the kitchen.

"Now, Mr. Dodd, to what do we owe the pleasure of your company?"

"I'm looking for information about an officer who might have served with you in the siege of Vicksburg. I was told by young Mrs. Lofton, the Roundtrees' daughter, that you were very knowledgeable about the officers who served under General Pemberton."

An attractive lady in her middle years stepped through the door carrying a pot of fresh coffee. Both men stood as she approached.

"Mr. Dodd, I'd like you to meet my wife." Turning to include her, he said, "Anna Mae, Honey, this heah's Mr. Dodd from out west." He sat down on the wicker couch and patted the cushion next to him. "Come join us, sweetheart."

Nodding slightly, she sweetly smiled and gracefully seated herself beside her husband. "Ah'm pleased to meet y'all, suh. What is the honor of this visitation from one so far away?"

"It's rather complicated," Sam answered hesitantly as he sat down in the rocker facing them. "I'm a deputy sheriff and

I'm tryin' to get to the bottom of a number of fatal shootings that occurred in Montana. Two men from Mississippi were victims; both soldiered at Vicksburg."

Major Knowles interjected, "Honey, Mr. Dodd was askin' about someone who I might have served with during the war while in Vicksburg, just when y'all came out with the coffee. Martha Lofton, the Roundtrees' little girl, told him about us."

Before the major could continue, his wife visibly shuddered and with disgust asked, "Why'd anyone want to bring up those awful times?"

Knowles put his arm around his wife and hugged her. "Anna Mae, maybe y'all don't want to hear what we might talk about."

"No, y'all go ahead," she sighed. "It's nice out heah; ah'll just listen. Go ahead gentlemen, continue."

Sam leaned forward and inquired, "Did either of you happen to know a Colonel Raven?"

They looked at each other, then the major asked, *"Malachi Raven?"*

Sam's heart quickened. "Yes, that's the man."

"Yes, we both knew him. He sat in that very rocker you are sittin' in . . . in the spring of '63."

Sam was surprised by the comment and tried hard to hide his feelings. He and the Thirteenth Illinois Army Corps of ten thousand men had visited Port Gibson in the spring of '63, killing Confederate soldiers in the process.

Sam asked, "Was the colonel a close friend of your family?"

"No," answered the major. "He was a highly admired colleague of everyone on the general's staff. Raven had been wounded several times, gallantly leading his men. While recovering, he was assigned to Joe Johnson and had occasion to visit our city on official business. He was here with us when Grant crossed the river just to the south, at Bruinsburg. He, like many others, joined General Bowen's forces and finally retreated into the confines of Vicksburg's fortifications where he fought bravely in its defense."

"Would you know where Raven's plantation home was located?" asked Sam.

Major Knowles smiled. "Raven was of English and French Cajun stock. He's a Louisiana boy through and through. His people were cotton planters and owned sizable land near St. Francisville."

"Do you happen to know what regiment he was with?"

"I don't know about his original assignment, but in Vicksburg he fought in He'berts' Brigade—the Third Louisiana."

"He was such a handsome young man," added Anna Mae. "Why are you asking so many questions about Malachi? He couldn't possibly be involved in any killings. He was a Louisiana gentleman through and through."

"The colonel lives in Montana now," Sam answered solemnly. "People change. The West is harsh country."

"Not Colonel Raven," she emphatically stated, irritated by Sam's answer.

"You say Raven is in Montana?" Knowles asked, curious. "I never thought he would ever leave the bayou country."

"He's been in Montana quite a spell," answered Dodd. Trying politely to ignore Mrs. Knowles, Sam turned his attention to the major. "Do you recall the names of two soldiers from Mississippi, a Rob Hurtt or John Lewis?"

The major paused for awhile. "Not specifically. There were a number named Lewis who fought under the Stars and Bars. Were those two the men who were killed?"

"Yes, sir . . . they were. Major, did you by chance know of Raven's cousin, Dorsey Caine?"

"No, Sheriff, never heard of him."

"That's interesting. Dorsey was reportedly an officer under Raven's command."

"That may be possible. We Southerners have a lot of kin. Raven probably came from a large family. Lots of folks had their relatives fighting right beside them," replied the major.

"And on the other side, as well," Sam added sadly.

With an eyebrow raised at Sam's remark, Anna Mae inquired, "Were y'all in the war, Mr. Dodd?"

Both the Knowleses had obviously been too polite to ask about his empty sleeve. Crippled veterans were commonplace; amputated limbs and disfiguring scars of war were seen everywhere. This was the first question posed directly regarding his military service since he'd arrived below the Mason-Dixon Line. He wasn't about to lie and he wasn't ashamed of fighting for the preservation of the Union.

"Yes, ma'am. I was in the war."

"For the North?" she drawled.

"Yes . . . for the North." He settled back in the rocker, waiting for the next question which he was sure would be forthcoming. Mrs. Knowles' face was white, jaw muscles flexed under her pale skin. Her lips pursed tight together until her mouth was no more than a narrow slit.

"Earlier, suh," she spoke measuredly, "you seemed surprised when ah said Colonel Malachi Raven sat in the very chair in which you are now seated. Why was that?"

Sam sat quietly for a moment before answering. The major looked at his irritated wife and tied to placate the anger welling up inside her. "There, there, honey, the war's been over twenty years. I'm sure Mr. Dodd had little to do with the war down heah. Isn't that true, Mr. Dodd?"

"Well, Mr. Dodd," she piped in, "is that so?"

"No, Mrs. Knowles." Sam was straightforward, not wanting to be deceitful, but not wanting to elaborate either. "I was a squad sergeant, an advance scout for Grant's Army of the West. I fought south of this town, against General Bowen's men, the very day after Colonel Raven sat on this porch. That was the reason for my bein' startled."

With cold deliberation, she arched her head high until the tendons stood out on her neck. Her unblinking wide eyes piercingly fixed on Sam as she hoarsely shouted, "Did you kill anyone around heah?"

Sam was shaken by the gruesome question. "I was a soldier, ma'am. I was called upon to fight." He again vividly thought of the two men he had killed with his bayonet.

Unsatisfied and undaunted with his answer, she repeated, "DID . . . YOU . . . KILL . . . ANYONE . . . AROUND . . . PORT GIBSON?"

"Yes, ma'am, two. And both of them were trying to kill me."

Anna Mae Knowles bolted to her feet and while repeatedly clenching her fists, she hissed another question. "Do y'all feel any remorse for the sufferin' that y'all caused?"

Both Sam and the major stood up as well, her husband trying to calm her down. "Now, now, sweetheart, remember who we are. Mr. Dodd is a guest and means no harm."

Without responding, she turned on her heel and stomped into the house, slamming the screened door behind her. From inside, she cried, "David, get that evil murderin' *Yankee* out of heah!"

CHAPTER 23

MAJOR KNOWLES WAS UNMISTAKABLY FLUSTERED. Nervous, he looked through the door where his wife had just exited. Turning his attention to Sam, he said emotionally, "I apologize, suh, for my wife's behavior. The war was very hard on her."

Sam didn't know what to say; Anna Mae's outburst had left him more than uncomfortable. He knew how to handle men, but women? They were still a mystery to him. He reached up and tipped his hat to the major. "I think it's advisable that I leave. I'm sorry if I caused you any problems."

"Wait for me, suh; I'll get my hat and walk into town with you." Before Sam could object, Knowles had rushed inside and immediately returned with a wide-brimmed hat which he placed on his balding head. Motioning for Sam to join him, he started down the steps, exclaiming, "Come on, suh—it's such a nice day for a walk."

They covered better than half a block before another word was said. The major was the first to speak. "Did you like our Amanda's molasses treats?"

Sam was surprised by the question; it seemed so far afield, considering what had just occurred. "Yes, very much," he answered.

The major continued to talk about his maid. "Amanda's is an interesting story; would you care to guess her age?"

This, too, puzzled Sam, but he offered a guess. "Well, I would say maybe fifty-five to sixty."

"Would you consider barely over forty?" stated the major. "My wife found her in the field behind our barn. Anna Mae thought she was dead, nothin' but gray skin and bones. Her clothes were rags and the poor thing was covered with grime and lice. It took courage just to touch her. She brought her back to our house, fixed up a room for her out back, and nursed her to health. Amanda's been with us ever since."

"What happened to her, causing her to be on your property?"

"She was an innocent casualty of the war. Some of the plantations hereabouts were burned, destroyed along with the crops. Many slave owners were killed or fled for their lives. After the fall of Vicksburg, there was no law to speak of and anarchy reigned. Slaves either starved to death, stole to survive, or depended on food from the federals. No one could work the fields; our draft horses were taken to pull the Union cannon or they were led off by the Yankee bummers. Rovin' bands of plunderers terrorized the womenfolk. With their men off fighting in distant states, they daily were in a livin' hell. It was a dark time for every Mississippian."

"I thought the Northern troops helped maintain order," Sam stated.

"Not that you could count on," replied Knowles. "Around here, they brought in Negro troops to keep order—hardly a comfortin' thought to the ladies." Knowles stopped walking and faced Sam. "Are you aware that over twenty-five thousand Negroes flocked to Vicksburg? They called it Freedom City. What a cruelty that was—those poor souls foolishly lookin' to their Northern liberators for food, clothing, and shelter. They threw together shanties, and some lived in caves; their lot was a pathetic tragedy.

"Many slaves weren't as fortunate as Amanda and thousands starved to death. Disease was running rampant; the yellow fever and dysentery killed more. The streets were overflowin' with slaves lookin' for their so-called liberators to care for them. Some Christian folk formed the Freedman's Aid Society and tried to help . . . but it was a thankless task. Just as they were making some progress, more Negroes would arrive followin' General Sherman. His army was like a magnet, with them trailin' along after him. About ten miles of 'em, accordin' to one of his generals."

Sam knew that to be true. The same thing happened in Sherman's march across Georgia and South Carolina as hordes of slaves followed in their wake, creating untold problems.

The major continued. "Did you know, suh, that only one in ten Southerners owned slaves? Most of us did not and many of us didn't even believe in slavery." Not waiting for a response, he went on. "Ah don't think it's known that there were tens of thousands of Negro Freedmen here in the South and that more than two thousand of them owned slaves themselves."

"That, I didn't know," responded Sam. "Why are you telling me all of this?"

"I want you to know why that kind and gentle wife of mine behaved so badly. I don't want you to think poorly of her or of our hospitality. We are Christian people, suh, not prone to uncivil behavior."

"So am I," Sam spoke softly. "We pray to the same God and read the same Bible; yet for four years, we tried to kill each other . . . can you explain it? I still have trouble with it."

"Maybe too many of us didn't read enough of Scripture," Charles Knowles answered thoughtfully.

Sam smiled. "That's the best explanation I've heard and I do believe you're right."

They continued to walk, side by side, without conversation. For some unexplainable reason they both looked down at their feet and, at the same time, skipped, each trying to get in step with the other. At once, they broke into laughter and Sam joked, "I never was very good at drill."

"Neither was I," admitted Knowles, smiling.

"I've read very little about happenings in the South after the war. Maybe because I went to Colorado shortly after the fighting ended."

"Very little was written about the evils of Reconstruction," stated the major. "Absolute censorship was imposed upon our press and criticizin' the carpetbaggers could get you a long term in jail. We had a dictatorship forced upon us. Many white Southerners were denied the vote, while every male Negro could do so, whether he could read or not. We had to take a loyalty oath to be able to vote and if the scalawag registrar didn't believe you, he could arbitrarily deny you the franchise. By stackin' the deck in their favor, the abolitionist-Republicans maintained their majority and imposed insufferable restrictions and taxes upon us all. The Yankee press wouldn't tell the truth, and the Southerners couldn't."

Sam took it all in, listening intently. "I don't think it'll console you one whit or make you like him any better, but General Sherman hated the Northern correspondents as well. I remember how glad he was to hear that some members of the press may have drowned in the river. He was positively delighted when one of our gunboats sunk with four reporters on-board, saying, 'They were so deeply laden with weighty matter that they must have sunk.'"

Charles Knowles chuckled, then countered with, "In a private letter to a friend, Jefferson Davis said of the newspapers, 'Their malignancy begotten of ignorance can be overcome by neither truth or reason.'"

"I doubt if there was much else they had in common, other than both graduating from West Point," commented Sam.

Major Knowles sighed heavily. "Although we're all Americans, our customs *do* differ, North and South. We both honor the men who founded this nation; we have the same heritage but seem to know so little about it." Then, with a sparkle in his eye, he quipped, "Mr. Dodd, do you know which states were the first that wanted to secede? We Southerners weren't the first—did y'all know that?"

"No, I didn't," Sam said with a grin, "but you must be joking."

"No, suh! In 1814, the Hartford Convention was held in New England an' those highbrow Yankees considered leavin' the Union. They wanted to be free of us Southern aristocrats; leastwise, that's what they said. Those cold, blue-nosed New Englanders talked about formin' a *Northern* Confederacy—can you believe that?"

Sam laughed. "Well, if that had happened, I'd guess you would have fought those Northern traitors in order to preserve the Union."

The major grimaced at Sam's novel assumption and took a moment before he spoke. "Ah would like to think," he said very slowly, "that we would have let them secede . . . but the more I think about it, you may be correct. Havin' a bunch of Yankees settin' up their own country would have been seen as an assault on the memory of all the highly revered Southerners who formed this great nation. Washington, Jefferson, Madison, Monroe, Patrick Henry were all magnificent sons of the South." He was now beaming from ear to ear. "Yessuh, preservin' the Union to keep a bunch of damnable Yankees from seceding . . . *that*, suh, is a principle worth fightin' for."

"Major, I sense no bitterness in you. Didn't you hate us? I certainly held no love for the South."

"My dear Sheriff, if anyone could hate the North, I did. It is easy to do so, in general, but difficult to do in particular."

Sam was enjoying this bright, good-natured son of the Confederacy walking beside him. "Major, you'd make a mighty good Westerner."

"Why, thank you, Mr. Dodd, ah'll take that as a compliment. However, I must conclude from your comments about Colonel Raven that not all men from the South make particularly good men of the West. From what I knew of him, he would have been an asset in any part of the country."

"The war changed quite a few men," answered Sam. "The story around Big Timber is that the colonel lost his wife during childbirth and then the federal soldiers set fire to his plantation. That could have embittered him sufficiently to leave Louisiana."

"I'm truly sorry to hear he turned bad. The last time I saw Malachi was at the surrender of Vicksburg. I was exchanged for a Yankee officer and joined General Hood in the defense of Atlanta. I have no idea where he was sent."

"You say Raven was in Vicksburg at its surrender?"

"Yes, he was. I distinctly remember talkin' to him about the conditions of surrender that Grant set forth. They were most lenient and a surprise to all of us. We expected much worse."

Sam said, "I was told by folks in Big Timber that Raven was wounded badly in the fight for Atlanta and returned to his home before the war had ended, only to find it ravaged and destroyed. They claim he was so disheartened, he left for the West."

Sam went on to tell him about his Vicksburg visit with Lieutenant Koopman and the cold reception he had received. Knowles was not surprised. "Many of our young officers became highly dependent on whiskey. It became a problem of such magnitude that General Bragg issued orders forbiddin' it as early as the summer of '62. The War Department later had the generals suppress its consumption amongst all ranks, officers as well."

The major shook his head and added, "Didn't do much good; the boys just got more secretive and more inventive. Durin' the lulls in fightin', the boys dreamed up a lot of ways to make liquor, callin' it by all manner of things—bust-head, pop-skull, rifle knock-knee, just to name a few. After the war, when we were faced with the disaster of the so-called Reconstruction, many of our young men couldn't shake the bad habits they had acquired." Turning to Sam, he remarked, "I hear it was a problem with the North as well."

"You bet it was," replied Dodd emphatically. "It was a *big* problem . . . from top to bottom. General Grant himself had a low tolerance for the stuff, but he had the good sense to appoint a teetotalin' Lieutenant Colonel by the name of John Rawlins as his aide. His main duty was to keep ol' Ulysses out of the red-eye. Did a pretty good job of it, from what I hear."

Knowles added a few more comments on the subject of contraband alcohol, then talked about his service with Hood during the siege of Atlanta. Sam listened with great interest, since he was also there, fighting for the other side.

"Pardon me, Sheriff, for ramblin' on. We fought that battle once and I think that is enough. Best we think about the good of tomorrow rather than concentratin' on the seeping wounds of yesterday. I sincerely hope my wife didn't offend you."

"I was a part of the misery Sherman's army inflicted, assigned to his headquarters' staff from Vicksburg 'til the war's end. What we did in Mississippi pales compared to what the troops carried out in South Carolina."

"Y'all blamed South Carolina for starting the war; isn't that true?" asked the major.

"They fired on Fort Sumter," Sam answered simply.

"It was a good thing my wife didn't know you were close to Sherman; no tellin' what she would have said." Knowles' voice grew subdued, as he explained, "Anna Mae lost her mother when she was very young. All the family she had was her younger brother, Charles, and her father. Charlie was too young to enter the regular army and her father was too old, so both of 'em joined the local home guard. When Grant's army crossed the Mississippi, they took part in the resistance and fought with General Bowen to protect Port Gibson; both were killed just south of town."

The long walk to the depot came to an end. Sam looked up the tracks—north toward Vicksburg, on the pretense of searching for the train. He did not want Charles Knowles to see his face when he hesitantly asked, "Did her father have a full beard?"

"Why do you ask?" inquired the major.

"Did he?"

"No—'cept for sideburns, he was clean-shaven."

Sam's shoulders relaxed, as if a great weight had been lifted. He quietly said, "That's good to know, Major . . . for me, that's very good to know."

CHAPTER 24

SAM FEASTED HIS EYES AS HE DROVE the buggy through the little town, never having seen a more picturesque place than St. Francisville, Louisiana. Pulling back on the reins, he slowed the trotting Morgan mare to a walk so as to miss nothing. Even the melodic songs of the mockingbirds were a fitting musical accompaniment to the beauty of the setting. Stately oaks draped with pale gray moss loomed in every spacious yard.

Victorian and Georgian homes lined both sides of the streets. The warm air was heavy with the scent of magnolia and roses accented by a faint touch of wood smoke. Sam took a deep breath, drinking it all in. A strange sensation passed through him taking him to the faraway Western mountains and Montana, leaving him puzzled. *Magnolias shore don't smell like yellow blooming sage. Wonder what it could've been?* Looking up at one of the big oaks, he thought, *You, ol' feller . . . would've been firewood in quick order in Big Timber.* Sam suddenly brightened as he finally made the connection. *That's it, the distinct smell of burning oak.*

Newly settled Western towns like Big Timber hadn't been around long enough to consider beauty as a criteria for building anything. Practicality, affordability, and necessity were the dominant rules in frontier architecture. Makeshift wooden or sod structures, tents, and hastily slapped together rectangular brick-and-stone buildings were common. The only regard for style was in the false fronts added to some of the more recently built saloons.

Nope, Big Timber sure isn't St. Francisville—leastwise, not for another hundred years. This is so clean and pretty, I wish Mary were with me; she would take kindly to this place.

It appeared the war had passed by this lovely Southern town. Sam wondered why. Maybe because it was out of the direct pathway between Natchez and Baton Rouge or maybe, like Port Gibson, it was too beautiful to burn. He knew it wasn't the beneficence of the Northern commander, General Banks; his army could be tracked by the scorched fields and farms in their wake. The citizens of Louisiana, and Texas too, bore no affection for the politician-turned-soldier. Nathanial P. Banks and his army of New Englanders were universally hated.

Sam remembered clearly the vehemence displayed by Colonel Raven towards Yankees who occupied Louisiana—especially the soldiers of the Forty-first Massachusetts Regiment who he accused of turning his family's plantation into cinder and ashes. Sam was curious about Ravenswood, the family home, and wondered what it looked like now twenty years later. In less than an hour he'd see for himself.

Having inquired at the post office, he discovered Ravenswood was now owned by the Peter Ross family and was told they would probably have a good idea as to what happened to the Ravens.

The postmaster's directions to the Ross place were plain and simple. "It ain't difficult to find," he said. "Just follow the white fence that branches off River Road."

It would have been impossible to miss. Miles of four-rail whitewashed fence bordered the well-kept gravel road leading to Ravenswood. Down the entranceway, immense towering live oaks bracketed the cobblestone leading to the mansion. Their branches almost touched, forming a shady canopy over the wide causeway.

Expansive flower gardens lay on three sides of the sparkling white-painted residence. Camellias and lilacs abounded, as did red, yellow, and pink roses in first bloom and the usual profusion of azaleas. As Sam approached, he noted that the roof was of copperplate having long ago turned green. A wide porch and a balcony supported by large Grecian columns spanned the entire front.

Sam was confused by the plantation's bustling activity; Negro gardeners were hard at work and in the distance, he could see the planting of new crops in the freshly plowed fields. It seemed to be the epitome of the gracious living of the pre-war Confederacy, the South that Sam remembered in Mississippi and Georgia . . . before the fires. *This can't be Raven's property. There are no signs of destruction and, for sure, this house has been here for longer than twenty years. The colonel's plantation site must be nearby.*

A gray-haired butler answered the door. The diminutive, stoop-shouldered black man looked up at the lanky rancher towering above him and proceeded to stare at the tall-crowned Stetson on Sam's head, then down to his high-heeled boots. Finally he drawled, "May ah help y'all, suh?"

"My name is Samuel Dodd." Having noticed the look of inspection from hat to boots, Sam added, "From Montana. May I please speak with Mr. Ross?"

"Come in, suh, and wait right heah in the hall." Glancing up again to the brim of Sam's Stetson, the butler asked, "May ah take yo' hat, suh?"

Sam, like most ranchers, didn't like to remove his Stetson unless it was absolutely necessary. Some wore their hats indoors and out; a few had even been known to sleep with them on. But Sam acknowledged that he wasn't in the West so, reluctantly, he gave up his wide-brimmed hat to the butler.

A smartly dressed white-haired woman emerged from double doors; her very walk commanded attention. There was no doubt . . . she was the lady of the house, refined, attractive and accustomed to respect. With a bold twinkle in her blue eyes, she said, "Moses tells me that we have a gentleman from the Wild West in our home."

Sam blushed slightly and muttered, "Yes, ma'am, reckon you do."

"Moses also tells me you've come to see my husband but, unfortunately, Peter isn't here. May ah be of any help?" She extended her bejeweled right hand. "Ah'm Pamela Ross."

Sam smiled and nervously gripped her outstretched fingers, not knowing whether he should shake it or kiss it. He chose the former.

"Mrs. Ross, my name is Sam Dodd. I'm a sheriff's deputy from the Territory of Montana trying to find out about a Colonel Malachi Raven, an officer who fought for the Confederacy. I understand his former home is nearby and that your family now owns it."

Gracefully, she turned a full circle with her arms stretched wide. "*This* was once Malachi's home."

Sam frowned. "It was my understanding the Raven plantation was destroyed during the war."

"As you can see," Pamela Ross happily stated, "it isn't true. Ravenswood was built in 1810 by Malachi's grandfather and it's been a working sugarcane and cotton plantation ever since. Even durin' the war, our work didn't cease. The only difference was the Yankees took our crops."

"I thought the federals were 'specially punitive to the families whose sons served in the Confederacy."

"Usually they were, but few men were as shrewd as Artemas Raven, Malachi's father." She pointed to a portrait of a dignified looking elderly man. "That was Artemas. As soon as the Yankees took New Orleans, he swore allegiance to the North and brokered an agreement with General Banks. A few others followed in his footsteps. He even entertained Yankee officers here."

"It seems Malachi took after his father," remarked Sam.

"Heavens, no!" she exclaimed. "Malachi was mortified by his father's behavior. He'd have rather seen Ravenswood in cold ashes than have seen one stick of our sugar flavorin' one Yankee's coffee. He and his daddy never spoke to one another again."

"When was the last time you saw Colonel Raven?"

"Oh, we saw him many times right after the war; in fact, right up to the time he left us." Sadness reflected from her eyes. "He was such a decent man; we all hated to see him go."

"I thought you said he and his father never spoke again."

"They didn't. Artemas died just before the war ended. Malachi came home for the funeral and, too soon thereafter, he left us as well. We still miss him terribly."

Sam said nothing, but considered, *She should see him now. She'd be shocked at the transformation. Reckon the fight with his father and losing his wife were the miseries that drove him west. In all probability, there must've been something left to get him started in the cattle business.*

"How did the death of Raven's wife during the birth of his son affect him? I'd suppose it must have changed him some," said Sam.

"The death of his wife?" She laughed. "Such news is a shock to me. Where did you hear a silly thing like that?"

It was Sam's turn to be shocked. "She isn't dead?"

"Mercy sakes, no. Believe me," she winked, "ah'd be the first to know. You see, she is very near and dear to me."

Sam was totally baffled. "How about his son, J.D.?"

"Ah don't know about any J.D., but the Raven heir is doing very well. He is in his last year at the University of Louisiana, graduatin' at the top of his class," she proudly exclaimed.

Before Sam could clear his befuddled mind, she confused him further. "Would you like to pay a visit to the colonel? If so, please accompany me." Without waiting for a reply, she turned on her heel and rushed out the front door. Sam obediently followed, his mind awhirl searching for answers, his brain now crammed with crosscurrents of contradictions. *What's she getting at, do I want to meet the colonel? Is Raven here? Has he left Montana and returned to Ravenswood? That can't be! Raven's son isn't attendin' college in Louisiana; J.D.'s still gotta be back in Montana. What is this woman talkin' about?*

Walking along the pathway, the dignified Mrs. Ross chatted about the history of Ravenswood, its bountiful crops, the beauty of its gardens. Sam paid scant attention, for he was trying to figure out fact from fiction, separating what scraps of truth he had pieced together from the lies and half-truths he had been fed. He was thoroughly confused; however, it now occurred to him that the poor woman might be daft. The path led to a sheltered grove of stately oaks sheltering a small cemetery yard, enclosing a stone mausoleum. "He's in there," she said reverently, "lying beside his daddy, mother, and granddaddy. One of these days ah'll, too, rest beside him. You see, Mr. Dodd, Colonel Malachi Raven died a few years after the war from wounds he received at Vicksburg. He was a true gentleman and a wonderful husband as well."

SAM PACED ABOUT THE GUEST ROOM mulling over the confounding events of the day. Mrs. Ross invited him to supper and to stay the night; and though he graciously declined, she had fervently insisted. She wanted him to meet her second husband and was eager to hear more about the fictitious Colonel Raven. Sam was grateful for the hospitality, especially the evening meal, which was unusual but much to his liking. It consisted of oyster soup, a rice dish with crawfish and okra, and a delicious corn bread with small jars of clover honey near each plate. Sam and Peter Ross enjoyed a brandy on the veranda until the mosquitoes drove them indoors. They talked of cattle, crops, and the growth taking place out west. Nothing was discovered as to who the false Raven could be, although his hosts were fascinated about the circumstances surrounding him.

Sam retired early, needing solitude to mentally sift through the tangle of facts and assumptions that tumbled around in his brain. They had to be sorted out, categorized, put in order. He felt both elated and depressed at the same time—actually delighted to find the Elk Track Raven was a fraud, a pretentious fake, but discouraged that it wasn't reason enough to accuse him of murder.

Truly, he felt further away from the truth. Just this morning he thought he knew Colonel Raven, *but tonight? Who was this pretender?* Many a man went west and changed his name; using an alias was no sin in Montana. Matter of fact, it was downright impolite to ask questions about a man's past. More than a few had been shot or had his nose busted for putting it where it didn't belong.

Raven's past must be darker than the inside of a witch's hat. Sam had little doubt that his hidden identity was the key. The two murdered cowboys from Mississippi must have known him earlier on, *but where . . . Vicksburg, Atlanta, maybe even before the war? Raven could have given them money to shut them up. How else could a couple of old waddies like Hurtt and Lewis come up with so much gold? If the phony Colonel Raven didn't get his large stake from formerly owning a Louisiana plantation, where did he get it? Was he a thief? Did he hold up stages, rob banks, win at gambling, find gold in New Mexico? Was he ever really in New Mexico?*

Sam smacked his forehead with the palm of his hand in frustration, foolishly hoping to jar loose some rationality. He had to cleanse his mind completely of all the erroneous information he had picked up in Big Timber, concocted to create the sympathetic illusion of a wounded Confederate officer and gentleman. *Was he ever really a soldier?* Sam felt reasonably sure that he had been. The man he talked with at the Elk Track Ranch had to have fought at Champion Hill and Vicksburg. He knew too many details about the battles to have just read about them, yet he was dead-wrong about the circumstances of the Vicksburg surrender.

How come the false colonel had misread the facts . . . was it pure hatred or his unwillingness to concede any good in General Grant? That was a distinct possibility; the loathing he had for the North wasn't a pretense. He thought how the saliva had flowed to the corners of his mouth and the venom had literally seeped from his pores. The only reliable fact that Sam could go on was the assurance the man was at Vicksburg . . . but as an enlisted man or an officer?

"Sort of like lookin' for a needle in a haystack and I haven't found the haystack so far. It's a jumbled patchwork of deceit and lies; so much so that I'm talkin' to myself out loud. What am I really sure of? The man in Montana is a fraud. There couldn't possibly be two Colonel Malachi Ravens with plantations in Louisiana. So, it is obvious he stole the name and knew of the real Raven."

But why would he use the name of a real person? Did he believe no one would ever suspect? It doesn't make much sense, but then liars are often trapped by their own folly.

I've spent months away from home and feel no closer to the truth. Sticking around here, it could take years to find out who this Raven really is. Best I go back and confront the phony and see what he has to say. At least, I can keep him from pretendin' to be somethin' he's not and stop him from besmirchin' the name of the real Malachi Raven.

Sam smiled mischievously. *I wonder how ol' Homer Dills is goin' to feel when he finds out his daughter is marryin' the son of a gold-plated fraud. Well, as the Good Book says, the folly of fools is deceit.*

In a better frame of mind, Sam thought about how much he missed Mary and the children. *It'll be so good to see their beautiful faces again.* With that pleasant picture, he reached in his knapsack and pulled out his Bible. He opened it to Ecclesiastes and thumbed through the pages. When in need of wisdom, Sam found solace in meditating on the words of Solomon. He read in Ecclesiastes 7:8: "The end of a thing is better than its beginning and the patient in spirit is better than the proud in spirit."

Sam put the Bible aside and, again spoke out loud. "Maybe this is the end of it; finding out that Raven isn't Raven might be all there is to it. But maybe not. Best I be patient like the Good Book says and not jump to any more conclusions."

The tired and still perplexed Westerner extinguished the lamp and crawled into bed. Sleep came quickly.

CHAPTER 25

"Grits for breakfast!" Sam was more than pleased. He explained that he hadn't had them for a long while and that the dish was a common companion to eggs and ham during his youthful years in southern Illinois. Grits were not so popular in the West, where potatoes were usually piled high beside the eggs. Sam ate with gusto, accepting a second helping of buttermilk cakes topped with an abundance of butter and sorghum molasses.

"So, y'all headin' back to be with all those wild Indians," teased Pamela Ross.

"Yes, ma'am! Have to shoot several of 'em every mornin' before I can enjoy breakfast," joked Sam, "or else they might get some rebel ideas like the Indians you have hereabouts."

"Well," exclaimed Peter Ross, "you must know about our Chickasaws and Choctaws. They were fiercely loyal Southerners and made good soldiers, faithful to the Confederate cause to the end."

Sam wryly remarked, "Good thing the Sioux and Blackfeet didn't join up with you Rebs or we would still be fightin'." They both laughed at his good-natured humor.

Sam was somewhat surprised when he met Peter Ross, being older than expected, many years Pamela's senior. When they were at the grave site she told him about her difficulty in trying to manage Ravenswood alone, especially with an infant son after her husband passed away. Peter was her next-door neighbor and widowed as well. When he offered to manage the plantation's business for a share in the proceeds, she gratefully accepted. It didn't take long before their dependence and mutual respect for one another grew into a deep affection, culminating in an exceptionally happy marriage.

"Mr. Dodd, how soon y'all be headin' home?" asked Mrs. Ross.

"Very soon, ma'am—in fact, today."

"Did you find your trip fruitful?" inquired her husband.

"Somewhat. I'm still in the dark over the reason for four men dying and my son's being shot. I certainly haven't enough evidence to arrest anyone. You can't lock up a man for usin' a false name."

Sam helped himself to more pancakes, then said, "It's puzzling why the impostor chose the name of Raven. Could they have looked enough alike to have fooled anyone?" Then, answering his own question, he stated, "He didn't seem to have fooled the two cowboys."

"Would you like to see a picture of the *real* Malachi Raven?" asked Peter. "Pamela, don't y'all have a tintype of Malachi somewhere?"

"Why, yes ah do, dear." She was fairly animated in her willingness to show Sam the likeness of her deceased husband. Turning to Sam, she said, "Sheriff, if y'all are curious, come right along with me to the library."

"Yes, ma'am, I'd be happy to."

Once more Sam followed along behind her. The impressive library was filled with a wide variety of rare books, portraits of family members, and the intricate paintings of birds done by the local St. Francisville artist named Audubon. An ornately carved set of mahogany chess pieces was ready for play beside a large black-oak desk in the corner and many other quality items. The room reeked of refinement and wealth.

Pamela Ross took a leather folder from the bottom desk drawer and placed it on a table. She carefully opened it and picked out a photograph of a young man in uniform. "This was when Malachi was in military school. Wasn't he a handsome boy?"

Sam nodded affirmatively. She was right. He stood tall, was dark complexioned and appeared gallant in his posture . . . a fine example of a young southern Louisiana aristocrat. Sam tried to imagine what Raven would have looked like at that age. Both were tall and dark-haired; however, their facial characteristics were not at all alike. The real Raven's features added up to handsome, while the impostor had a swarthy look about him. There was really only a slight resemblance between the two.

"Your former husband looks to have been pretty tall."

"Oh my, yes he was. Malachi stood over six feet; he positively towered over others." She selected another photograph and handed it to Sam.

"This is a picture of him when he graduated from West Point. See how much taller he was than the others?"

"Sure do," answered Dodd.

"And, here he is several years later, near the end of the war. The poor dear looks so serious."

"Yes, he does," agreed Sam, *and much older and gaunt,* he thought. *Nothing ages a man faster than gettin' shot at.*

"I'm sure y'all have seen enough. Ah can't look at these without being saddened." She returned the pictures and began to close the folder.

"Wait . . . what was that big one? I thought I saw a group of officers, maybe his regiment?" asked Sam.

"I didn't bother to show you that one because Malachi wasn't in it. It was given to him by General Pemberton. It's a picture of the officers in charge at the defense of Vicksburg. Some of Malachi's closest friends are pictured."

"I saw a head and shoulders sticking up over the rest. I assumed it was your husband."

"No, it wasn't him," she answered, closing the leather folder.

A strangeness overcame Sam. He felt as though a hundred pricks of cold needles were lightly touching his skin, traveling up his back and arms. He had to steady his hand as he reached for the folder and his voice carried an edge of excitement as he asked, "May I see that picture, please? The one with all the men!"

"The one of the Vicksburg officers?"

"Uh-huh, the one Pemberton gave him."

Pamela Ross reopened the folder and picked the photo from the rest. She frowned at the change in Sam's demeanor and was a bit startled as he practically snatched it from her hand.

"Yep!" he said excitedly. "That could be him."

Standing a full head above the rest of the officers was a bearded major with heavy brows shading his deeply recessed eyes. Sam's heart quickened. "Do you have a magnifying glass I might use?"

"Why, yes, of course." Searching through the top drawer to the desk, she found one and handed it to Sam.

He moved the glass slowly before fixing on the proper distance to clearly view the man in question. *It's him!* There was no doubt in Sam's mind that he was looking at the pretender, scowling from out of the past, leering from the faded tintype, as if to say, "So . . . you found me at last."

ALTHOUGH THE DISTANCE FROM ST. FRANCISVILLE to Baton Rouge was short, the train ride to get there seemed to Sam to take forever. He spent most of the journey, oblivious to the lush green countryside. His mind was fixed on the new pieces of the puzzle he had obtained by visiting Ravenswood.

Tucked inside his bag, carefully protected by his clothing, was the photograph. Pamela Ross was kind enough to let him show it to Lieutenant Colonel Woodrow L. Jenkins, the man she identified standing beside the tall one in question. She said that if anyone would know who he was, it would definitely be Colonel Jenkins, the adjutant to General Baldwin of the Louisiana Seventeenth.

Peter Ross had warned Sam, "Sheriff, keep a close eye on that Rebel. Woodrow Jenkins is what we call a true son of the South; he actually refused to surrender at war's end. He would rather have been bitten by a passel of cottonmouths and chewed up by a 'gator than forced into signin' a loyalty oath to the damnable Yankees. He and a number of fellow officers fled to Mexico. Some of the others went down to South America; quite a few migrated to Brazil. They simply refused to accept defeat, hoping that the South could one day rise again. Jenkins, at least, was finally lured back here sometime in '77 at the tail-end of the Reconstruction."

"That's truly not the only reason," Pamela coyly interjected. "The blonde tresses, dimpled smile, and pearly teeth of the youngest daughter of General Archer had a lot more to do with it than anythin' else. Woodrow was smitten by that charmer the first time he laid eyes on her." She added with an impish smile, "Y'all got to understand the captivating charms of a Southern belle."

Ross glanced at his lovely wife and grinned. "Smitten or not, the sheriff better be careful of what he says around Jenkins. That good ol' Louisiana boy has yet to surrender. He showed absolutely no mercy to any Yankee durin' the conflict, even bragged about shootin' some Yankees over them stealin' a few chickens after Lee had surrendered at Appomatox."

"I'm a true Westerner now," Sam said, with a grin. "Maybe that will count for something. Besides, I'm investigating the murder of two Confederate veterans."

Sam hoped it would make a substantial difference. He had no intention of reviving his Civil War record for Colonel Jenkins.

THE SIGN ON THE STAIRWELL READ, "Colonel Woodrow L. Jenkins, CSA, Attorney at Law." An arrow pointed upstairs. Sam smiled at the fact that he still preferred to be addressed as

Colonel and had the initials *CSA*, representing the Confederate States of America, prominently displayed after his name. *I
guess Peter was right; Jenkins hasn't given up as yet.*

Sam knocked on the door, expecting to hear a stern, milita-
ristic response. He was pleasantly surprised at the friendly and
mellow drawl that greeted his ears. "Y'all come right on in."

Seated behind a small desk piled high with papers and
opened books was a stocky, middle-aged man with gold-framed
reading glasses perched low on the bridge of his nose. As he
looked up over the rims, he smiled warmly and said, "Good
day, suh, have a chair and . . . pardon, suh, but there's no place
to sit." Law books and client file folders were scattered everywhere—on the tables, the couch, the floor, and stacked deep
on the opened drawers of the file cabinets. Getting quickly to
his feet, Jenkins hurriedly grabbed the stack of folders on the
chair next to his desk and placed them precariously atop the
already large number on the cabinets. "There," he said with
satisfaction. Patting the back of the now-empty chair, he took
off his glasses and gestured to the empty seat. "Sit down, suh."

Woodrow Jenkins wore a gracious smile from the moment
Sam entered the room. "Peter Ross wired me you were comin'."
Scanning Sam's attire, he added, "What's a Western lawman
doin' in Baton Rouge?"

"Peter didn't explain?" asked Sam.

"No, he didn't," answered Jenkins, whose voice changed
slightly after Sam had spoken. "All it said was you were from
out west." Changing the subject quickly, he asked, "Lose your
arm in the War Between the States?"

"No," Sam answered abruptly. "I'm here to see if you can
identify someone for me." With that, he bent over and pulled
the tintype from his satchel.

Before he could show it to the attorney, Jenkins quietly asked,
"Are you a Yankee?"

Sam looked into the clear, gray eyes staring at him from the
now expressionless square face. Apparently, he wasn't about to

stop his questioning until he found out if Sam had fought in the Civil War.

Sam returned his gaze directly. Calmly, but with firmness, he said, "Yes, and I was with the Illinois Thirteenth Infantry. We were on the other side of the line from you at Vicksburg."

"That was under the command of McClernand, wasn't it?"

"That is correct," answered Sam.

"Were you an officer?" He spoke barely loud enough for Sam to hear.

"No, I was a sergeant . . . an enlisted man."

The following question was so hard to hear, Sam had to ask Jenkins to repeat himself. Clearing his throat, he asked it again, but with a distinct edge to his voice. "Didn't McClernand lose his command after Vicksburg?"

Sam feared what was coming next. Jenkins knew perfectly well who had succeeded McClernand. He came directly to the point with his answer. "Yes, he did. McClernand got on the wrong side of Grant, who removed him from command and turned us over to General Sherman. I spent the rest of the war under his authority."

"You fought in Georgia?"

"Yes."

"In South Carolina?"

"Yes," Sam matter-of-factly exclaimed, "and Mississippi, Tennessee, North Carolina, and in Virginia too."

Then, Jenkins asked quietly, though with sarcasm and through clenched teeth, "Did you take part in the burning and looting?"

"No. I was with Sherman. I wasn't detailed to do so, but if I'd been ordered to burn, I most certainly would have complied." Sam leaned forward as he said, "I was a soldier, Colonel, and I tried to stay alive by bein' a good one." He sat back and hesitated just long enough for his words to penetrate. "I believed in what I fought for and I believe in it now. I haven't changed my mind one whit."

Sam could see the colonel's jaw muscles flex and pulsate as he bit down on his teeth, obviously trying to hold his temper. Measuring every word, he said, "There was no honor in the way you Yankees fought, no honor at all. No pride in your manhood, none whatsoevah! None but cowards bring about starvation for women and children."

The colonel's harsh judgment got under Sam Dodd's skin and he, too, fought to contain his emotions. "Sir, there is no honor in war, only death and destruction. The object of battle is to anni-hilate the enemy and bring them to their knees. We weren't engaged in an Old-World battle where kings fought kings with mercenary soldiers. There were no kings in this fight—just com-mon folks fighting for conflictin' causes. All of the states and all of the people were involved, civilians as well. The people of the Northern states were pitted against former neighbors to the South. Plain and simple, we won . . . you lost."

Sam leaned closer to the angry lawyer and between clenched teeth, added, "Did you like the stink of the bloated, dead bod-ies of our comrades at Vicksburg as the ripened in the summer sun? I didn't!" Sam tempered the anger in his tone and added, "Did the mothers of your dead cry any harder than ours . . . *did they?* If burnin' your crops and homes hastened the end of the war and saved one life, then I say Godspeed to General William Sherman."

Jenkins was white, the blood now drained from his face. "How dare you, suh, speak to me like that!"

Sam immediately replied, "Do you want to settle this right now? Are you ready to challenge me to a duel?"

Startled and confused, the honor-bound gentleman was both angered and offended by Sam's forthright remarks. The colo-nel boldly raised his chin as he stated, "I'd be so obliged."

Like a shot, Sam countered, "Then I get the choice of weap-ons and where it will take place . . . correct?"

"That is correct, suh!"

"In that case, I choose right-arm wrestling, here and now,

on the edge of this desk." With that, Sam scooted the chair up close and turned his right side toward Jenkins.

A bewildered colonel exclaimed, "But, suh, what are you doin'? You don't *have* a right arm."

"By gum, you're right," answered Sam. "I guess I must concede defeat, sir. You win. Now, does that make you feel any better? Colonel, we both fought one bloody war; need we fight another? I still have four children I've got to raise and a wife to look after. I'm here tryin' to find out who murdered two of your veterans and I need your help, not your ire."

The jutted jaw relaxed and Jenkins' hand went to his full head of gray-streaked hair. He rubbed his scalp for several moments, then said, "A challenge to arm-wrestle . . . and by a one-armed Yankee at that. If that don't beat all."

SAM HANDED THE OLD PHOTOGRAPH to Jenkins and asked him to identify the tall, dark officer.

"Why, that's Major Jacques Du Bois of the Louisiana Artillery. He was in charge of the river batteries for the Eighth, an excellent man with a 7.44-inch rifled Blakely canon. Du Bois gave the federal gunboats fits." A look of sorrow crossed his face. "Jacques was very courageous. He died before Vicksburg surrendered."

Crestfallen, Dodd asked, "How did he die?"

"Drowned in the river," answered the colonel.

Sam's interest quickened. "Are you sure? Was his body recovered?"

"No, but he was never to be seen, thereafter. Several who were with him were discovered later, their bloated bodies washed up on the banks."

"He's not dead," insisted Sam. "That Reb is still very much alive."

It was Woodrow Jenkins' turn to be caught off guard as he blurted out, "You must be joking!"

"No, I'm positive your Major Jacques Du Bois is in Montana, as we speak, pretendin' to be Colonel Malachi Raven."

Colonel Jenkins was visibly unnerved by what Sam had just attested to. He dropped low into his chair, letting Sam's information sink in. He got up and paced about the room, still deep in thought. Finally, he stopped short and asked, "Has he been doing well?"

"What exactly do you mean?" responded Sam.

"Does he have wealth? Or, is he poor?"

"Poor . . . not hardly. He's probably the richest and one of the most powerful ranchers in the Montana Territory."

Jenkins was again shaken by Sam's candor. He crossed the room and opened the door. "Sheriff Dodd, could you return here tomorrow morning, about ten? There are others who must hear your story."

There was a finality about the way he made the request that left no alternative. Sam picked up his satchel and left with neither of them uttering another word.

CHAPTER 26

IT HAD BEEN A LONG TIME SINCE Sam had awakened to the melodic warbling of a mockingbird. He lay in bed, enjoying the great imitator mock its' feathered friends. He thought of another bird by the name of Raven who should be called "Mockingbird" for his imitation of the real thing. Maybe today, this morning at ten o'clock, he would find out more about this Southern bird, now residing in Montana, and the strange flock of vultures that surrounded him.

The strange manner of Colonel Jenkins, especially his sudden dismissal of Sam after he found out that Raven—or Jacques Du Bois—was still alive, intensified Dodd's curiosity to a painful degree. Conceivably, in a few hours, he'd have some idea why the murders occurred. More sleep was now impossible, so he dressed and went outside into the warm and muggy morning air. He felt uncomfortable and sticky after walking just a few blocks. The heavy cotton shirt clung to his back and sweat was trickling down his neck. Tipping back the Stetson, he mumbled, "Wish you were straw," then loosening his bandanna and wiping his face, he said. "Whew! Today's goin' to be a corker."

The sun had yet to push up over the eastern horizon and what coolness was left of the morning was disappearing fast.

In the quiet, few people were out on the streets. Sam caught sight of an inviting, hole-in-the-wall café with a brightly colored sign advertising, "Mae's Country Kitchen." There were a half-dozen stools along a counter facing two women who were busily taking care of the patrons—one over the wood stove and the other, serving up the orders. At one of the small tables, three men were heavily engaged in conversation. It looked like a friendly place, clean and neat, and the aroma of coffee made Sam suddenly realize how hungry he was.

Briefly, the talking stopped when Sam entered, then slowly picked up again after he sat down at the counter. The café appeared to be a neighborhood gathering spot and Sam was obviously an outsider, a rare sight at six in the morning—rarer still with Western boots and Stetson. Without a word, the stoic-faced waitress poured Sam a cup of coffee and pointed to the chalkboard where the morning menu was displayed. He smiled at the expressionless waitress and ordered, "Biscuits and gravy and a side-order of bacon, if you please."

At the sound of his Northern accent, the cook turned around, raised one brow, and stared at her new customer. Across her apron was embroidered, "Mae." Turning her attention back to the stove, she deftly tossed two eggs over in the skillet. The humidity, along with the heat from the stove, clearly made for very uncomfortable working conditions. Mae was middle-aged and pleasant to look at, even though her hair was in disarray and her forehead was beaded with sweat.

From a corner table came the rumblings of a heated political discussion. A mustachioed old curmudgeon was adamant: "George, thar ain't no how a Democrat could evah git elected ovah those nigger-lovin' reptilicans like President Arthah. Dey'd rig de vote fo' sho'!"

"Now, Davey, don't ya be too fixed on dat," responded his portly Cajun companion. "Ol' President Hayes warn't too bad a sort, considerin' he be a bluebelly Yankee."

"We ain't goin' to elect no Democrat fer a hunderd yars

dats a fak, I gar-ron-tee. De swamp run dry fo' dat happens fo' sho'." Davey interrupted his diatribe to call out, "Linda, darlin', fetch me dat coffeepot, do ya heah?"

The waitress, presently peeling potatoes, raised her head just enough to give him a look which seemed to say, "Ah'm busy—y'all get it yourself."

Mae slid the large plate under Sam's appreciative nose. Generous slices of sugar-cured bacon were still sizzling-hot. A huge blob of bright yellow butter floated in the middle of the creamy sea of thick, white sausage gravy covering huge buttermilk biscuits. Sam had never tasted better and he stuck around for an hour or so, enjoying several more cups of coffee. The little café was getting crowded as the morning wore on and he was taking up precious space. The glare of the waitress told him it was time to leave.

The time passed slowly while he walked about Baton Rouge. He happened by the bridge over Ward's Creek where Mary Lincoln's brother, Lieutenant Alexander Todd, was killed— accidentally shot by his own Confederate soldiers.

What a strange war, thought Sam, *where the close kin of the president's wife fought on the other side. How great must have been her agony.*

AT A QUARTER BEFORE TEN, Sam headed back to Jenkins' office on Laurel Street. He eagerly climbed the stairs to the balcony, two at a time. Through the window, he could see others had arrived and, from appearances, they had been there awhile. Coats were draped over chairs and hazy cigar smoke hung in the air. Sam knocked . . . and the door was immediately opened by Jenkins. "Come on in, Sheriff. Ah have some people ah want you to meet."

Two neatly dressed middle-aged men were standing beside the desk while another, much older, extremely dignified-looking gentleman sat up straight in the chair behind it.

Colonel Jenkins introduced Sam, starting with the younger two. "Sheriff Dodd, the gentleman to your right is Captain Daniel Richey and to his left is Major Staats." Sam stepped forward and extended his left hand which, in turn, both shook with their right without commentary. "Now, Sheriff," he deferentially said, "ah'd like you to meet General Pierre Gustave Beauregard."

The general nodded politely while remaining seated behind the desk. "Good mornin', suh. We heah you have quite a story to tell."

Sam was impressed by the dignity and carriage of the man before him and awed by his reputation. Beauregard was considered one of the great Confederate leaders, often mentioned in the same breath with Joe Johnson and Longstreet. Only Robert E. Lee and Stonewall Jackson received more adulation. *This here is the general who started the war by firing on Fort Sumter and commanded the Rebel forces at Shiloh. What is he doin' here? What possible interest could he have in this matter?*

Sam's momentary silence prompted the general to restate the question. "Would you tell us, suh, what y'all know about Jacques Du Bois? It is of great interest to us all."

"I'd be happy to, General," Dodd firmly stated. "But under the condition that you tell me all *you* know about him."

They looked to the general, then at each other. After a moment, they all nodded affirmatively. Sam proceeded to relate the whole story to them—the murders, the Elk Track Ranch, the deceptions, the outright lies, and the political clout Raven's wealth had afforded him in the Northwest Territory. Sam left nothing out, even including his trip to Vicksburg and the providential trail that led to the photo at Ravenswood.

Allowing for multiple interruptions by the officers, it took several hours for Sam to complete the entire saga. After he had finished, the general politely asked, "Would y'all give us a few minutes to confer? What y'all have told us is most disturbing. We must ruminate upon it."

Sam nodded in agreement and stepped outside. Sitting on the balcony steps, he lit his pipe. The early afternoon sun was peeking from behind large white cumulus clouds forming in the sky. Though he wasn't hungry, they reminded him of Mae's gravy and biscuits. In the distance came the crack of lightning and the rolling rumble of thunder, a late-afternoon rain in the offing. Sam had barely finished his pipe when Jenkins opened the door and beckoned. "Come on back in, Sheriff. The general would like to talk with you."

Sam scrambled to his feet and reentered the smoke-filled room. The general greeted him solemnly. "Mr. Dodd, what ah'm about to tell you must be kept in the strictest confidence until all of our suspicions are confirmed. We agree the man in question could well be Major Du Bois, but until we are sure and can determine a proper course of action, we will need your word of honor to treat what we are about to tell you as privileged information . . . a secret." Looking up at Sam, he asked, "Do you agree, suh?"

Sam nodded his head, and said, "Yes, General, you have my word."

Beauregard motioned to Captain Richey and Major Staats and requested that they do the briefing. For the next hour or more, Sam became completely engrossed, hearing of one of the most bizarre escapades of the entire Civil War period.

Two months before Grant had crossed the river and surrounded Vicksburg, the real Malachi Raven escorted a shipment of gold there from the Confederate capitol in Richmond. The gold was to be transported by boat down the Mississippi to the Red River, then across Louisiana into Texas. From there it was to be taken into Mexico for the purchase of guns and ammunition because the Confederate coast had been blockaded by federal warships. Mexican harbors were open to foreign shipping, but no one would sell merchandise to the Confederacy without receiving hard currency.

Because the Union's army and gunboats, under Banks, had made travel on the Mississippi and Red Rivers too dangerous, a new overland route had to be established. Colonel Raven was awaiting assemblage of a mule train to carry the gold when Grant crossed the river and surrounded the town, leaving no opportunity to sneak such a valuable shipment out of Vicksburg by land. General Pemberton received orders to smuggle out as much of it as possible if the defeat of his forces seemed imminent. The Confederacy needed the gold desperately since, by then, their paper currency was considered practically worthless. The only likely route to keep the valuable metal safely in Confederate hands was to float it out, downriver.

Union picket boats guarded the lower waterway day and night but a few Rebs had been able to escape by drifting quietly past the boats, lying low behind floating logs. Moving a raft of heavy gold was a whole different story, not to mention exceedingly dangerous. Inasmuch as the river current only traveled about four miles an hour, whoever was chosen to guide the logs had to be in the water for at least five hours, in order to make it by the last of the Union guards. As risky as it was, the attempt had to be made. If the raft were discovered, the gold was to be sacrificed and allowed to sink to the bottom of the river rather than have it fall into Yankee hands. Eight powerful swimmers were selected to float alongside and guide it around anchored federal gunboats. Their plan was to meet up, downriver, with members of the Texas Cavalry, waiting with a team of mules.

The gold was coated with a black paint, placed in dark leather bags, and securely tied to the raft of logs. On a moonless night, six disguised enlisted men and two officers took to the river and disappeared into the murky waters. Two weeks had passed before the swollen body of one of the enlisted men was found, miles downriver with a bullet hole in his head. None of the others was heard from again. It was assumed the daring venture was a failure, discovered by the picket boats, and that the remaining men either drowned or were also shot. The gold? It was presumed to be on the bottom of the river.

Sam listened carefully to every word and when the captain stopped talking, Major Staats added, "Lieutenant Colonel Donald Novey was in charge and the second officer was Major Du Bois."

Sam jumped in quickly to ask about the enlisted men. "Could one of them have been a Dorsey Caine?"

"There was no one by that name," answered Captain Richey. "But, could you describe him to us?"

"Dorsey is a powerfully built man, pretty hairy, one hundred eighty-five pounds, a wide, flat face." Sam then added, "Oh, yes, long arms—very long arms and sloping shoulders."

"That rather fits the description of one of the men, a Sergeant Duval. Uh, let's see, the more ah think about it," said the captain, "Major Du Bois was quite insistent that Duval come along."

"Why was Major Du Bois picked to be a part of the crew?" asked Sam.

"We called for volunteers, those who knew the river and were also particularly strong swimmers. The major was a Louisiana boy, raised around the swamps," stated Major Staats. "We surely had no reason to doubt his loyalty; he hated Yankees and his war record was exemplary."

"What was this Du Bois like?" inquired Sam. "Did any of you know him well?"

"No, ah didn't," answered Staats.

"Nor me, either," added Captain Richey.

"I was acquainted with him slightly," said Woodrow Jenkins. "He was born and raised not far from here on a small plantation, near the junction of the Teche with the Atchafalaya. His family were cane and cotton farmers. Their place wasn't very large, a few slaves and a lot of hard labor. His mama and brothers ran the place; never knew much about his daddy. The boys were constantly gettin' into fights."

"Over anything in particular or just youthful nonsense?" asked Sam.

"They would scrap with anybody and everyone; they even battled among themselves. Jacques was a hothead, even killed a man in a duel. Shortly thereafter, probably to avoid prosecution, he joined the Louisiana Artillery as a lieutenant. In fact, he was put in charge of a light artillery unit. He was an excellent cannoneer and fought in several engagements before he was assigned to the Vicksburg defenses. His family place was right in the path of General Banks' army, while he was chasin' our General Richard Taylor around the bayous. I wouldn't be surprised if the Du Bois property wasn't completely burned, like the rest."

"You said he was a hothead?"

"Yes, quick to anger, proud, considered himself quite a ladies' man. That's what brought about the duel. Seems he said somethin' improper to a young lady from one of our finest families. The lady's brother was incensed by his advances and heated words were exchanged, culminatin' in the brother challenging Jacques to a fight. Du Bois was a superb marksman and chose pistols. He shot the rash young man between the eyes. The seconds for the deceased claimed Du Bois turned too soon and fired as his opponent whirled about, taking advantage of the moment. Observers for Du Bois claimed to the contrary. It made quite a stink but was quickly forgotten when the Yanks invaded New Orleans."

"Du Bois has a son—did you know that?" inquired Sam.

"Ah didn't even know he was married, but then ah really didn't know him very well. As young men, we associated with, well . . . we had different friends, socially."

Jenkins seemed slightly embarrassed by his answer, but Sam pressed on. "Are you saying the Du Bois family wasn't too highly thought of?"

"Frankly, suh, ah believe it is unbefittin' to speak of another man's mother, but present circumstances require it." Clearing his throat, the colonel continued. "Mrs. Du Bois was an extremely beautiful Creole woman who reputedly used her female wiles for monetary advancement. Her male friends included some of Louisiana's most prominent."

General Beauregard interjected, "No call for embarrassment, Woodrow; what you're sayin' is common knowledge."

"Thank you, General," Jenkins said, blushing. "There are some things that don't need discussin', but it does have a bearing on knowin' about Jacques Du Bois. He desperately wanted to be a part of Baton Rouge society, but the purported sins of the parent . . ."

". . . Shall be passed on to the future generation," finished Sam. "So, guess he wasn't accepted as a social equal; is that right?"

Colonel Jenkins nodded.

The conversation continued for another hour. Bits and pieces of information which might come in handy were exposed. It was now quite clear to Sam, and all assembled, that if the man impersonating Raven was really Du Bois, the motive for the Montana murders was all too apparent. The men who helped Du Bois transport the gold were undoubtedly also murdered, or had to be a part of the conspiracy. Everyone agreed that some action had to be taken.

"We must first be absolutely sure that the man in Montana Territory is Du Bois. The only way to confirm our speculation is for someone who knew him to travel west and positively identify him." Looking directly at Colonel Jenkins, the general continued, "That appears to be you, Woodrow."

"Ah'd like to go too," stated a determined Captain Richey. "Colonel Novey, the officer in charge of that gold, was a personal friend of mine. Unfortunately, my dear wife has been in declining health for several years now. It would be a serious hardship for her if ah was to leave her side. Ah truly regret not being able to accompany y'all."

Major Staats stepped forward and forcibly spoke out, "I would also like to accompany Colonel Jenkins." Staats was of slight stature, usually pacing about, a bundle of nervous energy. Now, he was standing stock-still, uncompromising, like a miniature Stonewall Jackson. "What Major Du Bois did was despicable. Not only did he murder for his own gain but he struck a mortal blow to the Confederate cause. He escaped down the river, which means he successfully ran the blockade. That gold was intended to buy guns and ammunition for our men. Who knows how many died because of his treachery. If he is still alive, I personally want to see him hanged."

"As do I," stated the general emphatically, "but not until he stands trial and is convicted by a jury of his peers." He looked each man in the eye before adding, "Bring him back heah and we'll try him in Vicksburg for the murder of Colonel Novey and all the rest."

Everyone but Sam implied agreement. Aware of his reticence, Beauregard asked, "Don't y'all concur, Sheriff?"

"It's not that I don't agree, but I can tell you right now—it isn't goin' to be easy. It could take a small army to bring him in."

General Pierre Gustave Beauregard lifted his aristocratic head and smiled. "Why that, suh, fits us perfectly; we of the South have nevah had anything else but a small army."

CHAPTER 27

THE TRAIN TRIP BACK TO MONTANA was long and dreary. The Pullman cars crept northward to Nashville, then on to Chicago for a lengthy layover before passengers had to board again. In Minneapolis they transferred, for the last time, to the Northern Pacific Railroad . . . only to run into more delays. Now, it was west across the Dakotas, out of the states, and into Montana Territory.

Early on, the three travelers had much to talk about but as each day passed, the hours of silence between them grew. By the time they'd reached Chicago, idle conversation had almost ceased entirely. Sam wasn't, by nature, given to talking much anyway. Rehashing the Civil War brought back the bitter past. Major Staats, being a nervous sort, had the irritating habit of drumming his fingers on the back of the seat. Periodically, he would get up abruptly and pace up and down the aisles. Colonel Jenkins brought along two valises crammed with legal briefs. He spent much of his time poring over the papers and, between train transfers, sent telegrams to his clients.

Sam had already telegraphed his messages west. Before leaving Baton Rouge on June 4, he sent two wires. One of which was to the sheriff in Laramie asking it be delivered to his son,

David. He wanted David to join them in Big Timber on or before June 13. The other wire was to Sheriff Sanford in Bozeman, requesting he be there on the same date.

Sam was engrossed in determining the best way to have his Southern companions observe Du Bois, surreptitiously. He had previously mulled over the variety of alternatives, such as riding out to the Elk Track and confronting Raven face-to-face. *Will that be wise? Hardly.* The Elk Track hands were a hard-case lot and there were too many of them. Raven—or Du Bois— wouldn't budge without a fight; neither would Dorsey Caine.

Raven and his henchmen would resist like cornered rats, having little to lose. Should the four of them go out there, they'd be better off taking the sheriff and some extra men along. But putting together a large enough posse in a town as small as Big Timber would arouse suspicions.

If they waited around until Du Bois happened to come into town, they wouldn't be there two days before the whole place would know of their presence. Could they possibly approach the Elk Track unnoticed, sneak up close enough to observe Du Bois without being seen? *We'd be safer sneakin' up on a wide-awake mama grizzly and stealin' her young,* thought Sam.

Waiting in town 'til Raven—or Du Bois— showed up could take months, time that none of them could afford to lose. *Is there a way to entice Du Bois into Big Timber?*

The answer came to him while thinking about David and the broken heart his son was probably still carrying around inside. Losing Deborah Dills had to hurt—real bad. Sam couldn't help but reflect on the thoughtlessness of Mrs. Dills, sending them a wedding invitation, announcing June 15 as the happy date.

That's it! The wedding! Raven will have to be in Big Timber for the marriage ceremony! Sam chuckled at the irony of it all. Mrs. Dills was goin' to help in the capture and arrest of her daughter's new father-in-law, the four-flushin' Colonel Raven.

The train should have easily gotten them to Big Timber before the fifteenth. Even with layovers, transfers, and waiting in railroad depots, the trip should've taken less than ten days. But, a washed-out bridge in Minnesota and a missed connection in St. Paul caused the loss of several days.

Sam was anxious as they pulled into Big Timber, mid-morning of June 15. He didn't like having too many people know that he was back in town; the fewer who knew of their arrival, the better. They had planned to get in late at night, not in broad daylight. Their intention was to get off the train individually, pretending not to know each other. Then, they would go directly to the Bramble Hotel, secure rooms, and wait until a meeting could be set up with David, the sheriff, and whatever deputies Sanford brought along.

Their delayed arrival had already knocked that plan awry. To make matters worse, and much to Sam's chagrin, the station was bustling with activity. He was astonished to find so many people. In actual fact, they met a welcoming committee greeting the arriving wedding guests. The depot was alive with commotion as women hugged and kissed and men shook hands and clapped each other on the back. Everyone was dressed in their finest and clearly in a festive mood. Sam recognized a state senator from Miles City and heard another gentleman greeted as "mayor."

Mr. and Mrs. Dills moved from one dignitary to another in obvious high spirits, introducing themselves and others. Although Sam tried, he couldn't avoid catching the eye of Mrs. Dills as he stepped from the Pullman car.

"Coming to the wedding, Mister Dodd?" she strained venomously, through clenched teeth.

"Now, Matilda, you and Homer *did* send Mary and me an invitation, didn't you?" Sam wanted to add, *and do we have a wedding surprise for you!* Instead he said, "Wouldn't miss it."

Luckily, no one other than Matilda Dills seemed to notice Sam's presence. He inched his way along the platform, trying to move unnoticed through the throng. Suddenly, he saw shocked recognition flash across the face of a man coming directly at him. Sam was more than relieved to see him brush by, intent on greeting someone else behind him.

In a shout loud enough to wake the dead, the man exclaimed for everyone to hear, "Colonel Woodrow Jenkins and Major Staats! What in the world are y'all doin' in Big Timber?"

Before either could speak, the stranger turned happily to his wife and companions, announcing, "Honey, friends, this here's mah former commandin' officer, Colonel Woodrow Jenkins, and this is Major Staats. Glory be! Two of the fightin'ist Rebs that evah manned the Vicksburg ramparts."

Major Staats was the first to step forward and grasp the outstretched hand, "Sergeant Brulte!"

The sergeant beamed at being recognized. "Yes, suh, Major. Ah'm pleased y'all remembered me."

A warm smile broke across Woodrow Jenkins' face as he also graciously extended his hand. "I remember you too, Sergeant. Weren't you one of our most able couriers? I recall you were wounded pretty badly gettin' through the Yankee lines and, as I recollect, you were cited for bravery."

Sergeant Brulte drew himself up proudly. "Yes, suh! And y'all was the man who gave me the citation!"

Jenkins remembered it well. The sergeant had risked his life many times, sneaking through the Union lines with important messages, dressed as a Yankee soldier. Had he been captured, he would have been summarily shot. Jenkins was aware that he should cut the visit short, but to be rude to such a good man? Never . . . especially in front of his wife and friends. They reminisced as if time didn't matter. Finally, Staats interjected, "Sergeant, we have to be movin' along now; but tell me, what brought you west?"

"Ah'm a saddle maker and figured there was greater opportunity out heah for me an' mah family. We opened a leather shop in Miles City an' have been doin' quite well."

One of Brulte's friends added, "Ol' Jamie got himself elected to the Montana House of Representatives a few years back. He's one of the best Democrats we got."

A man standing close by, taking in the entire conversation, barged forward and interrupted the good-byes. "Colonel, my name is Denny Walters and I'm with the Capitol's leading newspaper, *The Helena Herald.*" In non-stop fashion, Walters asked, "What brings you all the way from the South to our Montana Territory?"

Turning to the reporter, Jenkins politely answered, "Ah'm now in business, Mister Walters, and so is my colleague here, Mister Staats. We've come to discuss the purchase of cattle. Could y'all excuse us so we can bid farewell to our friends?"

"Well, are you here to buy cows from Colonel Raven out at the Elk Track Ranch?" inquired the pushy newsman, ignoring the colonel's request.

"Maybe. We've many folks to see," interrupted Major Staats. "We expect to have some contact with him as well as others." With his back to the reporter and his attention on Sergeant Brulte, the major smiled and said, "Excuse us, Sergeant, but the colonel and I have some folks to meet at the hotel. It sure was a pleasure seein' y'all again."

"Likewise," grinned Jamie Brulte. "If y'all evah pass through Miles City, ah'd be pleasured to see ya."

They shook hands and moved apart . . . all except the reporter, who stayed alongside the colonel, interjecting other questions. Jenkins stopped short, faced the bothersome writer, and said firmly, "Pardon me, suh, but ah just don't have time to talk to you. Would y'all excuse us please?"

Undaunted, the journalist pushed on, "Did you know Colonel Raven during the war?"

Jenkins was startled by the unexpected question. "Ah didn't know him personally, but have heard of him."

Then to Staats, Walters asked the same question.

"Ah don't think so," responded the major. "Excuse us, please." Deftly using his shoulder, he wedged between the aggressive reporter and the colonel and, turning their backs, walked away. One more question was hurled in their direction, "Do you intend to be at the wedding this afternoon . . . between young Raven and the Dills girl?"

Simultaneously, they turned and Staats answered, "No, we are not. *Who* did you say was getting married?"

It was the reporter's turn to look puzzled. "Haven't you heard about the big event?" He motioned to all the people still at the station. "It's why there are so many people here. Why, this is the biggest social event in the Territory. Folks are comin' to Big Timber from all over. The territorial governor will be here, a pack of legislators, and even some of the copper-mining bigwigs. Both Marcus Daly and W.A. Clark will be here, feudin' and fightin' as they usually do. This is a bigger event than the legislature passin' our State Constitution earlier this year."

"No, we're not here to celebrate any wedding," stated Jenkins. "As ah said before, we're here on cattle business."

Finally recognizing they had nothing more to offer, the inquiring reporter spotted another newsworthy person and drifted away. Sam joined them as they headed toward the hotel.

"Who was that following along with you?" he asked. Although his face darkened when he heard the word "reporter," Sam shrugged his shoulders after they'd related the conversation. "No use gettin' upset if the hog's out of the wallow. Chances are, Du Bois won't smell trouble unless that reporter gets upwind of 'im. Your names won't appear in the papers until it's all over. Mrs. Dills seein' me shouldn't raise any suspicion, just their curiosity. By the time the Du Bois clan wakes up, they'll be under arrest."

THE BRAMBLE HOTEL WAS PACKED, with no rooms available, and neither a David Dodd nor the sheriff were among the registered.

"Where are they?" fumed Sam. By now, it was well past ten o'clock and the wedding was to commence at two, in less than four hours. They needed a place to stay and meet with the sheriff; he had to be in town, somewhere. At the hotel, they learned how the Dillses had splurged and, with plenty of financial help from the Ravens, were making a big showy display out of the wedding, attracting statewide attention. They had put on a rodeo the day before and this morning, horse races were staged west of town. This evening, a huge dance was planned honoring the newlyweds.

There wasn't a soul who hadn't heard about the stag party thrown for J.D. the night before; the revelry was the talk of the town. A giant-sized tent was shipped in by freight to accommodate the ceremony, since Big Timber had no church or facility large enough to hold even an average-sized gathering, much less the enormous throng that would be attending the event. The Northern Pacific Railroad Company parked extra Pullman cars on the sidings, accommodating the overnight guests. Tents and covered wagons were scattered along the river; even a number of Indian teepees were in evidence.

Sam had never heard of a wedding being so large or given such importance. He asked Jenkins and Staats to pick up their bags and follow him up the slope to the home of Doc Collins. "Maybe the good doctor will have a place for us to rest our heads."

It was unusually hot for June as the sun radiated blistering waves on the high mountain plateau. Sam's Southern companions weren't used to exertion at four thousand feet, nor were they accustomed to the frigid evenings in store. They were already aware of the dry air sucking the moisture from their bodies. "Whew," muttered Colonel Jenkins as he dropped his bag on the porch. "If this was back home, ah'd be drippin' wet, through an' through. But look here," he said while gazing downward, "not a damp spot on mah shirt. How long does it take for a man to get acquainted with this strange climate?"

Sam laughed heartily. "Wait 'til this afternoon when the wind comes up. We all change our boots to ones with lead in the soles. Keeps us from gettin' blown into the next county. Sometimes the breeze gets so bad, you can only walk in one direction."

Jenkins lowered his head and closed one eye in wry disbelief and said, "Dodd, have you ever been in a Louisiana cyclone?" Without waiting for a reply, he continued, "One day durin' the war, some know-nuthin' Yankees were marchin' across a cotton field when one of our smaller cyclones passed, twistin' and twirlin' right through their ranks. Before y'all could say Dixie, it screwed every man in the whole regiment seven feet into the ground. As one of our Cajuns would say, 'Whut yo tink abot dat?'"

Sam grinned from ear to ear, truly enjoying these Southern gents. Both had been the epitome of propriety and all business during their first few days together, but now, they were relaxed and engaging, sporting a dry sense of humor that matched the Montana summer.

Sam's knock brought Amy to the Collinses' door. Before he could utter a greeting, she jumped up with a cry of joy and threw her arms about his neck. "Oh, Mr. Dodd, what a wonderful surprise!" Quickly glancing behind him, she asked "Is David with you?"

"No, Amy, he's not." He saw the immediate disappointment written on her face, so he added, "But I expect him to arrive at any time."

She blushed crimson. "Oh, that is such good news." Then noticing the two men standing near Sam, she opened the door wide and graciously invited them inside.

"Amy, is the doctor home?" asked Sam.

From behind the door came the gruff voice of Jason Sanford: "No, he's not but I shore am . . . 'bout time ya got here. I'd given ya up for dead!"

IT TOOK SEVERAL HOURS to bring Sheriff Sanford up-to-date. When Sam finished the long account, he asked, "Jason, you've been around the last couple of days and know the lay of the land; how do you think we should approach this identifying business, seeing if Raven is really Du Bois? By the way, have you seen him around?"

"Funny you should ask," replied Sanford. "I haven't seen hide nor hair of the colonel. You would expect to see him everywhere at the weddin' goings-on of his only son, wouldn't ya? He wasn't at the rodeo and he didn't show up anywhere last night. Saw plenty of Dorsey Caine and Elk Track hands, but no Colonel Raven. Peculiar, huh?"

"I would venture a guess," said Major Staats. "Too many people here, like our seein' Jamie Brulte at the train station. Ah'll bet he's not the only Civil War veteran who's about."

"You're probably correct," said Colonel Jenkins. "And if y'all are, Du Bois will make only a cameo appearance at the wedding. Y'all better plan for that contingency, a distinct—"

He was interrupted by loud rapping at the door.

Sam was amazed by the speed with which Amy ran to the entrance and hurriedly pulled it open. It was David but, for him, there was no giddy shriek and no hug. In fact, she stepped back demurely and uttered, "Hello, David, your father is expecting you. He's in the parlor."

David nodded politely and smiled, "Hello, Amy." Without another word, he quickly brushed by her on his way into the living room and warmly greeted his father.

Sam caught a glimpse of Amy as she fled for the kitchen with her head turned away, but not before he saw her crestfallen look and the tears welling up in her eyes.

CHAPTER 28

COLONEL MALACHI RAVEN LOOKED DOWN from the window of the Bramble Hotel at the rowdy crowd gath ered below. He was watching one of the cowboys riding backward down the dusty street, precariously perched on his galloping mount, one hand on the cantle and the other firing his six-shooter skyward. The horse suddenly veered right and jammed to a stop while the cowboy went left, disappearing in a cloud of red dirt. Spectators and passersby applauded wildly as his cohorts helped him to his feet and carried him into the nearest bar. Raven recognized them as J.D.'s friends, still celebrating last night's stag shindig.

"Dorsey, where did all these people come from? Ah didn't know there were this many human critters in Montana."

"Me neither," his rugged companion replied disgustedly. "It's the doin's of that Mrs. Dills. Ah bet that witch even invited the king of England. I hear'd she even sent an invitation to President Chester A. Arthur and that Democrat, Grover Cleveland." Dorsey looked around for a spittoon but couldn't find one, then spotted the full water pitcher to serve his needs.

"Jacques, did ya see the letter the Dillses sent out?"

"No," responded Raven. "Ah saw the invitation though, and it was bad enough. What did the letter say?"

"That ol' bat wrote that her little girl was marryin' the son of Colonel Raven, Confederate war hero, and that you was one of the richest cattle barons in the West. She musta mailed it to every politician and newspaper in the Northwest Territory."

"Where did she get the money to do all this?" Raven angrily spat out. "I had no thought it would be such a big affair. Is that stupid storekeeper rich enough to afford all this?"

"It ain't that fool Homer Dills that's footin' the bills. From what ah can tell, he ain't got a bed-pot to piddle in. They're gettin' the money from J.D."

"What! My son?" This was so incredulous, he grabbed the drapes in his fist in order to steady himself.

Dorsey looked over to the irate Raven. He didn't look well. Slowly but surely, he had been loosing weight. His cheeks were sunken, and his usual ruddy complexion was becoming a sickly, ashen gray. The sizable crowd on hand, brought to Big Timber by his son's generosity, was adding to his already distraught condition.

"That's right, Jacques, they're gittin' the money from J.D. But you have no cause to get mad at him; he still doesn't know who we really are. Not tellin' him the truth was a mistake," scowled Dorsey. "That Dills gal's got Jefferson twisted around her little finger. She said she'd marry up with him and her heart's desire was a big weddin'. Said it would please her mama." Dorsey walked over to the window and watched the crowd below mingle about. "It might please her ma, but it could get us hung if we ain't careful."

Shaking his head, he said, "We was sure we picked the perfect spot to get away from everyone when we came here. Can't believe it's been twenty years. All there was here was Crow Indians, lots of tall grass, and the ghost of that lady on Crazy Mountain."

Pointing to the people below, Dorsey continued, "Now look at it—crawlin' with folks and too many of 'em Southerners who came up here in the last ten years. As I said, we better be careful . . . " he spat again into the pitcher, "or we'll git spotted by someone who knowed us back when."

"You know I didn't want J.D. to grow up knowin' how we got all that gold. I figured he might amount to somethin' if given half a chance." Raven turned to Dorsey and looked proud. "It's worked out that way too. He's got a real future in politics when Montana becomes a state. He's got money, he's handsome, educated, and after today, he'll have a beautiful, ambitious wife on his arm. Those two will go far. As for you and me, we can keep out of sight around the Elk Track 'til we turn to dust. Nobody's goin' to find us out there."

"Oh yeah, we didn't do too well when those two Texas boys spotted you . . . what was their names?" asked Dorsey.

"John Lewis and the big-nosed one was Hurtt. We took care of them satisfactorily."

"Think so? What about that Dodd feller pokin' around?" Dorsey reached under his neckerchief and rubbed his neck. "Ah still got rope burns from that stinkin' lawman's lariat. Ah intend to kill 'im slow, if ah ever get the chance."

"That's all over. He's gone back to Colorado and took his kin with him. All we have to do is get through today and make sure the out-of-town people don't get a good look at us. We have to be at the wedding, but we can arrive late. Most everyone will already be seated and will only be seein' me at a distance and I doubt if anyone could recognize you; you're forty pounds heavier and you've changed a lot. Because of my height, I tend to stand out more. Quit worryin'; neither of us looks anything like we did twenty years ago."

Dorsey laughed sarcastically. "Your long legs ain't the biggest problem, little brother. Taking the name of Raven wasn't too bright. Me pickin' the name Caine seemed fittin', considerin' all the men we did in. Y'all shoulda picked Jackson or Smith . . . but oh no, ya had to use Raven."

Raven snapped at Dorsey, "Stop callin' me your little brother; someday, someone's goin' to hear ya."

A cruel smile crossed Dorsey's face. "We sure don't have the same daddy but Mama Du Bois dropped the both of us. We're brothers, whether you like it or not."

Raven straightened up erect, then said, "My sire was Artemus Raven. Mama told me so. I have every right to the name."

Dorsey laughed. "The only right we have, dear Jacques, is to be called bastards. Liza Du Bois bedded some pretty fancy gentlemen and did right well. She never told me who my daddy was, but no matter, we had a fine mother. We are the by-products of her lovin' and she was good to us. She raised us up instead of givin' us away like some doxies do."

"Well, it wasn't the same with me," smugly stated Raven. "Mama assured me Artemus Raven would recognize me as his son . . . one day. Our sweet mother said he even proposed to her after his wife died. Please, Dorsey, don't call her a doxie."

Dorsey smirked and boorishly replied, "Believe what you will, little brother. Believe that rascal Artemus was going to set you up as King of Ravenswood, believe that lecher was really a kind and gentle father instead of the old rogue he really was. Believe Mama was a lady. Why, you can even believe there's a ghost lady wanderin' around the Crazies with an ax in her hand if you want. But also, believe this . . . you better stay in this here room, out of sight, until the weddin' starts. You're right about goin' late. We can then slip in by the side of the tent and take our seats up front, where our backs will be to everybody."

"I believe she's up there," Raven muttered nervously.

"Who's up *where?"*

"That crazy ghost; I saw her."

"Come now, little brother," joked Dorsey. "You been hittin' the bourbon too hard."

Defensively, Raven blurted out, "I've seen her twice. Once on the trail back of the ranch, then again up in the high timber." He appeared to be truly frightened and one corner of his mouth began to twitch.

"You're lettin' imagination get the best of ya. Ah've seen things that coulda looked like a ghost. You know, like twirlin' leaves caught in the wind, snow droppin' from tree limbs, funny noises cuttin' through the aspens, maybe white patches of ice— any number of things. Yore mind's playin' tricks on ya."

Raven again gazed out the window, but now his eyes were fixed on the rugged Rockies. "Ah dream about her, Dorsey. Ah see a filmy, shiverin' mass of light, misty-like in the form of a woman, gliding silently up behind me, ax over her head . . . then she fades away into black rippling water. *And ah see the swollen face of Colonel Novey, bobbin' up and down, eyes and mouth hangin' open, then he's slowly sinkin' into the Mississippi.*"

Facing his brother, he grimaced and was trembling. "Ah've had this same nightmare many times . . . too many times. Dorsey, do ya ever think about any of the men you've killed?"

"No," he replied matter-of-factly. "Why should I?" Before Raven could respond to his indifferent reply, there was a knock on the door. An aggressive voice called out, "Colonel Raven? Are you there? My name is Walters, from *The Helena Herald*, and I'd like to have a few words with you."

CHAPTER 29

Y'ALL KNOW THIS SAM DODD FELLER is a bluebelly Yankee," wisecracked the irascible Doc Collins, as he was introduced to the Southerners.

Ignoring the doctor's caustic remark, Sam said, "We needed a place to meet with the sheriff and I figgered you were the most kind and hospitable man in Big Timber, so why not impose on the lovable Doc Collins."

"Humph!" was his reply. "Whatya doin' back here, Dodd?"

Once again, Sam related everything he had discovered in the past few months, since leaving Big Timber.

"You mean to tell me Raven isn't Raven? Incredulous!" stated Collins.

"Yep, we're pretty well convinced that bird's name is Du Bois; leastwise, that's what we're here to find out. Jason's gone into town to locate his deputies and find out if the so-called colonel is here in Big Timber and whether or not he is expected to attend the wedding. We figure it's our opportunity to identify him as Du Bois. Among the confusion of everyone arriving, Colonel Jenkins and Major Staats can slip in without being noticed. They should be able to get a close look at Raven and see if he really *is* Du Bois. And if he is, the plan is to signal

Jason, who will be close at hand. He and two of his deputies will get Raven and Dorsey aside and arrest 'em on the spot, right after the ceremony. We should catch them totally by surprise."

"Isn't that a bit dangerous, arresting him in front of all those people?" asked the doctor.

"It just might be, but the longer we wait, the greater chance he'll discover us bein' in Big Timber," answered Sam. "Mrs. Dills spotted me at the train depot and an old Rebel acquaintance recognized both the colonel and the major at the same time. Some newspaper reporter took it all in and asked some very nosy questions. Raven could already know that somethin's up; and if he gets suspicious, he'll run for sure. But if he shows up at the wedding, it's fair to assume he doesn't know we're here."

"David and I should stay out of sight until the wedding starts. Then we'll move up somewhere nearby where we can help if need be. Should either of us be seen by Caine or Raven, they might get pretty leery, pretty fast. There's not much doubt that Matilda Dills would tell the Ravens about seein' me at the train station. But more than likely, they'd have no chance to talk until the reception, after the ceremony."

"It still sounds pretty risky to me," the worried doctor somberly stated. "Anything goes wrong, somebody's goin' to get hurt."

"We agree," said Sam. "But what's the alternative? We certainly can't try to have Raven arrested while he's surrounded by his men at the reception. Only during the wedding ceremony will he and Dorsey be isolated. From what I understand about formal weddings, the family is usually required to sit up front—the bride's kin on one side and the groom's on the other."

"You surely are right there," came the excited voice of the doctor's wife as she entered the room. "From what I hear, they have even shipped in a big pipe organ from St. Louis. Doesn't that beat all?" Martha Collins set out a tray of coffee and lemonade on the sideboard. "Every woman from miles around has ordered new outfits for the occasion. It's all we've talked about for the last two months. I thought you gentlemen might like some refreshments."

As they eagerly helped themselves and graciously thanked their hostess, Sam asked Martha Collins to tell him more about the wedding. She happily complied, going into the most minute detail.

David Dodd, sitting quietly in the corner, couldn't help but overhear every word and with each elaborate detail of Deborah's ceremony, he became more forlorn and depressed. He finally got up and silently went outside to sit on the porch steps. Having been home in Colorado had helped push Deborah to the back of his mind. But being here in Big Timber, having her so nearby, the heartache was burning a hole in his youthful chest. To make matters worse, she was marrying a man he despised. The revolting image of J.D.'s hairy arms around her slight frame caused him to shudder.

He jumped to his feet, the welled-up frustration forcing him to move about. The growing anger and righteous indignation felt like an erupting volcano in his head. The injustice of it all produced an all-consuming rage. He slammed his fist into his palm and kicked the ground. *Blast it! We were the ones to be married!* He thrust his hands in his pockets to keep from pounding them into the nearest tree and stomped around the side of the house. He was thrown off his guard when he saw Amy in the backyard, hanging up clothes to dry. She immediately noticed his dour expression and the red flush in his cheeks. "David, what is it? Aren't you feeling well?"

"No, I'm not," he gruffly responded. "I don't feel good at all. I'm not snake-bit or anything like that, but I shore got the miseries." David felt compelled to tell somebody how lousy he felt. Who better than sweet, understanding Amy. He certainly couldn't burden his father with his woes. Just the thought was mortifying and made him feel silly. He couldn't tell his mother; after all, he was a grown man. That's what little boys do. He sure wouldn't dream of telling another man and have him think he was a simpering, love-sick weakling. Amy was his friend; she already knew him well, having spent so much time nursing him back to health. She was like a good pard who would sympathize and sense the ache he felt inside.

David began to talk and couldn't stop, rambling on and on, completely unburdening himself. Amy listened while she worked. Faster and faster, she reached into the basket for the damp shirts, then socks, then drawers, ramming the clothes pins into the line, securing them for eternity.

Finally, she could take it no longer, the red having risen precipitously from her neck to her forehead. She faced David, her blue eyes sparkling with anger. "David Joseph Dodd . . . yer stupid, dumb as a board!" she spat out angrily. "Ya don't know when you are well off. That huzzie would haf made you a lifetime of unhappiness and sorrow. Yer lucky to be rid of her."

David was shocked and backed up a step as she moved threateningly toward him, waving a clothespin under his nose, speaking loudly in Norwegian and highly accented English.

"Whaa . . . what are you saying?" he stammered. "I . . . I don't understand Norskie!"

"Good thing you don't! I just said some things a good Christian woman shouldn't say!" Without seeming to take a breath, she continued to sputter. "Have you holes in yer head to want that woman? When you was sick and dyin', was she by yer side? No! When she could have married you, did she? No! When you went back to Colorado, did she go with ya? No! Would she make a good mama for yer children and care fer you through thick und thin? No! Does she love the Lord like ya do? No!" Putting both hands on her hips, she went on. "How thick can yer head be, David Joseph Dodd? She didn't love ya, not one whit . . . she loves herself!"

With that, Amy suddenly began to sob, pulling her apron up about her eyes. Then just as suddenly, she stopped the tears and went back to hanging up the laundry while David stood dumbfounded, with his mouth agape.

"David Dodd, don't ya come moon-eyed around me again, tellin' me yer troubles. I've got plenty of my own." Beginning to cry anew, she threw a wet towel at him. "Git out of here; I have work to do."

David beat a hasty, confused retreat around to the front of the house, just as his father emerged from inside. Unable to miss the bewildered look on his son's face, he asked, "Anything wrong, David?"

"I don't rightly know, Pa." He looked around behind, to see if he had been followed. "But one thing for sure, palaverin' with a gal can be mighty unsettling and downright strange. Pa, how long did it take before you came to understandin' women?"

Sam laughed, "Son, the longer I try, the less I know. I still can't figger out your ma, much less the rest of 'em."

"So, there's no use tryin'," concluded the still-perplexed young man.

"Not on that score," Sam chuckled some more. "Leastwise, not that I know of."

"They're sure hard to figure out—worse than a jughead mule, not to mention mighty frustratin'. Sorta makes a man want to pick a fistfight or at least, hit something," responded David.

Sam smiled. "Davey, there was a wise Polish man by the name of Winnike who claimed that, historically, many wars were started by kings needing to vent their frustration over their inability to figure out the wiles of a queen."

"Pa, that truly makes sense . . . it surely does."

"SAM, I CAN'T LOCATE RAVEN ANYWHERE . . . and that makes me nervous," stated the sheriff. "He's got to be holed up somewhere, 'cause everybody's expectin' him to be at the wedding and the party later on." Jason Sanford paced back and forth on the Collins' living room carpet, offering Sam,

Colonel Jenkins, Major Staats, David, and the two deputies his assessment of the present circumstances. "Too many things can go wrong," he muttered.

"Did you see Dorsey around?" asked Sam.

"Nope, and that bothers me too," declared Sanford. "I didn't see hide nor hair of either of 'em. J.D. and his sidekicks are over at the hotel gettin' all duded up for the festivities and drinkin' the bar dry. It'll be a wonder if J.D. will be able to stand up durin' the ceremonies. The bride and her party are at home, waitin' 'til they're picked up by a fancy carriage. I did find out that there's a side entrance to the tent where the family and the minister will enter in after the guests are there. I'm told that's when everyone's seated, the organ starts up, and some gal starts to sing. When she's through warblin', the bride and her pa will march down the middle aisle on a bright red carpet they've rolled out to cover the dirt. It shorely is a fancy affair!"

"Jason, where do you think it'd be best for Jenkins and Staats to sit?"

"I'd say about halfway up, on the left side. I intend to be right up front, just a few rows back. I'd like to be closer but they've roped off six rows on both sides for family and visitin' dignitaries."

Jason walked over to the window and peered outside. "The wind's comin' up. In an hour or so, it could be blowin' real hard. I went out to that monstrous tent to look it over just before I came here, and the canvas was already flappin' and crackin' so loud I don't know how anybody will be able to hear the organ, much less the preacher."

"Sheriff, have you seen many of the Elk Track hands in town?" asked Colonel Jenkins.

"There's some here, but I can't say I know all of 'em. There's lots of men around, all done up with ties and coats who look durned uncomfortable, and quite a few are packin' iron."

"That means they're carryin' guns, doesn't it?" inquired Staats.

"It shore does. Shoulder holsters, hoglegs, plenty of tools to blow out yer lamp," responded the sheriff. Looking directly at the two Southerners, he asked, "Are the both of you heeled?"

"Do you mean, are we armed?" asked the colonel.

"That's what I mean," said Sanford.

Colonel Jenkins opened his coat, displaying a nickel-plated .41-caliber Colt Lightning snugly stuffed in his belt. Tucked in the small of his back was a holstered .32-caliber Sharps pepperbox with carved ivory grips. Major Staats pulled back his coat to display a .32-caliber Smith & Wesson backup in a shoulder holster. "Will this do?" he asked.

"If yer good with it," said Sanford. Looking over the assembled men, he said, "Well, let's be on our way. We all know what each of us has to do."

Sam halted them before they started for the door. "There's just one more thing."

"What's that?" asked the sheriff.

Sam smiled, then said, "Well, gentlemen, we begin by bowing our heads."

CHAPTER 30

Jason Sanford was right; the wind might well be a factor. Men were scurrying around driving additional pegs into the dirt, trying to firmly secure the large tent to the ground. The wedding carriage had just arrived and the bride and bridesmaids were having a difficult time keeping their wedding apparel in place. Each had to hold onto their hats, while desperately attempting to control their dresses and flower bouquets. Mrs. Dills was having a terrible time holding up her daughter's very long bridal train. The entire affair looked rumpled and chaotic.

Both Sam and his son stood in the shadows of a nearby building, close enough to see what was going on but not near enough to be recognized. Conversely, they had some difficulty clearly identifying the faces of the guests. The tent was soon packed and late arrivals were being turned away. There was no space left inside and few wanted to stay in the gale that was pushing in upon them. Although several people were put off by not being allowed to enter and were visibly upset, they were courteous enough to endure the wind in order to greet the bride and her father who were waiting eagerly for the procession to begin.

"Why all the waitin', Pa? Why doesn't the blasted wedding begin?" snarled David.

"I think it's because the colonel hasn't arrived." They had already seen Dorsey ride up with J.D. and two others. They tied their mounts by the side entrance to the tent. But as yet . . . no Raven.

Out of a billowing cloud of dust a dozen or so riders came into view, heading straight for the tent. "Oh, oh, here he comes," said Sam, while moving back into the shadows. Conspicuous in the midst of the Elk Track horsemen was one man, taller in the saddle than the rest, dressed in a white suit. "That's him for sure. Dang! Why does he have such a band of men with him?" A worried frown crossed Sam's brow. "I smell trouble— lots of it."

No sooner had the colonel dismounted and gone immediately into the tent than the pipe organ began playing. Though faintly, they could hear the voice of the soprano soloist over the howling wind. They watched as most of the Elk Track hands moved around to the windward side of the cloth structure. Two were left behind holding onto the horses' reins. All were armed.

"David, there's going to be big trouble. I think Raven knows somethin' is up."

As soon as Sam had spoken, the strains of the wedding march began and a wind-blown Deborah Dills, on her father's arm, disappeared into the folds of the tent. During the second refrain of the melody, they heard the distinct sound of pistol shots, followed by panicked shrieks and shouts of terror.

Simultaneously, the Elk Track hands scattered on all sides of the huge tent, slashing the ropes and letting the gales of wind do the rest. Barely escaping the collapsing structure, Raven and Dorsey emerged, guns in hand. The enormous sheets of canvas enveloped the frightened guests as the muffled screams and cries of the injured merged into an ugly wail, clearly heard above the howling wind.

Surrounded by their men, Raven and Dorsey galloped off at a dead run toward the river. "Get to the horses, David. We can catch them before they cross the river."

"Aren't we goin' down to help the folks under the tent? Deborah, Mrs. Collins, and Amy are under that mess."

Sam quickly looked at the wreckage and then back to the direction where Raven and the rest had fled. "You get over there and help. I'll follow Raven." He grabbed the horn and vaulted into the saddle, ramming his spurs into the beast, forcing him to explode into action. At a frothy, full-bore pace, Sam and the mount pounded through town after the fleeing band. They would pass the river ferry and head upriver where they could comfortably ford the water without too much trouble.

Crossing the Yellowstone would slow them down, at least enough for Sam to get there. Topping the rise above the ford, he spotted them in the river, halfway across. Leaping from the saddle, he pulled the Winchester from the scabbard and jacked a round into the chamber. Sam sat down and leaned back, leveled the rifle over his knees, and fired a round in front of the lead horse.

"Raven!" he shouted. "Stop or I'll have to kill ya!"

The shot galvanized them into frantic action, spurring their broncos unmercifully. The few horses who had any footing started to lunge and buck while those chest-deep in the river struggled mightily. Raven hunched over the far side of his stallion, keeping his men between Sam and himself, affording no target at all. Dorsey, however, managed to turn his gelding partially around and wildly fire his six-shooter, kicking up dust all around Sam.

With steady calm, Dodd brought the iron sights to a bead on Dorsey. Kapow! Thud! He could almost hear the unforgettable sound of bullet hitting flesh and bone. Dorsey buckled in the saddle but stayed astride the horse. Another rider turned to help, only to have Sam's second bullet take him high in the chest, knocking him into the fast-flowing river. Jacking another round into the chamber, Sam dropped one more rider before they escaped behind the cottonwood trees.

Sam mounted and unlimbered his rope. Then, riding to the river's edge he lassoed the dead and pulled him to the nearest bank. Fording the rushing water, he found the other ranch hand leaning against a stump—still alive but fading fast. Sam's .44-40 had caught him high in the lungs; air bubbles were visible in the blood seeping from the gaping chest wound. His eyes were still open but the opaque glaze of impending doom was in his blank stare. Sam cautiously approached, rifle leveled at his head. He kicked his pistol out of reach, then tried to make the dying man comfortable. Experience had taught him that the rider's soul would soon be departing.

The dying man whispered that he wanted a drink of water. Sam walked to the river's edge and partially filled his hat with cold water, but by the time he returned, there was no need of it. He'd never seen either of the dead cowboys before. Both appeared to be in their forties and looked as hard as the river rocks on which they lay.

Sam dumped the water out of his Stetson and put the wet hat back on his head, then sheathed the Winchester in the scabbard and got back up on his horse. Looking down at the crumpled body, revulsion and a deep melancholy encompassed him. As flies gathered around the bloody face, several gray-colored scavenger birds were already gathering on the nearby brush, waiting for Sam to leave. No one hated killing more than Sam Dodd. But here, by the confluence of the beautiful Yellowstone, lay two more men whose lives he had ended. It was a bitter thought, bringing bile to his mouth. He dismounted and respectfully straightened out the legs and torso of the dead cowboy and crossed his hands on his chest. Sam then took off his coat and covered the upper body and face. Mounting once more, Sam rode into town without looking back.

PANDEMONIUM REIGNED UNDER the heavy canvas. Pushing, shoving, frightened people were looking for any way to escape the suffocating conditions under the collapsed tent. The center support poles had crushed several people and trapped others, while most had finally worked their way from beneath the edges. David was helping cut holes in the canvas to let grateful souls out. It was a full half-hour before they could get to those trapped under the downed poles. Amy and Martha Collins escaped with minor scrapes and the vast majority were slightly bruised physically, but highly disturbed emotionally. All the guests were dirty and disheveled, as were their fine clothes, ruined in the rush to flee from under the sweltering canvas.

Matilda Dills had swooned and her husband and daughter were trying to revive her. What was left of Deborah's wedding gown was a torn and dusty mess. The skirt and flowing train were gone, as were her veil and shoes. The bridesmaids were last seen disappearing through the clouds of blowing dirt.

The minister's body lay still, under a frock coat placed respectfully over him. Propped up against a wagon, Colonel Jenkins was wounded and unconscious, being tended to by Doc Collins. A concerned and anxious Major Staats stood close by.

"How bad is it, doctor?" inquired Jason Sanford.

"Just a bad scalp wound," Doc Collins answered casually. "The colonel will feel like he's been kicked by a mule for a number of days, but he'll live. A couple of centimeters to the right and we'd be shippin' his bones back to Louisiana." Turning to the major, Collins asked, "What happened in there? I was in the back of the tent when the shooting began and didn't see a thing except the tent fallin' on our heads."

"Things didn't work out as planned," replied Staats. "We arrived too late to pick our seats; the place was already jam-packed. They weren't even going to let us in until that, whatever his name is, reporter butted in and called out Colonel Jenkins' name. Mrs. Dills overheard and insisted that one of the ushers find us some seats. He took us way up front and squeezed us in real close to the family section."

"Yeah," a sarcastic sheriff added, "you were practically sittin' in my lap."

"It was hot under that tent, folks were crammed together, and everybody was sweating buckets. People were grumbling and highly irritated, especially all the dignitaries standing there in front of us. We couldn't figure out why the ceremony was being delayed. Then, Du Bois arrived."

"So . . . it was Du Bois," said the sheriff.

"No doubt about it," the major emphatically stated. "As he entered, right away the music started and the lady began to sing. Du Bois kept his eyes to the front, talking to his son, but everyone in the first few rows kept slapping him on the back and offering him their congratulations. The minister came over to ask that the family take their places. Just then, Woodrow took out his handkerchief to wipe his face as Du Bois turned to find his seat. He spotted us immediately."

"I bet you shocked the life out of him," remarked Doc Collins.

"Actually, it didn't seem to. He almost looked like he was expecting us, because he said something to the man beside him and, like greased lightning, they drew guns, took aim, and fired. Jenkins caught the first bullet and fell forward."

"How did you miss bein' hit at such close range?" asked David.

"The reason is lying right over there." Staats motioned to the body of the minister. "He jumped in front of Du Bois and shouted something about no guns in church and took the bullet meant for me."

"I got knocked aside by some senator and his wife tryin' to get out of the line of fire," said Jason. "Next thing I knew, I had a mess of canvas on my face and people squirmin' about me, also tryin' to get away from the shootin'."

As they stood nearby, the tent was being pulled away, exposing two more casualties—a woman who was struck by a stray shell and a small girl, crushed in the panic of the crowd trying to escape. Matilda Dills had recovered and was sobbing loudly. Her husband spotted the group by the wagon and came stomping over in a boiling rage. Dills pointed at David and yelled to the sheriff. "Arrest that man! He's gotta be the cause of it all! Arrest him, I say!"

"Don't get your bowels in an uproar, Homer. David didn't have anythin' to do with it. The blame lies at the feet of Colonel Raven, or usin' his real name, Jacques Du Bois."

Homer stood in shocked, numbed silence as Jason filled him in on Du Bois' nefarious background. "Your daughter is a very lucky little lady. She was just minutes away from sharin' a wagon tree with a stud from that clan."

Homer Dills pulled himself up to his full height of five-foot-three, stuck out his chest, and exploded at the top of his voice: "I don't believe a word of it. Lies, all lies made up by those jealous Dodds!" With that, he turned on his heel and strutted back to his family, defiantly kicking the dirt every step of the way. They watched his mouth flapping and his wild gesturing in their direction. With scowls on all three of their faces and noses in the air, they began the long walk toward home.

"Some people shore have a heap of trouble with the truth," commented the sheriff.

Moaning softly, Jenkins began to blink his eyes. He closed them again and mumbled, "Ah know ah'm not in heaven; my head hurts too much. Must be hell or Big Timber."

"Some dudes have said there's not much difference," piped in Doc Collins, wryly. "How's your head? Hurts a bit, don't it?"

The colonel hesitatingly touched his sore head, and moaned, "Well, ah guess ah'm alive."

Looking at David, Jason asked, "Where's yer pa, son?"

David looked away toward the river and just then spotted the familiar, mounted figure loping toward them. "He's ridin' up now, Sheriff. He took off after Raven, hoping to catch 'im before he and his men crossed the river."

Sam swung down from the bay and saw Jenkins on the ground. "Is he goin' to be all right?" Then noticing the figure under the coat, he asked, "Who is that?"

"Some little girl got trampled in the panic and a lady was wounded by a stray bullet. Otherwise, all the rest will make it. There shore are a lot of unhappy people though, wonderin' what's goin' on," answered the sheriff. Gradually, a crowd had been collecting around the wagon, looking for answers. Through the assemblage pushed the disarrayed but excited reporter, glasses knocked askew, jacket tousled and ripped.

"Sheriff Sanford, I'm glad I found you." Spotting Jenkins and his bloody wound, the reporter gasped, then in rapid fire, asked "Wha . . . what happened to the colonel? Who fired those shots? Who's that over there, covered up? Any idea why the tent caved in? I just saw Mr. Dills and he said it was the fiendish act of the Dodds. Any truth to that?"

A large gathering huddled around the sheriff, drinking in every word as he placed the blame where it rightfully belonged. Amid wails and whispers, he informed them of the alleged Colonel Raven's background. When he concluded, the crowd quickly disbursed to spread the shocking news. The delighted reporter ran off to the telegraph office with the story of his life.

Jason Sanford joined his deputies helping with the few remaining injured and the removal of the deceased. In the waning hours of daylight, making his way back to town, he knew it was time to talk with Sam Dodd and to form a posse.

CHAPTER 31

DAVID WANTED TO KEEP WALKING up Main Street to Deborah's house, to see how she survived the collapse of both the tent and her wedding! He was pretty sure she hadn't been physically hurt but wondered how she was handling the onerous news about the Raven family. David was more than curious to know if she had changed her mind about marrying J.D.

Surprisingly, he was equally concerned about Amy. When he last saw her, leaving the wedding site, she was limping badly. More than once, he'd contemplated her scathing tirade against Deborah and wondered about the truth of it. He came to the intersection of the two roads where he had to make up his mind—to the left, to see Amy . . . or to the right, to the Dillses' home. He started one way, then the other. Thoroughly disgusted with himself, he turned around and headed back to the center of town where the men were gathering.

I really don't have much time, anyway. The posse should be close to ready and within the next hour, we'll be leaving. Why should I bother to see either one of 'em? Deborah threw me over for a low-down snake and that blonde Norskie gal just bawled me out good. Why should I give a hoot about her? I made the stupid mistake of sharing my thoughts and look what it got me . . . a good tongue-lashing! My just desserts for confidin' in a woman!

The street was inordinately crowded, hot, and dusty. The wind was whipping up the fine red dirt and pulverized horse dung into miniature whirlwinds. Many of the people who were going to attend the reception were frequenting the local bars instead, since all events had been canceled. The few cafés and two hotel eateries were jammed to the rafters, as were their lobbies. The Northern Pacific Railroad depot was a sea of disgruntled dignitaries, using their influence to catch an earlier train home. Wagons and buggies loaded with rumpled occupants were leaving town as well, all looking glum. Cowhands were loitering outside the saloons repeating the stories being circulated about the Dodds, the questionable Ravens, and the posse being formed. Folks were overly warm and irritated. It was a far cry from the pleasant day everyone had planned.

David's thoughts were mixed. He was more than delighted that Deborah was still single, but bitterly disappointed that Raven had escaped. His father had bet they'd gone directly to the Elk Track where, if they chose to wage a battle, they could effectively hold off a small army. A myriad of emotions raced through his body as he trudged through town.

Near the Fast Buck Saloon, one of the waddies darted inside as soon as he spotted David walking down the boardwalk on the far side of the street. David recognized him as Emmet Pratt, the son of Lory Pratt, a rancher over Livingston way. J.D. had picked Emmet as his best man—a good choice, for both had reputations as wild ones, rogues of the first order.

David wondered if J.D. might be in there drinking, since the Fast Buck was his favorite watering hole. He was curious as to how much J.D. knew about his father's background. If by some chance he hadn't known, today's chaos must have been quite a jolt to him, as it was to the Dills. Come to think of it, he probably hadn't been told. It was common knowledge that

Raven had spoiled J.D. rotten, and even gloated over the benefits he could shower on his son, giving him every material thing he desired. J.D. reveled in his Southern heritage and gained a devil-may-care reputation that sure didn't include the Puritan ethic of hard work and sobriety. He was a dashing, good-looking hellion and proud of it. Brawls, gunfights, and high living were J.D.'s trademarks. To a much lesser degree . . . so were Emmet Pratt's.

Two peas out of the same pod, thought David. Awhile back when he was a deputy, he had to rough up Emmet a bit in order to quiet him down. Emmet was roaring drunk, riding up and down Main Street, shooting up store signs and showing off to his equally drunken friends. Firing into the air was tolerated but drilling holes in private property was not.

Called in to tame him down, David walked into the street and hollered at him to quit, but Emmet turned his horse around and tried to run him over. David leaped nimbly aside while at the same time swinging his right arm in an arch, catching Pratt in the stomach with his fist. It was a savage blow, knocking him clean out of the saddle as he rode by. Stunned and groggy, Emmet sat up in the dust, holding his middle while retching all over himself. David locked him up for the night in the back of the feed store.

The next morning, Emmet was sullen, stinking, and seething with hate. Several of his cronies had witnessed the perfunctory manner in which the deputy had disposed of his rowdy behavior. Embarrassed, he had no intention of forgetting the humiliation he felt at David's hands; retribution was in his bloodshot eyes. There was certainly no love lost between Emmet Pratt and David Dodd.

David felt no sorrow over the present plight of J.D. Raven. Even though he had no responsibility for his father's past thievery, his hands were still dirty. David remembered his good pal, Cal Davis. *J.D. participated in the plot to dry-gulch Cal and me, sendin' that fake telegram enticing us to go to Melville. He has Cal's blood on his hands. What's that quote from Jesus that Pa is always sayin? "A good man out of the good treasure of his heart brings forth good things and an evil man out of the evil treasure brings forth evil things." That's a fact. A lot of evil has come out of that famil—*

"Dodd! Turn around!" The threatening voice of Jefferson Davis Raven cut through the hot afternoon air like a diving hawk after prey. "Turn around or I'll shoot you in the back, you son of a stinkin' lying dog!" A torrent of raucous, abusive curses poured from J.D.'s lips; loathing drenched every word.

David turned slowly to see J.D. push through the swinging doors of the Fast Buck Saloon, followed by Emmet Pratt and several others, into the bright late afternoon sun. J.D. staggered into the dusty street, stumbling around the horses tied to the hitching rail, still swearing profusely. He showed all the signs of being full of whiskey, reeling from side to side, having difficulty standing up.

David walked toward him. He saw that J.D.'s gun was still holstered, but that his hand was twitching close by. David caught sight of Emmet Pratt—as he stepped into the street and casually leaned against the hitching rail—to Raven's left. David quickly noted that the leather loops used to secure their Colts were unfastened and both had their holsters strapped to their legs, facilitating a faster draw. David removed the loop over his .44 as well, and ignoring the foul language measurably asked, "What can I do for you, J.D.?"

"What can you *do* for me? You can *die* for me! You and that one-armed skunk you call yer pa been tellin' a pack of lies about my father and Dorsey. You've tried to turn my woman against me and have sullied up our good name. For that .
I'm goin' to blow holes in that lyin' hide of yours!"

"You're drunk, J.D., in no condition to take on anyone an' I don't want to have to shoot you," turning slightly to Emmet Pratt he added, "or you either, Emmet."

"You can bet you ain't goin' to shoot me," slobbered J.D., "because you know I'm danged good with a gun. I could be blind pie-eyed and still blow holes in that sanctimonious body of yours before you could clear leather. Ain't that right, Emmet?"

Pratt nodded and called out to David, "You're a dead man, Dodd, and ya got it comin'."

As he started to straighten up, David shouted back, "Don't go movin' around too much, Emmet; take one more step and I'll kill ya."

"Now listen to that there," sneered Raven. "He's going to *kill* ya, Emmet. Ain't that a leg-slapper?"

All of J.D.'s friends, watching from the boardwalk, laughed . . . all but one. He was sober enough to see that David wasn't intimidated by the arrogant talk. He knew the Dodds were not to be messed with. They had a reputation for not backing down. Looking to stop any possible bloodshed, he called out, "Aw, J.D., come on back inside; cool down and let's have another drink." Several of the others were getting nervous as well. What they thought would be bantering rivalry was becoming much too serious.

J.D. looked over his shoulder to his cohorts and shot back, "I'm comin', but not before I finish off this lyin' piece of horse dung."

Though David had had enough of the cussing and bravado, he didn't want to fan the flames any further. "Your pal is right. You and Emmet are just on the prod and lookin' for trouble. Better sober up before someone gets hurt."

"I told Deborah you were nothin' but a stinkin' coward and you couldn't carry my boots," sneered Raven. He cleared his head to remember the last time they went at it and what had incited David. Deborah was his weakness; she was the way to sucker him into a gunfight. He had to force Dodd into drawing first, sure he was fast enough to beat him. He couldn't be the first to slap leather and have to face a murder charge. So, he continued to use Deborah's name, intimating his own personal relations with her, saying things that no man should infer about a decent woman.

As J.D. spoke, the blood began to rise in David's face and he slowly realized that Raven wasn't as drunk as he pretended.

Raven was obviously trying to force him to make the first move, confident in his ability to gun him down. Emmet Pratt was his backup, his witness. David didn't want to fight but he couldn't back down; nor did he dare to turn his back on them and walk away. J.D. continued to taunt him as he moved menacingly forward, arm ready, hand over gun.

"I'm gonna kill you, Dodd!"

David was resigned. *If death is going to come, let it be now. It's time to force his hand.* Calm and cool, he said so all could hear, "Don't let anything but fear stop you."

Raven's brow furrowed and as the significance of David's words sunk in, his lip curled and his right hand streaked to his .45 Colt. With blinding speed, he drew the gun and fired. He was fast—faster than David, but not as accurate. David inched to the right as he cleared leather. His father had taught him that when drawing fast, the tendency was to jerk the trigger on the first shot . . . Raven had done just that. His bullet grazed David's left arm just as the .44-caliber slug from David's gun tore through J.D.'s right eye.

Emmet Pratt stood frozen as J.D.'s head was thrown back by the shock of the 200-grain slug entering his brain and knocking him over into the frightened horses. In drunken anger, Pratt clumsily grabbed for his gun. David yelled, "Don't do that!" But . . . to no avail. Emmet was intent on firing, determined to avenge his friend. Making sure not to kill him, David shifted his aim and shot at his right shoulder, jerking him backward, but not enough to stop Emmet from getting off one round, hitting David in the upper leg. With the searing pain of lead tearing his flesh, he fired again, sending a deadly bullet into Emmet. This time . . . he aimed for the heart.

David stood there, in too much agony to take a step, a profusion of blood spilling down his leg. Two bodies lay grotesquely in the dust, both trembling . . . twitching in the last moments of life. Violent death was always ugly, the spirit being hard pressed to leave the body, departing in jerks and spasms.

He looked over at the stunned bystanders, still on the walk-way. One of them said, "We saw it, Dodd. You gave 'em every chance."

David pulled off his belt and drew it tightly around his leg, trying to stop the flow of red . . . then he limped up the road to see Doc Collins.

CHAPTER 32

THE LARGE POSSE MILLED ABOUT the livery stable, anxious to leave. Someone shouted, "Let's be movin', Jason. They'll be in Canada by the time we git goin'!" Sanford had insisted that each rider provide himself with enough food and ammunition for an extended manhunt. Whether the Ravens holed up or vamoosed, the chase could be long and dangerous. Some had been slow in getting their gear together, knowing there was little chance of making it to their first destination by nightfall. Reaching the Elk Track Ranch before dark was out of the question.

"Jason, do ya really think anybody's going to still be around when we get there?" asked one of the posse.

"Anyway," asked another, "wouldn't meetin' us head-on be foolish for them to try? Shootin' Injuns is a lot different than holdin' off the law."

"There's little doubt it's the first place they'll head for," answered Sanford. "How long they *stay* is another matter."

Sam didn't believe the Ravens would stay put, there being no likely reason to stick around. They were sure to grab what gold was available and head for parts unknown. The only thing that might keep them at the Elk Track was the physical limitation of

Dorsey. Sam wondered how badly he had been hit. If they decided to fight it out, it could be bloody.

The sheriff had plenty of capable fighting men with him; some of them were Civil War veterans, both Yanks and Rebels.

Sam was sorry David wasn't with them and had to remain in Big Timber. Fortunately, his wounds were more painful than fatal. J.D.'s bullet just scratched his left arm while Emmet Pratt's lucky shot entered and exited the fleshy inside of his thigh, barely missing the bone. Once again, it would be quite some time before he could comfortably sit in a saddle. Colonel Jenkins was another problem. The dizziness persisted, but he still insisted on being a part of the posse. With some trepidation, the sheriff allowed him to be included.

It was a bone-weary, dusty ride to the outskirts of the vast Elk Track spread, where the body of armed men topped the high rise and halted, allowing the horses to blow. They had ridden the animals hard to reach the upper plateaus of Swamp Creek before dark and were now silhouetted black against a fiery sky. Over several draws and within view of the next ridge lay the valley's entrance of Dead Crow Gorge, the narrow pass to the ranch headquarters.

Major Staats nudged his mount up next to Sam. "Dodd, how often do you Westerners get spectacular sunsets like this?"

Sam had been too busy thinking about tomorrow to notice the magnificent panorama of the rolling high plains with their lush, waving grass. The magic of the red evening sun turned the glistening white snow, on the peaks above, into rich cream. Close to the horizon, thin wisps of clouds were crimson slashes painted across the pale blue sky. The wind was moving down from the higher elevations, cooling the land below, making the tall green and gold grass come alive.

"Believe it or not, this happens pretty regular," smiled Sam. "If you're fond of weather changes and pretty sunsets, you'll love Montana. Fry one day, freeze the next 'midst colored splendor. Heard they even had snow flurries on the Fourth of July last year."

"I'd guess they don't get hot spells in January," chuckled the major.

"Shore do!" joked Sam. "Last year in late December, it heated up to five degrees below zero and several folks in Big Timber came down with sunstroke. All the schools in the territory closed down 'til the heat wave passed."

Staats started to laugh but stopped suddenly as he glanced toward Jenkins. The colonel was slipping to the side, close to falling from the saddle. He called out sharply to his friend, "Woodrow! How y'all feel?"

Jenkins waved his hand feebly and, pushing down on the stirrups, straightened himself upright. "Ah'm just fine, Major. Don't y'all worry about me."

Staats gave a worried look to Sam. "Do we have much farther to go? Woodrow looks like he's ready to drop."

Sam agreed. "We made a mistake in allowin' him to talk us into lettin' him come along. We don't have far to go now, but to be on the safe side, let's ride abreast of him." Both spurred their mounts and moved alongside the colonel and stayed by his side until they reached the creek where they intended to camp for the night.

As they gathered around the fire to discuss their next move, Jason asked Sam to let them know what to expect tomorrow.

Kneeling, Sam took a stick and drew in the dirt the layout of the ranch and the fortifications. He detailed the narrow canyon entrance and the high granite walls, then pinpointed a high spot halfway through the canyon. "There's a lookout bunker right here. It's very well-situated to spot anybody coming through the pass. One or two men might sneak through, undetected, on a dark night . . . but not a whole posse. Any of you familiar with the Elk Track layout? Anybody been here before?"

Everyone looked at each other, then shook their heads. Sam went on. "Before we ride in, someone's got to scout ahead and see if a lookout has been posted at the top of the canyon. We could be trapped like snakes in a sack if they plan an ambush in that narrow pass." He looked about seeking a volunteer, but when no one immediately stepped forward, Staats squatted down beside him. "I'll go."

Sam looked kindly at the brave Southerner. "Thank you, Major, but it looks like the lot falls to me. I seem to be the only one who knows the area and best I go it alone. If there's someone guarding the pass, maybe I can get close enough in the dark to take him out without him sounding an alarm. If there's any trouble, I'll be back before sunrise."

"And what if you don't show up by then?" asked Sanford.

"Then come on in," replied Sam. "That will mean there's no lookout or I've taken care of him. I'll meet you at Swamp Creek right at sunup."

He nodded agreement . . . nothing more to be said. Sam swung into the saddle and disappeared through the pines and into the night.

An hour later, a bright moon hung like a newly minted silver dollar in the diamond-studded sky. Sam rode to the edge of the illuminated valley. Fearing exposure, he continued along the dark pine shadows bordering the valley's floor. He carefully approached Dead Crow Pass and tied his buckskin up short to a tree. Hugging close to the rocks, Sam entered the pass and slowly worked his way upward along the trail. Finally, he recognized the rock outcropping where he could get a good view of the lookout post above. Noiselessly, he moved around the granite boulders and in the moonlight, could see it plainly. Remaining still, he waited patiently until his neck began to cramp. Having seen and heard nothing, chances were good that no one was up there in the stone fortification.

Time to get going. *No, hold on.* Just as he was about to step out into the open and relieve his neck muscles, he saw a faint glow of red appear, then quickly vanish. Someone had just taken a deep drag on a cigarette. Sam froze, motionless behind the rocks. Within seconds, he heard the unmistakable sound of someone relieving himself, then nothing. Whoever was up there was conscientious, capable, possessing the rare discipline necessary to fulfill a sentry's duty.

Sam had been keeping a watchful eye on the changing shadows as the moon traversed the heavens. He figured he'd need at least another hour before the trail would be dark enough to slip deeper into the canyon, allowing him to climb up, get behind the lookout, and approach him from above. Waiting patiently, crouched against the granite, Sam had time to rest his bones and gather his thoughts, concentrating on the need for stealth to reach the top without being detected. With the above approach, he was hoping to get the drop on the unsuspecting guard.

One furtive step at a time, Sam moved up the trail, staying close to the shadowed side. He slowly cut up the draw, crossing the path which led to the lookout post. Nonstop, he inched his way to the top. He found it to be flat, covered by scrub sage and a few small junipers, affording little cover. He crept as close as he could before discovering that the last twenty yards or so were loose shale rock. Sam was grateful the wind was in his face when he spotted the sentry's horse, tied off behind a scrubby pine.

Sam had no trouble picking out the figure of the man behind the barricade and could have shot him with ease, but the echoing gunfire would alert the ranch. He was sitting with a rifle across his lap, attentively peering over the stone fortification at the trail and valley below. His back was mostly unprotected, allowing for an unrestricted view were he to turn around. Sam had no alternative but to lie and wait. Maybe he would nod off, put the rifle down, or have to relieve himself again—anything to catch him off guard.

Time was now of the essence. It had taken a long time to get this close but he might as well be miles away, the loose shale making the last of the stalk impossible. The guard was showing no signs of drowsiness, no yawns, no stretching—just constant vigilance. Getting impatient, Sam contemplated calling out to him, demanding he drop the rifle. But what if he didn't, and there was gunfire?

As the moon drifted over Sam's shoulder, it dawned on him that if he stood up, the guard would only be able to see a silhouette and not be able to readily identify him. It could be a disadvantage and risky, and even a crazy idea.

Why not? he thought. He quickly sneaked up to the side of the horse, startling it intentionally. It shied away, but let out a whinny loud enough to alert the guard. With haste, Sam aggressively strode over to the startled lookout, saying in a loud whisper, "I'm here to relieve ya, pard!"

"Hey," came the response. "It's about time ya showed up." The guard put down his rifle and started to gather his things as he lazily asked, "Who is it . . . that you Clyde?"

"Yep, it's me! Who do you think!" Sam slammed the barrel of his gun down hard across the forehead of the unsuspecting guard, knocking him unconscious. Looking down at the prostrate figure, he again whispered, "It's me, sneakin' Sam Dodd—and you're under arrest."

"WHAT DO YOU THINK WE SHOULD DO, Colonel?" asked Sam. All four of them were crouched on one knee, peering through the brush at the ranch in the distance. Jenkins had the telescope, observing the outer walls and tower guarding the entrance. The morning light was touching the top of the canyon walls and before long would reach the roofs of the Elk Track structures.

Without taking the telescope from his eye, the colonel said, "Ah see no men on the walls and only one in the tower by the gate. He has a rifle in his hands. Other than that, there's little movement. Seems quite peaceful."

"There could be plenty more up there in a matter of minutes," commented Major Staats. "They must have been expectin' us or there wouldn't have been a lookout."

"Somebody's likely to get killed tryin' to scale those walls," stated Jenkins.

"I'd bet most of Raven's hands don't know the trouble their boss is in. Makes me wonder how much they really *do* know," said the sheriff.

"There's a way to find out," suggested Sam. Motioning for them to follow, Sam crept back into the trees, out of view, to where the other men were waiting. The lookout guard was gagged, leaning up against a tree. Sam drew his pistol, leaned down and quietly said, "We're going to ungag you, but don't cry out or I'll have to raise another knot on yer head . . . understand?"

The man stared docilely at Sam and nodded. When Major Staats removed the bandanna stuffed in his mouth, he blurted out, "Why didya go and hit me on my haid? It shore smarts."

Sheriff Sanford bent over and said, "We'll do the asking. Are Raven and Dorsey at the ranch?"

"Was last night. We was settin' around the cookhouse havin' supper when them an' a bunch of the boys came in ridin' hard. Raven was madder'n a swarm of hornets. They carried Dorsey inside, all bloodied up. The colonel tossed me a Winchester an' told me to git movin'. That's when he sent me up to the lookout to see if anyone was comin'. Told me to fire a shot in the air if I see'd anybody." The dazed cowhand looked around. "Who are all you folks an' whatya doin' up here . . . what's goin' on?"

"You tellin' us you don't know?" asked the sheriff.

"If I'da knowed, I would'na asked!" he answered. "I been settin' up thar on a cold rock since the sun went down tryin' to figger out what's all the fussin' about. I been watchin' hands gallop this way an' that, some ridin' in, then some come ridin' out. Then, it got real quiet. Next thing I knowed, I got knocked on the noggin." Holding up his tied hands, he pleaded, "Could ya take the ropes off? I gotta itch."

"It's all right, Major, untie his hands," said the sheriff.

Staats reached over and cut the cords and immediately the cowhand began to scratch his stomach and arms, emitting sweet sounds of relief. "The little buggers jest don't let a body alone."

"You say several riders left the Elk Track?" asked Sam.

"Yep. Saddled up new hosses an' went by me at a dead run. What's goin' on, anyway?"

"How many men were here at the ranch when Raven and the rest of the crew left for town?"

"Maybe two, plus the cook. Ever'body else went in to see J.D. get hitched and maybe to get drunk fer free."

"Looks like the rats have deserted the ship," said Jenkins.

"We still should keep our guard up. Jason, maybe it'd be a good idea if you rode on up to the man at the gate tower and tell him who you are. We'll cover you and if he makes any hostile moves, we'll open fire," stated Sam.

Jason grunted, "Good idea." He called over the deputies who were carrying Sharps rifles and gave them instructions. Crawling to the edge of the creek embankment, they leveled their rifles at the tower and waited as the sheriff cautiously moved into the open and walked his horse toward the gate. At three hundred yards, he shouted out, "Elk Track Ranch! I'm Sheriff Jason Sanford. I'm here on official business."

The man in the tower shouted back. "Don't come any closer, whoever you are. I got orders to shoot anyone who comes around!"

From behind the sheriff, one of the deputies stood up and yelled, "Jasper Shank, that you up there?"

"Who's out thar callin' my name?" barked the ranch cook who was manning the gate.

"It's me, Jasper—your friend, Horace Gow. Put down that gun, Jasper, afore ya git shot. That's Sheriff Jason Sanford yer talking to."

Jasper put the rifle down like it was a hot branding iron, "Sheriff Sanford? Why didn't ya say so?"

Jason smiled and rode up closer. "Anybody else around?"

Jasper leaned out, "Nobody here but Dorsey, the colonel, and me. Ever'body else took off last night, skedaddled outa here, gear and all. What's goin' on? The colonel put me out here last night and told me to shoot anyone who came close."

"Good thing you didn't," Jason said, as he motioned to the posse to move forward. "Where's the colonel and Dorsey?"

"They're up at the main house. Dorsey's shot bad. The colonel's takin' care of 'im."

"Better fan out, men, and check all of the buildings," commanded Jason. "Don't take any chances."

Jason and Sam, along with the two Southerners, slowly approached the ranch house with their guns drawn. Moving up the steps to the entryway, Jason and Sam stood, backs to the wall, on either side of the door while Staats and Jenkins covered the back. The sheriff reached out and banged hard with his fist, "Come on out with your hands high!"

The heavy door blew open and rocked on its hinges as shotgun blasts erupted from inside. Before the racket had died down, Sam spun a half-turn, stuck his arm around the corner, and fired all six rounds from his revolver, then pulled back to reload as Jason did the same. Sam quickly sneaked a look, then ducked away, inviting another blast. None came. He looked again, darting back . . . then three more times, before slipping rapidly inside. He crouched down by the door frame and scanned the entire room, over the sight of his gun. "Come on in, Jason—it's all over."

Slouched in a chair facing the door was the bloodied, dead body of Dorsey Caine, still holding the shotgun in one hand and buckshot reloads in the other. His shirt and pants were caked with dried dark red from the wound received at the river. Fresh blood seeped from the hole in his forehead. There wasn't a trace of Jacques Du Bois, alias Colonel Malachi Raven.

CHAPTER 33

"S AM . . . COME OVER HERE and take a look." The extremely excited voice of the normally sedate Colonel Jenkins reverberated through the spacious room. He and the major were on their knees beside the large buffalo rug they had thrown back. They had removed several floor boards, revealing a hidden compartment. "Ah felt some give when ah stepped on the rug. Reckon in their haste, they weren't careful to put the slat back in place. See here what ah found, wedged between the side wall."

Between his thumb and forefinger, the colonel was holding onto a small gold coin which he handed to Sam. "That's an 1854 three-dollar piece, minted in New Orleans. No question in my mind where it came from." He was trembling with anger and flushed in the face. "Traitor! It makes me sick to my stomach that a Confederate officer could do such a dastardly act. Ah'm ashamed even thinkin' about it."

Suddenly, Jenkins began to weave unsteadily on his feet. Both hands went to his head as if to keep his troubled and throbbing brain from exploding. Appearing befuddled, he murmured, "Ah . . . ah better sit down." He took one step, then as though all life had left him, he crumpled to the floor.

The sheriff and Staats rushed to pick him up and quickly carried him into the adjoining room. His pulse was weak, erratic, and his skin reflected the ominous gray cast of the very ill.

Sam spoke up authoritatively, inferring no compromise as he addressed Jason and Staats. "Major, you'll have to stay with the colonel until he's well enough to ride back to Big Timber. This is no country for a sick man. And if he gets any worse, waste no time sending a rider for Doc Collins." Facing the sheriff, he said, "Jason, you have a posse to direct and a number of Elk Track hands to round up. I've got an idea which direction Raven headed and every minute I stick around here, he's gettin' farther away. Agreed?"

With the affirmative nods, Sam rushed out of the room.

Major Staats turned to the sheriff after Sam's hasty departure and with a touch of humor, remarked, "Are y'all sure he wasn't an officer?"

THE TRACKS WERE FRESH, no more than ten hours old. Two horses, one with rider, had been through the narrow way directly behind the ranch. The trail to the plateau above was well-hidden behind brush, scrub oak, and large boulders—a mere slit in the mammoth rock face the only clue to its existence.

Sam soon found it to be tough going—in fact, perilous. Dismounting frequently, he led the mare upward, over large rocks, squeezing between boulders. He could tell he wasn't the only one having trouble negotiating the narrow trail, noting the fresh scrapings of leather on the rocks and judging the marks were made by Raven's pack saddle.

Several times the buckskin balked when forced to scramble up the incline, tossing his head in defiance. Sam had to constantly coax him to keep moving, cajoling the gelding along with words of encouragement.

The difficulties on the narrow lower trail paled by comparison when they reached the switchback, nothing more than a slash cut into the side of the rock face, leading precipitously skyward. Sam sucked in a deep breath as he encountered the challenge ahead. *Hey, boy, that's hardly wide enough for a goat, much less me and you.* He quietly slid to the ground and led the hesitant, frightened animal up the path hugging close to the granite face. With every new step Sam felt more exposed. His heart was pounding as he stopped to rest. *I feel like I'm naked in church!*

Glancing up, Sam knew a rifleman situated on top could pick him off with ease. *If Raven's aware I know about this miserable excuse for a trail, he could be waiting with a rifle, ready to send me to my Maker.* He looked down into the black chasm below, then back along the narrow precipice. There was no place wide enough to turn around. Raising his head skyward, he muttered, "Well, Lord, no way to go but up." With all the care he could muster, he began to edge forward again along the granite wall, each stride bringing more apprehension. Making matters worse, the trail was getting slick from seeping water.

Every few yards or so, the mustang slipped backward, jerking Sam awkwardly as he scrambled to right himself. Each time he stood fast, shivering until urged forward again. He stroked his head and neck, calming the buckskin with a gentle voice. "Well, ol' feller, reckon the only place you've been ridden is around the flats of Big Timber . . . 'cause you shore aren't no mountain horse—that's a fact. You're better than them others I used, but you're still a good for nothin'. You may be a tough old range horse for the flatlands, with a good constitution, but you've an irritatin' habit of tossin' your head back when I ask you to do somethin' you don't like. I could break you of that, but now isn't the time. Come on, only a few steps more and we'll top the ridge." Sam inhaled a deep breath of relief when, at last, they emerged into the scrub pine on the rim. *Thank You, Lord.*

Raven's tracks looked to be a little fresher. *It must have taken him some time to get two animals up that trail with that bum leg of his. I wouldn't doubt I've gained at least two hours on 'im—maybe more.*

It was now apparent that Raven had no intention of hiding out at the Elk Track with the others, but had planned a delaying action allowing him time to escape. Placing a lookout in Dead Crow pass did the trick of slowing down his pursuers. Sam found it peculiar that Dorsey Caine was willing to be sacrificed, staying behind with a loaded scatter-gun in hand. Maybe Dorsey knew he was about to die anyway and wanted to take others down with him. Caine was an enigma, a hard one to figure.

Sam knew for certain that Raven would be constantly on the lookout to see if he was being followed. But so far, he was making no attempt to hide his tracks, perhaps believing his lead was too great to overcome. *He may be right,* Sam thought. *A lot depends on how well he knows these mountains.*

By early afternoon he was beginning to realize Raven wasn't that familiar with the high reaches of the Crazies. He appeared to be wandering aimlessly and unsure of any direction. Raven had changed his route below the snow line and was traversing the mountain, taking an erratic course. At one point, he rode into the deep timber, then back out again, unable to penetrate the thicket. There were signs indicating he was stopping often, maybe needing to limp out the soreness in his bad leg. Also, Sam came across a recently drained whiskey flask left behind at a resting place.

By late afternoon, Sam could see he was closing the gap and it was time to exercise great caution. Raven had crossed an immense, open sage-and-rock-covered bowl. Fingers of glacial snow reached down from above, melting into several small streams, gushing over the face. With no juniper or pine to conceal his movement, Sam would be fully exposed once he rode into the bowl, with only a few large boulders and outcroppings to hide behind. *If Raven's in those pines on the far ridge and he's sober enough, he's bound to spot me.*

Sam waited in the junipers, glassing the far side. It was blinding looking into the disappearing sun perched just above the ridge. *Is he over there or did he keep moving?* Sam didn't want to try crossing the expansive space until dark . . . but it would mean waiting another hour. Frustrated, and taking a calculated risk, he jabbed the mare with his heels and rode out into the open, exposed as a liar before the Lord.

The buckskin picked his way gingerly across the bowl. Suddenly, he tossed his head and balked at crossing one of the streams of rippling water. Sam again jabbed his spurs hard into his flanks, egging him forward. Repeatedly, the gelding threw his head back hard, then . . . KAPOW! He caught the bullet meant for Sam. The crack of the rifle shot echoed throughout the basin as the buckskin collapsed in a heap, dropping as if slammed in the skull by a sledgehammer.

Sam dove headfirst from the saddle, away from the falling horse. Together, they tumbled down the slope, coming to an abrupt stop on a ledge of stones, wedging the body of the horse between Sam and the assailant. He inched free and reached over to draw the rifle from the scabbard as more bullets thudded into the animal's side. The stock was badly split and the action jammed . . . the rifle was useless. *Blast it, I can't let him know my Winchester's busted!* He raised it just above the horse's belly, giving Raven a clear glimpse of the barrel.

As the sun moved lower, it cast a long shadow over Sam's refuge, allowing him to safely peer over the dead horse without presenting a clear target. It was a faint sound and he was too confined to see but, in the distance, he picked up the unmistakable ring of horseshoes hitting rock as they moved away.

Sam rolled over on his back and took inventory. His face was harshly bruised and bleeding and his right shoulder ached something awful. He flexed his legs and twisted about . . . nothing was broken. Staying well behind the horse, he waited patiently for the night to close around him. Sam realized that Raven could have ridden off, walked back, and be up there right now waiting for an easy target. *I've already made one big mistake by bein' impetuous; no sense making two in the same day.* Darkness came quickly enough.

Sam rummaged inside his saddlebags, struggling to find his stash of antelope jerky and dried fruit. As he gnawed on the welcome provisions, gradually satisfying his aching, empty stomach, he racked his brain figuring what to do next. He was in a real fix, dozens of rugged miles from the nearest civilization and on foot, the curse of the cowman. Worse still, Raven was making his escape.

Lord, what can I do . . . give up and go back? One of the Psalms flashed across his mind, *"I rise up before the dawning of the morning, and cry for help. My eyes are awake through the night watches." . . . What's the next line? Doggone, I can't remember. Oh, yeah, "They draw near who follow after wickedness."*

Sam thought about the words. *Follow wickedness, go after him? On foot? Now, that's a different idea. Me hobbling along and him on horseback. He has a rifle and me with just a sidearm.* Sam dismissed it as a foolish, intellectual perversion of the Good Book. Throwing the saddlebags over his shoulder, he grumbled aloud, "There's enough grub here to last me a few days and, with any luck, I can be back in Big Timber by late tomorrow."

He had ventured only several paces when the rim of the full moon peeked over the black horizon. The great white illuminated ball rose as if it were a giant lamp, hung up in the sky, lighting the landscape, creating stark shadows. He stopped and looked back. The few steps had already eased the stiffness from his legs and made the ache in his muscles more tolerable.

I reckon Raven wouldn't expect to see me follow on foot; in fact, he might just slow down, thinkin' I've given up. With optimism fresh in his mind, Sam adjusted the saddlebags more comfortably and began a slow jog up the trail after his prey. In awhile, sweat came from the shuffling pace he had set for himself and the warm dampness felt good. *How many times did I trot along like this, scouting for General Sherman? Too many to count. Must have covered half of the South.*

But now he was twenty years older, a grandfather and, having just turned forty-four, he wondered how long he could keep it up. Sam surprised himself with the endurance he still possessed. The arduous work of running a large cattle ranch demanded much of him physically, keeping him in good shape, and he was grateful there was no flab on his lanky frame.

Tracking Raven proved to be no problem, what with following two shod horses by a well-lit sky. Sam determined he was headed north, for the valley between the Crazies and the Little Belt Mountains and then . . . on to Canada. The hours passed swiftly as the bright moon moved from the horizon to overhead, past midnight.

Somewhere, sometime Raven would have to stop and rest. *That bad leg of his must be givin' him fits. For sure, he hasn't stopped for the last couple of hours. Spotting me on his trail must have put a scare into him.*

Sam knew he was closing in on Raven, sensing his evil presence nearby when he paused to listen. *What was that?* Straining his ears, he caught the slight yet distinct rustling of hooves and the creak of leather, followed by tumbling rocks. Raven was less than a quarter-mile away, most likely near the small, heavily timbered valley below. Sam continued his persistent, ground-covering lope, anxiously approaching the fleeing villain.

So I'm closing in; then what? Raven had a rifle. Sam had only his handgun. He would have to get near, very near, before he would have a chance to apprehend him. Sam hoped Raven would stop for a rest again but, obviously, he'd been spooked by Sam's pursuit. Time was becoming critical, daylight was only a few hours away; in the summer months dawn came early.

Sam stopped momentarily to scan the landscape before him. *I've got to get up ahead of him before it gets too light . . . and that's not gonna be easy. Raven's out of sight in the pines; time to close the gap. Maybe up ahead I can find a way to get around him.* Sam quickened his pace and began to run down the rocky slope. Once more, the exertion soon drenched him in sweat, but at the same time increased his exhilaration as the distance between them rapidly decreased. *If I keep this up, I can catch him before he gets out of the timber. His rifle won't do him much good in there.*

As Sam entered the trees, he abruptly slowed down. The forest blocked out the moon, making it much darker and the trail more difficult to see. He stopped again to listen. Just ahead, he could hear the sound of snorting horses breaking noisily through the bramble and lodgepole pines. Sam eagerly moved forward, throwing caution to the wind. Just a hundred yards ahead was the unsuspecting Raven, preoccupied with the task of trying to guide his animals through the dense lodgepole pines and deadfall.

All Sam had to do was close the distance immediately, before Raven broke out into the open. *It might be now or never. There's no way he'll hear me with all the racket his horses are making. I might even surprise him enough to disarm him.* Sam moved to the left of the trail, leaping over decaying deadfall, gliding swiftly closer, circling the rider as a wolf stalking a grazing deer, waiting for the right moment to pounce. Raven was cursing, plainly exasperated as he struggled with the pack animal in tow. Apparently, the mule had gone to the opposite side of a tree, tangling the lead rope in its branches.

The time was ripe to close in, to move quickly before the rope was free of the limbs. Sam stepped over and through a maze of fallen timber, balancing precariously on a large, decaying log which was lying across a small marsh. He got a good look at the thrashing pack mule's flank. Suddenly, the rotted log gave way, crashing Sam to the ground, twisting his right leg beneath it. The pain shot through his knee unmercifully, causing him to grimace and clench his teeth in agony. It took superhuman effort not to cry out and warn the colonel of his presence. Cold sweat covered his brow as he gingerly inspected his leg. It was sticky with blood from a puncture wound but otherwise, not broken.

He didn't move until he was sure the noise of the violent fall hadn't alerted Raven. *Guess not.* Sam could still hear the thrashing around of his animals. The colonel must have finally freed the lead rope because the swearing had stopped and he heard the horses slowly moving away in the dark, oblivious to what happened just yards behind them.

Sam tried to get to his feet, but fell at the first attempt. The slightest pressure on the twisted knee shot darts of agony throughout his whole body. He leaned back on the log, shoulders slumped, totally dejected as he listened for the sound of Raven's outfit becoming dimmer and dimmer.

Sam was not a cussing man . . . but he thought about it now, for his predicament was intimidating and the alternatives few. The chase was obviously over; there was no catching Raven now. He would have to return to Big Timber, hobble back on his badly wrenched leg. Reaching to his belt, he pulled out his knife. He selected a sturdy limb and fashioned a crutch he could lean on.

Sam had just taken a few grueling steps when he heard the first shot. Immediately dropping to his good knee, another shot rang out, then a terrified shout. . . . "Git away from me!" . . . followed in quick succession by a scattering of pistol blasts and a bone-chilling scream. "You're dead! Get away from me!" The high-pitched voice was frantic and raw, with ugly terror lacing every syllable. Then in the death-chilling silence, Sam realized *he* was not the target. An uncontrollable quiver ran down Sam's back, for even in the height of battle, he had never heard such manifested fear.

Raven's being attacked by a grizzly or a pack of wolves! Sam tossed the crutch aside, drew his gun, and moved agonizingly through the pines. Stalking silently, he soon came to a small clearing where the two horses were calmly grazing . . . unattended. *Where's Raven?* From the far side of the little meadow, he heard a low moaning. Soundlessly, Sam limped his way through the clearing and saw him, sitting with his legs spread wide, huddled up against a fallen log. Raven's shoulders were hunched over and his hands were trembling, unsuccessfully trying to reload his pistol, dropping unspent shells to the already littered ground.

"Drop the gun, Raven," demanded Sam, as he leveled his .44 Colt at Raven's head.

"Didya see her?" Raven's voice broke. Paying no attention to Sam's command, he continued the attempt to load his gun, still dropping the shells between his legs. "She came right at me, had an ax in her hand . . . g-gli-glidin' across the meadow. Ah . . . Ah shot her an' she disappeared, then . . . " With his eyes wide in horror, "Then she . . . she came at m-me again." Raven's lower lip was quivering, his slobber glistening in the bright moonlight.

Sam holstered his Colt and reached down, then took the gun from Raven's shaking hand.

THE NORTHERN PACIFIC LOCOMOTIVE spun its massive iron wheels, crunching the traction sand between wheel and rail. Amid clamor and whistling steam, the terrain began to move by. Colonel Jenkins and Major Staats waved their farewells from the rear platform. A manacled Jacques Du Bois, alias Colonel Malachi Raven, was beside them. Jason Sanford and Sam Dodd stood by the tracks, watching as the train disappeared to the east.

"Sam, you did a danged good job bringing in that scum. It took a lot of nerve trackin' him down on foot."

"I'm not the one that got him," smiled Sam. "He was driven loco and captured by that lady-ghost of the Crazy Mountains. I just gimped over to him and plucked the gun from his hand."

"You tellin' me you believe in ghosts?" joked the sheriff.

"Well, for a minute, I almost did. I hauled up those heavy packs stuffed with bags of gold and paper money and hung 'em in a tree. Then, I tied up Raven and secured his hands real well to the pack saddle. He was docile as a lamb and tetched in the head—kept mumblin' to himself. When I swung up on his horse to lead us out of the clearing, Raven began to scream again. Frankly, him yellin' and what we saw whittled two years off my life real quick. Scared the dickens out of the mounts too. They were flinchin' all over the place."

"You told me what happened before, when you rode in with Raven," interrupted Jason. "Over near the Yellowstone, there's a whole passel of geysers. One, I hear, is a real dandy."

"This was just a little one, but when that steam came out of the ground, hit that cold air and the bright moonlight bounced off it, she looked pretty spooky to me. I'll tell you, my heart jumped a few beats, not to mention what it did to Raven. He started screaming and yelling all over again. Took me quite awhile to quiet him down and to get him back on the packhorse."

Sam was still thinking about the eerie illusion when Jason interjected, "Sam, that's a very sick man. Wonder if he'll live long enough to stand trial."

"All depends whether or not the devil has more evil work for him," answered Sam. "His kind lives a long time."

"How about you—going back home to Colorado?"

"You bet, as soon as David feels he's fit to travel. Should be no more than a few days."

"Sure you don't want to stick around Montana and be my number-one deputy?" kidded Jason.

Sam laughed heartily. "My lawman days are over. I'm headin' home to raise a bigger herd of cows, breed some good Morgans, and watch my grandson grow up." Then with a more serious face, he spoke with firm conviction. "Jason, I'm tired of killing; I've done too much of it. I'm particularly thankful that I didn't have to shoot Malachi Raven."

"Well then, how about comin' with me to the Bramble Hotel and we can kill off two of the biggest steaks in the county. I'm hungry!"

"That's the kind of fatality I can deal with," Sam said, grinning. "And maybe we can kill off a gang of beans too."

CHAPTER 34

A S USUAL, THE TRAIN WAS LATE. For thirty minutes, Sam watched David pace up and down the platform. Something was definitely bothering him; so much so, he was ignoring his painful leg. His wound was far from healed, but David insisted on leaving early, having had more than his share of trouble in Big Timber. They were going home, finally . . . leaving behind both good friends and grievous memories in the shadow of the Crazy Mountains.

Sam leaned against the station house wall and looked up at the peaks rising eleven thousand feet and thrilled at their glacier-capped beauty. He would miss that awesome mountain range; he had grown quite accustomed to viewing its panoramic majesty and was a bit fascinated by the mystery surrounding it. His appreciation of the scenery was interrupted as David approached, handing his father a letter.

"Pa, what do you think about this? I just got it today, from Deborah."

Sam took it from him and asked, "Son, are you sure you want me to read it?"

David, tight-lipped, nodded.

Dearest Darling,

My heart almost broke when I learned you were leaving town without seeing me, but I can understand why. I have been so terribly foolish and cruel to you. It's no wonder you never want to see me again. I don't blame you a bit.

Difficult as you may find this to believe, I was happy—actually overjoyed—when the wedding didn't take place. The doubts in my mind over loving Jefferson were growing daily. I wanted to call it off but the pain it would have caused my parents was too great to bear. They were so looking forward to our marriage. Alas, I was torn between my love for you and duty.

Mother and Father were overcome emotionally by the tragedy of J.D. losing his life in the duel. I, too, was shocked by it all. When it was declared to be self-defense, my heart sang with joy.

Fate has placed her hand in this tangled web and pushed us apart. My heart aches for you to forgive me. Can you? Don't leave without letting me hear from you.

All my love,

Your devoted Deborah

Sam handed the letter back to his son without a word.

"Well, Pa, do you have any advice?"

"Son, when it comes to affairs of the heart, I can't advise you. She obviously wants to see you and make up. That decision is solely yours."

"She hurt me terribly, Pa . . . but I just can't help thinkin' about her." Clearly disgusted, David rolled the note into a ball and threw it down on the tracks, just as the train was pulling into the station.

Nothing more was said before they climbed on-board and selected their seats. As the train began to slowly move out, David jumped to his feet and put his hand on Sam's shoulder. "Pa, I have things to take care of. I've got some bridges to mend." With that, he limped through the aisle and hurriedly dropped from the moving train to the cindered track below. Sam craned his neck to see him disappear inside the depot.

"SAM, WHAT DO YOU THINK DAVID'S GOING TO DO?" asked Mary as she bustled about the kitchen, getting ready to serve the family supper.

"Your guess is as good as mine, sweetheart. I'm a poor one to ask. All I can tell you, I've said before. Our son was very agitated when he left the train."

"Don't you think he should be home by now?"

"He should . . . but he isn't," answered an exasperated husband. "Sweetheart, we've been over this conversation a dozen times. He'll get here when he gets here and I hope it's soon. I could sure use his help with the st—"

Interrupting, Matthew, Daniel, and Betsy came bursting through the door. "Ma . . . Pa . . . riders are comin'," shouted Matthew.

"Yeah," added Daniel, "and I think one of 'em is David."

"Yes," Betsy excitedly exclaimed, "and he's got a lady with him."

Mary looked quizzically at Sam, then back to the three children as they all rushed to the porch. "Sam, a *woman?*"

"I guess he brought Deborah back with him. He said he couldn't help thinkin' about her. Reckon they made up."

Mary smiled. "Let's hope so. I want him to be happy."

Betsy asked, "Mama, who's the lady with David?"

"That's Deborah Dills, Betsy; she used to live close by."

They all gathered on the porch, impatiently waiting for the approaching riders to come close enough for a warm welcome. There was no question, one of them was David and his companion was a woman.

Daniel looked up at his mother and frowned. "Ma, I didn't know that Deborah Dills had blonde hair!"

ABOUT THE AUTHOR

H.L. RICHARDSON (Ret.) is a twenty-two year veteran of the California State Senate and, although he was born in Indiana, proudly calls California home. Founder of the nationally renowned Gun Owners of California and Gun Owners of America, Richardson has focused his extensive political career on the preservation and protection of our Second Amendment rights.

An active hunter and outdoorsman, Richardson remains involved in state and national politics, is a popular speaker, and continues to provide colorful media commentary on a host of issues. He is the author of two successful humorous political books, *Slightly to the Right*, and *What Makes You Think We Read the Bills?* The latter is used as a text in political science classes throughout California. He has also written for numerous national publications.

In spite of his significant business, political, and hunting activities, Richardson has deftly combined his love of writing and extensive knowledge of the West to author a series of western novels for Word, including *The Devil's Eye*. He has also written a contemporary political romp, *Split Ticket*.

Richardson and his wife Barbara have three children, and six grandchildren, and reside in the Sacramento area.